Prai

"Atmospheric and heartfelt, Sara Ackerman's *The Shark House* is a dazzling portrait of the beautiful, important, complex relationships between humans and nature, humans and science, and humans and one another. The author's passion and respect for Hawai'i—its people, its creatures, its land, and its sea—shine on every page. Readers seeking to be transported into a world of rich culture, vibrant descriptions, and fascinating characters will fall in love with this book."

—Gabriella Saab, author of *The Star Society*

"An immersive, evocative setting; a unique and compelling mystery; a tenacious, courageous heroine working in a man's field—*The Shark House* has so many things going for it, but it's the emotional depths this story swims in that make it absolutely unforgettable. Stunning, brutal, and hopeful all at once, *The Shark House* will sweep you away."

—Lee Kelly and Jennifer Thorne, authors of *The Antiquity Affair* and *The Starlets*

"*The Shark House* shimmers with a potent mix of drama, danger, and atmosphere you can feel. Drawn along by its restless, romantic current, you'll discover that what swims beneath the ocean's surface is less startling than that which lurks in the dark reaches of memory. Dr. Minnow Gray is a thoroughly modern heroine—smart, strong, and self-possessed, yet full of tenderness toward the misunderstood objects of her affection. If women had a Shark Week all their own, this book would be it."

—Erin Bartels, award-winning author of *The Lady with the Dark Hair* and *The Girl Who Could Breathe Under Water*

The shark house

OTHER BOOKS BY SARA ACKERMAN

The Guest in Room 120

The Maui Effect

The Uncharted Flight of Olivia West

The Codebreaker's Secret

Radar Girls

Red Sky Over Hawaii

The Lieutenant's Nurse

Island of Sweet Pies and Soldiers

The shark house

a novel

SARA ACKERMAN

The Shark House

Published by Harper Muse, an imprint of HarperCollins Focus LLC, 501 Nelson Place, Nashville, TN 37214, USA.

ISBN 978-1-4003-4798-8 (ePub)
ISBN 978-1-4003-4797-1 (TP)
ISBN 978-1-4003-4799-5 (downloadable audio)

HarperCollins Publishers, Macken House, 39/40 Mayor Street Upper, Dublin 1, D01 C9W8, Ireland (https://www.harpercollins.com)

Library of Congress Cataloging-in-Publication Data

CIP data is available upon request.
Art Direction: Halie Cotton
Cover Design: James W. Hall
Interior Design: Jen Overstreet

Printed in the United States of America

25 26 27 28 29 LBC 5 4 3 2 1

For Marilyn,
who introduced me to my first shark

GLOSSARY

A few notes on Hawaiian words and pronunciation:

The vowels are phonetic—*a* (ah/uh), *e* (eh), *i* (ee), *o* (oh), *u* (ooh). Each vowel is sounded out; for example, *kuleana* is (koo-leh-AH-nah).

The *'okina* is a glottal stop, or a sort of pause, similar to the sound between the syllables of "uh-oh." In print the correct mark for designating an 'okina is a single open-quote mark. Diphthongs (i.e., when two vowels appear together) are blended if there is no 'okina.

The *kahako* (i.e., a line over a vowel, as in Haleakalā) is a macron, which lengthens and adds stress to the marked vowel.

A few word and names you'll find in the book:

Kaupiko (Kau-PEE-koh)
Kiawe (Kee-AH-veh)—in Hawaiian, *w* is sometimes pronounced as a *v*.
Koholā (Ko-ho-LAH)
manō (mah-NO)
Nalu (NAH-loo)

The shark house

From the journal of Minnow Gray

Hawai'i, November 25, 2017

"We are born of sharks. From the beginning of time, sharks have swum through our lives and our islands, sleek as river stone, elusive and ever present. They are our protectors, our ancestors, our future."

When I first heard these words, spoken by a Hawaiian man I've come to know, I felt like I had returned home to a place I had known only in my dreams. The words were electric and touched me in such a deep way, I realized everything I had believed until that moment was just a human presumption. I thought I knew sharks, but really I knew nothing. In the passing years the words have only grown louder and have pulled at me in a way nothing else ever has.

Looking back, I see that Hawai'i and I were destined for each other, that it would only be a matter of time until I found my way to her looming volcanoes, rocky coastlines, and living blue waters. There were things I needed to learn about myself and things I needed to learn about the sharks, and to realize that shimmering thread of connection. No one thinks of sound when they think of sharks—they think instead of serrated teeth and gaping mouths and dorsal fins. But when I close my eyes, I can still hear the sound of that tiger shark breaking water behind me like a sea-dappled missile. Something fierce and beautiful to behold—and deadly.

I thought I knew sharks.

CHAPTER 1

The Invitation

Huaka'i: *trip, voyage, journey, mission*

Carpinteria, California

February 1998

Minnow felt the shark before she saw it. She always did. A prick of her senses and she spun around in the dark water until she spotted the enormous animal looping around in a wide, exploratory circle. As it closed in, she could sense its agitation. She glanced around to see where the boat was, but there was no sign of it. The dark edges of panic began closing in . . .

And then she heard a loud, jolting ring.

It had taken her a while to fall asleep, by way of counting octopuses, but she had finally managed to drift off. Without turning on the light, she fumbled for the phone, knocking it onto the wooden floor in the process. It was probably a wrong number, and the intrusion annoyed her, cutting into her fiercely guarded sleep time.

"Hello?" she mumbled.

"May I speak with Dr. Minnow Gray, please?" said an unfamiliar voice.

"Speaking."

"Minnow, this is Dr. Joe Eversole from University of Hawai'i. I'm sorry to call so late in the evening, so I'll get right to the point here. I think we have a problem. And I'm hoping you can help."

Oh shit.

She sat up and switched on the light. "Don't tell me there's been another incident."

A slight pause. "So you're familiar with our . . . situation."

The way he said *situation* caused an itch under her skin. What had been happening in Hawai'i was more than a situation, and it alarmed her on many levels.

"Of course I am. Sharks are my world."

Anyone with a television or newspaper knew what had gone down in the past few days. A deadly attack and a missing person along the same rugged stretch of Hawaiian coastline, plus shark sightings galore.

He spoke in rapid fire. "Got it. And yes, there's been another incident. This one not fatal, but the victim is in bad shape, and it's got me worried because this is number three, not to mention the near misses. People are freaked out, and I worry what's coming next. It could get nasty."

"What kind of help are you looking for?"

"Well, I'm short-staffed. Our whole team is in Australia for a symposium, and I could use a white shark expert who knows their shit. Someone to help me figure out what's going on—why all in this location. I can't say for sure yet, but my guess is this latest is another white shark." He paused to catch his breath, then added, "I was hoping you might be able to come out to Hawai'i for a week or two. Maybe more."

"What about Doc Finnegan? I'm surprised you didn't ask him."

Men were top of the food chain in this field—in all of marine biology, really. Doc Finnegan was a leading white shark researcher with a big ego and territorial tendencies. He was also her mentor. Doc had spent time in Hawai'i, so he seemed like the natural first choice.

"Yeah, I tried to get him, but he's in Guadalupe for the next few weeks. He's the one who recommended you."

Of course. She knew that. But dropping everything and jetting off to Hawai'i was a big deal. Especially now. There were so many reasons to say no, number one being she had scraped together and earmarked nearly all her savings to finally get a vessel of her own, and aside from that she had seventy-four dollars to her name. Her new little nonprofit, Sea Trust, wasn't even off the ground yet, and she had been planning on writing grant proposals and securing funding and a hundred other things this week. Not to mention her therapy sessions. Leaving now would derail everything.

She tucked a misbehaving lock of hair behind her ear. "As much as I'd love to, I don't think I can swing it," she said.

There was a long pause. "This is a chance of a lifetime. A known great white in Hawai'i. Could be a game changer for you."

Somewhere between those words was the unspoken truth of her predicament. A way of letting her know he knew of what had happened on the Farallon Islands last season. The events that had broken her a thousand ways.

Joe was right, though. It could be just what she needed. A chance to gain a foothold on her own, since there would be no going back to the Farallones. Not now, not ever.

"*If* I say yes, could you pay my way there?" she asked.

"I can pay your way and house you."

Her next words unspooled on their own. "Hold off on the housing, I may have a connection on the coast. When do you need me?"

"Is tomorrow too soon?"

Yes.

"I'll see what I can do."

The next morning, she showed up at the airport without a ticket but managed to find a seat on a plane to Honolulu, where she would transfer to a smaller plane headed for the Big Island. On the five-hour flight over, Minnow took the time to review the few facts she knew about the series of incidents, rereading newspaper clippings and notes she had taken while watching the news. On top of the now-confirmed two incidents and one missing swimmer, there had also been a kayak bumped by what was reported to be a massive shark, and a surfer knocked off his board by something "big, dark and very strong."

The first fatal incident occurred five days ago. A twenty-three-year-old man and his father were surfing a remote wave when the son and his board were thrown out of the water. The father had allegedly witnessed the whole thing. There had been so much blood that the whole area around them had turned red. They made it to shore alive, but the son died soon after.

Minnow closed her eyes. A hazy picture formed in her mind.

Red water, golden kelp leaves, a beam of sunlight.

Just as fast as it arose, the image disappeared. Whether it was a memory or something conjured by her imagination, she couldn't be sure. In the past few months, more of these pictures had begun to appear during waking hours, and it felt like the hypnotherapy was knocking something loose inside her.

According to the most recent article, the man's surfboard had not been found, but the search was still on. Bitten boards were often full of clues indicating the species involved. A shark sometimes left a perfect jaw imprint, better than a dentist could have taken. And even better if there was a tooth or a tooth fragment lodged in the foam of the board. Right now it sounded like all the scientists had to go on was the way the flesh was torn and the nature of the encounter to lead them to their conclusions. She hoped Dr. Eversole could provide more details.

The other death—presumed death, at least—was murkier. A swimmer had taken off from Niu Bay toward a passing pod of whales. He'd left his wife and daughter onshore and swam out to sea and up the coast until he disappeared from view. Visiting from California, and in Hawai'i to train for the IRONMAN Triathlon race, he was reported to be a very strong swimmer. But he never came back. According to the papers, a helicopter pilot involved in the search had seen a shark "the size of a small whale" in the area.

To be sure, Minnow was not in the business of flying around the country investigating shark attacks. Attacks on humans—especially fatal ones—were rare events. And when you got down to it, humans killed far more sharks than sharks killed people. Scores more. In the past year in US waters, there had been only two confirmed deaths by shark, while humans killed *two million* sharks. The thought caused her a blink of sadness.

Weary from another nightmare-plagued, shitty sleep, she closed her notebook and looked out the window at the cloudless sky. The situation at hand was unusual. At least a few white sharks migrated to Hawai'i each year, that was known. Many of the ones they had tagged ended up venturing out to the central Pacific in late fall and early winter, but they usually weren't *foraging*—scientist speak for "hunting." So, what was happening here?

From the journal of Minnow Gray

Guadalupe Island, September 8, 1994

It was hard to tell where I left off and the shark began. She was that close to me. Longer and broader than most I have seen. Magnified by the water, her exquisite blue iris looked into me with a searching, ageless curiosity. She reminded me of my shark on Catalina but smaller, maybe seventeen feet. I resisted the urge to hold my hand out to touch her because I didn't want to startle her. The feeling was sublime, as always, and I got choked up.

Once she faded away into the blue, I glanced back at the guys in the cage. Through their bubbles, I saw them all give an enthusiastic thumbs-up. The rush hit me then, and I felt like I'd just been injected with an elephant's dose of adrenaline. I didn't want to come up for air, but I had to; my lungs were screaming.

Am I afraid? *People always ask me this, and I struggle to answer. The great white shark elicits a deeper kind of fear. One buried in the dark parts of our psyche. I think maybe the fear is so huge and so old, it turns into a kind of acceptance, if that makes any sense at all, and I tell them that I'd rather die swimming with a white shark than live in a world without them. There are so many things more dangerous that we humans have become habituated to. When you realize that, everything changes.*

Because the one thing I know for sure is this: We are not in control. Not one bit.

CHAPTER 2

On Hallowed Ground

One hānau: *homeland*

Big Island, Hawai'i

February 1998

The Kailua-Kona airport was a little oasis in the middle of black fields of lava. The smell of jet fuel mixed with an onshore salty breeze and notes of plumeria. Not as hot as Minnow had expected, but that was February for you. Either way, the temperature was miles warmer than Santa Barbara, and she had left her boots and beanie at home, along with her cracked and cumbersome wet suit and any expectations of what the coming week would bring.

This was her first trip to the Big Island, and on the approach, she had not been able to tear her eyes away from the many gradients of blue. Midnight, noonday sky, and sandy shallow turquoise. Outlines of coral reefs stood out like lace, beckoning. And up the way, coconut trees clumped together along white sand beaches. The island seemed to be making its best attempt at dazzling her, belying the recent tragedies in these very same waters.

While an undergrad, Minnow had spent some time on O'ahu studying hammerheads in Kāne'ohe Bay but had never ventured to any of the outer islands. Now she was thinking what a stupid move that had been. Uncle Jimmy had always talked up the Big Island and his days there just after college as a dive instructor by day, waiter by night. But he had never taken her there, too busy running his bakery back home. Even though she called him Uncle Jimmy, he was more father than uncle, raising Minnow since she was seven.

After gathering her small suitcase and dive duffel, Minnow walked out to the curb where she saw a sunburned man with a shock of wet red hair and dark glasses walking her way.

"Minnow Gray, I presume?" he said.

She'd purposely worn her Greenpeace T-shirt.

"Dr. Eversole, a pleasure to meet you."

He held out a hand. "Please, call me Joe."

In real life, Joe seemed much smaller than he'd looked on television, but when he shook her hand, his grip was as firm as steel.

"I'm so damn glad you pulled this off. Things are heating up even as we speak."

"How do you mean?"

"Let's get you loaded and on the way, and I'll fill you in on everything."

He led her to an old Toyota truck covered in patches of rust, its back window lined with faded and peeling stickers. *Big Island Love. FBI. Live Aloha. Surfing Sucks, Don't Try It.* The back was full of crumpled wet towels, a mask and snorkel, swim fins, a cooler. All of it dusted in black sand.

"Who else is here with you?" she asked.

"My intern Nalu came over from O'ahu with me. He's back at the harbor, rinsing off the boat and meeting a friend for lunch."

"Is anyone else coming?"

He shut the tailgate and opened her door without answering. Minnow climbed in, a funny feeling swirling in her gut.

"No."

She waited for him to get in and slam the door, then said, “So it’s just us two?”

He drummed his fingers on the steering wheel. “Us two and Nalu.” He swallowed hard, then said, “And damn, I hate to do this to you, but there’s been an emergency and I’m flying back to O‘ahu on the six-thirty flight. My wife went into premature labor and I need to get to the hospital.”

Minnow turned to him and for the first time noticed the puffiness under his eyes. This was most unexpected and not good news, but she mustered, “I’m sorry, I hope everything is okay.”

“I think so. It’s just a few weeks early, but this is Christina’s first, and they may have to do a C-section, so I need to be with her.”

“When will you be back?”

“As soon as I can, but it’s hard to say. I’ll connect you with Tommy Warren, head of Department of Land and Water Assets, better known as DLWA, and Mayor Lum. You can update them both until I return. Tommy’s actually Lum’s nephew.” He handed her a flimsy ID card with her photo glued on. “Use this if anyone questions you.”

She felt a strange sense of weightlessness. “So what is it exactly that you want me to do in the meantime? I have no authority here. No one even knows who I am,” she said, second-guessing her split-second decision to hop a plane over here without a plan. But the allure of a white shark in Hawaiian waters had been too enticing to pass up.

Joe hung a right onto a two-lane road surrounded by old lava flows, the black surface shimmering in the midday sun. “Like I said last night, the state is under a lot of pressure to do something about these attacks. First and foremost, we need to maintain a presence and look like we are on top of the situation. Hell, just look like we’re doing something—anything. Having a white shark expert on the island will help in that department. But this is new territory for all of us. We’ve never had a cluster of attacks like this. And I know tiger behavior but not white. Not like you do.”

Minnow squinted out into the glaring sun and felt the backs of her thighs melting onto the car seat. The last thing she wanted to be was a pawn. "Am I here just so you can check a box?"

"Look, none of us want this to end up with another shark-culling event, which is a real possibility. So first of all, I'm hoping you can get a read on what's happening to cause these attacks, and then also help sway the powers that be to prevent a culling event. Maybe talk to the press, too, as a voice of reason. Mass hysteria is not something we need."

That, she understood. "I'll do what I can and collect as much information as I can, but you know sharks are unpredictable. What if we find no reason?"

"Just do the best you can. I've already done a preliminary report on the first attack, and I can show you what I have back at the hotel. Yesterday the fire department and navy divers gave up the search for Hank Johnson, the missing swimmer, but I want to keep looking for any sign of him. As for yesterday's attack, the victim is still in and out of consciousness, so you'll want to interview her when she comes to. Or maybe I should say *if*."

So the victim was a woman. For some reason Minnow had expected a man. She had seen the dramatic headline in the paper this morning—*Man-Eater Still on the Loose in Hawai'i*—along with a few facts from the article. Less than two miles from where the first attack happened. Critical injury. No other details. The headline was wrong, though. White sharks did not discriminate between men and women.

"What can you tell me about the sharks? I know you believe the first one was a great white, but is there any reason to believe yesterday's was also one?"

"Yes. There have been several sightings this last week, so you can talk to those guys too."

"Haven't you already spoken to them?"

"To all but one, and you might glean something more. I also want you to keep combing the area, and keep an eye out. Sounds like there have been more tiger sharks around, too, if you talk to some of the fishermen. Something seems out of whack."

"What are you doing about it?"

"We have shark signs up at the beaches near the incidents, but not everyone listens."

"Will I have access to a boat?" she asked.

"Yep, and I have a stipend for you. Seventy bucks a day. It's all I could get."

Not much but better than nothing. "I'll need a car."

"I'm leaving this for you and Nalu. He can drive you around. My buddy lent it to me, it's his farm truck."

She got the feeling he was leaving something out but knew he had other things on his mind. Still, she planned on pressing him as soon as they got to the hotel.

On the way into Kailua-Kona town, they passed a boat harbor and a historic fishpond before turning down Ali'i Drive, where they met up with the ocean. A short pier jutted out, and tourists cruised the sidewalks scantily clothed and burned pink from the sun. A manicured green lawn spread out around several old houses and a stone church. The setting was beach-town-touristy vibe meets old Hawai'i.

At his hotel, a spaceship-shaped building, Joe took her to a late lunch. They sat at a table off by itself and he ordered a pint of beer right off the bat. Minnow stuck to *lilikoi* juice, which the waitress told her was passion fruit and that she swore by it. Joe excused himself and returned with a stack of manila folders. When he finally took off his dark glasses, she saw he had sea-blue eyes with a pronounced pterygium on one—too much time in the sun and salt water. He surveyed the ocean, a stone's throw away, dark and choppy now from an onshore breeze and a blanket of clouds.

"These waters are hands down the most beautiful in Hawai'i. All the way from South Point up to Māhukona area. You have this incredibly unique coastline that is mostly lava and little sand. That makes for clear water and burgeoning reefs. Plenty of fish. And plenty of sharks. Not as many as Maui, mind you, a veritable tiger pupping ground, but Hawai'i Island has its fair share." He paused to gulp down half of his beer.

"Have you ever seen a white shark in Hawai'i?" she asked.

"Never. Historically, there are accounts, but they are few and far between," he said, then added, "as I'm sure you know."

She did know. Anything there was to know about white sharks in the Pacific, she had made it her business, her life.

"Can I see the photos?" she asked.

He slid her a file. "We don't have much, other than what the emergency room staff took. I'll warn you, they are gruesome."

Minnow made sure the waitress was nowhere around, then opened the file with *Stuart Callahan* scrawled on the front. The first photo was a close-up of a thigh with a clean, half-moon-shaped bite mark that spanned from hip to knee. Each tooth left a gaping red hole. She fought back the bile rising in her throat.

"Oh my God, the shark has to be huge," she whispered.

"What's your guess?"

She hadn't seen a bite so big. Ever. "At least eighteen. Probably twenty? I'd need to measure it to be sure."

"I was thinking the same. According to my measurements, the shark would be twenty feet long," he said somberly.

"Only one bite?" she asked.

Joe nodded. "His father used his surf shirt as a tourniquet and got him to shore alive, but by the time he went for help and returned, Stuart had bled out."

It would have been impossible to stop the bleeding from such a wound on his hip. But a father would have to try. Her heart went out to him, and she suddenly felt woozy. The thought of a father witnessing his son's brutal death brought to mind her own story but in reverse. Only, Minnow had no recollection of the morning her father died. Perspiration beaded on her forehead.

"Is Mr. Callahan still on the island?" she asked, trying to keep her voice level.

"Yes. He and his wife own a home at Koholā, and they spend their time between here and Palo Alto. They're loaded, from what I gather. Private jet and the whole nine yards."

"Did he get a good look at the shark?"

"When I interviewed him, he was still in shock and still sedated, so I tried to make it brief. You might want to hit him up again. He told me he saw his son and the surfboard go skyward and a huge dark mass launch up, displacing a ton of water. There was a brief thrashing, and then the water turned red."

Her blood ran cold picturing it. "Terrifying."

Joe took another swig, finished the pint and set it down hard on the table. A small amount of froth remained on his lip. "To put it mildly. But we know tiger sharks don't generally jump out of the water like that, so that was our first clue that we were dealing with a different beast."

Tiger sharks were nothing to be messed with, and they were responsible for the most shark-related fatalities in Hawaiian waters. Even Minnow knew that.

"Were any teeth or fragments found?"

"Not with this one. That's why I kept looking for the board, but it still hasn't shown up."

"Do we have a description of the board?"

"Orange shortboard, shaped by Dick Brewer." He pulled out a small digital camera and offered it to her. "I still need to get to Longs to print out the pics. As you can imagine, I haven't had a second. They're in chronological order."

There were more photos of the injuries. The evidence pointed to a classic great white attack, the animal coming from underneath with enormous force and stunning its prey, then biting. But humans weren't on the white shark menu, so after a bite or two, the shark would have swam off without actually consuming Stuart.

Beyond the injury shots were pictures of a point break with perfect peeling right-handers, a surfer's dream, allowing them to ride the waves all the way into the bay. Minnow kept flipping through the photos. Turquoise water and roping blue lines of surf. Then another of a boulder-strewn cove. Joe narrated as she looked through them.

"That's where the Callahans were surfing. It takes twenty minutes to hike in from where they parked. Mr. Callahan had a tough choice to make: stay with his son while he died or leave Stu alone and go for help. Stu was a big guy, around one eighty, so there was no way Mr. Callahan could carry him all that way."

Minnow felt for the father. Felt for the son, who had been left on a bed of sea-smoothed coral and lava rock under a small heliotrope tree. This was her second time in as many years investigating an incident, and it reminded her why she preferred the business of studying shark behavior and observing them in their natural habitat, far away from any people.

"So, what about yesterday's incident?" she asked, after Joe had shown her the rest of the photos, which were purely location.

He scratched his head. "I'll tell you something that's been nagging at me. Two years ago, a white shark was reported in these waters by fishermen, and we had a diver disappear. And two years before that, we had another missing person, a boogie boarder. He was never seen again, but his shorts washed up ashore shredded the following week. What do you make of that?"

The two-year timing was interesting because it followed the white shark migration pattern. "White sharks have a two-year cycle. Especially the females. Their gestation period is sixteen months."

"So this could be the same one returning?"

"Not necessarily. They aren't always that predictable."

But one was, she knew.

He pushed the other file toward her, but when he saw the waitress coming, he quickly pulled it back. He ordered another beer and Minnow took another glass of the ice-cold, tart lilikoi juice that tasted like summer and winter shaken together.

When the waitress left, Joe shoved the folder back her way. "I'm surprised this hasn't leaked already. Hold on to your bikini."

Minnow glanced up at him. "What do you mean?"

"I mean we are well and properly screwed. There literally could not be a worse possible victim and the press is going to be all over this in the next day or two."

A victim was a victim was a victim. But when she opened the folder and saw the first photo, she immediately knew what he meant.

From the journal of Minnow Gray

November 1, 1992

White sharks are not white. They're slate gray, the color of wet ash left over from a bonfire on the beach. Whoever named the animal must have seen it from underneath, looking up at its marble-white underbelly. In science speak, it's called counter-shading, *a form of camouflage. And it reminds me of the first time I saw a white shark while I was* in *the water.*

From the journal of Minnow Gray

Farallon Islands, September 3, 1995

They call them the Sisters and I've yet to see one. Top of the food chain giants, all female, at least seventeen or eighteen feet and massive. That's longer than this Boston Whaler we are in, and I am acutely aware of this fact.

When a shark makes a kill, you can often tell by the clouds of birds overhead and a radio call from the spotter up in the lighthouse—what they call Shark Watch. As soon as it happens, I follow Gordon or Max and run to the landing and help them swing the boat, which hangs on a crane, out over the water. With arms carved from hard work, they winch the boat down several stories of crumbling cliff into the roiling sea. We speed out, catching air at the crest of a large swell.

So far, we are above water, not in it, where strangely I feel more at ease. There is only one man who dives down there and he goes alone, gathering urchins below his boat. Ron Elliott is famous around these parts and the guys talk about him with a kind of awe. I want to know more about him and have asked Max to introduce us when the time is right.

But back to the kill out near Great Arch Rock. There is red all around us and the sharp smell of seal, and I gag when I see the body, ripped in two. Gordon slows the boat and we drift, searching for any signs of shark. This patch of sea is crawling with white sharks at this time of year, and it feels dangerous to be floating in such a small vessel with who knows what swimming around below us. We've brought underwater video cameras affixed to poles, and Max and I lower them.

Neither of the men say anything, and I can feel our collective heartbeats going through our feet and into the fiberglass hull of the boat. White sharks can "hear" your heartbeat in the water, and if one came close enough now, I wonder if it would home in on ours. This is my first time out with the guys in the boat, and I try to keep cool, but my hands are trembling.

Then Gordon yells, pointing. We both turn port and the boat leans uncomfortably. "Holy shit," Max says. First we see the boil and then a tail fin breaking the surface. Everything is quiet and the shark cuts toward us, fast. I hold my breath and watch as its sleek black form darts under us, sending the Whaler rocking. My eyes must be wide, because Max grabs my arm, almost tenderly. "It's okay," he says. This is not my first rodeo, but something about the myth of these islands and the dark foreboding water gives my skin a chill. And then it comes around again.

She *comes around.*

At the same time, both guys say, "Greta!"

I've just seen my first Sister. Or maybe I've seen one of these beauties before, just not here. But I don't tell them that.

CHAPTER 3

The Other Victim

***Kaikuaʻana**: older sibling of the same sex, to address someone as such is a sign of respect; older sister*

If Minnow hadn't known better, she would have sworn the woman was dead. Pale as milk, with a tangle of wet hair spread out around her like seaweed, her face cut across by a four-inch gash that sliced into her upper lip. Even in this state, she was beautiful. And even in this state, Minnow knew exactly who the woman in the photograph was.

"Angela Crawford?" she said, her voice hushed.

Angela Crawford, Oscar-winning actress and soon to be ex-wife of actor Bradley Stone. The biggest couple in Hollywood, another casualty. Minnow felt sad for anyone whose life was so microscopically scrutinized, but there was a price for everything, a balancing of scales. Nature preferred homeostasis, and even movie stars could be classified in the natural order of things, *Homo sapiens* that they were.

"The shark didn't know who she was, apparently," he said with a shake of his head. "She and Zach Santopolo have been staying at the

Kiawe resort, flying under the radar and doing a good job of escaping the paparazzi. But this is going to blow up, especially if she dies."

Zach needed no introduction either. Hottest man alive, or so *People* magazine said. These kinds of people interacted with their own kind. And like many animals, they followed a certain hierarchy.

"How did it happen?"

"One of the hotel's owners lent them his motorboat and a driver, and they were following along a school of spinner dolphins south of Papio Bay. Angela wanted to swim with them, so they went ahead of the pod, anchored and jumped in the water, hoping to intercept. She was on a boogie board floating around in about eighty feet of water, looking like lunch. According to Zach, there was a huge explosion, like a bomb went off. She got rammed and then shoved about fifty feet through the water."

To a shark, people on boogie boards resembled seals, a favorite meal of the great white. Minnow had seen firsthand what happened when you floated a seal decoy around an aggregation of white sharks. The decoy never lasted long.

"No more photos?" she asked.

"There are photos, but they wouldn't let me take any of them out of the hospital. There's a burly dude standing guard who wanted to search me when I left, but I talked him out of it. Movie stars don't interest me. The lower half of her arm was barely hanging on, the docs were most likely going to amputate, and there are bite marks all along her right side and several ribs broken. She's badly bruised and lost a ton of blood, but luckily for her, they had the boat and a cell phone and were able to get her to the hospital pretty darn quick."

"Did any of the witnesses get a look at the shark?"

"Zach said it was hard to tell what he was seeing. He saw the thrashing and lots of red and that the animal looked almost black and was as wide as the boat. He thought maybe it was a whale, but then it went under. The ocean went still and he thought for sure it was going to come for him next, but it never came back. The boat driver sped over and scooped him up. He saw about the same thing as Zach, except he said the dorsal was probably three feet high."

"Any tooth fragments?"

"Nothing."

"She hit her with hurricane force, didn't she?" Minnow mused.

"Like a motherfucking freight train."

They sat for a few moments in silence and Minnow looked out on the water, thinking about the Sisterhood on the Farallones and where these behemoths went when they left the rocky offshore islands. Recent satellite tags had shown something surprising: They didn't hang out up and down the coast as previously thought. They ventured out into the deep blue Pacific, spending much of their time roaming the high seas. They moved fast, sometimes covering as much as sixty miles in a day, and they dove deeper than anyone expected, at least a half mile down, maybe more.

"I wonder if one of the Sisters is here. That would be something," she said, half to herself. Suddenly before her was the possibility of a hunt and what would happen if a Sister was caught. Her veins turned to salt.

"The Sisters?"

"When I was working at the Farallones, the shark project guys there called the posse of big females 'Sisters'—collectively, 'the Sisterhood.' They're all over seventeen feet and wider than a Ford truck," she said with reverence.

Whenever she thought of these sharks, which was often, she felt an overwhelming tug to go back to those dark, savage waters. These animals possessed a magnetism all their own, and she was caught up in their field, sure as night.

"Ah, I'm familiar with the project but not the term. How long were you there for?"

"Three seasons," she said.

Shark seasons. September through November.

This seemed to impress him. "Damn, you must have seen some rad shit."

What went on underwater at the Farallones was wilder and rawer and fiercer than anyone could ever imagine, but she had to laugh. "'Rad shit' is a good way to put it."

It felt good to release the tension twisting through her body as she'd listened about the incidents and studied the photographs. No doubt she would have dreams tonight. They always grew more violent in times like these.

"Speaking of rad shit, I just want you to be prepared for the media circus that's going to descend on this island once people find out about Angela. And even more so, if they get wind that Zach Santopolo was with her. Are you sure you're okay to be here without much backup?" he asked, looking her in the eye and holding her gaze.

No backup was probably closer to the truth.

"I came here to find out what I can about the shark—or sharks—so nothing has really changed in that regard. Everything I learn can help us understand their movements and motives better, and therefore our future conservation strategies," she said.

"Spoken like a true scientist. I knew I was making the right call by asking you here. Now, let me get packed and you can drop me at the airport on your way up the coast."

"What about meeting your intern, Nalu?" Minnow asked.

"We'll pick him up on the way," he said, glancing at his watch. "Where exactly are you staying?"

"With Woody Kaupiko. His family has a place called Hale Niuhi, on the coast near the Kiawe."

His eyes widened. "Woody Kaupiko, huh. How'd you get an invite there?"

"My uncle knows him from way back. Why?"

He shrugged. "Just that it seems you would need a connection to get in with that family. They aren't known for being warm and fuzzy, especially the older brother, Cliff. Word is, he's shot at a few boats that came too close into the bay there."

In her line of work, Minnow was used to outlaws and outliers, so the news hardly fazed her.

"My uncle never mentioned that. Just that Woody is a well-respected waterman and that the house is pretty rustic, at best."

"I guess you'll find out soon enough."

They pulled into Honokohau Harbor and were greeted by a giant white anchor and rows of struggling coconut trees, alongside a dry dock. Boats in different states of disrepair littered the sidewalk. Boat harbors always felt like home to Minnow, and this one was no different.

When they reached the water, Joe pointed toward the harbor mouth. "We have a whole shiver of sharks living out here. They came for the discarded fish parts and never left. As far as tigers go, they're quite tame, though. I've done a few dives with them." He paused as if he were lost in a memory. "Some of the local fisherman refer to them as 'the kittens of Honokohau.'"

Minnow smiled. "There's a misnomer if there ever was one. But I like it. How big are they?"

"The biggest one I've seen is Laverne. Fourteen feet and thick. Man, when you see those stripes it stirs something deep inside. Never gets old though, does it?"

She had to agree. "Never."

Joe honked when they pulled up in front of a restaurant on the water's edge, a greasy-looking joint. A minute later, a dark-skinned, long-haired young man with a ponytail came out. He looked all of twenty.

"Here's Nalu, my main man. Don't let his good looks fool you, or his laid-back attitude. The kid has more going on upstairs than most of the professors in my department."

Minnow was being left here with a boat, a truck, and a kid.

Nalu cruised on over to the truck, obviously in no hurry. "Dude, I thought you forgot about me."

Joe and Minnow both climbed out and introductions were made.

"Howzit," Nalu said.

"Minnow is staying next to the Kiawe, so you'll need to pick her up and drop her off there, or vice versa. I expect you to help her out while I'm gone and give her whatever she needs," Joe said.

Nalu raised an eyebrow. "Roger that."

Even with the harbor's strong smell of salty air and fish, he reeked of marijuana, as though he had walked through a cloud of burning buds.

Minnow offered, "I'm happy to drop you back at the hotel and take the truck."

"Nah, I'll drive you. Make sure you make it to your place okay."

She wanted the truck. And her freedom. "I have directions, I should be fine."

Nalu slung his backpack into the back of the truck. "Those roads in the lava are pretty heavy, and camouflaged. Not a good idea to go alone."

Joe nodded. "Better to go with a local."

So, her fate was sealed. Ride with the stoned intern and be stranded until morning.

Five minutes after she and Nalu had dropped Joe at the airport, Minnow rode with the window open and hot wind blowing in her face. The Bangles' "Walk Like an Egyptian" played on the radio, fading in and out of static, and Nalu moved his head forward and back along with the music. For some reason it made her smile. On one side Hualālai rose up, green and sloped and shrouded in clouds. The volcano's gentle girth appeared to take up the whole island until they crested a hill where the gentle slopes of another shield volcano came into view and two more in the distance off to the right. These were even more substantial. Across the channel a fifth peeked above the clouds.

"Haleakalā," Nalu said. "Maui."

"Which one is the tallest?"

He pointed, his tan arm remarkably well designed. "Mauna Kea. Almost fourteen thousand feet. Mother of the *'āina*—the land."

"I didn't realize they're that high."

"Taller than Everest when measured from the sea floor."

"So it gets deep out there. How far out?" she asked.

"Not very. The seafloor drops away pretty quick on this whole island. Aside from a few seamounts southwest of us, and Lō'ihi, our youngest volcano off the east side, we are surrounded by midnight and abyss. We even have our own trench, and trough."

The trench she had heard of but not the trough.

"Trough?"

"Kind of like our own moat. The weight of our islands depresses the lithosphere, which is already fragile from the hotspot below. We're living dangerously out here," he said.

"How deep is the trough?"

"About eighteen thousand feet at her deepest. And in her shallows, we have mesophytic coral ecosystems inhabited by many of our own Hawaiian brands of fish."

Nalu flipped seamlessly between surfer dude and science nerd.

"So what's your take on the attacks?" she asked.

The sky had darkened even more, and a fat drop of rain plopped on the windshield.

"I think it's the same one," he said, "because our concentration of white sharks is low and all reports mention the extreme size of this thing. What are the odds of there being two massive white sharks here?"

"Low to none."

He took off his shades and set them on the dashboard as they drove into a sheet of rain. "You're the expert. What do you think after talking with Dr. Joe?"

The way he said it made her wonder how he felt about her being here. The pecking order of scientists was a real thing, and as an intern he was bottom of the rung.

"I would have to agree, and yet I don't believe we have some man-eating monster here. There has to be a reason the shark is hanging around," she said.

"If there is, we'll find it."

"I'm surprised there's been no sign of a whale carcass or something. No big runoff events?"

"Nope. But that doesn't mean there isn't a carcass of some kind out there. The ocean hides things, you know that."

She knew it absolutely did. Swallower of boats and submarines and lost souls, keeper of secrets and all kinds of sublime aquatic life, most of which humans had never seen.

"How did you get into sharks?" she asked.

He sat quiet for a few beats. "When I was in high school—I went to Kahuku on the east side of O'ahu—all the spots we surfed were big-time sharky. We just kinda accepted it, you know? Then one day my friend lost his foot. Got nailed by a tiger. The next day, a group of guys went out and caught three big sharks, pulled them into the beach at Hukilau and laid them all out. One of them was huge—like fourteen feet, and pregnant. They were so proud, and all I could think was how beautiful this animal was. Seeing her lying there dead with her mouth open just seemed so senseless. It really haunted me."

"I'm sorry," she said, knowing firsthand the pain of seeing something like that. "About your friend. And the shark."

He nodded. "I used to love to fish. I never did after that."

She understood.

"Did you keep surfing?"

"It took a while before anyone went out to that break, except guys from the mainland. But eventually we did, and over time we forgot."

"Tragedy happens, but the world keeps on spinning, doesn't it?"

He nodded. "I still surf plenty, but I pay more attention to my *na'au.* When I get that shark vibe or if it feels weird before I go out—murky water, guys fishing—I stay back."

They shared a few moments of fin-filled silence before she decided to clear the air. "I'm here to help you, you know. Not to step on your toes or get in your way."

He tensed. "I never said you were."

"Just putting it out there."

They moved out of one deluge toward another, passing a wide-mouthed bay with a black sand lagoon to one side. Beyond that, they paralleled a longer stretch of cliffy coastline with no trees or foliage and no sign of life. Then they hit an area with rambling, delicate-leafed trees Nalu called *kiawe* but Minnow knew as mesquite, growing straight out of the crumbly lava. *Inhospitable* was the word that came to mind.

Five minutes later, Nalu slowed the truck and they bounced off the pavement onto a narrow rocky shoulder. One spindly bougainvillea with a few pink leaves stood alone in the black, looking forlorn and out of place. Rain bucketed down and Nalu turned his wipers on high, swishing guppy-sized drops.

"I think this is it," he said.

The barely perceptible road down to the house swung back the way they'd come and ended up at a thick, one-bar gate built into a mound of lava. He stopped and they looked at each other, neither making a move to get out.

"Is this kind of rain usual? I thought this was supposed to be a legitimate desert," she said, as the windshield began fogging up.

"Afternoon convection. Not uncommon," he said.

She reached for her door latch. "I'll get the gate."

He opened his door and jumped out, fast like a ninja. "I got it. What's the combo?"

"Six-seven-six-six."

When he climbed back in, he was dripping. The truck rattled through the *a'a* lava, what Nalu said was the crumbly, slow-moving kind, and they crunched their way toward a hazy gray ocean. The truck rattled, squeaked and scraped over the lunar terrain, and Minnow was just waiting for a tire to go flat.

"It would be nice if I could *see* something," she said.

"You will in the morning."

"Speaking of tomorrow, I'd like to get on the water early to see where the attacks happened and get a sense of the area, then go to the hospital later to check on Angela. What time is sunrise here?" she asked.

"Almost seven."

"What time can you be back here?"

Judging by the trip today, the drive here from the hotel, without stops, would take forty minutes give or take.

"Depends on how late I stay out tonight," he said with a goofy grin.

"Sounds like you have your priorities straight."

"Joke," he said. "I'll be here bright-eyed and bushy-tailed at six thirty. Will that work for you?"

"Perfect."

They came upon a sharp fork in the road.

"Turn left," she said. "Woody says the right goes to the Kiawe. Do you know how far it is from here?"

"If we had kept going on the highway, we would've hit the turnoff anytime. Too bad you aren't staying there, the place is legendary."

"I could afford to stay there for about half an hour, if that," she said.

He laughed. "Yup, sounds about right."

A little farther on, Minnow could just make out a hand-painted sign on a coconut tree that said, *KAPU! No trespass.* She cracked the window and saw the ocean next to them, gray and choppy. No beach, just lava up to the edge of the water. And then a house appeared, flanked by coconut trees. Red roof, brown wooden siding, thatched fronds over an extended porch. No other cars were in sight.

"Where is everyone?" Nalu asked.

"Woody said he'll try to make it down tomorrow or the next day. He sent me detailed instructions on how to open up and get the generator running since there's no electricity."

He seemed surprised. "So it's just you?"

"For now."

"What are you going to eat tonight?"

The clouds had obliterated any sign of a sunset, other than a hazy orange out over the ocean where she imagined the horizon must be. Everything else was draped in a monochromatic gray.

"I had a late lunch with Joe, so I'm still full, and I have an apple and trail mix. I'll be fine."

She grabbed her bags from the back and climbed out. The rain had slowed to a featherlight drizzle and felt refreshing on her skin. Not icy cold like California rain, this felt like a caress, a welcome. Something about the place felt vaguely familiar, almost as though she'd been here before. Maybe Uncle Jimmy's old photos were now coming to life. In all honesty, she was happier to be here than she thought she'd be.

"Thanks for the ride. I'll see you in the morning," she said, then shut the door and moved toward the house.

Walking on crushed lava and bleached-white coral fragments, she made her way around to the back, following Woody's instructions. Behind the house, hidden earlier by trees that could have come from the pages of a Dr. Seuss book, a large network of ponds meandered toward another red-roofed house. She could still hear the truck idling. Nalu, she guessed, was debating whether to be a good human and help her or do the bare minimum required.

In her mind this was exactly what separated the bad interns from the good ones: a willingness to do the most mundane and unforgiving tasks *without* being asked. Anything from scrubbing nine months' worth of bird shit from the picnic table to volunteering to help pull up the anchor in frothing ten-foot seas, where a rat pack of white sharks circled below.

On a narrow back porch, she set down her things and pulled out a flashlight so she could see the numbers on the lock. It was so rusty, it felt like it would crumble in her hands, but eventually she slid the combo into place and the lock popped open. She pressed the door, but it didn't budge, so she pushed with her shoulder before finally resorting to kicking. The door swung open into musty blackness.

Where the hell were the windows?

From the journal of Minnow Gray

Farallon Islands, September 1, 1995

Getting the invite here feels like I've won the lottery, and I have Doc Finnegan to thank. The house where we scientists stay is decrepit, wind-battered and as unwelcoming as they come. The guys here say it's haunted, and not just by mice. I can believe it. Windows rattle, floorboards creak and unnamed things howled a few nights ago when a storm hurled breaking waves in over the rocks. I'm still getting settled, but I know I'm going to love it.

Yesterday I had a crash course in Farallon history from Max, the head of the shark project, and I have to admit, I'm fascinated by the island's dark past (and if I'm honest, by him too). Over the past few hundred years, these rocky islands have been home to shipwrecks, rapacious seal hunters, egg collectors and lighthouse keepers. Death and disease ran rampant, and being here, I can see why. But I am more than happy to overlook the bleak, barren land and the ghosts and vermin in exchange for a few months at what is essentially a block party of oversized sharks.

CHAPTER 4

The House

Hale: *house, building, lodge, hall*

Minnow stood on the porch wondering what kind of weirdness she had gotten herself into. Her beam swept across the inside of the house and she heard the scurry of rodent or insect somewhere in the dark recesses. A gust blowing in from behind stirred up the faint smell of decay and memories of the first time she had stepped foot in the old house on Southeast Farallon. This felt like a tropical version, but here she was alone. Hoping Nalu had changed his mind about leaving, she peered around the corner. But the crunch of rolling tires and taillights pulling away gave Minnow her answer.

There was one consolation, though. Upon closer inspection, she saw the house was, in actuality, all windows. It was also all one room, dormitory style, with a kitchen off to one side. Along three of the walls were ropes on pulleys to pull up the boards blocking each window. Quickly she went to the closest wall and began unlatching the screens, pulling up the boards, and tying them off on a cleat. Fresh, salty air blew in and the sound of the surf out front filled up the house, completely changing the vibe from suffocating and stuffy to possibly habitable.

Once she got everything open, she found a battery-powered Coleman lantern that surprisingly worked. From her bag she dug out the paper with Woody's instructions for turning on the water, the generator and the propane-powered fridge and stove, and began reading. According to Woody the gasoline-powered generator was out back in a cobwebby shed and started on the second pull, the propane tanks were easy, but the fridge would require her to lie on the peeling floor and stick her arm way back underneath to light the pilot. That could wait until tomorrow when Woody came. *If* Woody came.

The eight beds were twins, all soft and saggy. She picked the one on the ocean-side corner and set her bags on a card table next to it. Under the warm glow of incandescent lights, the house felt more inviting. A small doorway opened into the sliver of a kitchen that felt more like the galley on a boat than an actual kitchen. But as long as she had a place to lay her head, she would make do.

Faded photographs hung along one wall and she walked closer to inspect them. Old family pictures of a beautiful, smiling couple with three young kids, two boys and a girl. The father looked part Hawaiian, the woman, white. In some they were holding fish, in others playing ukulele. Always sun-kissed and smiling.

Off to the right there were some newer ones. A series of portraits. One in particular caught her eye. A close-up of a dark-haired man wearing a coconut hat, green eyes creased around the edges and looking straight into the camera with a half grin, as though in on some universal secret.

She had seen a much younger version of him in a photo album of Uncle Jimmy's. Woody Kaupiko, a man he spoke of with uncommon admiration. Someone who was born of the sea because his ancestors depended on it. Looking around at all the shells, driftwood and Japanese glass fishing floats, she felt that connection in her bones. She looked forward to meeting him but also felt a shiver of nervousness.

Off the kitchen another door opened onto a concrete deck area under a trellis of some kind of twining plant. She noticed at the far end another smaller house. All of it bordered by a lava rock seawall and a certain kind of rustic charm. She let herself out and walked to the edge. Again, she felt a strange familiarity. Maybe the scene reminded her of Catalina and the rocky edge of the sea or of the Farallones.

The beach out front, if you could call it that, was all sea-smoothed pebbles, clattering as the waves rushed in and out. Minnow stood there for some time, wind on her face, feeling the invisible pull of the ocean. She thought of her father, now dimmed through the fog of time, and wished he were here. He would have loved the ruggedness of this place and its proximity to the water. But she also often wondered how he would have felt about her chosen profession—though the profession had really chosen her. Studying and trying to save the creatures that cut his life short seemed such a strange twist of fate.

When she was younger, school had been her least favorite thing. One day in first grade, she'd snuck out during nap time, walked down to the beach, torn off her clothes and jumped in the water as naked as a piece of whittled driftwood.

That night at home, her parents had gotten into a huge fight over it. The fights usually started the same way—over something Minnow did or didn't do. Or something Bruce did or didn't do. Layla seemed to take personal offense at everything, as though these perceived transgressions were done specifically *to* her.

The truth was, her mother had been the furthest thing from Minnow's mind that morning. She'd wanted to be near the fish and sharks and circling gulls. She wanted to be surrounded by seaweed and dolphins and shell-stealing hermit crabs. Not chalkboards and notepads.

"Minnow, you can't keep doing these kinds of irrational things," her mother would say. "It worries me and it makes us look like bad parents."

Then Bruce would stick up for Minnow. Always. An alliance that had formed early on, its grooves only deepening as time passed.

Until they didn't. Until Bruce was gone.

A vicious attack, they said, when really it was just one bite.

But one bite was often all it took.

I miss you, Dad.

As she stood there on the rock wall, a wave lightly splashed her, reminding her of where she was. Her gaze swung north, and she realized the flickering lights in the distance must be the Kiawe. By all accounts, the resort was one of a kind. A haven for rich people who wanted to pretend they were camping on a remote island in the Pacific, but with all the amenities of a five-star hotel. No Vienna sausage or Tang there. And instead of a building, the resort sprawled out in a village of thatched-roof huts, home to its own restaurant, poolside bar and spa. Minnow had seen photographs in the magazine on the way over, and though the Kiawe wasn't her style, it looked pretty cool—if you were a gazillionaire.

Funny thing was, in his instructions for opening the house, Woody had mentioned he had a running tab at Reef House Restaurant and the Saltwater Bar, so Minnow could mosey on over anytime she wanted. Just follow the white coral path. She figured that tomorrow night she might take him up on it, depending on how the day went and whether he showed up. She had no way of reaching him, so she'd just have to wait and see.

After sitting on the wall until the sky turned an inky black, she went back inside to eat her apple. She decided to call it an early night and brushed her teeth, turned off the generator, pulled off the bright floral coverlet on the bed and slid into the crunchy sheets. Weary as she was, sleep terrified her because she knew what was coming. But her eyes kept closing as she tried to read *The Perfect Storm* by lantern. Eventually she switched off the lantern and hoped the ocean would lull her to sleep. It did not. Instead, her mind wandered to old memories, and to sharks.

From the journal of Minnow Gray

August 18, 1993

We call them white sharks, *not* great white sharks. *Why? Because there is no lesser white shark so there is no reason to have a greater white shark. Except I would argue you could use* great *to mean "large" or "superior" or "substantial," which all define the* Carcharodon carcharias *perfectly.*

CHAPTER 5

The Man

Kane: *male, husband, man*

One of Minnow's earliest memories was of sitting on a rock at the edge of a deep drop-off, watching a perfect triangle of a fin slice through the water while her father skinned a fish. The shark was close enough that the large, blue-ringed eye met her own and something knowing and alive passed between them.

Then a few years later, when she was old enough to go in the water alone, she would swim in the tiny urchin-filled cove below their house on Catalina Island, waiting for her father to return from one of his dives. Little by little she would venture farther out toward the mouth of the bay, where her mother told her never to go. But limits were not something Minnow understood well. In her mind, a limit was a line you crossed once the adults had stopped paying attention.

One particular day, soon after she'd turned six, had been burned into her memory like an old film, and she watched it play through her mind as she lay in bed unable to sleep. The water that day had been unseasonably warm and she had made it out to the edge of the cove, where the bottom fell away sharply, the point of no return, and she thought of her mom's warning. But after diving down and seeing a school of neon orange garibaldi, she followed them into a kelp forest in the open water. Their scales caught the sunlight and gave them a magical iridescent look. In fact, everything in the water that day took on a magical hue. Even the big shadow that swam above her, blotting out the sun.

She looked up in anticipation, believing it to be her father's yellow kayak, and she was excited to tell him about the fish she had seen. But what she saw was much bigger than the kayak, and glowing white, as though containing its own light source. Momentarily forgetting she needed air, she watched the animal slowly circle around her. She held on to a stalk of slimy kelp to keep herself down.

There was a largeness to the creature that caught her off guard. And an oldness too. Minnow floated wide-eyed as the shark assessed her, then slid back into the beyond, the final swish of its tail a wave goodbye.

Over the course of the next year, Minnow's forays took her farther out of the cove and up and down the island coast. Some days she would see the shark, some days she wouldn't. Every so often she would see a different shark but none as big as the first and none she felt so friendly with. And so her obsession began.

When no one was looking, she would poach a fish or two from her father's bait box and slip down to the rocks at the point, tossing them out. Something she realized now was not the smartest idea. *Her* shark was a female and she called her Luna. On her dorsal fin, Luna had four slits. The cuts were deep but had long healed over and now gave her fin a feathery look. They made her easy to spot from above or below. Now, with years of research under her belt, Minnow believed Luna was possibly a Sister.

Thud.

Minnow woke to the weight of something landing on her shoulder. Quick as a darting eel, she brushed off whatever it was and flung it as far away as possible, then switched on her flashlight to see a large brown spider scurrying away. *Oh fuck*. Give her a shark over a spider any day. Across the room, she saw a broom and dashed over to it, miraculously managing to steer the spider out the door.

It took her heart about fifteen minutes to slow, and she lay awake awhile longer, listening to the Hawaiian night sounds. While earlier the house had been warm enough for just a sheet, now a chill had crept in and she swaddled herself in a bug-proof cocoon of blanket. Every so often a fish jumped in the pond, making a light splash in the stillness. If she didn't count the spider and the task that loomed in the morning, Hawai'i was really quite lovely.

Eventually she drifted off again and fell into a dreamless slumber that ended when she heard the sound of a rumbling engine before it cut off. Moments later, a wide beam of light shone in her eyes, disorienting her. She looked at her watch. Six twenty-two. The light moved up to the ceiling and pinballed around, then went dark. It was coming from the ocean.

Minnow shook out her clothes from yesterday, slid them on and ran outside with the Coleman lantern. "Hello?" she called.

"Yo, it's me, Nalu," said a voice in the dark.

Relief and confusion flooded in.

"What are you doing?"

"I said I'd pick you up."

She wanted to protest but could find no real argument. He'd said he would be here and he was.

"It was faster this way. No backtracking required," he added.

In the dim light of dawn, she could see the boat was tied off to a mooring float maybe fifty feet out.

"How will I get out there?"

He turned the light on again, blinding her. "Swim?"

Bad idea.

"I have a lot of gear."

"I'm sure there are surfboards there, just borrow one. And no rush. I'll drink my coffee and watch the sky."

Just hearing the word *coffee* made her mouth water. And he was right. There were surfboards here, and even a small kayak. Minnow brushed her teeth and gathered her gear before pulling the red kayak onto the rocky beach. The ocean had calmed in the night and she managed to get everything aboard and paddle out with no trouble. This water was nothing like launching at East Landing on the Farallones, where any misstep could turn you into chum.

Nalu helped hoist her stuff up and she tied the kayak to the old Clorox bottle buoy. His hair was wild and loose and had taken on a life of its own in the night. He smelled like weed again too. By now the eastern sky behind Mauna Kea was splashed a coral red. But until she had her coffee, Minnow could barely process anything that was happening around her.

She nodded to the small paper cup he was holding. "You don't have any more of that, do you?"

He gulped back whatever was left in his cup, holding his mouth open to catch the last drop. "Nope, sorry, not enough hands this morning."

"Okay, well, I need coffee."

She had seen a can of Folgers on the kitchen shelf that, along with most of the other goods, looked prehistoric.

He glanced around. "Hmm. No real options in the area."

"What about the hotel?"

"That bad, huh?"

"Unfortunately, yes."

All her attempts at quitting caffeine had been embarrassingly unsuccessful. Nor did she need a headache today of all days. There was too much on tap.

He shrugged. "You're calling the shots. But I'm down if you wanna try."

"If we manage to snag some, I'll buy your next cup," she offered.

"You're on."

They buzzed up the coast full throttle, a few hundred yards offshore. The vessel was an older, twenty-two-foot Boston Whaler with a beefy Yamaha engine, the perfect size and plenty of juice. Minnow preferred the smaller boats because they were easier to get in and out of and nimbler around rocks and surf. Nalu stood at the helm, stance wide, hair tousled in the wind. He didn't say another word until they approached the Kiawe less than ten minutes later.

"Thar she blows," he said.

"Can you drop me on the beach?" she asked.

"I'll get as close as I can, but you're gonna have to get wet either way."

Within the crescent-shaped cove two motorboats and a catamaran were moored, plus a sailing canoe anchored in the middle. Minnow stripped to her swimsuit and held a folded, frayed towel in her hand. The bottom of the bay was mostly sand, so he dropped her in waist-deep water and she waded to shore. Just before seven thirty, the beach was empty, but she could see a few guests at tables around the bar area, all heads turned her way. Wrapping the towel around herself, she made her way up to the wooden deck, barefoot and half naked, her favorite way to be.

The Saltwater Bar was the polar opposite of Hale Niuhi. Sleek, freshly oiled teak furniture, leather-bound menus, and bursts of gardenias on every table. Shiny silverware, cloth napkins. An older couple wearing straw hats and loose linen clothing. Minnow noticed a long table at the far end covered in bowls of fruit, muffins and pastries. Next to those were pitchers of juice, all backed by a row of pineapples. Her mouth puckered.

"Can I help you?"

Minnow jumped and her hand flew to her chest. "Oh gosh, you scared me. Yes, I'm looking for coffee."

The pretty young woman did not smile. "Are you a guest of the resort?" Though from the cold tone in her voice, it was obvious she already knew the answer.

"No, but I'm staying next door."

"Next door? There is no next door here, ma'am."

Nothing worse than being called *ma'am*.

"Just down the way, at Hale Niuhi," Minnow said. The woman looked at her blankly, so she added. "At the Kaupiko property."

For anything else Minnow would have retreated back to the beach and moved on, not wanting to hassle or draw attention to herself. But not coffee.

"I was told by Mr. Kaupiko that he has—"

An older gentleman wearing a shirt in the same green print suddenly appeared behind the bar. "George, can you please show this woman back to her boat?" the woman asked.

George smiled and Minnow stepped over to the bar. "Good morning, George. I'm staying at Woody Kaupiko's, and he told me he has a running tab here. All I need is two cups of coffee and I'll be on my way. Please."

His smile widened. "Why didn't you say so?"

"I did say so."

Minnow turned, but the woman had already left them.

"No worries, Lina is new and Woody nevah been here long time. So what brings a pretty *wahine* like you to Hale Niuhi?"

His pidgin accent reminded her of her time in Kāne'ohe as an undergrad, subtle yet so distinct.

"Business."

He laughed as he set two paper cups on the counter. "What kine business you in?"

Sharks, she almost said, then caught herself. That was certain to open a big can of worms and she wasn't in the mood for that. "Research."

"Research for what?"

"A book."

It was partly true. She had an *idea* for a book, and journals and notebooks full of notes, but had never quite started. A memoir. But first she needed to remember.

"A Hemingway type, huh? That's gotta be the best spot for writing. No one around for miles to bother you."

Minnow felt her right cheek heating up and sensed someone at the far end of the bar listening in on their conversation. But she kept her eyes on George, who was about to pour some cream into the coffee.

She held up a hand. "Black, please."

He motioned toward the back table. "Care for any food, then? You look like you could use some plumping up."

It was true. Since breaking it off with Max, she had lost seven pounds on her already thin frame. Still, she hated when people pointed it out.

"Thanks, but I have to get going."

"Not without our famous mango muffins. Woody would never forgive me. I'll pack a few to go for you so you can grind 'um later," he said, taking off for the kitchen.

Minnow turned slightly to see where the boat was but instead made eye contact with the man at the end of the bar. He looked to be alone and had a newspaper spread out in front of him, which he quickly glanced back at. She tried to look away but found that she could not, and stood rooted to the floorboards. His gold-tipped hair came out of his hat in loose pieces, and his face was dusted in freckles. The way he stared at the paper, a little too intently, made her think he wasn't really reading it, merely pretending to.

Then he looked up at her again and fixed his eyes on hers. Yellow-green, like kelp on a sunny morning. She felt like she was being studied, the same way she would have studied a new species of shark or any number of undersea creatures.

"Hey," he finally said, no smile.

"Hi."

He wore a long-sleeved T-shirt, red surf shorts and rubber slippers, and seemed out of place. Maybe he was a lifeguard, early for work.

"What's your book about?" he asked.

The question caught her off guard. "My book?"

"You told George you were writing a book."

She laughed self-consciously. "Oh, right. Well I haven't actually started it yet, I'm still in the brainstorming phase."

"What's it about?" he asked again, not rude but not friendly.

His face was all angles, as though whittled by the wind. And he was handsome. The kind of handsome that usually came with a boatload of trouble.

"A memoir. About my life," she said, grasping at words and wondering where her brain had gone. "Nothing that interesting."

One side of his mouth lifted ever so slightly. "Sounds like a guaranteed bestseller."

The way he said it, all sleepy-eyed and nonchalant, irritated her. "Actually, I think it could be a bestseller, not that it's any of your business."

She turned to leave, but her eyes caught a word in bold at the top of his newspaper.

Shark.

He tracked her eye movement and held up the paper, as if for her to see.

Shark Hunt on Table.

Minnow stepped closer. "Excuse me, would you mind if I have a quick look at your paper?" She practically snatched it out of his hands and scanned the front page. No mention of Angela Crawford, at least there was that.

> State and county officials weigh in on the possibility of a shark hunt in the wake of deadly attacks on the Big Island's Kohala Coast. It wouldn't be the first time sharks have been targeted in the aftermath of an attack. From the late fifties to the mid-seventies, close to five thousand sharks were culled in attempts to make Hawaiian waters safer. The

> tally includes 554 tiger sharks, the second most common shark responsible for attacks on humans, after the great white.
>
> "We need to make sure our waters are safe," Mitch Hamada, head of Tourism Authority, said. "And if there are sharks on the loose with a taste for humans, that won't be good for business."

She stopped reading, disgusted. "They have no fricking idea," she said, handing back the paper. "Thanks."

"The sharks or the Tourism Authority?"

There was no sarcasm in his tone, and she realized it was an honest question.

"Actually, both."

"Have you been following the story?" he asked.

"Yeah, I read the papers. Why?"

For some reason she was still bothered by his off-the-cuff bestseller comment and wanted to get out of here and back to the boat.

"It just seems like a visitor staying in the middle of a bloody triangle might want to know what's lurking out there," he said.

"Last I checked, sharks *live* in our oceans. Big sharks, little sharks, old sharks, new sharks. And they do not *lurk*, they swim. Because if they stop swimming, they die."

He looked slightly amused. "Sounds like you have an opinion about it. I like that. Too many people these days are incapable of thinking for themselves."

Now she was curious. "Do you have an opinion about these shark incidents?"

He held his mug with both hands, as though he needed to be warmed up. He stared into it for a while, then said, "Not really."

His whole demeanor changed and she wondered why. Then George returned with a plastic bag full of goodies.

"You come back anytime, and tell Woody, if he ever shows up, that Uncle George says *aloha* and to come on ovah." Then he leaned closer and lowered his voice. "By the way, did he tell you what Hale Niuhi means in Hawaiian?"

"No, what does it mean?"

George stepped back, fiddling with his mustache. "I think better he tell you. There's a story behind it."

Of course now she was dying to know, but there was no time for stories and George seemed like a long-winded kind of guy. She thanked him and left, juggling the coffee and muffins and her towel, which kept slipping down past her hips. When she reached the edge of the sand, her head half turned back to the bar. The man was watching her. Her heart ramped up a few beats, and she turned away before she could do anything stupid, like smile.

From the journal of Minnow Gray

Guadalupe Island, July 4, 1996

Lots of people say that white sharks have a soulless, dead stare. That has not been my experience. I was fifteen when I saw Jaws*. I didn't want to go, but Sandy's mom offered to take a bunch of us to a drive-in showing and I felt obligated to say yes. I remember so clearly that line in the movie where Quint says, "Ya know the thing about a shark, he's got . . . lifeless eyes, black eyes, like a doll's eyes. When he comes at ya, doesn't seem to be livin' . . ."*

As with so much in life, it all depends on the light. Today a sixteen-foot adult female known as Cat made pass after pass an arm's length away from me while I was in the cage. The morning sun illumined the blue ring of her iris outside of the black pupil. I could see her tracking me each time she swam by and there was nothing dead about those eyes. Sorry, Quint.

CHAPTER 6

The Search

***Moananuiākea**: the vast Pacific Ocean*

Morning on the Kohala Coast. Calm, oil-slick water, blue and blue and more blue. Black and black and more black. Lava leveling everything in its way until it meets the ocean. Few beaches. All around, mountains rising from the water like pyramids.

Everyone on Oʻahu spoke about how different the Big Island was, but being here made it feel so much more alive. As if the island vibrated at a higher frequency. And something about the sheer bulk of those volcanoes made her feel tiny but also part of the fabric of the place, as if she were woven into the morning by air and water and sunshine.

Nalu kept the boat moving at a good clip as they headed to the point break where the incident with surfer Stuart Callahan happened. While laypeople threw around the word *attack*, Minnow preferred *bite* or *incident*. Much of the time, people died from a shark bite rather than an all-out attack. White sharks are notoriously curious, and since they have no hands, they use their mouth to investigate things. And those mouths are home to seven rows of serrated teeth, with a conveyor belt moving in a new tooth when an old one falls out.

The point was about eight miles south of the Kiawe and a mile south of an enclave of billionaire homes known as Koholā. The water was so smooth, Minnow was able to drink her coffee without spilling. When they arrived at Bird Rock, the name of the surf break, she was still bone dry.

"Why is it called Bird Rock?" Minnow asked.

Nalu pointed to a scattering of dry rocks off the point. "Because there's usually a bird standing on one of those rocks."

"What kind of bird?"

"*'Auku'u*. Heron."

He turned off the motor and they floated forty yards or so outside the bay. Beneath the surface, coral heads in a myriad of yellows and purples and reds spread out in all directions. The benign beauty made it hard to believe what horrors had happened in this exact spot a week ago. A body vibrant and alive and riding waves one minute, then bleeding out the next.

Today there was no surf and it was hard to imagine waves rolling in here.

"Is this where they were?" she asked.

"From what I hear, there's an outside break when the surf is bigger and another smaller one here. The waves were sizable that day, and Stuart and his dad, Sam, were out there."

She could see the coral shelf for another forty yards or so, and then the water turned a deeper shade of blue. "Looks like a big drop-off out there."

"It gets deep fast."

She paused, thinking. Steep drops were notorious for attracting sharks because the upwelling of cooler water mixing with warm was often a place where fish hung out.

"Did you guys have a look underwater?"

"No. We've been tight on time."

"Let's go farther out. I'd like to get in," she said.

They were already here, so they may as well see the underwater topography.

Nalu drove them out and dropped anchor. The sun burned down hot, and Minnow couldn't wait to submerge herself. Though Nalu had brought tanks, she wanted to free dive. It was her preferred method of being in the water, less encumbered. For her sixth birthday, her father had given her an oval-shaped mask that had quickly become her most prized possession. She carried it everywhere and even slept with it next to her feather-soft pillow. Since it came with no snorkel, she had been practicing holding her breath and noticed she could stay under for longer periods of time. Her goal was to grow her own gills, though she never told anyone that.

While she pulled out her mask and fins, Nalu just stood there.

"Are you coming with me?" she asked.

"Do you want me to?"

"Two sets of eyes are always better than one."

He surveyed the water around the boat, first starboard and then port, almost as though he was afraid.

"You think it's still hanging around here?" he asked.

"I doubt it, but there's only one way to find out. And anyway, I want to see the topography for my incident notes."

Not looking too excited about the prospect, he slowly peeled off his shirt and grabbed his gear, spitting in his mask and nodding over at two three-prong spears, which lay along the side of the boat. "You need one?" he asked.

Minnow held up her dive knife. "I have this."

Not that a dive knife or a three-prong would do much in the event of an ambush attack by a large shark, but that was a risk you took.

As soon as she jumped in, she turned a slow three-sixty, surveying her surroundings. The silent blue of the water immediately dissolved all thoughts of the world above. Toward shore, coral shelves and clumps and heads lay beneath schools of yellow tang and a whole menagerie of colorful reef fish. Her gaze swung around and followed a ledge with a narrow channel leading away from her, walls lined with red pencil urchins and spiny urchins bigger than her head. Visibility was incredible, an easy eighty feet or more. It was easy to tell where the surf break was—a large flat table of rock much shallower than the surrounding area sat just outside of them.

Minnow looked up at Nalu, who was still in the boat. "Looks beautiful, all clear," she said.

"This is some of the clearest water on the coast. All rock, no sand."

He slid into the water gingerly, like he was trying not to make any splashing sounds, and she wondered what was going on with him. Though she did have to admit, there was something unsettling about entering the water in the exact spot something so violent had happened.

"Let's look around outside first and then follow the ledge in toward shore," she said, ducking under and swimming toward the coral shelf where the waves presumably broke.

The way the sunbeams shone on the fish scales made them look like swimming kaleidoscopes, and the purple puffs of coral almost undulated beneath her. As surreal and lovely as it was, swimming in new waters always gave her a shiver of nerves. You never knew what was just over the next rock or moving in from the deep.

They swam across the shallow shelf, and Minnow counted four large tiger cowries, a small snowflake eel and one small octopus, who quickly turned from mauve to mottled brown, like seaweed. Nalu swam down and poked at it with his spear. Not wanting him to kill the little creature, she tapped his shoulder, causing him to swirl around fast and pop his head out of the water.

His eyes were big. "What?"

"Don't hurt it," she said.

He let out a big exhale. "Not planning on it. Sometimes they like to play tug of war."

A big relief, since octopuses were one of her favorite animals—shy and inquisitive and feisty. She had gotten to know a few in her underwater ventures. One had even tried to steal her camera, grabbing on with two tentacles and refusing to let go.

By the time she put her head under again, Nalu's octopus was gone. They swam to the far edge of the ledge, where the bottom fell away fast. Rays of sun disappeared in the abyss, and she understood very clearly why an attack had happened here.

While smaller sharks, especially blacktip and whitetip reef sharks, patrolled these rocky shallows, mature white sharks usually stayed in cooler, deeper waters. She could easily imagine a large white shark cruising along the drop-off, not actively hunting but with an eye open for seal, turtle or even a baby whale. Her large tail would have been swishing slowly back and forth, no hurry, nothing to fear. Stuart had definitely been in the wrong place at the wrong time.

Minnow swam down six feet or so and hung there. Her body felt relaxed in the warm water, but her mind was acutely aware of that curtain of blue, the line where visibility ended, the space to always keep your eye on. Sharks were masters at approaching on the periphery, often from behind. Their vision was much better than a human's, and you could bet they saw you before you saw them. But now, nothing moved in toward them. No dark shadow from the deep, no swift swimming ghost.

They circled around the coral mountain with Nalu staying close on her heels, and Minnow felt like it should be the other way around, with him being the local. As they entered the bay, narrow cracks opened up in the coral, and when Minnow dove down to peer inside one, she came face-to-face with a gold-flecked moray eel with half its body out of the hole. Reflexively, she backed away and then swam up for air.

Nalu came up a few seconds later. "Grandfather *puhi*," he said.

"*Puhi* is 'eel'?"

He nodded. From her brief time here, she remembered a few Hawaiian names of sea creatures. *Honu*, turtle. *Humuhumunukunukuāpua'a*, triggerfish, *manō*, shark. She'd need to shore up on the multitudes of fish names with the books in the house, faded and water-stained as they were.

At its deepest, the bay was only twenty feet or so, and Nalu seemed more relaxed in the protected waters, going off on his own and pulling up a giant helmet shell to show her. The sun toasted Minnow's back through her top, and she wanted to keep going, following every little curve and cove along the shore, but there was so much to do back on land. Arranging a visit with Angela Crawford was high on her list. As was getting in to see the mayor. If she could win him over, half the battle was won.

From the journal of Minnow Gray

February 4, 1991

Galeophobia: *an intense, irrational and persistent fear of sharks. Many scientists believe this fear is not innate in humans. That means we are not born to fear sharks. I believe I am proof of this.*

CHAPTER 7

Settling In

***Manō:** shark*

Early afternoon they unloaded at the boat harbor, Minnow feeling crisp and toasty and already turning pink. This time she dropped off Nalu at his hotel, stopped for groceries and headed back to the house. With no word when Woody was coming, she slithered onto the floor and tried to light the fridge. It took a few snaps, and then she saw the blue flame of the pilot light flick on. Same as yesterday, a thick layer of cloud cover had materialized midafternoon, stacking up against the flanks of Hualālai and spreading down the mountain minute by minute. Minnow ate her peanut butter and honey sandwich on the patio in the shade of the trellis above, a tangled thicket of woody vines.

In the light of day, she could tell no one had been here in a while. Leaves and sticks and sand had piled up on the concrete deck pad, and the grass out front toward the ocean was overgrown and strewn with coconut fronds. When she was done eating, she did a quick tidy up of the place, then called the hospital on the ancient rotary phone. Dr. Eversole had given her Angela's room number and said not to ask for her by name but just to refer to her as *the shark incident patient.*

"North Hawai'i Community Hospital. How may I direct your call?"

"I'd like to speak to the nurses' station for room 206, please."

The phone rang and rang and she almost gave up, but a harried-sounding voice finally answered. "Aloha. East wing nurses' station."

"Hi there. I'm a shark biologist working on the recent attacks. And I'm calling to find out how and when I can speak with the shark incident patient in room 206. My name is Dr. Gray."

There was such a long pause that Minnow began to worry that maybe Angela hadn't made it. "Yes, well, we can't give out any personal information without patient consent. And no visitors at this time."

"I'm not a visitor. I've been hired to work on the case."

"Hired by who?"

Good question. "By the university—the state." Though she couldn't even be sure who exactly she was working for.

"Hang on. I'll need to go check," the nurse said.

As she waited, she watched a fat gecko scurry down the weathered wooden post, a mongoose weave in and out of the bushes, and a gray heron land on a rock out front. At least she wasn't alone.

Five minutes later, the nurse came back on. "The patient is sleeping and the doctors are busy, so I don't know what to tell you."

At least Angela was alive.

"Is there any family I could talk to? The man who was with her in the water? Please, I'm doing my best to figure out what's happening and prevent any more incidents."

She knew she was dancing around the obvious, but she wanted to remain discreet since she had no idea how many people knew.

"Why don't you give me your name and contact info, and I'll pass it on," the nurse said.

There was a yellowed sticker on the side of the phone with faded numbers, but it was illegible. "I don't know the number where I'm staying. I'll call back tomorrow."

Frustrated, she hung up. It was hard to imagine Angela Crawford lying in a hospital bed up in Waimea, possibly fighting for her life.

Angela had burst on the scene the same year Minnow graduated from college, almost a decade ago, causing a firestorm with her appearance in the movie *Hour of the Hawk*, opposite Kevin Costner. Strangely, Minnow bore a resemblance to Angela, and watching her was like watching a more striking version of herself: a mess of long dark hair, porcelain skin and a fiery spirit that came alive on the screen. It was her passion for hawks that made Minnow take notice of her, even though she knew Angela was only playing a role. That was her gift—to shape-shift into whatever character she played.

Since then, Angela had become America's favorite wild card—making blockbuster after blockbuster but also occasionally starring in low-budget indie films. It was something Minnow had admired in her, that independent streak and the desire to take on roles for the love of the story, not for the money. But that was the weird thing about famous people—you somehow felt like you knew them, when really, you only knew the characters they played, not their motivations and desires, hopes and fears. And despite Angela's fame, Minnow simply wanted to meet the woman who'd just had a devastating encounter with a massive white shark and lived to tell about it. Something like that was bound to bring anyone down to earth.

When Minnow called Mayor Lum's office, his secretary put her right through. Nalu had briefed her on his background. Hawai'i County mayor, retired attorney, smart and charismatic, and a guy whose favorite pastime was going to Vegas.

"He'll smile and make nice, but don't trust the guy as far as you can throw him," he'd warned.

It would've been nice to meet in person, but his office was in Hilo, close to two hours away, and she had serious doubts the truck would even make it that far.

"Miss Gray, I appreciate you for flying out here so quickly," he said. "I understand you are somewhat of an expert on great white sharks."

Miss? She had introduced herself to the secretary as *doctor.*

"No problem, Harry. And yes, white sharks are my specialty."

"Despite what people are saying, our waters are generally pretty safe. I want to remind people of that. I want *you* to remind people of that. So, do you have any updates for me?"

"Nope, nothing new. I'm just getting started, but tomorrow I'm going to try to interview the most recent victim. It'll help to take some measurements and hear her story, and I'm also determined to find Stuart's surfboard. That would at least tell us if it's the same animal."

"I'll tell you what I told Dr. Eversole. Spring break is coming up next month, and with it the Kiawe Roughwater Swim. We've got people coming from as far away as China, and our businesses count on this race to keep them going. If you don't have this thing figured out in two weeks, I may have to authorize a shark hunt. Open season—"

Her stomach twisted in on itself. "I strongly advise against that."

"There's a shark out there hunting people in my waters, so advise away. I'll do what I need to protect our interests."

"Mayor Lum, shark hunts have been shown to have a detrimental effect on the ocean. We need our apex predators to keep things in check. All the shark hunts here in the past did nothing but mess things up—other big fish proliferate and eat the reef fish, which causes microalgae to explode, and that makes the coral susceptible to bleaching. Give us the time we need and we'll figure this out. Plus, we believe the great white sharks head back to the mainland sometime in April."

He blew out into the phone, and she pictured him sitting in his office with a thick head of white hair, smoking a cigarette. "April is a long way off. Plus, it's not like we would be taking sharks all over Hawai'i. Just along this coast."

"I should also add that white sharks don't *hunt* humans. They most often bite out of mistaken identity or curiosity."

"Curiosity, my ass."

"It's true, Harry." Conversations with men who knew it all usually never went well, but she was determined to at least keep those two weeks—she could find out a lot in that time. "Do I at least have your word on the two weeks?"

He paused. "Sure, why not?"

"In the meantime, it would be great if you could let the press know that under no circumstances should anyone be out there hunting sharks on their own."

"Fine. And in the meantime, you keep me posted on any updates. I'll let Vera know to expect to hear from you."

"Will do."

"I don't take this situation lightly, Miss Gray."

"It's actually Dr. Gray, Mayor Lum. And neither do I. There is nothing light about any of this, and believe me, I know as well as anyone what it's like to lose a family member in a shark incident. Like I said, sharks are my life."

The average person did not understand how someone could revere sharks, but she had come to terms with that long ago. People did not love sharks. Most of them feared them in the deepest part of their brains. She was an anomaly.

He paused, blew smoke again. "Then you know what I'm dealing with."

"Absolutely."

Minnow lay on the wall by the water, looking up at a rose-streaked sky and keeping an eye out for the first star. Winter sun was not supposed to be as strong, but her sunburn made her back feel hot and sticky. She should have worn a rash guard top, but the water had lured her in with its perfect temperature. Cool at first but lacking the icy shock of California. And the longer she stayed in, the more her body felt right at home. No threat of hypothermia whatsoever.

Once darkness came, she went out back to turn on the generator. The shape of the coconut trees against the starlit sky caused her to stop in her tracks and stare up for a minute. A fish plopped in the pond nearby, and a bird screeched. There was something to be said for the barren beauty of the lava fields. It was a little bit eerie and isolated, but when she thought about it, what did she have to worry about? There was no one for miles, and no dangerous wild animals. On land, at least.

After wolfing down two black bean quesadillas with fresh salsa, she dusted off the large daybed, pulled the Big Island relief map off the wall and began creating her own map of where the attacks and sightings had occurred. The Kiawe was really located at the center of it all. At no other time in history had Hawai'i had a situation like this. It nagged at Minnow that a large white shark would remain in the area and wreak havoc like this. In her experience, unless they were at aggregation sites, foraging or reproducing, white sharks usually traveled. She was missing something important; she could feel it in her gills.

The phone rang, splitting the silence and causing her to jump clear off the bed. No one had her number here because even she didn't know it.

"Hello?"

"Ah, there you are. I was beginning to wonder if you made it," a man's voice said with notes of pidgin.

"Woody?"

"None other. Look, I was gonna try come down tomorrow, but I'm stuck on a job, so I should be there day aftah. You good?"

"Yes, I'm great. This place is incredible. I feel so lucky to be able to stay here, thank you."

"How about the *manō*—the sharks?"

"Well, I'm just getting the lay of the land, and I hope to talk to the victim in Waimea tomorrow," she said. "Have you ever seen any white sharks in the area?"

A loud laugh. "Girl, we got plenty to talk about when I come down there. But yeah, I seen 'um. Bumbye, you go eat at the Kiawe, and we'll talk story when I come."

Funny how the voice fit so well with the photos on the wall. Deep, gruff, but with a smile behind it all.

"Sounds good, I can't wait to finally meet you after all these years."

"Same, girl, same."

"Oh, and what's the phone number here? I need to give it out to a few people I'm working with, if that's okay."

"It's 882–6266. Easy to remember—882-MANŌ."

From the journal of Minnow Gray

December 6, 1991

I came across a term today that stopped me in my tracks. I've never heard the word soundscape *until this moment, and knowing that a word like this exists makes me feel seen (and heard, ha). The definition is this: the full range of sounds present in a particular environment, such as crashing waves, seagulls, dogs barking, and every acoustic phenomena one might find at the beach, as perceived by the listener. It turns out some people are extra attuned to soundscapes (that would be me to the extreme). Even more intriguing is the idea of a* soundmark, *a sound unique to an area (like landmark). Oh my God, I love science.*

CHAPTER 8

The Boat

Mauna Kea: *the highest mountain on Hawai'i; literally, "snow mountain"*

Sometime in the night the surf picked up. Minnow could hear the water raking in over the rocks, pounding. But when she woke in the morning, the waves were only shoulder high at their largest. On the south end of the rocky bay, a wave peeling left broke in only a couple feet of water. Waves meant surfers in the water and she prayed for no more mishaps, for the sake of both human and shark.

The sun was still behind Mauna Kea, and she walked out to the small pebble beach so she could get a better perspective of the mountain. It was hard to imagine snow on any of these peaks, but she knew it happened. Her cheeks cool in the early morning air, she closed her eyes and thought of her mother. Her long blonde hair and saltwater eyes, and how the light had never returned to them after Minnow's dad died. There were people who had lived this same horror in the past few weeks. Going about their lives one minute—blissful under the Hawaiian sun, enjoying the white sandy beach or the balmy sea—and the next, experiencing every person's nightmare.

When she arrived at the pier, Nalu was already in the boat, fiddling with the engine, and had a yellowed surfboard propped up against the gunwale. The harbor seemed extra quiet, and she realized it was because the crows and seagulls were absent. The only birds around were doves, cooing softly in the nearby kiawe trees.

"Morning," he said, hair wild and eyes bloodshot.

"Morning. Rough night?"

He'd either been partying or with a girl.

"Nah, all good."

Girl, then, most likely.

"You planning on surfing today?"

"It crossed my mind. Why?"

"Where you going to go? Bird Rock?"

His face paled slightly. "That would be a negative. But there's a break up north less exposed, shallow water. I figured if we were in the area, may as well check it out."

"I'd love to talk to any surfers we see up and down the coast, and fishermen too. See if anyone has seen anything."

"Good idea. Any luck with Angela Crawford?"

"No, but I'll go up there later today or tomorrow. The nurse stonewalled me."

"Understandable. That kind of fame—and injury."

Even with the swell, the ocean was mirror slick. They made good time, but still, driving so far burned a lot of gas. And time.

"What do you think about anchoring in the bay outside of Hale Niuhi? It was calm even with the swell. You could stay in the other cottage if you wanted to."

"Anchoring, yes. Staying there, probably not."

"Not enough girls here?"

He shot her a look, a smile cracking his face. "Something like that."

It was pretty obvious. With looks like that, he probably had half the girls in Kona lined up outside his hotel.

They came upon Bird Rock, and to her surprise four surfers were out. Three guys and a girl. Two were inside, two farther out, where Stuart was ambushed.

"Brave," she said.

"Or stupid."

"Or they have no idea. Maybe we should tell them, in case they haven't heard." Though that was unlikely, given the hype in the papers.

He slowed and pulled the boat alongside the guy farther out, twenty yards away, in deeper water. The other one had just caught a wave, all the way to the shore.

"Hey," Nalu called, "you hear about the shark incident here last week?"

"Yeah. They're out here, man," the guy said, scooping water with both his hands and showering himself with it.

"Were you out here last week?"

"Anytime there's waves, I'm out here. Gotta get 'em while you can, this side."

"He's right. Maui blocks the swell," Nalu said to Minnow.

"What about Wednesday?" Minnow asked.

The day Stuart and his dad were out.

"Who wants to know?"

A wave swung in and before she or Nalu could answer, the guy spun and caught it, leaving them hanging. But the other surfer paddled into the lineup, giving them a nod. An older local, covered in what appeared to be tribal tattoos on his forearms and chest.

"Brah," Nalu said, "you heard about the shark attack out here?"

The guy shrugged. "Pretty sure everyone on the island has. It happened once. Chances are slim it'll happen again in the same exact spot."

Not entirely true, but Minnow held her tongue.

"Have you seen any big sharks in the area?" she asked. "Or anything out of the ordinary—dead whales or carcasses of any kind?"

"Just a monk seal up at Kiholo last week, but it was lying on the sandy beach, fat and happy. You talk to Sly yet?" He nodded toward the man who had just caught the wave.

"We tried. He caught a wave in."

"He saw a fat shark out diving last weekend."

"What kind?"

"White, I think?"

When Sly paddled back out, he came straight to the boat and held on to the gunwale. "Who are you guys?"

"We work for UH. Just looking into the recent attacks and trying to learn more about the shark, nothing more."

"Yeah, we don't want this place shut down or turned into a shit show. And there've been a ton of boats out here lately. Gawkers and who knows what else."

It seemed unlikely that anyone would be able to keep surfers out of the water along this coastline, rocky and remote as it was.

She cut in. "No one's going to shut anything down. We're just trying to find out if it's the same shark, and if so, why it's hanging around."

"Then yeah, I saw it while I was spearfishing up in Opihi Bay last Saturday morning. The water was still turned up from the dying swell, I was out at the point in twenty feet of water, poking around for *tako* in a hole, when I got a weird feeling I wasn't alone. I spun around and saw a fucking submarine swimming by just at the edge of my visibility, maybe thirty feet away or so. I thought it was a whale at first, it was so big, but from the silhouette it became obvious it was no whale. It never slowed, never acknowledged me. Still, I climbed out on the rocks." He held up his hand and showed black in some of his fingers. "Got some *wana* in my fingers."

"Could you see from the surface if it came back around?" Minnow asked.

"The bugger was just passing through. Never saw it again."

"How big would you say it was?"

"Almost as long as your boat, maybe longer, wide as fuck."

"And yet here you are," Minnow said, curious.

In her experience, there were two camps of people. Those who let fear shrink their world and those who could quiet, compartmentalize or block out the fear and keep doing what they love. But there were also a rare few who seemed to be missing the fear factor all together. She'd met a couple of those, too, in this business. Not all of them were still alive.

"Surfing keeps me sane, and I don't like crowds. So, I take my chances," he said.

"Were you able to tell if it was a tiger shark or a great white?" she asked. When speaking with laypeople, she often reverted to using *great white*.

"White. Hundred percent. No stripes, and that girth." Another set rolled in and he eyed it. "Good luck, I have to head in now."

Sly caught the next wave, smooth as a bird. Once he was out of earshot, she said to Nalu, "Sounds like it could be the same one."

"Gotta be."

White shark females were much larger than the males. Even as a young girl in Catalina, Minnow *knew* Luna was a female, she was so huge. This knowing was something she took for granted. She thought everyone was the same way until her mother began chastising her for saying she heard the kelp singing or the laughter of pelicans as they flew in formation overhead.

"You have quite an imagination, you know that, little fish?" she would say.

"I wasn't imagining it."

Her mother would roll her eyes and say, "Sure you were. But imagination is a grand thing. Artists and musicians and writers all need vivid imaginations."

Minnow didn't argue. There was no point. She tried to go about her days, telling herself she was imagining all of these things. The very slow thud she heard as Luna swam past. A shark heartbeat. The whoosh of butterfly breeze against her cheek. Or the purring and grunting of the fish in the reef that no one else seemed to hear. But in her heart she knew they were as real as the ground under her feet.

They continued up the coast, scanning for any signs of a surfboard, but they were hampered by the swell, which smashed against the black lava. Once they passed the Kiawe, the cliffs grew higher and steeper, and they had to stay even farther out because of the backwash. Twenty minutes later, they came upon a larger bay with a black sand beach, small waves on the inside and a thick wall of stout coconut trees and a boat anchored at the far point. It looked empty and calm. No sign of dive flags anywhere. As they neared, Minnow could tell the vessel was expensive just by looking at its lines and the shiny paint job, dark hull.

Nalu whistled. “Nice boat.”

“Looks like a Robalo, top of the line. I see a few of them coming in and out of Santa Barbara.”

“I saw this boat anchored out front of the Kiawe yesterday.”

“I wonder if this is the owner of the hotel’s boat? The one Angela and Zach were on.”

“Nope. That was a Yellowfin.”

He cut the motor about thirty feet away, and they glided close to the boat, Minnow sitting on the gunwale in case they bumped up against it. A shelf of clouds had blotted out the sun, turning the water from iridescent blue to gray. Again, they scanned around for any signs of life but saw nothing.

“Whoever it is, they’re probably in the lagoon. You can’t tell from here, but there’s a narrow inlet you can swim through when the tide is high. It's a safe haven for turtles, which is why you'll also find tigers cruising."

"Is this where you were thinking of surfing?" she asked, surprised at his choice of surf breaks.

"Yeah, on the inside, but it looks like the swell isn't hitting here. Not enough west in it."

Minnow did not surf. Put her under the surface, where at least she could see a predator coming and she looked less like a turtle or a seal. For some reason, coming face-to-face with sharks did not scare her. It was the ambush that gave her nightmares and had her waking up in cold sweats, feeling as though she'd just emerged from the inky depths, seawater in her bed.

"Something smells rank," Nalu commented.

Minnow sniffed the air. "Smells like mackerel. We use it sometimes to draw the whites in for tagging. They love that oily, fishy scent."

"'Yeah, it's probably *'ōpelu.*"

"What's *'ōpelu?*"

"Mackerel scad. Baitfish."

They were close enough now to the boat that she could see the fancy navigation and gadgets on the center console. She knew there was money along this coast, and here was the evidence.

"What are you guys doing?"

The voice came from the water below and caused Minnow to lurch into the air. Nalu almost toppled over backward.

"Holy crap, you scared me," she said, looking down at the man in the water.

He wore a tinted dive mask, so she couldn't see his eyes, but there was something familiar about his voice.

Nalu opened his mouth to say something, but the man beat him to it. "Again, what are you guys doing so close to my boat?"

"Just checking to make sure everything was okay. We didn't see any flags, and with what's been happening around here, you never know," Minnow said.

No dive tank either.

"I was just setting my anchor. Nor do I need any help," he said.

Not friendly, not unfriendly. Gold-tipped hair.

Recognition dawned. This was the guy from the Kiawe—the one with the newspaper. She wondered if he recognized her in her large straw hat and dark glasses. He didn't seem to, and for some reason she wanted to keep it that way.

"Nice rig," Nalu said, eyeing his fishing reels.

For the first time she noticed they were gold and top of the line, just like the boat. There was also a large steel alloy hook attached to a pole. It made her curious. Who was this guy and why would he need such a big hook?

She had to ask. "Are you alone?"

In one swift movement he hauled himself out of the ocean and into his boat. She could now see that, shirtless, his body was tan and smooth like carved stone.

He glanced around. "Do you see anyone else here? And you still haven't answered my question."

"We're scientists, looking into the recent shark incidents," she said.

He stood quiet for a few blinks, then slid on a wet suit top and strapped a hefty dive knife to his leg. His back was to them, as if he had moved on and their conversation was now over. "I'm here to hopefully find some dinner on the rocks," he finally said.

"*'Opihi,*" Nalu said.

"Yup."

Minnow remembered the large black limpets from the rocky islands off Kāne'ohe, and how she had gagged when coerced into eating one by her fellow students.

"Have you seen any white sharks around this past week? Or anything unusual or out of the ordinary?" she asked him.

"I'm not from here, so I wouldn't know usual from unusual."

He then grabbed a mesh bag from the center console, where Minnow spotted a fish-finder the size of a large computer screen. How nice it would be. Her fish-finder was duct-taped to the grab rail and barely worked, registering rocks more than fish.

"Well, good luck getting dinner," she said, annoyed at how purposefully unhelpful he seemed. "And watch your back down there. Sharks often approach from behind."

"I have eyes in the back of my head, so no worries there," he said, before sitting on the gunwale and falling back into the water.

"Nice bloke," Nalu said, as they watched him swim toward shore.

"Is it just me, or did he seem extra touchy?"

"Probably just some rich *haole* wanting a piece of paradise. No aloha, that one."

Minnow wondered what exactly constituted "having aloha." And did she?

"I saw him at the Kiawe yesterday morning, drinking coffee."

"There's your answer."

"But he seems different than the rest of their clientele. At first I thought he might be a lifeguard or something, but those reels. And that hook."

With his tousled and amber-streaked hair and freckled skin, he had clearly spent some time in the sun. But it was more than that. He had this undercurrent of confidence in the water, around a boat. He reminded her of her own kind.

Nalu was still watching the man as he scrambled up on the rocks, timed perfectly with the wash of a swell. "He's definitely a fisherman—of more than just *'opihi*."

From the journal of Minnow Gray
Hawai'i, February 23, 1998

It was Rachel Carson, the *marine biologist I aspire to be, who so eloquently helped me understand why we see the sea as blue, and in Hawai'i this seems more the case than ever. Especially here on the Big Island. The water molecules and tiny particulate matter reflect sunlight back to our eyes, yet the ocean has absorbed the red and some of the yellow, leaving cool and glorious blue light. When you think about it, the blue we see is this subtle and ever-changing dance between the sun, the ocean and our eyes.*

CHAPTER 9

The Kiawe

***Honu:** turtle*

In her mouth, she tastes blood. A tooth has come loose, she realizes, and she coughs it up into her hand. More come after the first, tall triangles, serrated and sharp, and she can't get them out fast enough. The inside of her cheek is torn. There is no surprise these are shark teeth—it seems perfectly normal, except they begin to pile up in her mouth and she is choking and gasping for air.

"Hello? Minnow?"

A loud knocking woke her up, and it took a moment to orient herself. Saggy mattress. Salty breeze. Rustle of coconut fronds.

"In here," she said, wiping the drool from her chin as she sat up, slightly disoriented. Weird, there actually *was* blood on the back of her hand.

"Are you okay?" Nalu called.

"Yeah, I fell asleep."

"Sounded like you were croaking."

"Nope. I'm still alive. Just having a weird dream. Sorry to freak you out." The inside of her cheek burns. She must have bit it.

"I just need to grab the keys to the truck and I'll be on my way," he said.

"They're where you left them."

"Unless you need me to drive you to the hospital?"

By the time Nalu came through the screen door dripping wet and letting it slam behind him, she was alert. It would be nice not to be so tied to him and to have her own car and her own boat, but maybe this was what it felt like to have a younger brother tagging along.

"Not today. Stonewalled again."

When she returned to the house earlier that afternoon, she'd called again. This time another tight-lipped nurse told her that the patient in room 206 was not ready for visitors, even scientists on official business.

"I'll take you up there tomorrow," he said. "Maybe we can work our way in."

He was right, but there was a part of her that was also relieved at not having to come face-to-face with the reality of how fragile humans were in the mouth of a shark. She thought of her dream again and could almost feel how easily those teeth would pierce the skin.

A few chunks of bleached white coral marked the road that branched off from the driveway and headed to the Kiawe. Minnow wanted to walk over and see if the resort owner was around, maybe pick his brain. Joe hadn't told her much about him, just that he was distressed about the deaths so close to the resort—and he'd been all in for a shark hunt.

For most of the way the lava road hugged the coast, and the breeze off the ocean cooled her skin. When one short section curved away from the water, the temperature rose a good ten degrees, and Minnow felt like she was walking in a field of sauna rocks. The lava crunched underfoot, and she was glad to be wearing shoes, not slippers. Walking here midday would be brutal, she decided, and was glad she had waited for the sun to drop.

Twenty minutes later, the road ended at a crushed coral circle, where a person could park a car if careful not to drive into the ocean while turning around. Several big logs blocked vehicle access to the Kiawe, and she sensed Woody probably didn't want anyone driving down to his house, not the other way around.

Coming in from the road, you would never guess you were headed to an über-fancy resort. A one-lane road, a small burnished wood sign that read *Kiawe* nailed to a tree. A sandy path ran alongside the road, and she followed it until she got to a guard shack.

A man in a tight polo shirt popped his head out. "Aloha. Can I help you?"

"I'm headed to the Reef House for dinner."

He looked up the road as if expecting someone else. "Just you?"

"Yes."

"You walk here from Kona?"

She laughed. "No, I'm staying at the Kaupikos'."

"Ah. Have you been to the Reef House before?"

"No."

"Follow the road to the fork and turn right. You'll see the signs. And watch for falling coconuts," he said with a wink.

The foliage thickened, and the temperature cooled considerably among all the breathing trees. Small huts appeared here and there, set back from the road, with steep-pitched, thatched roofs. It felt like a ghost town but in a good way. Another burnished sign led her to a vast lawn with a much larger version of the huts right in the middle, lights strung up all around. The ocean lay just beyond a crop of lava rocks and coconut trees, none of which had any coconuts on them.

Minnow sat at the bar, since that would be her best shot at picking up any intel, and a small man named Chris greeted her in a singsong accent. "A special cocktail for the lady?"

She smiled. "Water is fine, thank you."

"No one comes to my bar and just orders water, love. I'll surprise you," he said, flashing a set of teeth so white and straight, they could only be fake.

A drink might do her good. "All right, just not too strong, please."

Several twisty, heart-shaped trees flanked the restaurant, adding much-needed shade and carrying with them a sweet woodsy scent. She took her time glancing around at the other patrons, most of them couples or groups of couples. A whole lot of linen, several straw hats, and most people in white.

A few minutes later, Chris set down a pale orange drink in a martini glass with a hunk of pineapple on the side. He stood waiting, so Minnow took a sip. Tart passion fruit, vodka, bubbles, and very strong.

"You like?" he asked.

Her mouth puckered, but she had to admit it was good. She nodded. "How long have you worked here, Chris?"

"Long time. Twenty years now."

"You must have a lot of stories."

He laughed. "Oh, I just make the drinks and keep my ears and mouth shut."

"Somehow I doubt that."

"What about you? What's your story?" he asked, scooping ice into glasses lightning fast and on autopilot.

"I'm a scientist."

"What do you study?"

She figured she may as well be honest this time. Word would get out anyway.

"Sharks. White sharks, in particular."

"Careful about saying the *s* word too loud around here. Mr. Sawyer won't be keen to hear it," he said, nodding toward a mustached man in white linen pants and button-up speaking to someone at a table.

Mr. Sawyer owned the joint, she knew from Joe. The sun, which now sat perched on a hill of clouds on the horizon, reflected in Sawyer's mirrored shades. He looked like he'd stepped off a boat from Central America.

"He's worried, I imagine," she said.

"Wouldn't you be?"

"I'd feel bad about what happened, but sharks will be sharks."

Whether Mr. Sawyer heard her, she couldn't be sure. But he glanced her way, said something to the guy at the table, then made his way over.

He took off his shades and gave her a once-over. "Have we met? I'm Don Sawyer."

She shifted uncomfortably on the barstool. "I don't believe so. I'm Dr. Minnow Gray."

"Ah, you didn't seem like my usual guests, and now I know why. I hear you're a shark whisperer. That true?"

She hated that term. "I'm a shark researcher. I study them, which requires that sometimes I get in the water with them."

"A brave woman."

In his late fifties or early sixties, he looked fit and his bronze skin was still flawless.

"We all have our fears, Mr. Sawyer."

"Have you learned anything yet? Like what kind of fucking monster is out there?" he asked, his bluntness catching her off guard.

"I just got here, so no. I'm hoping to find Stuart's surfboard and get a look at Angela's wounds, but so far I've had no luck getting in to see her."

"No satellite tags show anything?"

"Nope. They only ping when the shark comes to the surface."

"Well, this shark has been at the surface more than once."

He was right about that, but she knew there were way more untagged than tagged sharks swimming around out there. And there were also the conventional tags, with just an ID number and contact info of the scientists who tagged the animal. If this shark had one of those, it could provide valuable data on the animal's migration patterns.

"We don't know if the same shark was responsible. And if it was, there's still not a whole lot we can do about it unless we find something that's drawing it in, which is what I'm banking on."

"Regardless, pulling out a few of these big boys would go far to alleviate fears and probably save some lives."

Her throat constricted. "Pulling out?"

"Hooking, shooting, what have you."

The words gutted her, and she felt the hook go through her own cheek. "Trust me, that's not the answer," she said.

"Easy for you to say—you don't have blood on your hands. But if we don't do something, you probably will after the Kiawe Roughwater Swim."

She was beginning to feel like it was Minnow against the rest of the world. An all-too-familiar feeling when it came to defending sharks, and sometimes she wished she studied sea otters or dolphins.

"Something you *could* do to help would be to get me in to see Angela. Do you think you might be able to swing that?" she asked, changing course.

"How will I reach you if I do?"

She gave him Woody's number.

Then he leaned over to Chris and said, "Open a tab for her, and put it on the house. As long as she's in town."

"You don't have to do that," Minnow said.

"I need your help, Miss Gray, as much as you need mine. So let's work together on this, shall we?" he said, then turned on his heel and left.

Miss Gray.

There were no prices on the menu, and she ordered the macadamia pesto pasta and roasted carrot salad, thankful that her bill was on the house. Chris mostly left her alone because the house filled up for sunset. After dinner she crossed the lawn to a pair of empty Adirondack chairs and sat back to watch the blood-stained sky. At least that's what it looked like to her. Pressure was mounting for her to do something to stop the hunt, and yet she'd learned little and found nothing. She'd only been there a few days, but she was starting to feel pretty useless.

Suddenly she noticed the silhouette of a man leaning against the coconut tree in front of her. He threw a rock and it skipped across the surface of the water, each tiny splash catching the last remnants of light. In the semidarkness she hadn't even known he was there. Then he turned and hopscotched toward her on the small tufts of grass between the lava. The tiki torches lit up his face, and she saw it was *'opihi* man. He froze when he saw her.

"Hey," she said.

"If it isn't the author."

He wore jeans and an aloha shirt, and she realized this was who Sawyer was talking to at the table before he came over.

"I didn't see you there. You blended in with the tree," she said.

He stopped a few feet away, hands in his pockets. "Yeah? I was starting to think you might be following me."

He *had* recognized her then, earlier in the boat.

"Definitely not," she said.

After a moment of silence he said, "Pretty evening, but then every evening is pretty here."

"It takes the breath away. You said you aren't from here. So where *are* you from?"

"Far away."

He was standing just a little too close, and part of her hoped he would sit in the chair next to her, while the other hoped he'd leave her alone with the stars and the lapping waves.

"A man of vagueness, I see."

"Pacific Northwest. Washington. What about you?"

"California."

"So how's that bestseller coming?"

Her cheeks heated up. "Great. How about those *'opihi*? You cooking them up for dinner in your hotel room?"

"Nah, they didn't last long enough to make it back here. I like 'em raw and slippery."

The way his eyes bore into her as he said it caused a hitch in her breath. "I will never understand how anyone could actually enjoy eating limpets and oysters and urchins."

"Variation of species. It's how we survive, isn't it?"

Again, pinning her to the chair with his eyes.

"I guess so, but still. Yuck."

To her surprise he actually smiled. Just a hint. "So are you really writing a book, or was that just your pickup line?"

Her ears caught fire at that last comment. "Full of yourself, aren't you? As for the book, it's still in the idea stage. I have notes and journal entries, and I do have quite a story to tell, but . . . I haven't gotten very far."

"What kind of scientist are you, exactly?" he asked.

"I did my doctorate on migration patterns of white sharks."

A faraway look came over his face. "So let's be honest. You're here for the shark incidents, not to write a memoir."

She felt like she had to defend herself. "Yeah. I was called here on account of my knowledge of white sharks, but sharks have been my whole world for a long time, and I was hoping to have some distance and time here to gather my thoughts."

That last part was looking less likely, though, with everything going on.

"That's an unusual statement, especially coming from a woman," he said.

"Which part?"

"That sharks have been your whole world."

The sky darkened behind him, which only made the tiki torches brighter, casting dancing shadows across his face. From the deck of the Reef House, a slow, sultry steel guitar started up.

"It's true," she said.

"You seem kind of young to have a PhD," he said.

People always thought she was younger than she was. Probably because she was thin with owl eyes and a dark fluff of wavy hair. Here her curls were more like ringlets of seaweed. "Yeah, I get that all the time. I started early. What about you? What brings you to these waters and this hotel"—she realized they didn't know each other's names—"Mr. . . . ?"

"I'm Luke. And you are?"

"Minnow."

Again, one side of his mouth flickered. "Minnows are freshwater fish," he said, as though she might not know.

"To be fair, they also live in brackish water, but yes."

"And you're a saltwater fish," he said, in all seriousness.

She laughed. "You're perceptive."

"So I've been told."

It was hard to tell what was going on here, and she realized he'd dodged her question.

She came at it from a different angle. "That sure is a nice boat you have. Do you do fishing charters?"

The muscles in his jaw flexed. "I'm working on it."

"How come you're staying here at the Kiawe?"

A line of tension rose between them, palpable as the salt air on her skin.

"Are you staying here?" he asked.

"No."

"Then what makes you think *I'm* staying here?"

"My bad. I guess I've seen you both times I've come here, so I just assumed."

He glanced over at the Reef House and the trees out front, all strung through with lights. It felt to her like he wanted to walk away but couldn't quite get himself to. As though there were some invisible fishing line holding him in place. A lead weight.

"Those lights are going to disorient the turtles. They were all over the beach this morning," he said. "Have you seen them yet?"

Something wasn't quite adding up. Why would he care about the turtles? To his credit, though, he was right. But why the evasiveness about where he was staying?

"No, and maybe you should tell Mr. Sawyer to shut down the light show. Looks like you know him."

"I do. And he's not the kind of man who likes being told what to do."

Minnow was growing more curious about Luke by the minute. "How did you know about light and turtles?"

"I read about it somewhere."

Minnow knew that turtles were a regular part of a tiger shark's diet but less so a white shark's. It was all in the teeth. While a tiger had curved and highly serrated teeth, good for sawing through shell, a white shark's teeth were designed to grab on and slice into dense marine mammal skin.

"Is it nesting season?" she asked, surprised she hadn't thought of this before.

If there were plenty of turtles on the beach here, it would certainly be a draw for large sharks.

"Beats me," he said.

Behind her, Minnow heard voices approaching. Women laughing. One of them called out. "Hey, Captain Greenwood, how about a midnight boat ride?"

Minnow turned. There were three of them, arm in arm. White teeth, bare shoulders. Young.

"It's not even eight o'clock yet, stupid," another said.

Minnow looked up at Luke, who seemed to be assessing his options. "Damn," he said, and she couldn't be sure if he meant *damn* because the women were gorgeous or because they were obviously drunk and beelining toward him. Or maybe both. He was still standing in place when they swarmed him, oblivious to Minnow.

One held up bottles of champagne in each hand. "Look what we got! Bubbles for days."

Luke stepped back a couple feet. "Not tonight, ladies, sorry. And I'm pretty sure we said sunset cruise, not midnight cruise."

The one with the champagne had thick hair down to her waist and wore a low-cut gauzy dress that showcased her small, firm breasts. Together the women smelled like a flower garden.

Minnow stood up. "I'd better get back, but my advice to you all is that if you go out there at night, stay in the boat."

They seemed to just notice her.

"Oh no! We interrupted something," one said.

"It's fine. I was just leaving," Minnow assured them. "Enjoy."

She looked at Luke before she turned away, and for the first time caught a better glimpse of the tattoo on his forearm. Was that a shark? Her eyes moved up and met his, and he folded his arms on his chest.

"We aren't going out on the boat tonight," he said to Minnow, as though he had to explain himself.

"Makes no difference to me. But I have to walk back on the lava in the dark, so, bye," she said.

As she moved off, she heard one of the girls saying, "What about skinny-dipping? I heard there's that glowy stuff in the water here."

"Bioluminescence," Luke said.

Minnow couldn't wait to see him again and get a better look at his tattoo. He seemed different than your average fisherman. And there was still that itch in the back of her mind that told her he was hiding something.

From the journal of Minnow Gray

April 22, 1991

There is so much truth to this, it stopped me in my tracks:

We are not afraid of predators, we're transfixed by them, prone to weave stories and fables and chatter endlessly about them, because fascination creates preparedness, and preparedness, survival. In a deeply tribal way, we love our monsters.

—E. O. Wilson, Harvard sociobiologist

CHAPTER 10

The Patient

***Nai'a**: dolphin, porpoise*

Minnow woke in the middle of the night, hit by a wave of panic. She had been dreaming of spiny sea urchins surrounding the house, leaving no path for her to escape. Her eyes flew open and her heart pounded against the inside of her chest. The odd fluttering sensations made her wonder if maybe this time she really was having a heart attack. Alone in the boonies in Hawai'i. She sat up, feeling the need to flee but having nowhere to flee to. *Just breathe. Four seconds in, hold for four, four seconds out, hold for four.*

But as she was holding her breath, Minnow felt her palms go clammy. Suddenly her head began to feel lighter, as though floating away from her body. Yep, for sure she was dying, so she started to cry—big, heaving sobs. She sat there for a few minutes, her body tensed into a ball on the bed, clutching the thin blanket in her hands as tears streamed down her cheeks.

After a time, as her therapist had promised, her lungs loosened and the tension began to slowly drain away. *Remember, the attacks will subside on their own. You just need to ride them out. Your body knows what to do if you let your mind stay out of it.*

So, why did her left foot burn like someone had shoved a fire poker into it?

She sat up, felt around on the card table, found the lantern and turned it on. There, on the top of her foot, between the tendons of her big toe and second toe, was a red mark. Upon closer inspection, she saw two tiny holes in the middle of it. She knew enough to know what it was.

Instinctively, she flew off the bed—again, yanked her top sheet off and shook it out. Something long and red and leggy flew off the sheet and disappeared in the darkness. The idea of such a heinous bug crawling on her while she slept was almost too much to bear. This was worse than Mexico with its giant scorpions or Australia with its spiders. She had no idea how poisonous centipedes in Hawai'i were, but she remembered seeing a first aid kit on a shelf in the bathroom. By the time she came back to the bed with the blue plastic box, her whole foot felt tight and hot.

Please, let there be antihistamine in here. But when she opened the lid, her heart fell. The box was full of fishing lures. This wasn't the first strange thing she'd found in the house. Last night she opened a drawer in an old dresser against the wall, looking for another towel, only to discover it was filled to the brim with small pieces of coral—all of them heart-shaped.

The pain began to run up her leg and she felt a wave of wooziness, so she lay back on the bed. What were you supposed to do with a centipede bite? Elevate the foot? Apply heat? Cold? She realized she had no idea. But the sky behind the house had lightened, thank God, so at least morning was here. The only person she could think to call was Nalu, at his hotel.

"Hello?"

"Hey, it's Minnow. I need help."

He yawned into the phone. "With what?"

"Can you come get me as soon as you can? I got bit by a centipede and I'm starting to feel kind of prickly."

A brief pause. "Can you breathe?"

"Yes, I can breathe, but my foot is ballooning up and I'm dizzy."

She could hear rustling around in the background. "On my way, Doc."

As Minnow lay in the emergency room bed waiting for the doctor, she could hear everything going on around her. Only curtains separated the beds, and nurses and technicians rolled equipment around, talked on the phone to someone who wanted to know what kind of cough medicine to give their baby, and gave coffee orders to an intern. There was a man in the bed next to her, groaning, and with only a paper-thin sheet separating them, she couldn't help but overhear he probably had a horrific case of food poisoning from bad sushi.

Right away, the nurse had given her an antihistamine, but the fire still seared all the way up to her knee. As she stared at the stark white ceiling, hoping for something to numb the pain, she wondered if this was the same bed Angela Crawford had been in. Maybe Minnow would even get the same doctor, the same nurse. Thinking of Angela made her feel almost silly for coming in with just two tiny pricks in the top of her foot, rather than large pieces of her body ripped and torn.

The curtain swung aside and a youngish woman walked in. "Minnow Gray? I'm Dr. Bush. I hear you had a run-in with a centipede?"

"I was sleeping, so I never really got a good look at it. But yeah, I'm pretty sure."

Minnow pointed at her foot, which was still ballooned up.

The doc leaned down and examined the bite. "Nasty buggers but generally not dangerous here in the islands. No trouble breathing, right?"

"Right. I felt pretty woozy, though. Tingly head, prickly hands and feet."

"Sometimes our own adrenaline does that to us, not the poison."

Minnow defended her reason for coming. "And the pain—it's off the charts."

Dr. Bush pulled out a stethoscope and listened. "Heart sounds good. The antihistamine should kick in soon. We'll give you something for the pain and you'll be good to go. If you want, I could call in an antibiotic to have on hand in case it seems like it's getting infected."

"What are the chances of that?"

"Pretty low."

She just hoped she could walk and put her fins on. "I'm in the middle of an important job and I really need my foot to be in working order."

"What kind of job?"

"I'm looking into the recent shark incidents on the coast."

Dr. Bush's face went white, but she didn't say anything, just looked down at the chart.

Minnow had to ask. "Were you here when they brought her in?"

Her.

When their eyes met, she had her answer already. The doc had the haunted look of someone who'd seen something they wished they could unsee.

"Wait, are you a reporter?" Dr. Bush asked.

"No, I'm a scientist. I study white sharks."

She sighed. "Yeah, I was here from the beginning. You think you've seen it all, and then something like this comes in. It shattered even the toughest of our crew."

"How's she doing now?"

"She's alive. Look, I can't really give out patient information—confidentiality and all that."

Suddenly Minnow had forgotten about her own bite. "What I really need is to talk to Angela herself, if at all possible, but I haven't had any luck getting through. Is there any way you can help me?"

Doc looked surprised. "You know who it is, then."

"Yeah, and trust me, the last thing I would do is go to the press with this. I'm just trying to put together the puzzle pieces. Is she in any shape to talk?"

"I thought you were here for that centipede bite."

A nurse came in holding a paper cup and two pills.

"I am, I swear, but I was going to come up here anyway, so I guess the timing worked out. Look, I really need to see her. *Please,* help me."

"Take those, and I'll see what I can do," Dr. Bush said, ducking out behind the curtain.

"What is that?" Minnow asked the nurse.

"Tylenol, and I have some lidocaine cream to rub on the bite."

Minnow swallowed the pills and lay back, head on the pillow, and let the nurse rub the cold cream on the top of her foot and lower leg.

A moment later, Nalu popped his head in. "You gonna make it?"

She rolled her eyes. "That remains to be seen."

"When do you get released?"

The nurse answered for her. "I just have a few forms for you to fill out, and then you're free to go."

"Good, because there is someone who wants to talk to you over in the main wing," he said, wearing a smug look.

"What? Who?"

He glanced at the nurse. "You know who."

Once the nurse left to get the paperwork, Minnow peered at Nalu. "How did you manage to get to her?" she whispered.

"I bribed the guard with malasadas."

"Oh, get real."

"No kidding. It turns out I went to school with his nephew, so we talked story for a while, and then he went in and spoke to her. She said you could stop by. Not me, just you."

"Was Zach around?"

"No sign of him."

Twenty minutes later, Nalu wheeled Minnow through the freezing hospital halls to Angela's room. Minnow felt ridiculous riding in the wheelchair, but the way her foot felt, limping there would have taken her half the day. As the guard let her in, she asked Nalu to give her a moment so she could have a word alone with the woman. A wave of nervous energy pulsed through her as she stepped out of the wheelchair. She was about to meet *the* Angela Crawford. There was no one else in the room at the moment and Angela lay slightly propped up, staring out the window.

Minnow spoke softly. "Hello."

Angela slowly turned her head and their eyes met. "Hey. You're the shark lady?" Her words came slowly, undoubtedly due to heavy medication.

"I am."

She was almost unrecognizable with her hair smashed up against one side of her face, no makeup, skin as pale as milk and the stitched gash that ran from her upper lip almost to her ear. But then she smiled, and there was no hiding who she was, even with her hugely swollen lip. "You're pretty. For a scientist," Angela said.

The words caught Minnow off guard, and she smiled as she walked closer. "Thanks, I guess?"

"Did they tell you the story?" Angela asked.

"I heard a secondhand report. But when we investigate incidents like this, it's really helpful to speak directly to the person involved."

Angela shifted under the sheet and then groaned. "I'm on some kind of horse tranquilizers or something, but I remember everything from that morning. It plays like a movie in my mind, except at times I'm sitting on the bottom of the ocean looking up watching the whole thing unfold. And then I'm there in the shark's mouth, and it keeps shifting perspectives. Weird, huh?"

"That kind of thing is common. It's your mind's way of trying to process the trauma. And we humans are masters at protecting ourselves in any way we can. We mask, distort, dissociate, block out, relive . . . you name it."

"So you don't think it's the drugs they've pumped me with?" Angela asked.

"Probably a little bit of both."

The butterflies about meeting Angela had completely disappeared. They were just two women in a room talking about the blurred lines between life and death.

"The weirdest thing is that my arm is gone. Just—poof—gone. And from what I gather, unlike with some species, human arms do not grow back," she said, cobalt eyes dropping down to Minnow's foot, which was wrapped tightly in gauze and aching badly. "What happened to you?"

"Centipede. Bit me while I was sleeping."

"Ouch."

"Yes, but . . . well . . . not as *ouch* as yours. How are you feeling now?"

"I hurt all over, even with the meds. Two hundred fourteen stitches, though I have to take their word for it. It didn't hurt while it was happening, though."

Angela's eyes teared up and she glanced back out the window. A sideways rain pelted the glass and hummed above them on the metal roof. Weeping pepper trees flailed in the wind, and mist hung low on the hilltops. Minnow remained quiet, giving Angela whatever time she needed.

"The shark left me a souvenir," Angela finally said.

"Oh?"

"Zach took it back to the room with him. He moved up here to some inn. A tooth."

This was news. "No one mentioned a tooth."

"He pulled it from my shin bone on the way in to shore. Zach seemed to think someone might take the tooth and try and sell it or do something weird, so he put it in his pocket. He tends to be paranoid, but in our world you never know."

Her words reminded Minnow of who she was dealing with. "I'd like to see the tooth. It can tell us a lot about the shark."

"I'll ask him to bring it."

"In the meantime, are you up for telling me your story?" Minnow asked gently.

Angela closed her eyes and remained silent for so long, Minnow thought she had fallen asleep. But then she said, "Even before we got in the water, I had this bad vibe. The ocean was clear and blue, but we were so far out and . . . I don't know, I just had this sense that we should just leave the dolphins alone and go back in. I even told Zach, but he was hell-bent on swimming with them. It was one of his bucket list items, so there was no swaying him."

Minnow remembered Joe saying that Angela was the one who wanted to go in, but she kept quiet.

"Zach is really comfortable in the ocean, but I brought a boogie board in with me just to hang on to. I grew up in Idaho, you know? The dolphins were still a ways off, and it was deep—deeper than any water I've swam in. I started to feel panicky but didn't want Zach to know, so I put on a good face, but my heart was jackhammering in my chest." She paused, rubbed her right shoulder, and winced. "They say sharks can smell fear. Is that true?"

"They can't smell fear, but they can pick up on a rising heart rate from pretty far away. It's an electro-sensory thing that helps them identify wounded or stressed animals—easy prey."

"That's why it came after me and not Zach?"

"Who's to say? You were also on the boogie board, so your outline was more seal or turtle-like."

"It all happened so fast. One minute I was floating in this pristine water, looking down at sunbeams, and the next something slammed into me. I remember thinking for a split second that somehow it was the boat, because the force was so strong, but there was this fishy, animal smell. I heard Zach screaming, "Shark!" and I went numb.

"It had my arm and the board in its mouth and it was dragging me out to sea. In my head, there was this voice saying to punch it in the nose—I guess I'd heard that somewhere—so I did with my other hand." She held it up and showed Minnow the laceration lines. "But I kept hitting teeth. Then something popped and I was free, just floating there as I felt the tail whack me and then disappear. I was in complete shock, and at the same time I seemed hyperaware that the situation was critical. The water was red all around me and that's when I realized my arm was mostly severed and I was probably going to die."

Angela's face paled and Minnow could see she was taking only tiny sips of air.

"Take it easy, Angela. Remember, you're safe now and you're alive. Deep breaths."

Minnow took a few long, deep inhales and Angela matched her. The tension in the room, which had begun to feel crushing, lessened.

"Again, I was above my body, looking down in this immense bloom of red, flowerlike around me. It was strangely beautiful, and I know this sounds crazy, but I didn't feel scared. There was almost this acceptance, like, *Hey, this is how it ends.* Then Stefan and Zach were beside me, and they pulled me out of the water and lay me on the floor of the boat. Stefan wrapped a leash around my upper arm and tightened it hard. That's the first time I really felt any pain. I asked him if I was going to die and he told me, 'Not today.' And that there was an ambulance on the way—he'd called on his cell phone. I'd seen it on the center console earlier and wondered why you'd need one out in the ocean with you. I guess this was as good a reason as any."

"Thank God he had it," Minnow said, knowing neither of them would probably be sitting here otherwise.

"One of the many little things that went in my favor that day. It was weird, though. Zach was pinching my ear really hard, and I asked why the fuck he was doing that. He said to distract me," she said with a hollow laugh. "As if that was going to do anything."

"He must have been scared."

"Oh, he was shaking in his boots, weirdly pale, with this blank look in his eyes. I'd never seen him like that. But then, I had never been attacked by a shark right in front of him, either." Angela looked up at the ceiling as if remembering.

Minnow brought her back a few moments later. "Did you get a good look at the shark? Its coloring, the shape of its nose. Like, was it blunt or more pointed?"

"Pointed. And it was dark—surprisingly dark. But when I caught sight of its underside, it was bright white," Angela said with a sigh. "I'm tired."

Minnow had a hundred more questions but decided not to push her luck. "I'll leave you be. But before I go, is there any way I could see your wounds? All signs point to a white shark, and seeing the bite pattern can help confirm. That and the tooth."

Angela pulled the sheet down as far as she could and leaned forward. "Can you help? This is as far as I can move. My ribs are cracked and I don't want to pull any stitches."

Minnow helped lift up Angela's hospital top, revealing a crescent-shaped wound that ran from her shoulder down the whole length of her side. The shark had been big enough to swallow her whole. She also wondered about the interdental distance present in the bite, essentially the distance between the tips of the most labial teeth that could help identify species. A measuring tape would be needed to help narrow her guess. But with Angela's description and the sheer size of the bite, there was little doubt in Minnow's mind.

A darkness came around the edges of her vision. Suddenly she was standing in the cove in Catalina, ankle deep in water. Nearby, a crow cawed. The middle of the bay was reddish, and she could no longer see her father, just the yellow kayak floating calmly. She shivered as she stood, soaking wet and terrified. There was nothing, no movement.

Fog smudged the edges of the scene, but Minnow was sure she was seeing an actual memory fragment, not a dream. Something that had been eluding her for her whole life.

"Minnow?" a voice said.

Was that her mother?

Louder this time. "Minnow? Here, sit."

Angela's voice brought her back into the room. The actress was patting the bed next to her, and Minnow obeyed. Her stomach clenched in on itself and her mouth watered with something tangy.

"It's a lot to see, I imagine. Strange, though, if you're squeamish being in this line of work," Angela said.

The Catalina memory began to fade, and Minnow grasped at it with her mind, clutching to keep it fresh. She wanted to stay there, to explore the deep folds of her psyche, to go just a little bit further back in time. She rubbed her forehead. "Sorry, it's not that. I was just . . . I was remembering something."

Angela looked more closely at her. "Did something happen to you?"

"No, my father."

Minnow had no idea why she was telling Angela this right now. Her own story had little bearing on anything. It was her private deal.

"I'm sorry. Did he survive?"

"He didn't."

The door opened, and a nurse and doctor burst in. By the looks on their faces, both seemed surprised to see Minnow.

"Ms. Crawford, how are you feeling today?" the doctor in scrubs asked.

"Everything hurts, but I guess that's a good thing. It means I'm alive," she said with a weak smile.

He looked at Minnow. "Your sister?" he asked.

Angela focused on Minnow, ice-blue eyes meeting her own and studying her face for a moment. "She could be, couldn't she?"

"I'm Dr. Gray, with the university. I study sharks."

The doc eyed her. "Could have fooled me. Anyhow, sorry to interrupt, but I want to do another scan, so I'm going to need to borrow the patient."

"No problem. We're pretty much done here," Minnow said, relieved she didn't have to get into her story with Angela.

"Actually, we aren't, but that's okay. Come back for the tooth tomorrow and we'll finish," Angela said. "Zach would have you sign a confidentiality paper, but I get the feeling I can trust you."

"No offense, but I don't care who you are, and I have no problem keeping it to myself."

One side of Angela's mouth curled up. "I knew it."

Minnow said her goodbyes and limped out the door.

From the journal of Minnow Gray

January 4, 1998

The dreams started the night my father died. Always underwater, always black-and-white. Not all of the dreams were bad. In fact, some were quite peaceful. But some made me wake up screaming in terror. Even caused me to run through the house and claw at the door, trying to break free. They haunted me. I remember the doc on the island saying they were just night terrors—lots of kids had them. My mom called bullshit on that as she took my hand and pulled me out the door. Her words stuck with me. "How many of those kids have witnessed their father bleed to death in the ocean from a shark attack?" she'd said.

After that, we took the ferry to Newport once a week to see Dr. Ralston, a kind old man who let me play with a sandbox and shelves and shelves full of figurines. He never said much, just turned me loose and observed from behind his oval glasses and narrow, finlike nose. On the first day I avoided the plastic sharks, but after that I couldn't stay away. They became the main players in my time there.

Dr. Ralston took copious notes and got very excited whenever I placed a man among the sharks, but over the next year the dreams continued full force. Even intensifying.

I heard my mom telling him, "I can't take the screaming at night."

"These kinds of things take time," he said, pleading with her to stick with the therapy.

We never went back. Mom couldn't afford it. Her income from the gallery was sporadic at best, and she'd had to get another job at the front desk of the Inn on the Cove. I liked that better than therapy because I had the run of the place, including the ocean out front. Though now Mom would go into a tirade if she caught me going in the water below my neck, which happened regularly. All the while, I had this feeling that my life would never be normal. I would never be normal.

CHAPTER 11
The Host

***Nalu**: wave, surf, full of waves*

Not a stitch of wind on the water. A throbbing foot and residue of the memory made Minnow restless, and she couldn't just lie around all day. After sharing cheese and pickle sandwiches with Nalu under the *hau* trellis and taking a quick catnap, Minnow insisted they go for a boat ride. Without the onshore breezes they'd had the past several afternoons, today burned brick-oven hot. A layer of sheen clung to every part of her body, and all she could think about was submerging herself in the cool blue.

Nalu thought the recent surf could have moved any surfboard or other parts up onto dry land and suggested they motor in along the rocky shoreline. The waves had dropped significantly, though a small surge still smashed white against the black lava rock. Nalu navigated the boat south, and soon a high layer of clouds laced themselves over the sun. Minnow sat up front, foot on a cooler, and kept an eye out.

"It would be hard to hide a surfboard in these parts, you'd think," she said. "They're so buoyant, and once it was on the rocks, it would stand out."

"Not necessarily. The waves were good size that day, and there are underwater lava tubes everywhere. It could have easily been shoved under, especially if it was broken in two."

Current lines snaked across the oil-slick surface, reminding her the ocean had its own conveyer belts that could move something far away from its original location. When they had gone far enough north without any luck, Nalu turned them around and headed back the other way. As they sat together in silence, Minnow kept trying to conjure the memory from the morning back to the forefront of her mind.

Why had she been standing in the shallows? Her mother had said she'd been out in the water, near her father, when it happened.

They motored past Koholā and Bird Rock, and he kept going south, farther than she would have, but she was grateful for the time just to sit and take in the land. To rest her foot and come up with ways to rid the house of cane spiders and centipedes. Though with all the ripped screens, gaps in the wood and cracks and crevices, that seemed impossible.

"Is there some local secret you know of to keep the centipedes out of my bed?" she asked Nalu.

That was when her eyes registered something foreign wedged between the pinnacles of rock.

"Look! In there, do you see it?" she said, hopping up and grabbing the binoculars.

Nalu backed off to an idle. "Could be a board, for sure."

He brought them as close as he could, up to the edge of a rock-filled inlet. It was definitely a surfboard. An orange one. Minnow dropped the binocs and pulled off her shirt. "I'm going in."

"Hang on there, Doc. I'll go. The last thing you need is *wana* in your already messed-up foot."

"I need to get in. I'll be fine."

They were about forty feet away, and Minnow hopped in the water with her mask. She put it on and did a slow three-sixty, taking in her surroundings. She was at the edge of an opening. Behind her the bottom dropped away fast. In front of her there was a coral-covered wall of rock teeming with fish. She swam through a break in the rocks, and when she reached the rocks where the surfboard was, she had to search for a place free of the black spiny urchin Nalu warned her about, where she could gain a foothold with her good foot. The small surge kept knocking her off, but eventually she managed to hoist herself up.

The surfboard had buckled in the middle and a giant bite had been taken clean out of it. Minnow carefully inspected the board for any teeth that might have lodged in the foam. There were none. But that didn't stop the chills from forming down the back of her neck. This shark was giant and the chances of there being two sharks this large in the area were almost nil.

Nalu remained stone-faced when she returned to the boat and handed him the board. "An orange Brewer. What Stu was riding." As if there were any question. "Any teeth?" he asked.

"No. But when I get the tooth from Angela, I can see if it's a match. I can already tell you it's going to be."

"Same shark in both incidents. That's not good."

"No, it's not."

Back at Hale Niuhi, Nalu left her with the ice from the cooler, and Minnow iced her foot while writing up her notes from the day. Her leather-bound journal, which she had refilled with paper more times than she could count, was sacred to her. Covered in water stains from the last ten years, it had seen more miles of ocean than most people had. Writing in it religiously was part therapy, part creative outlet, part science. Sometimes she was convinced these little notepads contained her soul. Drawings, poems, musings and meticulous observations.

She was writing notes from Angela's story and every new detail they'd gleaned so far when she heard a car engine. She sat upright and listened. It was definitely getting closer, and soon she heard the loud crunching of wheels on rock. The low sun had turned everything golden, and Minnow went outside to wait for the visitor, who she guessed would be Woody, and maybe his wife. A few minutes later, a beefy Dodge Ram rolled up. Minnow waved, staying on the paved walkway with her sore foot.

Woody jumped down and came over, taking her hands and studying her face for a moment. Warmth from his palms flowed into her. "Look at you, all grown up and gorgeous. You have your father's eyes, sure as the sun. How's it been here so far?"

Minnow felt herself wobble at the mention of her father. Here was a man who had met her father and whose memory she had yet to mine for stories. "It's been perfect. I can't thank you enough for letting me stay here."

"My pleasure. The house likes to be enjoyed. She gets lonely otherwise."

His words were nuanced with pidgin, and his eyes bore into her, turquoise like lagoon water. Sixtyish, tall and wafer thin, there was something comforting about his presence and his low, sandpapery voice.

"Can I help you unload?" she asked, stepping toward the truck, ready to brave the pain for him.

He looked down at her foot. "What happened to you?" Then shook his head. "Wait, wait, wait, don't tell me. *Wana* or centipede?"

"Centipede."

"Damn, we had rain down here on the coast last week, and those buggahs find their way inside where it's nice and dry and toasty. I should have told you to put your bed legs in the water buckets. No guarantee, but it helps."

"It's fine. The swelling is actually down a bit."

No way was she going to tell him she went to the ER.

"Think of it as initiation. A warm Hawaiian welcome," he said with a smile.

He had two heavy coolers, a duffel bag, a ukulele, and boxes of food, which Minnow helped him unpack. There was enough beer for an army.

When he moved out of the kitchen and into the main section of the house, he opened his arms, inhaled and said, "Ah, home sweet home."

The place had been growing on her. The roughness and remoteness, and how in the wee morning hours it was so silent, she swore she could hear the stars singing—something her father used to say and, as a young girl, Minnow believed to be true. Even now she listened for the sounds when she woke in the night. *The biggest stars have the deepest voices, and the small ones chirp like songbirds.*

"And don't you worry, I'll be sleeping on my cot out by the water. I snore, so Anna—my wife—banished me years ago and it stuck," Woody said.

"Will she be coming down?" Minnow asked.

He frowned, shaking his head. "She's at Volcano for the weekend with her friends. An artist *hui* she's part of. You ask me, it's a good excuse to drink wine and get a little crazy without any men around."

Minnow laughed. "I like her already."

A line on the horizon burned orange beneath the clouds, and Woody grabbed them both a cold beer and led her outside onto the seawall. Walking behind him, she noticed a tattoo of triangles around his ankle.

"Cheers," he said. "To our blessed *manō*. The sharks."

She tapped her bottle against his as he scanned the ocean with an expression that strangely reminded her of a contented dog.

"So tell me, what have you learned since you've been here?"

Minnow went through the days with him, leaving out Angela's identity, and how based on what she'd seen so far, the two incidents were likely the same shark.

"I seen the news today before I came down. Sounds like Lum might move up the shark hunt to next week. Sawyer and Warren, head of DLWA, was on there making their cases. Spring break and the roughwater swim," he told her.

All the air blew out of her. "What?"

"Nevah mind we the people are the trespassers."

"But he told me two weeks," she said.

"Politicians can be slippery. And anyway, what you hoping to prove that's gonna stop them?" he said, then emptied the last of his beer down his throat. Minnow had only managed one sip.

"Well, I was hoping it wouldn't be the same shark, or the same species of shark, and maybe we'd find that whale carcass or fishermen chumming or . . . something, I don't know."

"You found any of that yet?"

"No, but these large sharks usually cover a lot of ground, so to go out and indiscriminately fish is just slaughter. It's pointless."

"You're preaching to the choir, girl. And what if you found out this guy that disappeared was nailed by the same shark, then what?" he asked.

She had thought about that herself. "We may never know. And hypothetically, if it was the same shark, I would be certain something weird was happening. It's simply not in their nature to hang around and bite people."

Woody watched the water closely, his eyes catching fire in the last light. "The first thing you need to know is that the area to the south of us is known as Kalaemanō, literally 'Shark Point,' but it refers to waters all along this stretch of coast because of the many tiger sharks here. Places were named with great care and for good reason. Now, suddenly you get this fancy development, a resort and an open-water swim right in the middle of our tiger shark pupping grounds, and boom, recipe for trouble."

"But these attacks were not tigers. At least the two we have evidence from."

He crouched down and sat on the wall, feet hanging down to just above the pebble beach. Minnow joined him.

"My grandfather built this place, which used to just be a small fishing shack. This whole area was important for *pa'akai*—salt—and he collected and traded it, along with his fish. But he named the house Hale Niuhi, not for the salt or fish, but for the *niuhi* that swam these waters. The giant man-eating shark. Most people just call it Shark House."

Minnow had never been a fan of that term—it was misleading on so many levels, but she remained quiet out of respect. Had it been anyone else, she would have corrected him, but she knew Woody was on her side.

He continued. "My gramps knew the old ways and the new. Where to find the best salt, how they fed and trained the *'ōpelu* to stay in the area, and how to recognize and care for our family's *'aumakua*—the shark."

"And so your ancestors called the tiger sharks *niuhi*?"

He shook his head. "Not just tigers. My grampa and those before him knew of the sharks that came from across the sea, who came back year after year. They knew of the great whites."

"So the *niuhi* is a tiger shark or a white shark?" she asked, fascinated at this glimpse into the history here, of which she could tell they were just dusting the surface.

"Both. Any shark longer than twelve or so feet."

She nodded toward his ankle. "Is that what your tattoo is? Shark teeth?"

He held up his smooth, almost hairless leg. "Yup."

Someone like Woody would surely have his own opinions about

what was going on under the surface, but so far he hadn't offered much. Sharks were in his blood, as they were hers. She could feel it in the spaces between his words and see it on the lines in his face.

"What do *you* think is happening?" she asked.

"She's been here before, this one. Couple times, but only passing through. I'm curious what got the swimmer, because if that was a white shark, then we're treading in new waters. But my *na'au* tells me there's something going on to knock things out of balance," he said, resting his hand on his lower stomach.

Having him here gave her a new measure of hope.

From the journal of Minnow Gray

Farallon Islands, October 17, 1996

The team here has created a surprisingly popular Adopt-A-Great White Shark program to raise money to help fund their research. Max said at first people laughed at them, but they stuck with it and soon developed a passionate following. In exchange for a hefty donation, people get a photo card with the shark they want to adopt, a personalized certificate, a key chain and a stuffed white shark. My favorite part of the whole thing is reading the letters from these people who are obsessed with these animals. Little girls! Grandmas! Businessmen! One girl in particular is in love with Everest (named for the size of his fin) and she writes to him once a month without fail. I love her spunk. All those exclamation points! Really, Samantha is a girl after my own heart.

Dear Everest,

How is winter going over there? I hope you are not freezing to death! You are my favorite shark in the whole world! People tease me and tell me I can't love a shark, but I do. I love you! I hope I get to meet you one day. That would be fun!

Forever yours,
Samantha

CHAPTER 12

The Cave

***Īlio holo i ka uaua**: seal; literally,*
"dog that runs in rough water"

When Minnow woke in the morning, Woody was no longer on his cot. She found him on the far side of the fishpond, cleaning out long leaves from a dense pandanus tree hanging above. It was only six fifteen and semi-dark. When he saw her he waved but kept working. Minnow went in and started up the hot water and he loped in ten minutes later.

"Girl, you had me worried last night. Thought there was a catfight or something spooky going down," he said.

The dream surfaced then. In it her foot had come off and she and Woody and her father were swimming around searching for it—looking in holes, under towering blue coral heads, and in the sand. At the entrance to a giant cave, Minnow was about to swim in, but Woody grabbed her arm and made the universal shark sign, holding up his hand and moving it like a shark fin. She pulled free and swam in anyway, her father by her side. A moment later, a dense black shadow slammed into him and the water turned red all around them.

"I'm prone to nightmares," she said. "Sorry if I woke you up."

"Small kine haunting. But no worries, I was already awake waiting for the earthquake. To me it's proof that even though we've devolved, our animal instincts are still in us. I wake up every single time, a little before they hit. Did you feel it?"

That's right, there had been a quake too, a low drumbeat coming from deep in the earth. At the edge of the ocean, Woody had mumbled something that started with an *O*, then sighed and soon began to snore.

"I did. I was already awake too, and I heard you say something," she said.

"*Ōla'i*. Hawaiian for 'earthquake.'"

"Do you get them down here often?"

"Get 'um all ovah the island, plenty. Pele, she keeps us on our toes."

The kettle whistled and Woody pulled out the can of instant coffee. "This stuff is nasty, but I love it. You want some?"

"No, thanks. I brought a French press."

"Probably better that way. Anna calls my coffee 'toilet water' and says she'd rather drink out of the fishpond. I say it's what keeps me young. You two would get along just fine," he said with a chuckle.

They slowly sipped their coffee on the wall, with the sun rising at their backs. It felt like perfection, and Minnow wished she were here under different circumstances. Her foot was still swollen and an angry red, and she caught Woody eyeing it.

"I'll make you a coconut poultice. Heal you up fast. But first I want to go out with you in the water. We got some business to take care of."

"Nalu should be here soon."

Nalu arrived with glassy eyes and a hickey on his neck. The smell of weed that had been missing the last couple days once again swarmed around him.

As they shook hands, Woody sniffed the air. "Brah, is this how you show your respect to this *wahine* who came all the way from California to help our sharks?"

Nalu's face went red. "Uncle, I'm sorry. I had a shitty night's sleep and there was a roach in the truck, so I smoked it."

"We all had a rough night's sleep. That's what coffee is for."

"My bad."

"Don't show up around here like this again or you won't be welcome back. And I'll drive the boat this morning. I don't want some half-cocked kid at the helm," Woody said, nostrils widening.

Nalu shot a look at Minnow, who shrugged. She wouldn't want to be on Woody's bad side and for about a half second she felt bad for the guy, but maybe he would learn something. There was more here to discover than sharks, and Woody possessed a kind of old-world wisdom that Minnow recognized.

After filling a cooler, they swam out to the boat. Woody wore a pair of faded blue Birdwell shorts so thin that the seat was almost worn through and a big straw hat, nothing else. Nor did Minnow see him put on any sunscreen. But his skin was even darker than Nalu's and as smooth as a monk seal. He barked orders at Nalu, who obeyed like a frightened dog. Maybe this was partly a pecking order thing, a chest-pounding display of whose territory they were in. A common trait of males of most species.

The plan was to visit several places where Woody thought they might find Hank Johnson's body, or at least signs of it. He drove slowly, almost painfully so, and Minnow wasn't sure if it was because of his straw hat, which was held on loosely by two shoelaces tied under his chin, or because he was so busy talking. Both she and Nalu hung on his every word.

"This rock is where the manta rays hang out. The plankton get hung up where the currents converge. That inlet has one deep crack that funnels straight out to sea, bringing in colder water and bigger fish, *niuhi* included. See how the color of the water is different there? Plenty of freshwater springs running out from the land."

Behind was a backdrop of massive volcanoes, long and sloping, topped in clouds.

As they putted along, in the breaks between talking Minnow thought about the earthquake, imagining the fish sensing it, just as the humans had, only better. She had first learned about fish and earthquakes from a boat captain in Mexico, who told them that there would be no more fishing for the next few days after a good-sized quake had rocked the area. When she thought about the shark's electromagnetic sensitivity, it made perfect sense. Looking into it, she'd discovered that fish pick up seismic activity up to three Richter magnitudes lower than humans.

"What do you know about fishing and earthquakes?" she asked, curious about what Woody would say.

"Might as well call it a day if you're out fishing. The fish go dark. They know. Sharks too. In '75 I was in a cave grabbing lobster when three whitetips come shooting past me like they were late for a party. I should have followed them. Next thing, we were in a Shake 'n Bake box and I could hear the rocks grinding together. I thought the whole thing was gonna come down on my head. Now I pay more attention."

A mile or so down the coast, he slowed. There was no beach or trees or anything that might mark where they were. "See that skylight there? The hole in the lava? That's where we going," he told them.

Minnow followed his line of sight and saw a big round hole at the top of a tall dome of lava. It was a good thirty yards inland from the water's edge.

"What's in there?" Nalu asked.

"This cave collects things. I call it the blue room."

Woody grabbed the anchor and jumped in the water, sinking like a stone. No mask, no fins. When he came up, they all gathered their gear and jumped back in. Woody had a three-prong spear, Minnow her underwater camera. The sea here was so alive, when she closed her eyes and listened, she could hear the triggerfish crunching on coral, the rattle of *wana* spines, the screeching of an angry eel.

Woody was watching her when she opened her eyes. "If you swim down a couple feet, you can see the light at the end of the hole. Faint, but it's there. I've found things in the blue room after big swells. A cooler, a shoe, a boogie board. Even a glass fishing ball with the rope still on."

"The big one at the house?" Minnow asked.

"Yup."

Miracle it hadn't shattered against the rock.

Nalu, who had grown quiet, finally said, "How long do you have to hold your breath?"

"Long enough so you don't crack your head coming up."

Not a comforting answer.

"I'd guess twenty seconds," Minnow said.

"There's an air pocket halfway through," Woody added, "if you freak out or the surge pushes you out."

Minnow did a slow three-sixty to check the surroundings. Big slabs of smooth rock and boulders lined the bottom, with small colonies of yellow lobe coral popping up here and there. Visibility was good and she could see eighty feet out. Woody kicked toward the wall of lava they would be diving under, and she and Nalu followed. They all took turns dipping down and looking for the light.

"Just follow the light, and stay down on the bottom. You good to go?" Woody asked.

"Yes," Minnow said.

Nalu did not answer.

"Brah, you okay?" Woody asked.

Nalu nodded, but Minnow knew something was off. "You don't have to do this if you're uncomfortable, you know. It's a long breath hold."

He remained stone-faced. “Nah, I got it.”

“You sure?”

Woody looked at Nalu. “Stay right on my heels, I’ll keep an eye on you. We go first. Then you, next big surge,” he said to Minnow.

A moment later, the two men were gone, disappearing into the dark tunnel. She hovered, watching the sunlit bubbles coming off the rocks. She counted to twenty slowly. It seemed like nothing when you were relaxed and floating but entirely different when you were holding your breath under cold, hard rock. Suddenly a big dark torpedo came at her from the cave opening, so fast there was nothing to do. It went right past her, only inches away. But it wasn’t a shark, it was a seal. She could see the whiskers as it passed. The men must have spooked it.

Back at the entrance, Minnow watched for an incoming swell, small as they were, took a deep breath and dove under. The light appeared distant and small, but she kept her eye on it, swam just over the sand and came up on the count of twenty-one into a shallow, sandy-bottomed cavern with a small rocky shelf on one end, covered in smooth pink seaweed.

“Hooey. Always a rush, isn’t it?” Woody said, voice echoing off the walls. “Did you see our friend?”

“Hard to miss, and the last thing I was expecting was a seal.”

“Bet you was happy it wasn’t something else, though. Buggah was big.”

“Very.”

Minnow glanced around, taking in the bubble of lava they were inside of, realizing that the hole in the top was from a chunk of lava collapsing down into the cave. The whole roof was about six inches thick. Unsettling, to say the least.

“Any sign of our missing swimmer?” she asked.

Nalu was at the far end, near the pink shelf. “Hey, guys, look at this,” he called.

Minnow and Woody swam over and he held up half a swim fin.

"Do we know if our man Hank was wearing fins when he went missing?" he asked.

"Good question. Joe never mentioned it and I just assumed he wasn't. Since he was training."

They brought the fin back to where the sunlight poured in. The bottom of it was missing and the cut was jagged.

"Hard to tell for sure, but I would say this is a bite," Minnow said.

Woody inspected it closely. "Damn straight that's a bite. What else would it be?"

He had a good point. There were no barnacles or hardening or signs of disintegration, so the fin had not been in the ocean for too long. And a fin might slip off a person in the shore break or maybe slip off a boat or something, but there would be no real reason for a fin to get hacked.

"I don't know, but it's a body surfing fin," Nalu said.

"Are there any more people unaccounted for recently?" Minnow asked.

Nalu and Woody both shook their heads.

"Let's take this and we can find out about Hank," she said.

They combed the rest of the cave but found nothing but driftwood and a couple of barnacle-covered plastic bottles. On the way out Nalu stayed close to Minnow, and again she wondered about his odd behavior. For such a seemingly accomplished waterman, his obvious apprehension surprised her, but she didn't want to bring it up in front of Woody. The fragile egos of men were something she had learned all about during her time on the Farallones and their many expeditions to Guadalupe.

A Poem

by Minnow Gray, age 6

I saw a shark today.
A big one.
It had an eye and a fin and a tail.
The shark is dark.
I think I love it.

CHAPTER 13

The Press

***Hopena**: destiny, fate, consequence, result, conclusion*

After an early lunch of cheese sandwiches, Maui onion potato chips and crunchy homemade pickles care of Woody's wife, Minnow and Nalu went to the DLWA office in Kawaihae, next to the harbor. She was hoping to meet the director, Tommy Warren, face-to-face and share their findings and also see if their team had any updates. But from what Woody had told her, the DLWA guys were overworked and underpaid so she shouldn't expect a whole lot.

They parked in front of a small wooden one-room building equipped with several loud air-conditioning window units and surrounded by shipping containers and vehicles in various states of disrepair. As soon as she got out of the truck, Minnow was hit by waves of heat coming off the asphalt. Inside were four desks and a secretary with mounds of files on her desk. The place smelled like cigarettes.

"Can I help you?" the woman asked.

"We're looking for Tommy Warren."

"Not here today."

"When will he be in?"

"Mr. Warren spends most of his time in our Hilo and Kona offices, so I'm not sure. What you need?" she asked.

Minnow explained, then asked, "Has your team found anything new?"

"You'll have to talk to Tommy or Chad, but I doubt it. Once Search & Rescue calls off the search, we're out too."

"But what about the shark hunt Mayor Lum is talking about? Who will be in charge of that?"

"We would probably hire out local fishermen. Plenty of guys just waiting for the green light."

"Are people already out there fishing for sharks?"

"People can fish for whatever they want, but they won't get paid for it. The state pays these guys well. And as long as they aren't in fisheries management areas or taking summer crab."

A plaque on the woman's desk read *Janet Pahia.*

"Summer crab?" Minnow asked.

Nalu said, "Lobster."

"Four years ago on O'ahu, they took fiftysomething big tigers after an attack and a bunch of sightings," Janet said. "So, people gonna do what they need to."

Nalu nodded. "It was pretty much hysteria. The sharks had no chance."

Janet shrugged. "Better get them than they get you. At least that's how I see it."

There was no point in arguing. Everyone had their own theories about sharks, and yet they really had no idea what they were talking about. Taking out fifty apex predators from a relatively small area would have huge repercussions for years to come. And the shark who had done the biting was probably already on Moloka'i or Maui. Tiger sharks *moved.*

As soon as they pulled up into the hospital parking lot, Nalu said, "Oh shit."

There were vans and people all clustered around the entrance, and several photographers holding cameras with long telephoto lenses, as though going on a wildlife shoot.

"It was bound to happen," Minnow said.

"You sure you want to go in there right now?" he asked.

"I'm not sure of anything." Minnow was in no mood to be interviewed, nor was she prepared to make any statements to the press.

He nodded at a tall white-haired man dressed in an aloha shirt and wearing shades. "Look, there's Mayor Lum."

Wind blew a light rain sideways and the temperature was easily fifteen degrees colder than down on the coast.

"Let's just wait here for a minute and figure out our game plan," she said. "I *would* like to talk to the mayor."

Two black-shirted security guards stood in front of the sliding glass doors, arms crossed. A woman in a tight red dress stood off to the side with Lum, holding a mic up to him. If Lum got airtime, Minnow wanted airtime too. No matter that she was in jeans and a tank top and a borrowed flannel shirt of Woody's, or that her hair had coiled into a tangle from the brackish water shower.

"Let's go," she said, opening the door.

Nalu followed her, and as they approached he nodded to the two guards, one of whom was the one from yesterday. In his surf shorts and trucker hat, he looked like he could have been her son. No one else paid them any mind as Minnow walked near to where the mayor and newswoman stood and waited for them to wrap it up.

"So, in light of this new development, with Angela Crawford as one of the victims, will you be handling the case any differently?" the woman in the red dress asked.

Nalu whispered to Minnow, "That's Linda Moore. Channel nine."

"Not at all. I can assure you we will be organizing a shark hunt along the entire Kohala and North Kona coast if that's what our Shark Task Force decides is necessary."

Minnow's ears perked at the term *Shark Task Force*. Was there one she didn't know about?

Linda's hair whipped into her mouth. "Who makes up this Shark Task Force?"

"Scientists, DLWA members, a shark expert from California, fishermen, the Fire Department's Search & Rescue, Hawaiians. I'm assembling it as we speak, to determine our next course of action. We want to assure everyone that our waters are safe for swimming."

"It's the ocean, Mayor. Could you ever really say that with certainty?" Linda asked pointedly.

"Of course, but we want to assure anyone coming for spring break or the roughwater swim that this is no *Jaws* scenario. There's no cause for hysteria."

The guy was lying out of his ass, and Minnow felt a burning need to step in, but she'd have to wait.

"Did you bring in the mainland expert because the shark is a great white?"

"Yes. The shark that killed Stuart Callahan is believed to have been a great white."

"Why delay the hunt any longer?"

"A shark hunt is a serious matter, not one we take lightly. You know, the Hawaiians have a relationship with sharks and we don't want to step on any toes. It's a touchy subject among some circles."

"So you're weighing stepping on toes with losing toes—or more. Is that right?"

Lum cleared his throat, obviously uncomfortable. "You could say that, yes."

As soon as they wrapped up filming, Minnow walked up. "Excuse me, but I'm Dr. Gray, the white shark expert you were just talking about," she said, words blown this way and that in the wind.

Lum half smiled. "Yes, Dr. Gray, I'm glad you're here. And is this your colleague?"

Nalu laughed. "I'm just the intern."

Linda waved the camera guy back. "Oh, this is perfect. Do you have time for an interview, Dr. Gray?"

"Yes, I do."

Lum looked like he wanted to drag her out of there, but to do so would have made him look bad. A patch of blue sky opened up overhead, but the wind continued to howl. Linda seemed not to care, so neither did Minnow.

Linda introduced her and then got right to the point. "In your opinion, Dr. Gray, are we looking at the same shark in these three incidents?"

"I can't say for sure yet, but so far the evidence points to two of them being the same shark. And yes, it's a large white shark."

"How large?"

"Close to twenty feet."

A gasp. "And the third?"

"We have no body and no teeth or teeth marks, so it's hard to say about that one—or if it was even a shark and not a drowning. We're still looking, though."

"What are your thoughts on a shark hunt?"

"It would serve no point other than to decimate the shark population here." Minnow looked toward the camera. "So I strongly advise anyone who wants to take matters into their own hands not to."

"The waters would be safer, though, wouldn't they?"

"Not necessarily. Other sharks would likely move in. These large sharks are migratory. They travel."

"So why is the same shark hanging around?"

"That's what we're trying to determine."

"It's not normal behavior?"

"No, it's not."

"People aren't usually on the menu, is that right?"

"We are not part of the white shark diet. Tigers are a bit less discerning, but this was not a tiger shark."

A cloud moved over the sun, casting a dark shadow across the pavement, and Minnow realized she was chilled to the bone.

"Do you have any advice for people who may want to go in the water?" Linda asked.

"I would suggest that if you happen to be along that coastline, swim close to shore and with others. All of these incidents happened farther out in deeper water. But I would suggest choosing other places to surf for the time being. Sharks live in the ocean, so there's never any guarantee that you won't encounter one. But keep in mind that most of the time when sharks see humans, they usually just swim away. Sometimes they'll move in for a closer look, but the chances of a bite are slim. You're far more likely to be struck by lightning."

Linda paused, as if she were done. But she wasn't. "Tell me this, Dr. Gray. Would you be willing to swim in the roughwater swim in two weeks?"

Minnow wanted to say yes, but she paused. Would she? "I'm not a long-distance swimmer."

"But if you were?"

"Yes, I would do it. As far as I know, no one has been attacked during an ocean swim race here or anywhere else in the world. Sharks shy away from all that activity. Groups of swimmers, boats, Jet Skis."

"I guess most of us are hardwired to think of the movie *Jaws* when we think of sharks."

The words scraped hard against Minnow's cold skin. "*Jaws* did sharks a huge disservice. And they are still paying for it. That doesn't mean I don't feel terribly for the victims and their families—of course my heart goes out to them. But the answer is not a shark hunt, I promise you that."

Linda nodded. "Thank you, Dr. Gray."

Mayor Lum was nowhere to be seen.

On the way in to see Angela, Minnow stopped in the bathroom. In the mirror she looked less like a scientist and more like a woman who'd been adrift at sea for a week. But that didn't bother her. What bothered her most was the fact that right now, regardless of what the state was doing, anyone could be out there hauling sharks out of the water. Senselessly, ruthlessly, brutally. For some reason she had assumed everyone would wait until an official hunt was called. The inside of her cheek burned when she thought about it, and her skin crawled.

Nalu was waiting for her out in the hallway, shivering. "Did you hear what Lum said about a Shark Task Force?" she asked him.

"News to me."

"Me, too, especially since I'm apparently on it."

"There was a shark task force a few years back, maybe 1992? Woody might know more," Nalu said.

"Or Joe. But I don't want to bother him."

According to Nalu, there had been complications with the birth, so Joe would be on O'ahu at least another week.

She added, "I'll call Lum after we're done with Angela."

The guard at the door to her room looked at Minnow and said, "Just you."

Nalu stopped. "I'm with her."

"Not in there, you aren't. Ms. Crawford was clear—only Dr. Gray."

Minnow shot Nalu a sympathetic look before he turned and headed to the waiting room. As she walked through the door, she noticed Angela seemed to have more color this morning. But there was a sweet, almost fleshy smell hiding behind the antiseptic hanging in the room.

"Hey," Angela said with a smile.

"How are you doing?" Minnow asked.

"Hanging in there. My mom came last night, so that helps. Moms are the best that way, aren't they?"

Minnow sidestepped the question. "Where did she fly in from?"

"London. A beast of a trip to get here."

"Must be hard to be halfway around the world and get that call."

"She fainted, poor thing. I'm still just her wee baby girl," Angela said with a hitch in her voice. "So, Zach should be here any minute with the tooth. I mean, if he can manage to sneak past the cameras, which I'm sure he can because he gets off on that kind of thing."

"I suppose you'd have to if you want any kind of privacy."

What a crazy way to live.

"I hear the media is piling up outside. Bloody paparazzi soon to follow, I'm sure. I don't have the energy for it, so let them speculate. But while I have you all to myself, I want to hear about your father," Angela said.

Minnow winced, and Angela caught it.

"Please?" the actress said.

It was hard to say no to a woman who had just lost her arm to a shark. So Minnow told her what she knew about the day she lost her father, at least what she'd been told. And when she finished unspooling her story, she thought about the fragment of memory that surfaced yesterday. Maybe talking about it would jar something else loose, perhaps provide an answer to the question at the center of her being. *What really happened that cold, foggy morning?*

"What a thing for a child to go through. Hell, I wish I could hug you right now." She nodded down at her arm with its IV lines and her bandaged body. "But you know, these things that happen to us, they aren't accidents."

A sentiment Minnow had mixed feelings about. "I'm not so sure."

"I am. The answers may not be clear right now, but I am meant to be in this hospital bed for a reason. That shark and I were destined to cross paths."

"So you think it was my dad's fate to meet that shark too?"

Angela paused for a moment. "Pain and loss are the best teachers. So, whether you realized it or not, you were learning from the best at a young age."

In real life Angela was even more beautiful than on film. Maybe it was because up close Minnow noticed her small imperfections—a scar running through her right eyebrow, hair as messy as her own, chapped lips, a small murmur in her heart, audible in the breaks between words. She felt like the most real person Minnow had met in a while.

"By no means do I have anything figured out," Minnow said.

"You most certainly do, or why else would you be here?"

"I know sharks."

Angela stared at her. "It's not just that. You're intuitive. Perceptive. I recognize it in you because that's how I used to be."

"Not anymore?"

She shook her head. "Before I became an actress, I was into birds. I even majored in biology. If you can believe it, I was going to be an ornithologist—gulls, in particular. That all got derailed. I often wonder how my life would have turned out."

It was hard to imagine her being anything other than a superstar. But all famous people had a life before they were famous, with hopes and dreams like everyone else. The innate striving of the human species.

"It's never too late," Minnow said.

Angela laughed.

The door burst open without even a knock and a tall guy in a UPS outfit and shades came in, holding a big bouquet of red roses. "Delivery for Angie C."

Angela beamed. "What a delight."

He walked straight over to Angela, lifted his shades and kissed her long on the lips. When he pulled away, he glanced at Minnow as if noticing her for the first time.

"Zach, this is Minnow—Dr. Gray. The one who wants the tooth."

"Right. You're on the task force?" he asked, setting the flowers down on the counter where there was already a full garden.

Minnow stuttered. "Yes. Yes, I am."

He reached into his pocket and pulled out a ziplock bag. "Here you go. Weapon of mass destruction."

"Hon, don't call it that, please."

"Well, that's what it is, isn't it?"

His arrogance gave Minnow a bad taste in her mouth. "Technically, no," she said.

She opened the bag and held the tooth in her hand. Triangle. Serrated. Close to three inches. The possibility that the same shark attacked both Stu and Angela had now become a probability, and a high one at that.

"Don't mind him, he's just protective of me. So what does the tooth tell you?"

"Definitely a white shark. I can compare it with the bite marks in Stu Callahan's board, and I'll know if it was the same animal."

A long moment passed and Zach said, "You could be Angie's little sister. Has anyone ever told you that?"

"The doctor—" Minnow said.

At the same time, Angela said, "Dr. Giovanni."

"Weird. Anyway, Dr. Gray, as you can guess, Angie and I want our privacy, so mum to the press, okay? I mean, I know you have to tell them about the shark, but not one word about me being here, and no mention of Angela Crawford. Just say you can confirm a woman was bit and she's alive and being treated. Got it?"

She understood the need for privacy, especially because Angela needed to focus one hundred percent on healing. But she did not like taking orders from this guy. "As a rule, I would never give out a patient's identity, ever, so you don't need to worry about that."

"The press already knows it was me, Zach. I'd rather just give them a statement and keep them satisfied so they don't go digging around even more. Dr. Gray, if I write something down, would you read it to them?"

"Right now?" Minnow asked.

Zach shifted around on his feet, running his hand through his hair. "C'mon, babe, just let them wait. Those assholes never get enough, so just take care of yourself. They can wait."

Angela tried to lean forward, then yelped. "No, I want to do this. For the shark."

"Oh hell. I can't believe you just said that."

Minnow wished she could tiptoe backward out of the room and leave them to it, yet she was buoyed by Angela's words.

For the shark.

"I saw the news this morning. People are demanding they catch the shark that did this, and I want to let them know that I do not fault the shark."

Minnow could see that Angela's breaths were shallow, and red spots appeared on her cheeks.

"Tell me what to say and I'll say it," she said, reaching into her bag and pulling out her notebook, ready to seize the opportunity.

Zach picked up her hand. "This is stressing you out. Just do it later."

"I'll say more later but for now say this: 'Thank you for your concern and well wishes. I was bit by what authorities believe to be a great white shark here in Hawai'i. I'm healing well and expect a full recovery. From what I'm told, I was doing something I probably shouldn't have been doing, and I only have myself to blame.'"

By the time she finished, her eyes were closed and her voice trailed away. Minnow finished scribbling, then closed her notebook.

Zach stood up, ready to usher her out. "They have her pretty doped up, so maybe just hang on to that until next time you see her. She likes you, so I'm sure you'll be back. Angie's real picky about who she talks to, so consider yourself lucky."

Minnow stared him straight in the eyes. "I think I'll just do what she asked, but thank you. I'll check on her tomorrow. Good night, Mr. Santopolo."

From the journal of Minnow Gray

May 5, 1995

I am blown away by the recent data showing white sharks cruising in the midnight zones. We are talking up to three thousand meters down there, possibly more. They swim in darkness, but for what? I can understand the twilight zone, because we know the dense scattering layer is packed with small fish and other creatures on their menu. But the midnight zone? Doc Finnegan has a theory: giant squid. I tend to agree with him, but we need more info.

At thirty-three feet per atmosphere, we are talking a ridiculous amount of pressure on their bodies. They have clearly evolved to be able to withstand more than we ever could have imagined. Key adaptations: a large liver filled with oil to regulate buoyancy and the fact that their bodies are comprised of mostly water, which doesn't compress like air. Does this mean fish don't fart?

Most don't, with sand sharks and herring being the exception.

CHAPTER 14

The Swim

***He'e:** octopus*

Woody was passed out on the hammock when Nalu dropped off Minnow, so she went straight to Stuart's surfboard remnant and held up the tooth to the bite marks. A perfect fit, as suspected. She remembered Joe's words about the attacks two years ago and two years before that. Could this be not only the same shark that bit Stuart and Angela but also the one involved in those past incidents? She made a mental note to check up on those last attacks.

Next, she packed up a bottle of water and a bag of mac nuts and set out north, toward the Kiawe, in the kayak. So much was happening and she wanted to clear her head. She was beginning to feel like she'd been called here not for any knowledge she might possess but simply so the mayor or the state or whoever could say they had a white shark expert on hand. They'd checked their boxes, all right.

With thick cloud cover and a gray sky, she opted to go in just her swimsuit and an old straw hat she'd found on a shelf. Before putting it on, she inspected it well for scorpions or cane spiders or some as yet unknown vermin. It was a habit she'd formed in Mexico and it served her well. The coast was mostly rocky, but the ocean bottom here was shallower than to the south, with large fields of yellow and blue lobe coral and forests of finger coral. Every now and then, she jumped off with her mask and snorkel and towed the kayak behind her.

Even in the monochromatic light, the colors of the fish and coral popped. Turquoise parrotfish, yellow and black butterfly fish, yellow tang, even a large gold-specked moray eel, weaving among red pencil urchins and iridescent blue spiky ones. Eventually she came to a little inlet that hid a tiny black sand beach flanked by coconut trees. From the boat she hadn't even noticed it. This one she would have to come back to.

At no point along the way did she get that shark feeling. Sometimes it was just a light brushstroke up her spine, others a heavy pressing sensation. Granted, she was hugging the shoreline, but big sharks still came into shallow water. Maybe less often, but they did. She paddled into the bay fronting the Kiawe—Papio Bay, if she recalled the name correctly—and marveled at how idyllic it all looked. The Kiawe Roughwater Swim race started and ended right here, taking a north course and turning around a buoy a mile up the way. The race had been held every year for the past ten years. No incidents, no shark sightings.

Lost in thought about the race and what a beautiful swim it must be, Minnow failed to notice the figure sitting in the back of a familiar boat until she passed right by it.

"Minnow?"

She turned. It was Luke, backlit by a hazy sun.

"Oh, hey."

She kayaked over so she was alongside him.

"You look like a woman on a mission," he said, eyes sweeping over her skin and causing a strange warmth.

"I wanted to explore a little, and it's easier on this than a motorboat."

Up close, she noticed he was trying to untie a long rope with big, strong hands.

"Even better, just swim. Or are you afraid of sharks?" he said, lifting a brow.

She didn't laugh. "Ha. You're funny. I did swim part of the way. It was like an aquarium."

"You should see up north. Is that where you're headed?"

"No real plans. What about you? Are you coming or going?"

He paused, fingering the rope, as though he had to think hard about his answer. Minnow tried to get a look at his bicep, searching for the tattoo, but it must have been on the other side.

"Just got in. I was thinking about going for a long swim," he said, scanning the bay to the north. "Want to come?"

It almost felt as though he was testing her, and Minnow loved a good test. "Sure, let's go."

A wide, dazzling smile appeared on his face, dimples and all, melting something inside her. She watched as he strapped a dive knife to his leg, grabbed a mask and snorkel, peeled off his shirt and jumped in.

"No fins?" Minnow asked, when he came up for air.

"Nah, no need."

He dunked under again and disappeared for a time, and Minnow joined him in the water. Swimming around large predatory sharks, she'd become accustomed to wearing fins, but if he was going finless, so would she. They swam across the bay, and the sandy ridges beneath lit up as the sun burned through the afternoon haze. Minnow had to work to keep up with Luke, who flutter-kicked with feet so big she understood why he didn't need fins. Soon she fell behind and settled into her own pace.

When they reached the far point, Luke stopped and waited for her to catch up. Minnow observed him underwater as she approached, noting his complete ease and fluidity. As she got closer, the tattoo on his shoulder and upper arm came into view. Red and black, it looked tribal, but it was hard to tell what it was. A fish? A whale? A shark?

When she reached him, she was breathing hard. "Are we training for the roughwater swim?"

"I am. What about you?"

"Really, you are? Is that what you're doing here?"

As the words came out, she realized how much she hoped that that giant hook in his boat had nothing to do with sharks.

"I'll probably do the race. Though I wouldn't say I'm training. I would be out here even if there were no race."

"You're fast."

"So are you."

Minnow could swim for hours and hold her own against most, but Luke pierced the water like a dolphin.

"Not like you. Did you swim in college?" she asked.

"You could say that."

"What's up with all the vagueness?" Minnow said, swirling her legs to stay in place.

He moved closer and she could see the tiny water droplets on the tips of his lashes. "Was I being vague? Come on, we're running out of daylight."

Before she knew it, he was off again, leading her along a ledge just offshore, about twenty feet high and teaming with all forms of undersea life. He swam slower now, taking time to dive down now and then, picking up half-eaten cowrie shells or empty urchins. Being so nimble and at home in the water could only come from a lifetime spent immersed in it, and she wondered about his upbringing in the Pacific Northwest and how he ended up here.

Luke checked on her regularly, and she noticed how he also checked his surroundings continuously. Subtle but attentive, which was refreshing. Often it was Minnow having to keep an eye on those with her. Less experienced. Less aware. Being out here felt so freeing and she wanted to just keep swimming. Beyond the sunset, beyond the night. It had been a long time since she'd been out in the water like this with no agenda, no plan, just watching the fish—and Luke Greenwood.

He'd been right about the water this way. Shafts of late afternoon sun shot down, lighting up small patches of the ocean floor like lasers. When they hit another large bay, this one all black sand, Luke hugged the reef and led her in. Minnow spotted an octopus slinking along the bottom, with one leg reaching into a hole and feeling around. She watched it for a while, swimming along slowly, when she swam right into Luke's back.

He reached around and grabbed her arm. Instinctively, Minnow spun around, but she saw nothing unusual.

She popped her head up. "What is it?"

"I saw something big and dark move just out of visibility. Over there," he said.

They both scanned the surface in the area he'd pointed, and a moment later she saw a distinct fin. Then another. The idea of stumbling into sharks feeding made her hair stand up. Strange how she regularly, knowingly got in the water with giant white sharks, but now she felt apprehension. Maybe because she was in such unfamiliar water, but also she had to admit these attacks had rattled her some. Fear was an inherent part of the work she did.

Luke had let go of her arm, though it still hummed where he'd touched it. They were back to back now, when straight ahead, a shadow at least twelve feet long swam back into their range. Her heart started hammering in her chest. Good thing Luke had a knife. But the creature was wide, not long, and as its outline became clearer, she saw a wide gaping mouth and slow, graceful wings.

"Manta ray!" they both said at the same time.

It made sense, with tiny plankton thick in the water. The relief was palpable, and they hung there watching as the animal continued toward them, white underbelly splotched with black. Not far behind, another one sailed along, slightly smaller but no less magnificent. When it got to within an arm's length of them, the manta banked and made a wide turn, heading back in the direction it came. *Take me with you,* Minnow wanted to say. *This is where I belong.*

"How cool was that?" Luke said, eyes wide. "They'll loop around like this for hours."

Gone was the aloof cool guy, the vague fisherman. He was brimming with excitement, as was Minnow.

"Are they regulars out here?" she asked.

"I've only seen a pair in front of the Kiawe, on the point, just swimming and swooping and doing barrel rolls against me for what felt like hours."

Minnow wished they could stay and do the same, but the sun had dropped below the clouds, turning the horizon a burnt ochre. "We should turn around."

"Straight shot back. You wanna race?"

"Yeah, right."

"Just kidding. You lead this time, though," he said, sun reflecting in his watery eyes.

Something about the way he looked at her, as though he knew what she was thinking, threw her off-balance. She swam off without another word, racing daylight and thankful to go at her own pace. The bite on her foot was beginning to throb, but swimming finless could only be good for it. One beauty of ocean swims was that they healed anything and everything. Aches and pains, worries of the day, fractured hearts.

Every now and then Luke came up alongside her, and they'd make eye contact and the okay signal. Minnow looked back out of habit too, and he was always right there, drafting off her line. With him so close, she felt overly aware of every inch of her body and the way he might view it from behind. Every curve morphed and magnified underwater. By the time they swam up to his boat, the sun had dropped onto the horizon line.

Luke seemed to know what she was thinking. "I'll walk you back. I have a good dive light."

"That's okay, there's still light. I can make it back."

It would fade fast once the sun went down, though.

"Not a good idea," he said.

"Why not?"

"You really have to ask?" he said, climbing into the boat and holding out a hand for her.

She didn't take it. "Sharks?"

"Hard to believe I'm having this conversation with the premier white shark scientist in North America."

"So you're vague *and* you exaggerate."

He laughed. "You wouldn't be here if you weren't."

He was right, though, about the sharks. White sharks did often hunt at night, and large sharks tended to come in close to the shoreline. Their eyes were designed for it. Tiger sharks too—perhaps even more aggressively.

"I don't want Woody to worry about me. I've already been gone a lot longer than I expected," she said. Minnow never lost track of time like this and was annoyed at her own carelessness.

"We'll call him from the hotel phone."

Reluctantly, she agreed, and Luke grabbed a dry bag while she untied her kayak. She was about to paddle off toward shore when he said, "Can I catch a ride?"

Yes, it was an ocean kayak, but it was a one-person ocean kayak. Having Luke so close to her was a bad idea. "Are you afraid to swim?"

"No."

His eyes pinned her to her seat, causing a hitch in her breathing. "Um. Yes. If you want, sure."

She pulled alongside the boat and he hopped on behind her. She scooted forward, hoping he would set his dry bag between them, but he didn't. His legs went on both sides of her, lightly touching the outside of her thighs.

"You're shivering," she said.

"I get cold easily. Hence the ride in."

Minnow was intensely aware of his body a few inches from her back. All lean, hard muscle. Though cold, he still gave off enough heat to warm her skin, and being this close to him felt surprisingly intimate.

"What are you really doing here, Luke Greenwood? I know it's not just to swim and pick *'opihi,*" she said, now that she had him captive.

"I told you. Fishing charters, whale-watching tours, that kind of thing. I'm still ironing it out." His words were clipped, and again she had the sense the question made him uneasy.

Minnow had to ask. "You aren't fishing for sharks, are you?"

"The shark hunt hasn't gotten the green light yet," he said.

"From what I hear, people here have historically taken matters into their own hands. Decimating the shark population in the process."

"Yeah, well, I'm not from here."

The way he said it, she could tell this line of questioning was over.

"What made you leave Washington?"

A pause. "I was ready for a change."

"Did you fish up there too?"

"No."

A long silence swam between them, and she let it settle for now. The more she pushed, the more she could feel him backing away, and she wanted to keep him close enough to figure out his deal.

They left the kayak tied to a coconut tree, followed a torchlit path, and picked up two towels at the pool. From there he took her to the lobby, a Polynesian-style building with a high ceiling and open rafters.

Woody picked up right away. "Kaupiko."

"Hey, it's me, Minnow. I'm at the hotel. I went farther than I thought, so I'm going to leave the kayak and walk back. I just didn't want you to worry."

"I pick you up. Otherwise you'll end up face down in the lava. Happens all the time."

"That's okay, I have a light."

"Don't be stupid. Meet me where the jeep road ends."

He hung up.

Minnow turned to Luke. "Looks like you're off the hook. Woody's going to get me in his truck."

For a heartbeat she thought he seemed disappointed, but then he looked at his watch. "Sounds good."

"All right, then."

Back on land, things felt different between them. Stiffer and less ease, as though their long swim together had never happened. Minnow wanted to take him by the hand and lead him back out to the ocean. A strange but powerful urge.

"Oh, by the way, are you coming to the meeting here tomorrow night?" he asked casually.

"What meeting?"

"Sawyer offered to have a task force meeting here, I guess. I figured you knew."

"I saw Mayor Lum earlier at the hospital being interviewed, but he was gone before I finished talking to the news lady. It feels like he's avoiding me."

"I'm sure you're invited."

It wouldn't be the first time she was left out of the game. Wouldn't even be surprised if they had somehow invited Nalu and not her, boys club that it seemed.

Minnow studied him for a moment. "How did you know about it?"

"Sawyer."

Now that they were in a well-lit area, standing still, Minnow looked more closely at his tattoo. It was a Native American depiction of an orca.

"Beautiful tattoo," she said.

He glanced down at it, then shifted from foot to foot. "Thanks. So, you all good with your ride?"

"Of course. This path is the one that leads out, right?"

"Yep."

Minnow felt a strange inertia, as though her feet wanted to remain planted here in front of him. He stood there, too, unmoving, rubbing his tattoo. This time it was her turn to shiver, and not from the cold.

Eventually she snapped out of it. "Good night, Luke."

"Sweet dreams."

If only he knew.

From the journal of Minnow Gray
Hawaiʻi, February 24, 1998

They were so connected. So in tune with the world around them. I envy them that.

Pua ka wiliwili, nanahu ka manō.
When the wiliwili tree blooms, the shark bites.

—*Mary Kawena Pukui,* ʻŌlelo Noʻeau

CHAPTER 15

The Hunt

***Poi**: the Hawaiian "staff of life," made from cooked taro corms pounded and thinned with water*

Woody's truck was the kind you had to climb to get into, with the running board at mid-thigh level and the door above her head. Once inside, Minnow was surprised to see it was spotless and it smelled faintly like aftershave and flowers. He had the air-conditioning on high and Hawaiian music blasting from his speakers.

"Next time, leave me a note," Woody said, turning the music down. "I thought the kayak washed away until I saw your purse was back on the table."

"I'm sorry. I was feeling out of sorts after the hospital visit and not really thinking. I won't do that again."

"Anna said it was Angela Crawford who got bit out there, and it's all over the news. Big stinking deal. Da shark nevah care how rich or famous you are. Floating out in the deep on a boogie board like one sitting duck—who does that? That boat driver shoulda never let them in the water."

"It's true."

"Mainland guy. Comes here and doesn't know jack."

Minnow sat silent. Was that how he saw her too? "People need to be educated on how to lessen their chances."

"How about they just nevah come here in the first place? Every single one of these people was from somewhere else. To me that says something."

"I'm from somewhere else. What does that say about me?" she couldn't help but ask.

He grunted. "Yeah, well, you know the ocean. You've put in the time."

Back at the house, Woody grilled a fat steak for himself and looked at her as though she were crazy when she told him she was a vegetarian. But he quickly whipped out a tub of mac salad and poi from the fridge, along with a pot of already cooked rice. Minnow had tried poi on O'ahu, and it tasted like a cross between dirt and Elmer's glue, but this poi was sweet and thick and delicious.

"Waipio Valley, that's why," was all he said.

Minnow was so hungry, she could barely see straight and chased the poi with a bowl of mac salad topped with rice.

They were halfway through the meal when he said, "Mayor Lum called for you while you was out. Said they're having an informal task force meeting at the Kiawe tomorrow at six. He wants you there."

So she did have an official invite. "Did he say who else will be there?"

"No, but I told him I wanted to come. These waters are my front yard."

"As you should."

Once they finished, Woody set out two cold beers, told her to meet him out on the seawall and went to turn off the generator. All clouds had cleared, and it looked like someone had taken stardust and flung it across the blackest of nights. Only in the middle of the ocean could you see so many stars. She thought of Max, who loved stargazing, and was happy to have so much distance from him. But he would have been a good person to consult with about these recent incidents. No doubt he had heard about them. And that she was here.

Good.

The generator sputtered, then grew silent. A minute later, Woody sat down next to her, moaning about his hip. "You know why we have so many stars?" he asked, sucking down a long swig.

"We're on a tiny island in the sea?"

"That helps. But also, we have something called a Dark Sky law because of all the telescopes on Mauna Kea. So lights here gotta be a certain yellow wavelength—streetlights, that kind of thing."

"It's breathtaking," she said.

"You want to talk breathtaking, go up that mountain and try to walk ten steps. Thirteen thousand eight hundred three feet too tall for me. I like it down here, sea level."

"I'd love to go up there someday, but I'm with you on that one."

A satellite moved overhead, a tiny, steadily crawling pinprick, and then the shadow of a large bird flew past, barely visible except for where it blocked out the stars, wingbeats moving in time with her heart. Minnow closed her eyes for a few moments and could hear the Sally Lightfoot crab feet scurrying through the rocks as they nibbled on seaweed. The thought of them out there, going about their crab life just below her feet, brought her a strange heaping of joy.

"What do you call the Sally Lightfoot here?" she asked.

"What? I only ever heard of Gordon Lightfoot."

Minnow laughed. "The crabs. That's what they're called back home."

"They're *'a'ama* crab to us. Where the hell did they get Sally Lightfoot?"

"I have no idea."

It struck her that for all the immense tragedy and strangeness of the past week, the trip had also been full of tiny bright spots. The house—minus the bugs. The swims. Nalu. Woody. The warm, dreamy water. Even Angela. There was a connection there, sure as the sun. And then there was Luke. Enigmatic, gorgeous, and obviously hiding something. The jury was still out on whether he was a bright spot or not, but she'd enjoyed her swim with him today more than she wanted to.

"When was the last organized shark hunt on this island?" she asked.

"In '75 they tried to have one up at Upolo Point."

"Why, had there been an incident?"

"Nah, just for sport. 'Shark charming,' they called it. A man named Bowles decided he would make a day out of it, invite the whole island. My brother got wind of it, told him not a good idea, but he went ahead anyway. Cliff and I, we went up and made an offering to the ocean early that morning at Lapakahi, close by, warning the sharks of what was to come."

He stopped and sipped his beer, and Minnow's skin felt as though someone had pricked her with a million tiny needles. She wasn't sure she wanted to hear more, but he went on.

"You would not believe how many people came—thousands standing along the cliffs. These guys was selling hot dogs and shave ice and all kinds of crap, like one carnival. Brah, it was messed up. Bowles had gotten ahold of this dead cow, and his friends in a boat were dragging it back and forth in front of the cliffs. Every so often they would dump cans of blood from the slaughterhouse into the ocean."

"My God, that's sick."

"You're telling me. Bowles is one real macho dude, thinks he's Rambo. He was pacing along the edge with a harpoon, just waiting for the sharks to show. There was a few other guys sitting in director chairs holding rifles like they was on safari. Hawaiian safari."

The bitter taste of blood filled her mouth again, and she wanted to get up and run away from this story, away from the brutal acts humans are capable of—not in the name of survival, as with most animals, but simply because they could. And almost always, it was the men. "I've heard enough," she said.

"No, my dear, you have not, because get this: Not one shark showed up that day. Not one," he said, raising both hands in the air. "*Mahalo ke Akua,* someone heard our prayers. Because I've heard stories of the old days in those waters, and believe you me, they put one dead cow or pig in the water, and boom, get twenty big tigers within an hour or two."

She did not ask what they did with those sharks they attracted.

"Amazing."

"There are bigger things at play here, you better believe it. Mother Nature always gonna get the last word. So, even if Mayor Lum and his boys demand a hunt, we have the *'āina* on our side."

" *'Āina?*"

"The land. Wilderness. All of it, ocean too."

"I like the sound of it, but still, we need to prevent that from happening." She was curious about his brother Cliff. "What about your brother? Can he come to the meeting tomorrow?"

Woody slapped his thigh. "Hoooo, bad idea."

"Why?"

"Cliff is . . . unpredictable. He's the nicest guy, but you piss him off, watch out. Or not. Just depends on his mood that day, or which direction the winds are blowing. Or the phases of the moon."

He sounded a little bit like her mother, and in some ways Minnow too. She could always feel the pull of the full moon on her own tides. And it made her think of the Hawaiian proverb—not to go in the water when the *wiliwili* was flowering. Ancient knowledge.

"Where does he live?"

"Hawi. He works for the forestry department, backcountry. Luckily he found the perfect job for someone with his temperament."

"Maybe we need someone like him. Someone with a little fire, who people might sit up and listen to," she said.

"Let's see how tomorrow night goes, then we'll see," he said.

From the journal of Minnow Gray

Farallon Islands, November 1, 1996

We waited for the perfect weather, which in the Farallones during late fall can sometimes take a while. Max brooded all morning and I was picking up his nervous energy, but the sun was out and the water sparkled. It seemed like a risky thing to do in such a small boat (the Boston Whaler here is a mere thirteen feet, smaller than many of the sharks), and it wasn't well equipped. But that's one of the things I've learned about research—you do whatever it takes with as little as you have and somehow make it work.

We had two long metal poles with the PAT (pop-off archival tag) loosely attached. The second pole was for backup in case we dropped it, or worse. The plan was to harpoon the tag at the base of the dorsal fin and then if all went well, after a certain amount of time—in this case one was set for three months, one for six and another for nine—when the tag pops to the surface, it then will ping data to a satellite that tells us the water temps, the track the shark traveled and how deep it went. They had successfully tagged ten sharks last year, so it should have been no problem, but maybe it was having me on board that made Max uncomfortable. He worries about me more than he should and I find it both endearing and suffocating.

Anyway, I was driving the boat, and once we were ready he tossed the seal decoy over the side. It rarely took long for the sharks to come in for a closer look, and soon there was a flurry of fins. Max stood near the bow, perched like a heron. Before we hit the shark with the tag, he wanted to check its markings to ID it. There were a lot of moving parts and he kept yelling at me to speed up, slow down, go this way or do whatever. The sharks were cautious and circled the boat at a distance, but none went for the seal. Max was growing frustrated and so was I, so I suggested he drive and I take a stab at the tagging.

He has more experience with driving in this kind of scenario than I do. I don't like the idea of stabbing sharks with sharp objects, but their skin is tough and they are made out of cartilage, so they barely notice it. Eventually Huck Fin (a fifteen-foot male who always seems a little more curious than the others) came close enough to the boat for me to jab him. I had to lean way off the side of the boat to even have a chance of landing the tag. It all happened in slow motion from there.

In my excitement, I lost my balance and went over the side headfirst. Even before I hit the water, Max was grabbing at my foot, which I think made things worse. The icy cold stole my breath and I felt Max trying to drag me up and into the boat all the while yelling and cursing. Out of the side of my eye, I saw a large shape coming toward me, but it was moving slowly and I could tell there was no threat. At least not from that particular shark. I kicked my foot out of Max's hands, flipped over in the water and pulled myself into the boat with a strength I never knew I had. He was hyperventilating, but I was fine, if not a little shaken up, literally.

Next time I'll be more careful.

CHAPTER 16

The Tail

***Kahuna**: priest, sorcerer, wizard, expert in any profession*

There were lights on the water late last night or early in the morning—Minnow couldn't quite be sure. They could belong to anyone, she knew, since night fishing was a thing, but she wondered what was going on out there. After lying in bed for a while listening to the pulse of the rising sun, she rose and left Woody a note. She half walked, half ran to the Kiawe to get the kayak. The sun had just come up over Mauna Kea, and there was still a chill to the morning air.

As she walked, she stared down at the ground so as not to trip on the shadowed lava rocks. The movement felt somewhat hypnotic, and soon she was lulled into a trance.

There is a metallic, fishy residue in her mouth. She feels buoyant as she swims in the middle of a bait ball, looking for a way out. But it's hard to tell which way is up through all the fish. Every now and then, she feels herself bump up against something solid and large, and she backs away. But no matter which way she goes, she hits it again.

Then as quickly as it came on, the vision faded and she was back on the lava path. The experience had been like watching a slow-motion, black-and-white movie that she'd had a part in. When she got home later, she would write it down in her journal. Whether memory or dream, she couldn't be sure. It felt like a memory, only she couldn't remember ever having it happen. She shook it off and kept walking.

When she crossed over onto resort property, she saw several rental cars parked off to the side of the road just before the entrance. There were men in suits milling about and a guy with a huge camera zeroing in on the Kiawe sign. She pulled down her straw hat and ran the other way, hoping not to encounter any more of them.

On the way to the beach, she passed through the Saltwater Bar, led there by dreams of the mouthwatering mango muffins and hot dark roast coffee. Mr. Sawyer stood off to the side, almost in the bushes, talking to a man in a suit. Sawyer looked tired, and Minnow ducked past them and up to the bar.

George's eyes lit up when he saw her. "Aloha. You here alone this morning?" He glanced around as though he expected someone else.

"Yes, Woody was still asleep in his hammock."

"What can I get you?"

"Black coffee and a mango muffin, please."

"For here or to go?" he asked, eyes then moving to someone behind her. "Actually, you may want it to go."

Minnow couldn't help but turn around. The guy who'd been talking to Sawyer was walking right toward her, looking slightly disheveled but also familiar somehow. Wavy brown hair, scrunched brow. Was he a scientist? And then it hit her.

Josh Brown from CNN.

Immediately, she turned her back to him. Why wasn't he off chasing Bill Clinton and Monica Lewinsky?

"Yes, *to go* is a good idea," she said to George.

A moment later, she sensed a presence next to her, but she refused to look. She was in no way prepared to be on national television, especially in her hipster shorts and halter bikini top. Maybe later but not now.

"My sources tell me you're someone I should talk to," he said, smelling of chewing gum.

Minnow ignored him.

"Hello? You are Minnow Gray, aren't you?"

She winked at George, then half turned. "Oh, you're talking to me, sorry. What if I am?"

He dropped a card on the bar in front of her. "I'm Josh Brown, journalist with CNN. I'm covering the Angela Crawford shark story. Can we talk?"

When she thought about it, turning him down would be stupid. "I have a few minutes to talk, but no cameras right now, okay?"

He glanced down at her chest, then caught himself. He pulled out a notebook. "Fine. So tell me, have you seen Angela Crawford's injuries in person?"

Was that all he cared about? "No comment. Ask me about the sharks."

"Three attacks in a short period of time, same stretch of coast. All by a great white shark. Coincidence?" he said.

"That I can't tell you, but for future reference, we refer to them as *incidents,* since the shark bit and released the victims. Had it actually attacked, there wouldn't be anything left of either of them. And the third case, we have no evidence that says he was killed by a shark."

He scribbled, then said, "But we do know that two of them were white sharks, correct?"

"Correct."

"How big exactly?"

The size of this animal was going to wreak havoc in the American psyche, but she had to be honest. "Between eighteen and twenty feet."

Josh slowly looked up at her. "Jesus Christ. A monster."

She shrugged, trying to downplay it. "Not a monster. It's not uncommon for mature female white sharks to get that large."

A bit of a stretch but not entirely wrong.

"Is it normal for a great white shark to be hunting in Hawaiian waters?" he asked.

George produced her cup of coffee, and she took a sip before answering. "White sharks are seasonal visitors to the islands, so it's not unusual at all. But we can't say for sure if they come here to hunt."

"Aren't they always hunting? I mean, they have to eat, don't they?" he asked.

"We believe they can store food, so if they've recently had a seal or part of a whale carcass, say, they may not need to eat for a while."

"You see any seals or whale carcasses around here?"

"No."

"So the shark is hungry."

"I'm not going to bother guessing."

"So, as a shark expert, what is your recommendation on holding an international swimming race in these very waters in less than two weeks? Will the shark hunt make it safe enough?"

"The shark hunt is still on the table, but I strongly discourage it." She told him why, in detail.

"Why so willing to go to bat for these killing machines, Miss Gray?" he asked.

A term she intensely disliked. All predators were designed to kill efficiently, but the killing did not define them. "Because I've seen a different side to them and know they have been grossly misrepresented by the media. When a man in a neighborhood shoots someone, do we then go hunt and kill all the men in the area? It's a senseless and outdated way of handling the situation."

He stared at her for a moment and she thought he was going to counter her, but he said, "Point made. So if not a hunt, then what? You're here investigating, but to what end?"

"I still believe there's a reason the sharks—or shark—is hanging out here, and once we find that reason, we can act accordingly. In the meantime, I'm collecting data to further our understanding of them and the conditions surrounding these incidents. The more we know, the more we may be able to prevent future tragedies from happening. And to quote me, please use *Dr.* Gray."

He nodded. "I'm curious, what got a young woman such as yourself so interested in sharks?"

Minnow knew from past experience to say as little as possible to the press and to keep her personal life out of it. "I grew up in California."

A small laugh, exposing his famous dimples. "So did millions of other people. It just strikes me as a very specialized field of study, and not for the faint of heart. You must be tough as nails under that cute exterior."

Was he flirting with her? Josh fucking Brown.

"I'm good with a dive knife," she said.

"I'd like to see that."

"Not likely," she said, unable to help herself.

He smiled. "Look, I have to run, Dr. Gray, but are you staying here at the Kiawe? I'd love to continue this conversation, maybe even do a piece on you. I sense there's a lot more to your story."

"I'm staying elsewhere, but I'll be here later for the meeting. I'm sure Mr. Sawyer mentioned it."

"Affirmative. I look forward to being a fly on the wall."

The added media scrutiny felt like a screw in her chest being tightened inch by inch. "If nothing else, it should be interesting," Minnow said, grabbing her now lukewarm coffee and muffin and walking off toward the beach, feeling the burn of his eyes on her back. Why did men have to be so predictable?

Luke's boat was still there, and she paddled past it, then decided to loop around and do a little recon. Surprising that he wasn't already out on the water since she hadn't seen him in the hotel. In all honesty, she had been hoping to run into him at the Saltwater Bar, but she cut off that line of thinking. Spending more time with Luke would lead to nothing good.

Unfortunately, she was below gunwale level, so she would have to actually lean on the boat and stand up if she wanted to see anything. Which she did. She glanced around. The only people in sight were lying on beach chairs under umbrellas, reading books or magazines. She went to the far side and pulled herself up.

Nothing looked any different from the other day, but the tangy smell of blood clung to the surfaces of the boat and caused her to wobble. She almost fell backward into the water. She ran her finger along the edge of the gunwale and it came away fish scented. *He's a fisherman, Minnow; don't jump to conclusions,* she told herself. With a gravelly feeling in the pit of her stomach, she sat back down and paddled off.

The water glowed turquoise, magnifying coral heads and fish below. It was looking to be a stunning day, and yet she felt the weight of everything pressing down on her shoulders. She wanted so badly to solve this thing that, in many ways, was unsolvable. Because even if she did figure out what caused the shark to keep coming around, the truth of the matter was, you couldn't bring back the dead. Talking to Stuart Callahan's dad was not something she was looking forward to, but she had to hear his story. It was part of the job.

The Global Shark Attack File was maintained by the Shark Research Institute, and all of her data would be sent there once she could get back on her computer. The goal was to understand the factors that led to every shark encounter around the world—including boat and airplane disasters—with the hopes of minimizing future incidents, thus helping humans and sharks. Surfers made up the highest percentage of victims, though the percentage of surfers bit by a shark was minuscule.

With so much to do today, Minnow paddled a straight line back to the house rather than hug the shoreline and go in and out of coves. She was out beyond the drop-off, and she peered down but could no longer see the bottom, only rays of sun. She passed through several current lines, went off on a daydream about relocating to Hawai'i and was making good time when an electric sensation swept across her skin. That feeling she had when she knew she wasn't alone.

Moments later, behind her there was a *whoosh* and the familiar sound of water displacement. Trying to calm her heart, she slowly, so as not to rock the tiny kayak, turned. Thirty yards back or so, a tall fin sliced through the water, directly in her wake.

Oh fuck.

She altered her course, veering in toward land, and immediately began talking to herself—and talking to the shark. Time turned to molasses.

Curiosity, that's all it is. If she wanted you, you would have been hit already.

Deep breaths.

Hey, beautiful shark, I promise I'm not what you want.

Because of the angle, she couldn't tell whether it was a white shark or a tiger, but whatever it was, it was big. When she listened, she could almost hear its tail swishing from side to side, lazily, methodically. Nonaggressive but interested. If she picked up the pace, it would sense her fear, so she kept her strokes even. In her mind she willed it to turn and head back in the other direction. It didn't.

Minnow half turned again and saw that the shark was closer now, the fin even higher out of the water. It was hunting her, she could feel it. Her senses were on high alert now, and the smell of deep sea floated around her, brought forward by a light side shore wind. In light of recent events, paddling this far out in a tiny kayak by herself had probably been careless, but in the balmy blue seas it was easy to get lulled into complacency.

Now her arms burned and a voice inside mused that it would only be fitting to go out this way, the same way as her father. To be taken by something you love so much. The irony stung. In this line of work, the chance had always been there, looming. Now death was swimming after her with a tall fin and rows of sharp teeth.

Get ahold of yourself, Minnow!

These thoughts were so out of sync with how she usually felt when swimming with sharks, she wondered where they were coming from. Most likely it was all the hype and the collective fear out there in the world, beating down her defenses. She turned again and saw the fin get lower and lower in the water until it was gone, leaving a swirling boil in its place. At the same time, a cloud passed over the sun and the water turned from vibrant blue to gray.

If the shark was going to do something, it would be soon. Two frigate birds flew by overhead, hovering on the wind. Big, dark shadows in the sky. They flew on and left her alone but then circled around once more. It was eerie, as though they knew what might be coming, majestic scavengers that they were.

"What are you guys waiting for?" she said quietly.

Floating atop the surface of the ocean, she was now the sitting duck. The sitting woman who should know better. She thought for a long while about that and then felt a bump against the kayak, hard enough to send lightning through her but light enough to know this was not an outright assault. A long shady thing sailed past her, just beneath the surface. The shark's stripes were unmistakable, a signature of nature to camouflage the tiger against ripples of sunlight underwater. *Galeocerdo.* Thirteen million years in the making.

All tingly from adrenaline, she let her body and mind settle as the animal disappeared and sank into the deep. She somehow felt sure that it wouldn't be coming back.

From the journal of Minnow Gray

Guadalupe Island, August 2, 1994

Being out on the boat has always been my favorite place, with its freedom and adventure and seductiveness of the unknown. We humans must be hardwired for it to a certain degree in order for our species to survive. It's the dreamers and the risk takers and those who persevere who make history, isn't it?

There's also something about the space and silence out here that makes room for things to bubble up from my unconscious mind. Tonight I was lying on deck under the stars when I was hit with flashes from my childhood. The white of my mother's teeth when she smiled at me. My father singing along to his Neil Diamond record using a bottle for a microphone and making me laugh. Me tucked between the two of them on the bed during a thunderstorm, warm and cozy. I was so young when they died that every memory is something I guard with my life. My absolute worst fear is to stop remembering, because then they would really be dead.

CHAPTER 17

The Interview

***Niu:** the coconut (*Cocos nucifera*), a commom palm on tropical islands*

Woody was out mending a throw net when she got back and didn't seem too surprised about Minnow's tall-finned follower in the water.

"You were in the ono lane, that's why. Big sharks cruise there," he said, not taking his eyes off the knot in his hands.

"The ono lane?"

"Where the ono run. Forty to sixty fathoms, more so in Kona, but we get them up here too. You probably know ono as wahoo," he said.

Ah, yes. "Probably right where I was. How come you didn't warn me?"

"I was asleep."

Minnow told him about Josh Brown and the media stacking up outside the Kiawe, and that didn't surprise him at all either. Then he let her take his truck to see Sam Callahan at Koholā.

The wealthy enclave of Koholā was close as the *'iwa* bird flew, but she first had to drive out to the highway and then back toward the airport a few miles. From the main road everything looked so desolate, but there were signs of green as she drove down the smooth and winding road. There had been no sign to show her where to go, no indication of anything, really. But as with the Kiawe, and around Hale Niuhi, coconut trees surrounded water sources.

She stopped at a small gatehouse, gave her name and was directed to the Callahans' home down near the water. Everything on this island was on a slope, she realized, which lent itself well to sweeping views of the ocean and all the surrounding volcanoes. The house was surrounded by a tall lava rock wall with a wide burnished wood gate that swung open as soon as she pulled up. Giant smooth stones paved the drive and the yard was golf course green and just as manicured.

Mr. Callahan met her at the front door. He was tall, broad shouldered and built like he might have been a football player at one time.

"Dr. Gray, thank you for coming all the way out here to do this work. It's important," he said, shaking her hand.

The loss had already carved itself into his face, and his eyes were almost bleeding red.

"Mr. Callahan, I am so sorry about Stuart. I know how hard this probably is, so thank you for seeing me."

"Anything to help. My wife still can't talk about it, so pardon her absence."

"Understandable. It's really you I need to speak to anyway."

Over the course of her last few investigations, Minnow had learned she had to balance care and sympathy with a certain amount of getting to the point. They went outside and sat at a giant wood table, granite cool against her bare feet.

"Can I get you something to drink?" he asked, himself clutching a coffee mug that said *Pupule* on it.

"No, thank you." This was not going to be easy, and she wanted to be fully present.

"You know I talked to Joe Eversole already, but fire away."

"I mainly want to know about the water conditions, what you witnessed and any description of the animal. You probably know there is speculation that the same shark is responsible for all the recent incidents."

His chin quivered. "I wouldn't call what happened to Stuart an 'incident.' It was undoubtedly a premeditated attack."

Spoken like the personal injury attorney that he was.

"Tell me what you saw, Mr. Callahan. And if at any time it gets to be too much, we can stop and I'll leave."

He nodded, then began. "We have a golf cart we usually take to the south end of the course and then follow a coastal trail about a half mile to the point. That morning we could see the waves looked good, so Stu was frothing to get out there. As soon as I parked he took off at a jog ahead of me, and just before we hit the jump-off spot he tripped on the lava and skinned his leg pretty badly. He said the ocean would clean it and I didn't disagree."

Minnow pinched her forehead. "Was it bleeding when he got in the water?"

"It wasn't deep, but it was a good-sized abrasion, so there was some blood. Not too much."

Any shark within a quarter mile would have been able to smell the blood, especially if the current was drawing the water out.

"Any sign of something else in the water that might attract a shark? Dead fish or turtle, or anyone spearfishing?"

"Nothing that I saw."

"How big were the waves?"

"Double overhead. Six feet on the Hawaiian scale. Stu was all about learning the ways here."

"So the water in the bay was probably stirred up then, wasn't it?"

"Yeah, a lot of whitewater and foam when the sets came. But in between you could see the bottom easily."

Sam spun his coffee mug on the table and kept his gaze latched onto it, as though watching it might somehow rewind time.

"And then?" she asked gently.

"A couple sets had hit the outer reef where it breaks on bigger swells, so Stu paddled out there. I stayed put because I don't need to prove anything to anyone with my surfing. I go out, catch a few waves, but I do it mainly to spend time with my son." He stopped, took a deep breath. "So anyway, I was sitting there watching the horizon, watching Stu, when he went airborne. The sound was like a car accident, metal on metal, and when he landed, I saw the shark's open mouth clamp down on him."

"Can you describe the shark?"

"Black, big as a Chevy truck."

His hands had begun to shake, but other than that, he remained remarkably composed.

"The whole shark was black?"

"No, it was pearly white on its underside. When Stuart shot up, he came toward me, so I saw inside the shark's mouth too. Pink and fucking full of teeth. I had this crazy feeling like I was watching a movie in slow motion. Shock can have that effect. And in most cases—I've taken on hundreds—most people report time slowing down. Do you know why?"

She had an idea but could tell he wanted to be the expert here. "Why?"

"There are a few theories, and it may be that all are partly true. But when we're in fight or flight, we go into hyperfocus and we pick up every little detail, so there's an illusion of time slowing. It could also be because the amygdala becomes more active when we're scared and we perceive more, remember more, so it seems like more time has passed."

His lawyer brain had obviously kicked in and he was now in his element. He began spewing facts and stats and cases. Minnow patiently listened, soaking up the pain he was so valiantly trying to keep at bay, then steered him back to the case at hand.

"What happened next with Stuart? Once the shark let him go, did it come back around?"

He rubbed his forehead, now covered in a slick sheen. "They both went under, and I saw this huge tail thrashing for a few seconds, and then Stu popped back up. The water was red all around, and I couldn't tell if the shark was still there. I was paddling toward him as fast as I could and he was trying to yell but kept taking in water. Honestly, I didn't care at all about getting bit myself. My one and only need was to get to Stu."

"And you did," she said, hoping to offer even a feather of comfort.

"He was already white and I told him I loved him. He told me he loved me. We just kept saying it over and over on the way in—I had a longboard, so I laid him on that. I never saw the shark again. I was forced to make the most horrible choice ever. To stay with him or go for help. And in the end, my Stu, he never made it off of that lava field. "

And then he broke down in big, heaving sobs. Minnow let him cry, and she cried along with him. Loving sharks came with a price, and these human and shark interactions broke her heart a million times over. For a few moments she debated telling him about her father, but that would have done nothing to ease the ache. Instead, she said, "Thank you for sharing your story."

He sat forward in the chair, tears on his cheeks as his foot began tapping a mile a minute. "Here's the thing, Dr. Gray. My son loved the ocean and loved surfing. That morning started off so hopeful, so beautiful. Clear skies, clear water—I mean, when isn't the water clear down here? But then we got into an argument. He wanted to surf and I had set up a tee time at eight thirty with the VP of Volcom, whom I wanted Stu to meet. Thought maybe he could get a job with them, seeing as he was so into surfing and he wasn't really doing much with his life other than going on expensive trips, chasing waves. Bali, Tahiti, Fiji . . . Stu was there."

He sat there for a few moments, shaking his head, and Minnow thought maybe they were done. But he went on. "He flat-out refused to go, said I was meddling in his life and he could get his own job. A fight we had been having more and more lately," he said, studying her as though he was seeing her for the first time. "Do you have kids?"

"No," she said, holding back the explanations she often felt a compulsion to give.

The ocean is my one true love, so I haven't married.

I put my career first.

I have trauma, and I'm not sure I want to pass that on.

"Stu was our only child and now he's gone," he said.

Minnow felt her own heart squeeze. She wanted to wrap Sam in her arms, but there was an invisible wall between them she knew she shouldn't breach.

"We fought that morning and I didn't hold my ground. If I had, Stu would still be alive. I keep reliving that moment, the split second where I said, *Okay, I'll change it to tomorrow, but promise you'll come?* I was always a softy where he was concerned—to a fault. He promised, and off we went."

Her mother used to do that. *If only I hadn't been picking berries. If only I took you with me.* Minnow remembered thinking, *If only it had been Mom and not Dad.* In her child's mind, wishing she could trade one parent for the other, almost at will. Life without her father had seemed unfathomable. But eventually, somehow, life kept unspooling forward. And now here she was, sitting with a man facing almost the same situation as she had, only reversed, knowing that the only thing he could be sure of was that his life would never be the same.

Minnow thanked Sam for sharing his story and left feeling bruised and battered and gutted.

From the journal of Minnow Gray

Farallon Islands, November 25, 1996

My favorite girl, Gigi, is pregnant! She came up behind the boat this morning in that stealthy way that she has, showing off a new array of love bites on her face. It's the first time we've seen her this season and we were beside ourselves. A pregnant white shark is always a reason to celebrate. No one I know has ever witnessed a white shark give birth. We do know that they birth live pups four to five feet long after a yearlong (or so) gestation period. The eggs hatch inside the mom and the pups remain there for a few weeks, living on a milk-like substance that nourishes them and gets them ready for the wild. Because from day one, the baby sharks are on their own. For some reason this makes me feel a special fondness for them.

CHAPTER 18

The Task Force

*ʻ**Ono**: delicious, tasty, savory*

Woody must have been out in the water when Minnow got back to the house—though he left no note, so she used the time to add Sam Callahan's notes to her journal. Nothing new about the shark, but his guilt brought a new dimension to the story. Another reminder to kiss and make up after every fight.

She lined up photos she'd taken of the surfboard, the tooth, and the fin from the cave, which was still a maybe in the evidence department. She was still trying to reach Hank Johnson's wife, since no one thought to ask her if he'd had fins on, or if they did, it wasn't written in the report. She'd called the detective on the case, but he had no idea either. Also, Nalu was supposed to get on a computer and find out specifics of the attacks two and four years ago. That data could be invaluable. There were still so many missing pieces to the puzzle.

In preparation for the meeting, she wrote down her selling points against a shark hunt. The migratory nature of large sharks. The importance of apex predators. Hawaiian culture. Animal cruelty laws. It felt like everyone on the island was feeding on the fear, and fear had no place in science. Humans were so good at disrupting the natural order of the earth and its oceans without stopping to think of consequences down the line. So it was Minnow's job to be the voice of reason.

Woody emerged from the ocean with ten minutes to spare, put on a wrinkled aloha shirt, combed his hair with his fingers, and they were out the door. Even from the end of the lava road where they parked, they could see a line of cars parked all along the road into the Kiawe. At the gate there were two cop cars and a bunch of photographers standing around. Minnow wished they had come by boat since there was no other way around. It was all *a'a* lava, the crumbly kind.

As they approached, heads started turning their way, and she heard a shutter snap. Minnow looked down at the ground. In the days after her father died, Catalina Island had turned into a blur of press, all wanting interviews and photographs, and sticking their lenses where they didn't belong. Her mother would scream at them, then dissolve into tears, which scared Minnow. The feeling had remained with her. Instinctively, she picked up her pace. Woody did not.

"Relax, I got your back," he said.

She could sense the cameras pointing their way. *Click, click, click.*

"Is that Angela's sister?"

"No, that's the shark lady."

"Dr. Gray! Can you confirm that Angela Crawford lost her arm?"

"Is it true Zach Santopolo was with her?"

"Will Hawaiian waters ever be safe?"

Minnow kept her focus on the gate, not making eye contact with anyone. None of their questions warranted an answer, but she gave one anyway. "Hawaiian waters are safe. Excuse us, but we have a meeting to get to." And then, because she couldn't resist, she added, "And I study sharks, not movie stars, so no comment."

Woody nodded to the cop, who stepped forward, and they did some kind of half hug, chest bump thing.

"Bruddah, good to see you. We headed in for da shark meeting," Woody said in a thicker pidgin than he used around her.

The meeting was held in a large, open-air pavilion set back from the ocean, next to a large canopied tree. As soon as they hit the shade, the temperature dropped ten degrees. Minnow had dressed up for the occasion in a white linen button-up tied at the waist and ripped jeans. For the first time in days, she'd given her hair a proper wash, finishing up with a freshwater rinse out of a water jug Woody had brought down and left in the shower. Brackish was fine most of the time, but it left a lightly salted film.

A table had been set up out front, covered in a white tablecloth and full of drinks and platters of cheese and crackers and nuts. People stood around talking with drinks in hand, as though this were some kind of reception. She spotted Mayor Lum talking to the head of Search & Rescue, and Sawyer stood looking out at the water with Luke Greenwood and Nalu. Luke was pointing. Minnow followed their line of sight and saw a large fishing boat floating just off the point.

"Paparazzi. Guaranteed," Woody said.

"Theoretically, they could come ashore, couldn't they?"

"Yep. The beach is public in Hawai'i, all the way to the high water line."

A few minutes later, at five o'clock, Sawyer invited everyone to sit at the big round table in the pavilion. As they took their seats, Minnow realized she was the only woman there. Not new but still unnerving, as though sharks were somehow the responsibility of men.

Nalu sat down next to her, sliding a piece of paper in front of her. "Info on those two attacks—I mean incidents—you asked me to find out about."

"Can you summarize for me before we start?" she said, noticing Woody had gone for drinks and *pupus*—what they called hors d'oeuvres here in Hawai'i.

"No concrete evidence of anything. Only thing that might tie them to this shark is they were both on this same stretch of coastline. The day before the diver Kimo Kahapea disappeared two years ago, a large white shark was reported by a fisherman out by the buoy. Said it was as big as his boat. And four years ago boogie boarder Glen Torres was out during a freak swell at a place called Ghost Reef, known for big tigers. So there is no way to tie either of these to our present shark."

The Sister. If only Minnow could catch a glimpse of her, maybe even be able to identify exactly which shark it was.

"Good."

Someone pulled the chair out next to her, and she looked up, expecting Woody, but it was Luke. "Mind if I sit here?"

"Oh, I was saving it for—"

"He's over there. And seeing that this is the last seat . . ."

Her eyes buzzed the table and saw he was right.

"Of course."

Immediately, as soon as he sat, her right side began to heat up, same as that first morning in the bar.

"Nice jeans," he said under his breath.

Minnow shook her head, not even bothering to respond.

"I'm serious. People might mistake you for Angela Crawford in that outfit. It's not very science nerdish."

"Who ever said I was a nerd?" she said, turning to face him, then wishing she hadn't.

Sun pooled in his eyes, and the half smile he wore on his face said he was toying with her and enjoying it. She couldn't look away.

"You have a PhD in marine biology. It means you're a nerd."

"Say I did happen to be a nerd. What's wrong with being passionately enthusiastic and knowledgeable about something?"

"So you have the definition memorized."

She laughed. "How did you know?"

He got that faraway look again. "Someone once accused me of being a nerd, so I looked it up."

"A fishing nerd?"

"Nah, not quite."

"What exactly did you do back on the mainland?" she asked.

Across the table, Mayor Lum tapped a fork against his glass. "Aloha, everyone. Thank you for coming. I'd like to get started with quick introductions, and then we'll get into the meat of our purpose for being here." Though he didn't speak pidgin per se, he had this inflection that so many of the local people had. Almost old-fashioned.

They went around the table. Aside from the firemen and lifeguards, there was Tommy Warren from DLWA; Dave Morrow, head of the Kiawe Roughwater Swim; the district rep Tim Richmond; a police officer who called himself Dragon; Sam Callahan, who kept looking at her; and two local fishermen who both had been fishing this coast their whole lives. It made her wonder where Luke Greenwood fit in all this.

Woody went last. "My name is Woody Kaupiko, and I was born next door at Hale Niuhi. I could swim before I could walk, and my family used to be the caretakers of this *'ili*, this area. And I have opinions about this whole thing, so I appreciate being on your roster."

Mayor Lum nodded in acknowledgment, then took over again. He spoke slowly, swinging his gaze around the table and making eye contact with each person. "You all are here because you have a stake in these shark attacks or have experience or knowledge about sharks. You all know what's gone down, but we also have Minnow Gray with us to give us an update on what she and her intern have found out since her arrival. We'll do this roundtable style, each person gets a chance to speak, and then we'll open it up to questions. So Minnow, why don't we start with you."

The sun had gone behind a bank of clouds, dimming her light. She'd been hoping to go last, once she'd had a chance to hear what the others had to say, and she knew what she'd be up against, but all eyes were on her.

She smiled and took a deep breath. "Thank you, Mayor Lum, I'm honored to be here. Why don't I first present you with our findings and then go from there," she said, pulling out the photographs Joe had given her, as well as the ones Nalu had picked up from Longs drugstore just before the meeting. The tooth. The surfboard. The fin. Angela Crawford's wounds.

When she asked if anyone knew anything about Hank Johnson, one of the lifeguards said, "I remember his wife saying he was wearing fins."

"Did she say what kind?"

"No, but red. Easy to spot."

Damn.

"Okay, we're still waiting on confirmation from the wife, but I'll note it here," she said. "And though we can safely say the same shark that bit Stuart also bit Angela, that's really all we know. The incidents were a week apart and four miles away from each other, but as the shark swims, four miles is nothing. I know it's rare in Hawai'i for two shark incidents like this so close together, but it's happened elsewhere—Florida, South Africa, Australia. And the odds of another incident are close to zero."

She went on, outlining basic white shark behavior for those unfamiliar with the animals. From everything she'd seen all shark research in the islands centered on reef sharks and tiger sharks. The majority of people living in the islands probably didn't even know white sharks frequented their waters. When she was done with that, she launched into shark breeding patterns and how with white sharks, it can be thirty years until they reach maturity, and then they only give birth every few years.

"What I can't stress enough is that the role of these animals is critical to the entire ocean ecosystem. Sharks are great equalizers. And it doesn't take killing too many to upset their population for decades to come. Plus, evidence points to one animal causing the incidents, so a widespread hunt will have too much collateral damage while most likely not yielding the culprit, who is probably on her way back to the West Coast. My position, and that of my colleagues, is a hard no to any shark hunt, organized or—"

The older fireman cut in. "Girl, why does any of this matter? This shark, that shark. Bottom line, people are dying on our watch."

"Let her finish," Woody said.

"Organized or unorganized was what I was going to say. That's it."

Woody gave her a nod. The rest of the men, though, remained quiet. Even Luke.

"Any questions for the young lady?" Mayor Lum finally said.

Young lady? What a dickwad.

Sawyer held up a hand. "What about catch and release? Anything other than a giant white shark is let go. That way we'd ensure people feel safe enough to swim around here and enter the race, but we're not upsetting any natural balance."

She shook her head. "You still run the risk of badly injuring the sharks. There are all kinds of things to consider. The stress alone can sometimes kill them or leave them maimed with dislocated jaws. Leaving the hook in their mouths is cruel and can lead to infection and eventually death."

Woody jumped in, "Like the doc said, the shark in question is probably long gone, and what, you gonna go out there and just catch any kine shark? Waste of time. We hardly got any beaches over here, not too many people in the water like up north or in Kona. We need to just accept that when we go in the water we might meet a shark, and move on, no offense to any of the victims."

Minnow could feel the red spreading across Sam Callahan's cheeks. She avoided looking his way. Whoever had invited him had not been thinking clearly.

"So we know how you two feel about this. Let's hear from the rest. How about Ocean Safety, what is your recommendation?" Lum asked.

"When we see sharks, we put the signs up, and beyond that it's the individual's choice to go out," said Johnny Angel, a bearded man with tattoos up both arms. "In the case of the roughwater swim, we can beef up our escorts and do some scouting ahead of time. But I tend to agree with Dr. Gray—a shark hunt is wrong."

Minnow wanted to reach out and hug him. She was feeling like maybe things were going to go her way until Tommy Warren folded his arms on his chest and said in a slow, booming voice, "You know, the community is outraged, people are dying and we have a killer shark on the loose. Calls to our office of shark sightings have gone through the roof. We all know that Hank did not just drown out there and now you have a fin to prove it. The only way to nip this in the bud, especially now with national eyes on us, is to do a targeted hunt between Keahole Point and Kiholo. I have experienced guys lined up ready to go, and I don't think some chick from the mainland should be rolling in here and telling us what to do."

He caught her eyeing him and gave her a cold, hard stare. Minnow glanced down at the table in front of her, uncomfortable.

The district rep agreed with him. "My office is getting calls too. Hundreds of them. People want action. And this isn't just a matter of catching sharks; this is a matter of assuaging the fears of every single person on the mainland and around the world who is watching the news and shitting their pants. Even if the press is blowing it out of proportion, if we don't do something, all those happy tourists are going to take their dollars elsewhere."

What was wrong with these people? Had they not heard anything she said?

"Always about money, isn't it? Let those people stay home. Those sharks are our *'aumakua* and we stand by them," Woody said.

"You bet it's about money," Sawyer said. "How else do we feed our families? Not everyone had the luxury to grow up fishing and has a beach house. Nothing personal, because you know I have deep respect for you, Woody, but that's the reality here."

Representative Richmond folded his small, smooth hands in front of him. "Maybe your job doesn't depend on them. Or wait, does it? How many jobs have you taken at the Mauna Kea or Mauna Lani, Mr. Kaupiko?"

Woody's jaw tightened. "None of your business."

Suddenly Sam Callahan spoke up. "You would put the lives of a few sharks over people? I doubt you would feel that way if it had been your son, Mr. Kaupiko, with all due respect."

"My heart goes out to you, it does. But catching sharks is not gonna bring your boy back, and like the doc and the lifeguards say, shark hunts don't prevent shark attacks."

Sam began to tremble, then stood up. "If you'll excuse me, this is too much for me."

They all just sat there, and Minnow felt like she had to say *something*, as inadequate as it may be. "I'm so sorry, Mr. Callahan. We all are."

Once Sam was gone, Dave Morrow gave his two cents. "Not going to lie, we want to see this beast caught before the race. My phone has been ringing off the hook from entrants asking when the last date they can withdraw is. Talking about money, this race is a huge boost to your economy. This year we had 800 people signed up, but now we're down to 424. Do you know how many hotel rooms and rental cars that equates to? Because for every person in the race, they often bring family and friends. I'd hate to see one rogue shark ruin this forever."

Minnow fumed. "Sharks don't go rogue. That's a myth created by Hollywood."

Luke's leg started bouncing up and down. Minnow could feel it against her chair. It seemed like he wanted to say something, but he didn't.

They continued back and forth, the conversations growing more heated with each round. The mayor, DLWA, the fire chief, Sawyer and Dave Morrow were strongly in favor of a hunt, while Ocean Safety, Minnow and Nalu and Woody were not. Dragon the cop had no opinion one way or the other. He said he was purely there because of procedure. Neither side seemed to be able to convince the other. In all of this, Luke Greenwood did not breathe a word.

In the end Mayor Lum said, "Well, we covered a lot of ground. I think we have plenty to chew on. Right now we may not have our answer, but let's all think long and hard on what we've learned tonight, and I will reach out to each of you individually once I've made my decision. Meantime, keep me posted on any updates—sightings, new findings, incidents, large or small."

Again, Minnow got the sense this was all for show. The mayor had already made up his mind but wanted to appease the scientists and the Hawaiians, make them feel like they had a voice.

Sawyer took off his straw hat and wiped his forehead. "*Mahalo,* Mayor and all of you. Dinner is on me if any of you want to stay. Just mosey on over to the Saltwater Bar."

"I'm down," Nalu said to Minnow.

She was famished, and the idea of a five-star meal made her mouth water. "Let me see what Woody wants to do."

"I can drive you back if you want to stay."

She turned around to look for Luke, but apparently he'd already left and was nowhere in sight. Woody had his back to them and was staring out at the ocean and a yellow sliver of moon.

"You want to stay and grab a bite?" she asked.

He shook his head. "I have to get up early and head to Waimea for a job, and Anna wants to see me. But I'll be back in a day or two. You stay. The food here is *'ono* and I'm not going to be good company," he said, not even looking her way.

"Are you okay?" she asked.

"Are you?"

Her heart was full of lead. "No. That was shit. Why have shark experts if you aren't going to listen to anything they say? I have a bad feeling about what's coming."

"We'll talk when I get back. I'll leave my dive light for you behind the log, just in case," he said.

"In case what?"

"In case your plans change."

And then he was gone.

From the Journal of Minnow Gray

Farallon Islands, September 19, 1997

Something terrible has happened. It has to do with Wally, the shark we caught and tagged last season. For a while Max had wanted to try out a new method for tagging he insisted was safe for the sharks and would provide us with a lot more info on each animal. Everything appeared ready—we had a permit to use whale blubber to attract a shark and another permit to capture and tag one. I had pressed Max to use our old tried-and-true method, where the shark remains in the water, but Max wouldn't listen. He swore he had it all worked out. I had my doubts and should have stood up to him but knew it was pointless. No one knows more than Max. Not me, not anyone. At least in his mind.

What happened next was crushing. Wally ended up biting the baited and barbed hook, which was attached to a buoy. We then pulled him onto an underwater platform and tied him so he could be raised out of the water and we could draw blood, take measurements, and tag him. He was thrashing and pissed but hooked, so there was nothing he could do. A fourteen-inch steel alloy hook is absolutely bulletproof. Unfortunately, Wally bit the buoy and swallowed the hook and we could not get it out of his throat. I stuck my hand in through his gills, trying to wiggle it free, but it was lodged, and eventually we had to leave it in there. I fought to keep my cool, but I was shaking the whole time. All said and done, Wally was out of the water for twenty minutes. Stressed and hurt and scared. I could see it in his big, dark orb of an eye. When I glanced over at the Farallon Sanctuary observer, who was there to keep tabs on us, he gave me a solemn shake of his head.

Fast-forward to two days ago when Wally showed up in Fisherman's Bay with open wounds over his gill slits and along his left jaw. Not only that, but his lower jaw was hanging open, almost as though dislocated. It is obvious he's not in great shape and is suffering because of our fuck up. Gordon and a biologist from the National Marine Fisheries Service captured some video of him cruising below the boat, so I didn't get to see him in person, but watching that video made me livid. Max says there is no way of knowing if we did this. It could have been from a run-in with another shark. I say it was us, a hundred percent.

Despite the heartbreak of this incident, here's what completely unraveled me—yesterday I overheard Max telling the NMFS guy that it was my idea to use this new method of catching the shark. Had I not heard it with my own two ears, I never would have believed it. My boyfriend, my partner, my supposed love, blaming this whole ruinous thing on me. Rather than walking away like I should have, I busted in there calling him a liar and a shark killer and the world's biggest asshole. I'm sure I came off as hysterical, but I could not contain myself. Max looked me in the eye and said, "You wanted this, Minnow."

Turns out that's what narcissists do. They charm you and then mess with your head until you begin to question up from down and left from right. I think deep inside he knows I've been contemplating leaving him. His possessiveness has been slowly strangling me. That and the fact that he's begun to subtly but constantly put me down. I think he sees me and my shark connection as a threat, though to what I'm not sure. Maybe because he's the revered shark god and he wants me to remain in his shadow forever like a good woman should.

It's so twisted to think the man who knows me most intimately would blame me for this when he knows how much guilt I am already carrying about my dad. That's what hurts the most. I have more than enough guilt for one lifetime.

I'm hitching a ride back to San Francisco on a fishing boat tomorrow and doubt I'll ever come back, not as long as Max is here. I feel shaken and numb but also certain that this is the right thing to do. My departure is long overdue.

CHAPTER 19

The Statement

***Koholā**: humpback whale*

Minnow and Nalu sat at the bar sipping a rum and coconut drink that the bartender slid in front of them as they read over the menu. Surprisingly, no one else from the meeting had stayed. It was a weeknight and they probably all had long drives and families waiting at home.

"So what did you think?" Nalu asked.

"I have this feeling like I'm drowning. I want to do everything I can to help these sharks and educate people, but it's really all beyond my control. I wish Joe and the rest of the team were here."

"Joe said he'd be here next week if things go well, and the rest of the guys get back from the symposium on Friday. But what else are they going to say that you haven't already said?"

Minnow shrugged. "They're men, Nalu. And men listen to men."

"Huh. I never thought about it like that. *I* listen to you, don't I?"

Because you're practically still a boy, she wanted to say.

"You do, and I appreciate that."

He sat up a little straighter. "I promise to keep fighting this with you, whatever it takes."

"Thanks, Nalu. That means a lot."

As they waited for their food, every time the waitress—a cute blonde with a spray tan—came by to collect drinks, Nalu said something to her. *Why did they get umbrellas on their drinks and we didn't? Impressive how you balance all those drinks without spilling a drop. Do you ever swim after work, in the moonlight? What's your name?*

Dixie, it turned out.

When Dixie walked to another table, Minnow peered over at him. "Are you ever *not* hitting on some girl or another?"

"I haven't hit on *you*, have I?"

She made a face. "No, thank God. I'm almost old enough to be your mother."

"Not quite. Aunt maybe but not mother. And I know when someone is off-limits," he said, pausing to shove a handful of mochi crunch in his mouth. "But look who's talking. You think I haven't noticed the way you go all fluttery-eyed when you mention Greenwood?"

She almost spit out her drink. "Please, give me some credit."

"Why deny it? He kind of has that bad boy thing going, which chicks love. But do you want to hear my thoughts on him?"

Nalu had this way about him that made it hard to be mad at anything he did or said. And he was perceptive, she'd give him that.

"I can't believe we're even having this conversation."

He shrugged. "You want to hear it though, don't you?"

"Sure, tell me."

As soon as the words came out, she regretted saying them. Talking about Luke with someone else felt like bringing to life something that until now had just been a thought, a glimmer, a question mark.

"He's hiding something," he said.

"Tell me something I don't already know."

Dixie came back, loading up another round of drinks. The way she eyed up Nalu, chances were good that they'd end up at least exchanging numbers.

"What time are you off, Dixie?" he asked.

She looked at her watch. "Ten minutes. I've been here since eight a.m."

"Ouch, long day. Can I walk you to your car?"

She shot a look Minnow's way. "You two haven't even eaten yet."

Nalu held up his drink. "Oh, I'm not here to eat. We just finished up at the Shark Task Force meeting and I was thirsty. Dr. Gray and I work together and she's staying next door at Hale Niuhi."

"Dr. Gray must be super hungry, then, because I saw your order."

Mahi-mahi plate. Large order of fries. Margherita pizza. Caesar salad with mac nut croutons.

Minnow gave her a wide smile. "Nah, I'm taking the mahi plate back to Woody, and Nalu and I were just strategizing before he goes back to his hotel room."

She actually liked the idea of walking back alone under the stars with nothing but lava and ocean for miles.

Dixie leaned into Nalu. "Meet me by the fishpond behind the gym."

Once she'd walked off, he said, "Thanks, I owe you one."

"Just behave and be a gentleman."

"Always."

When the food came, Minnow ate a slice and a half and picked at the salad, wondering all the while how to sway the minds of those who wanted the hunt. Images of that beautiful, dead white shark on the dock in Catalina reared up, making it hard to breathe. That and the shark on the Farallones. Underwater, sharks were all speed and grace, but take them out of the water and they became limp, helpless, lumpy sacs. Right after her father's death, some of the divers on the island had taken it upon themselves to catch all the sharks they could, and it had been awful for Minnow.

"How's the food?" someone asked.

She turned to see Josh Brown, dressed in a tweed coat of all things. Thankfully, he had not been allowed in the meeting, but she figured he was probably lurking somewhere.

"It's great."

"Mind if I sit?" he asked.

"I was just leaving, so have at it."

He slapped his notebook down next to her. "How did the meeting go? I got Sawyer's take on it, but I'd love yours."

As much as she wanted to flee, talking to the press was partly why she was here, a way to the people. And Angela's statement still burned a hole in her pocket.

"Everyone made their points, one way or another, so it went well in that regard. But I still maintain that the evidence against a hunt is clear. In my mind there's really no other option."

"Sam Callahan begs to differ. I caught up with him after he walked out," Josh said.

"No one can blame him for feeling that way. Or Angela Crawford. But that's the thing. Angela feels differently."

He perked up. "How do you know?"

She fished around for the paper, pulled it out and waved it. "I have a statement from her."

"Hell, why didn't you say so in the first place?"

"Sorry, I forgot."

"You *forgot*?"

"Just momentarily. My mind was on other things."

It was true, she had been ruminating about the meeting, but now it dawned on her that she might be able to use Angela to help her persuade the rest of the task force.

"I need to get this on tape. Can you hang on while I get my guy? He's right over there."

"Yes."

While he went off, Minnow wet her hands and smoothed her hair with her hands. It was all she could do.

"You look good, no need to worry."

Luke had replaced Josh and was holding a frosty glass of beer, smiling at her.

"I'm not worried," she said.

"You could be hiding some seaweed in there and no one would be the wiser. Untamed suits you, though."

"Wow, two compliments in one night from you. I'm not sure how to feel about that."

In truth, it caused a strange lightheadedness that was not entirely unpleasant.

He looked into his beer. "Yeah, well, it's true."

"Having seaweed for hair has always been a dream of mine, ever since I was a little girl."

His face slowly turned back to her, one side of his mouth lifted. "You're serious, aren't you?"

"Completely."

A voice cut through the thick air. "Dr. Gray, we're ready for you. Let's go out front. On the beach, if you don't mind."

Josh and his camera guy were standing by the steps.

Luke saluted. "I'll be here if you need a drink after—I know I would. The press makes my skin crawl."

"Why is that?"

He shrugged. "I don't like the way they manipulate the truth. Some of them, at least."

"Fear and drama sell," she said. Then she added, "Will you come out there with me, for moral support?"

If he was surprised, he didn't show it. "I'm already there."

When she stood, her arm brushed his shoulder and she had the sudden desire to sit back down, shut the world out and talk. Just the two of them. Being so close, she could smell a tangy aftershave that reminded her of ocean. Or maybe it *was* ocean. He followed her out without a word.

Josh and his guy were standing under a coconut tree, clamping a bright light to a beach umbrella. "This is my main man Danny, and you are . . . ?" he said, eyeing Luke.

"A friend of hers."

It was like someone had flipped off his thermostat and the warmth she'd felt from him at the bar turned to cold, hard ice.

Josh ignored him and looked at Minnow, gaze slipping over her chest, down her thighs and back up. "This is freaking perfect. A shark scientist who could be a movie star. So, I need you to stand over here, across from me. I'll just ask you a few questions, and then we'll lead into Angela's statement. How does that sound?"

Minnow moved to under the coconut tree, facing the blinding light. "Fine."

"Okay, let's roll," Josh said.

She could barely see his face, only the outline of his coiffed hair.

In a somber tone, Josh began. "Aloha from the Big Island of Hawai'i, where a series of deadly shark attacks killed one man, possibly two, and left a third victim badly injured. With spring break and an international open-water swim coming up, state officials are considering a shark hunt to make waters safe again. Joining me now on the beach in front of the Kiawe is Dr. Minnow Gray, a great-white scientist from California who studies these beasts for a living. Dr. Gray, can you tell us what you know about the shark involved, because if I'm not mistaken, it's been the same animal."

Minnow stole a glance at Luke, who gave her a nod. "Yes, Josh. We do believe the same white shark is responsible for the bites of two people here along the coast, but the third is currently ruled as a missing swimmer since there's no evidence pointing otherwise."

"But the missing swimmer was within a mile of where Stuart Callahan was killed, was he not?"

"Yes, but there are far more drownings than shark incidents, so we can't jump to conclusions. We need evidence before we can make a determination."

"What kind of evidence are you looking for?"

"For one, his body has not been recovered, so that would be a first step."

"I understand you attended a shark task force meeting earlier this evening. Were any decisions made about how the state plans on stopping this man-eater?"

"First, it's not a man-eater. Shark bites are most commonly a case of mistaken identity. But also, a woman was bit, so the term is misleading at best. But more than that, it is extremely damaging to an animal that is greatly misunderstood. To answer your question, we are still investigating, but shark hunts are outdated and do more harm than good. Science now tells us this."

"What kind of science?"

"Shark tagging and tracking, mainly, which shows us how migratory these animals are. But also, we've learned about how important sharks are to the entire balance of the ocean."

"Would removing one predatory shark, who seems to have acquired a taste for human flesh, really make that much of a difference?"

She felt her whole body tensing and willed herself to relax. "Neither of these victims were consumed by the shark, so that tells us the opposite story. They were bitten and released. As soon as the shark realized they weren't seals, it moved on. Trust me, if this shark had a hankering for humans, there would have been nothing left of them."

"Maybe that's what happened to Hank, the swimmer."

"I don't operate on speculation."

A smile crept onto his face, and she could tell he was enjoying getting a rise out of her.

"Okay, so you mentioned a woman. Can you confirm for CNN that the woman attacked was actress Angela Crawford?" he asked.

She nodded, holding the folded note in her hand. "I can."

"Our sources tell us she's still in the hospital and was critically injured. Is she going to survive?"

"I have a statement from Angela here. I'll just read it to you."

"Brilliant."

Something moved in the shadows behind Josh and she caught a glimpse of Luke standing with his arms crossed next to the cameraman. When their eyes met, he gave her a thumbs-up. Her voice was a little shaky as she read, but she was so dang thankful for that last line.

From what I'm told, I was doing something I probably shouldn't have been doing, and I only have myself to blame.

Josh looked directly into the camera and smiled his famous prep-boy smile. "You heard that here first, folks. Angela Crawford has been attacked by a great white shark in Hawaiian waters, but she's alive and expected to recover. Dr. Gray, have you examined her yourself?"

"I have, as part of our investigation."

"Can you tell us anything more? Did she lose any limbs?"

"Patient confidentiality, Josh. Sorry, I can't."

"What a miracle she lived to tell."

"It is."

He smirked. "One last question. Your resemblance to Angela is striking. Have you ever thought about giving up sharks for Hollywood?"

What a douchebag.

"Never."

"Thank you, Dr. Gray, you've been illuminating," he said, then turned back to the camera. "Stay tuned for more live coverage tomorrow as this tragic and harrowing story unfolds. Back to you, Greta."

Once Danny turned off the light, Minnow went blind for a few seconds, unsteady on her feet. She felt a hand squeeze her shoulder and thought it was Josh, but it was Luke.

Josh was still there, though, and moved in a little too close. "I'd love to catch up with you tomorrow, Dr. Gray. Get a little more background on you and your work."

"It'll depend on how the day goes."

"I'll be here at five. Meet me then if you can?"

"No promises but maybe."

He handed her a card. "In case anything new comes up, call me anytime."

Still disoriented, she stepped out onto the beach and into the darkness. Luke came and walked alongside her and she could feel the heat coming off him.

"Now I know how the turtles must feel," she said.

"Yeah, that light could probably be seen from outer space."

It suddenly felt like the longest day on record, and all she wanted to do was climb into her saggy bed, rest her head on the hundred-year-old pillow and check out for a while.

"Well done, though," Luke said, walking toward the water.

"You think?"

"You kept your cool, which is probably more than I would have done. The guy seems like a slime."

"He rubs me the wrong way too. I don't know what it is about him."

"His smile is fake. It never reaches the eyes, which means you can't trust him."

Her vision had begun to adjust to the dark, and she could see the outlines of the boats on the water. "At least I got to make a few points. All that sensational jargon he uses, it's hogwash."

Luke laughed. "Hogwash? You sound like my grandmother."

"Yeah? Tell me about her, I could use a distraction." She dropped down onto the cool sand.

At first she thought he wouldn't answer, since he seemed so reticent to talk about himself, but he sat down next to her. "Granny June makes the meanest apple pie this side of the Rockies. She raised four boys who all went on to become national park rangers, and she sews all her own clothing. Still to this day. She lives in a cabin on the slopes of Mount Rainier and is friends with all the black bears in the area. Does anything in there sound familiar?" he asked.

She could hear the smile in his voice. "She sounds like a firecracker."

"Tough and sassy, all while being the kindest woman I know. She taught my brother and me how to shoot a gun and fly-fish when we were five, but she also fed foxes and raccoons out of her hand, nursed every injured animal that came onto her property, so much so that people would come to her before they'd go to the local veterinarian."

"Sounds like my kind of gal."

"You would love her. Everyone does."

They sat there quietly and the space between them crackled with electricity. Minnow could taste it on her tongue, the way she could taste a storm coming. Luke Greenwood was rubbing off on her, sure as the pull of the moon. So what if she had sworn off men for a while? Maybe she should make an exception in his case.

"Which park was your father at?" she asked.

"San Juan Island Historic."

"So your family lived out there?"

"We did. Friday Harbor."

"What a place to grow up."

"Have you been?"

"No, but it's on my bucket list," she said. "To swim with the orcas, that would be a dream."

Just thinking about the frigid water of the West Coast made her shiver. There was a different kind of beauty there. Cold and fog, giant beds of kelp, towering evergreen forests edging up against placid inlets or lashing, angry seas. For a moment she thought of Max on the Farallones but quickly squashed that. Max was past, and she wanted to live only in the present. Luke sat quietly, staring out at the warm Pacific just beyond their toes.

"There's something about islands, isn't there?" Minnow finally said.

"They are magic, for sure."

"I grew up on Catalina Island—until I was seven. I loved it there."

"Tell me about it. I've never been."

And so she did. All of it. Luke slowly drew closer to her, the way a plant tilts toward the sun, until she could feel his shoulder against hers. His touch somehow made it feel safe to let her past unspool into the evening. There was no expectation in it either.

"Will you ever go back?" he asked. "To live, I mean."

"No. Too much sadness."

"Makes sense. And I'm sorry for what happened. No one should have to live through that."

She shook her head. "No one."

"You didn't let it defeat you, though. Look at what you've made of your life."

"Oh, I don't know about that."

He leaned in. "Aside from all those letters behind your name, it looks like you've found your place in this world and you're willing to fight for it. I'd own that if I were you."

She nudged him. "Thanks for the advice. I'll work on it. But back to you and the orca . . . Now your tattoo makes sense. I'm guessing you've been in the water with them?"

"Hard not to up there. The resident pods you kind of get to know."

"Top of the food chain," she said.

"Yes and a whole lot more. Did you know the SRKW population is matrilineal, and they have their own dialect?"

His tone reminded her of herself when talking sharks. Confident, knowledgeable, enamored.

"SRKW?" she asked.

"Southern resident killer whale."

"Ah, right. No, I didn't. And is that a genetically distinct population?"

"Yep, and they feed on Chinook, mainly. Smartest animals in the ocean, hands down. I'd reckon they're smarter than a lot of humans I've met."

"So how come the son of a ranger who obviously loves the ocean didn't become a ranger himself?"

Minnow listened and could tell his lungs were big by how long and slow his breaths were. She also knew they had reached the end of this line of conversation and that a wall had gone back up.

"Long story, one I don't feel like getting into right now." He shifted uncomfortably. "What about you? How much longer do you plan on staying in Hawai'i?"

Once again, his evasiveness put her off. "As long as I need to." Which reminded her, there was one more question she needed to ask. "It didn't slip by me that you were the only one we never heard from in the meeting. Are you for having a shark hunt or against it?" A cool breeze skimmed across her skin as she waited for an answer.

"It's complicated," he said.

From the journal of Minnow Gray

June 11, 1992

She has such a good point here:

From a young age, I wasn't afraid of sharks—I was afraid of not *seeing them. Sharks don't just swim through the ocean; they tell its whole story.*

—Jennifer Homcy, marine biologist and captain

CHAPTER 20

The Buoy

Moe'uhane: *dream; to dream*

Minnow woke in the dark to the rumble of Woody's truck engine. She wished they'd had a chance to debrief after last night, but at least he'd be back, hopefully sooner than later. She looked at her watch. Five twenty. Knowing she wouldn't be able to fall back asleep, she got up, grabbed a few pillows, wrapped the blanket around herself like a mummy and made her way out to the seawall. She set the pillows down and lay on them, looking skyward and listening for the distant singing of the stars.

Sometimes it took her a while to quiet her mind and hear beneath the noise, but this early in the morning she needed no time at all. Lizard feet scratched down the closest coconut tree and somewhere just offshore a fin sliced through the water. She knew the sound, sat up, but it was too dark to see anything. A big shark swimming close by, not hunting, just being. It was obvious by her languid motion and slow heartbeat.

"Hello," Minnow whispered. "Please, go."

It made her think of Luna and her father and how those years when he was still with her lived so brightly in her mind. After he died, her whole world had gone gray. Even now, nothing carried the same crisp glow as it had in her youth, in The Before, as she often thought of it. Here on the Big Island, though, every now and then that same brightness had flickered on, the way an old television suddenly picked up a picture. She'd noticed it in the water. Or looking back at those pyramid-shaped volcanoes. Sitting next to Luke on the wet sand, his hand an inch or two away from her own.

When she'd asked that final question, her heart had been beating a mile a minute, and it scared her how much his answer meant to her.

It's complicated.

"How is it complicated?" she'd asked, fighting flames of anger.

"I am not for a big shark hunt where the whole island comes out to slaughter a bunch of sharks, but I do see how a targeted hunt could ease people's minds. It could even ensure things are done right. And I know you think this shark is long gone, but what if it's not?"

There was something tight in the way he spoke the words, something that made her wonder if he even believed what he was saying.

"What aren't you telling me, Luke?"

"You asked and I told you."

"Not about the sharks, about you. You can trust me, you know."

He rubbed his eye with a fist, then stood up. "It's been a long day, and I just don't have it in me to have this conversation."

She dug her feet into the sand. "I ask because I care. Does that make any difference?"

He backed away slowly. "I care too, probably too much. Good night, Minnow."

His voice cracked, and so did her hope.

Now, on the wall, she wept for the shark that just swam past and all the other sharks out there in these waters. For all future sharks, those unborn and those young and growing. With everything there was a tipping point, and she could feel that doing this thing, this hunt, would do so much more harm than good. And its echoes would be heard for years to come.

Tears wet her temples, and she drifted off for a time, then jolted awake to pink streaks in the sky. Only a few stars remained. Still fresh in her mind was a dream, though it didn't dissolve the way dreams normally did.

She is on Catalina in the cove where her father died. Morning light breaks through the fog here and there on the water. She is busy looking for shells in the shallows when the tide begins to come up, washing her farther and farther up the beach. It doesn't bother her at all. In fact, she loves going limp and letting the shore break roll her across the grainy sand. The water is frigid, but the cold never bothers her much.

Her mother has gone out for a walk and her father is sleeping in, and the morning feels like hers alone. The yellow kayak sits high on the sand, and she eyes it with longing. Maybe just a quick spin around the bay? No one would have to know. But her mother's insistent words are stamped in her mind. "You are never to take the kayak out alone, do you hear me? Between the fog and currents and sharks, you could easily just disappear."

A loud, crashing explosion brought her back to the seawall. Falling coconuts. Desperate to climb back into her memory, she curled into a fetal position and covered her ears. But the door had been shut.

What had happened in between this memory and the one from the hospital? She knew it would be the hardest thing ever to relive, her father dying right there in front of her, but she couldn't shake the feeling that things had happened differently than her mom had believed. Only by stepping back into her childhood mind would she ever know the truth.

Just now, she had been so close she could smell the blood in the air.

They sped over metallic-blue water, heading out to sea. Woody had suggested they check out the offshore buoys because large sharks often gravitated to them. Weather and wave FAD buoys—fish aggregation devices—were known to house entire ecosystems of saltwater critters.

Microbial reef was the scientific term for them. Microbes collected on the buoy, fish ate the microbes, larger fish ate the smaller fish and apex pelagic predators often swam through for lunch.

Minnow watched the high bank of clouds stacking up in the south with some interest.

"Is that coming our way?" she asked Nalu.

"This island has its own weather patterns, but my guess would be yes. See those puffy clouds overhead?" He craned his neck up. "Usually that means a storm is coming. But it could stay to the south of us."

A storm was the last thing they needed right now, and she prayed for the calm seas to remain. With Nalu driving, Minnow had the binoculars around her neck, ready to scope out other boats and any marine life or debris they came across. It was six miles out to the buoy, and already the sun burned hot on her shoulders. She was leisurely making sweeps of the horizon when suddenly a whale breached just ahead, its entire body launched clear of the water. So close you could see the barnacles on its fins. A thunderous slap when it landed.

"Whale!" they both yelled in unison.

Nalu let off the throttle and they floated, waiting for more. A moment later, a much smaller whale managed to get halfway out of the water, its splash a small fluff compared to the last.

"Baby," Minnow said, fullness welling up in her chest.

A pungent and fishy smell lifted off the water around them as a third whale—another adult—flung itself skyward. Eighty thousand pounds of grace and ancient intelligence. Minnow was no stranger to whales, and yet every time she came close to one, she had to gulp back sobs. Those eyes of theirs, they saw into her soul.

"Cut the motor," she said.

He did as instructed. Behind them, another slap. This time a tail twice as wide as the boat was long.

"Holy shit, we're surrounded," Nalu said.

If there were any large sharks around, none of them were getting close to this baby. Besides the mama, there were at least two other adults in the area.

"Escorts, right?"

"Gotta be."

Spreading out in the water below and reverberating through the hull of the boat was an eerie, high-pitched keening.

"Whale song, can you hear it?" she said, her whole being humming from the vibrations.

Nalu cocked his head. "Nope. Wanna jump in?"

She gave him a look. "That would be illegal, wouldn't it? Let's just let them pass and we'll be on our way."

A hundred yards. That was the law.

"You see anyone from DLWA around?" he said.

"No, but the laws are there for a reason. You know that."

From the north, Minnow noticed a yellow zodiac speeding toward them. And then another shooting out from the shore.

"What the hell?"

"Lots of people doing illegal stuff around here, chasing down dolphins and whales and mantas. Easy money, not a lot of enforcing of laws."

Angela and Zach for one, and look how that turned out.

She reached for the radio. "What's the frequency for DLWA?"

"Beats me."

"What do you mean?"

"I mean, I've never called them on the radio, not on this island."

The yellow boat came at them full speed, and Minnow waved her arms, but of course it did nothing to deter them. There was a whole line of what looked to be tourists hanging on to the rail, pointing and squealing. Maybe ten of them.

"Go over there," she said to Nalu.

He started the engine and moved toward the boat, which had positioned itself just downstream of the whales. When they were close enough, she called out again. "You need to get out of here."

"Yeah? Who are you?" the guy said.

Nalu held up a plastic sheath, like he was showing some kind of badge. "Brah, you heard her. We're with NOAA, and these whales are protected under the Marine Mammals Protection Act and the Endangered Species Act. You are breaking the law and we'll shut down your whole operation if you don't leave now," he said, in a surprisingly authoritative voice. It probably helped that he wore a trucker hat with a star on it, almost like a sheriff.

The boat captain, a skinny *haole* guy in a big hat, waved. "Roger that. We meant no harm, just passing by."

And with that, the boat turned and zoomed off toward Kona.

Minnow looked at Nalu. "What was that?"

"My school ID."

She laughed. "You are kidding me."

"Hey, whatever works," he said in that same deep voice he'd used to scare off the boat captain.

"Maybe Joe *was* right about you."

"What is that supposed to mean?"

"Nothing."

"Tell me."

She relented. "Just that you're a lot smarter than you seem. And not to let your good looks fool me."

A smile crept across his face. "You know that."

"But let me ask you this. I know you're smart, I know you love the ocean fiercely. But a few times now you've been almost frozen with fear. What's that all about?"

His smile faded, and he clutched the steering wheel. "Nah, just a little bit of nerves, nothing major."

"It's okay to talk about it, you know. We all have our fears, and no one would fault you for being scared of swimming into dark caves or around large sharks."

He turned on the engine and let it idle.

"Like I said, just nerves. I'm all good."

"All I'm saying is, when you try to stuff your fears, they grow, but when you expose them to the light of day—even thank them—that's when you gain the upper hand."

"How would you know? Doesn't seem like you're scared of much."

"Oh, the fear is there, but I've learned to compartmentalize it and give it its own little drawer in my mind, one that I can close whenever I need to."

"You make it sound easy."

"It's not easy, but I've had practice. And maybe it's not sharks so much as other things that really freak me out."

In the distance a whale breached, creating a huge splash with its enormous body.

"What could scare you more than a healthy twenty-foot white?"

"A shark hunt," she said, then thought for a bit, "or centipedes. Or some of my nightmares. When they're bad, I'm afraid to go back to sleep. Also, relationships."

All of these things had the ability to bring on the kind of full-body fear response ticked on by the amygdala. Racing heart, increased respiration and a laser beam focus.

"Yeah, well, I don't need any therapy sessions. And I'm this close to getting my master's degree," he said, holding up his pinched fingers. "But I appreciate your concern."

A motherly instinct—one that rarely surfaced—showed up now, and she wanted to hug him. All of him. But mainly the little boy trying so hard to be a man.

"Fine. But remember, keeping a cool head underwater can mean the difference between life and death. Yours or someone else's."

As they neared the buoy, a pack of frigate birds circled overhead, and Minnow could see several fishing boats in the distance. The water here was a deep marble blue, and she imagined the ahi and ono and mahi-mahi coming in to find a meal but instead ending up with a hook in their mouths and maybe fighting for their lives while a bunch of drunk guys on a boat reeled them in, or at least tried to. The lucky ones broke free.

"Let's hang around and see who comes near," she said.

The plan was to ask around and see if anyone had noticed anything out of the ordinary. Answers often came in the strangest places. You never knew.

They floated a few hundred yards off the buoy, watching the water, the other boats and the sky. Minnow thought the charcoal clouds were coming closer; Nalu didn't.

Finally, a small boat buzzed by, and she flagged it down. Not much bigger than theirs with no sun protection and carrying four guys.

"Probably best if you do the talking," she said.

They'd already been over what to ask, but she was feeling anxious, desperate for something new she could sink her teeth into.

"You okay?" the driver called.

Nalu nodded. "We're part of the state Shark Task Force, doing some recon out here. Have you seen anything out of the ordinary? Dead whales, large sharks, that kind of thing?"

Body parts, Minnow thought.

The guy who had been sitting on a cooler in the back stood up. "I seen a big tiger outside Magic Sands the other day. Ho, the sucker was long as this boat. Grinding some kind of carcass."

"Where's Magic Sands?" Minnow asked Nalu.

"Down south, past Kailua Pier a ways. Not in our wheelhouse."

"What kind of carcass?" Minnow called.

"Nothing big, hard to tell, but."

None of his friends had seen anything that stood out, but from the sound of it, they had only been out in the boat twice in the last month.

Over the next two hours, Minnow and Nalu floated and talked with six other fishing boats. There were all walks of life out here.

From the first guys—who, with any chop, looked in danger of taking on water—to a veritable yacht with a satellite antenna. Only one of the boats had a girl on it. No one had anything unusual to report. But the last boat, a salty old guy with a *Gilligan's Island* hat and a missing tooth had something interesting to say.

At first he told them he'd seen nothing, but after scratching his chin for a while, he said, "You know, last week I came upon a pile of what looked like chum just bobbing along in the current. Fish skin, a mahi tail, guts and pink water. Hard to tell what it was, but it struck me as odd."

Minnow cast Nalu a sideways look. "Where were you?" she asked the man.

He scanned the distant shoreline, as if trying to remember. "Um, this would have been north of the Kiawe, around the point and out maybe three-quarters of a mile. There's two current lines that come together out there semi-regularly. I've found all kind of neat stuff, collectables, glass floats, old bottles covered in barnacles, psychedelic jellyfish. I even found a surfboard once."

"Were there any other boats around when you came upon it?" she asked.

"Nah, most guys are outside Kona or closer to Kawaihae, and either farther in or farther out. It's kind of a no-man's-land in that zone."

"No sharks?" she asked, just to be sure.

"No sharks."

They headed in after saying goodbye, toward the area the old man mentioned, nibbling on peanut butter, honey and banana sandwiches that Nalu brought, care of Dixie.

The more Minnow thought about what the old guy saw, the more she became convinced it was no coincidence. Especially the location—so close to the three incidents. Because although she was not admitting it to anyone else but Nalu, she felt sure that Hank the swimmer had not been a drowning victim.

"That fishing boat could have easily just dumped its cooler contents," Nalu said, yelling above the drone of the motor.

"True, but what if someone was chumming out there?"

"Why would someone be chumming?"

"Shark-diving tours."

A light went on in his eyes. "You think?"

"They do it in Guadalupe. Make a ton of money too."

"No one does shark tours in Hawai'i."

"Not that we know about."

"Someone would have seen them," he said.

"Not if they're stealthy about it."

"Why would they need to be stealthy?"

"If they were chumming close to shore, breaking state and federal laws."

"And . . . ," Nalu said, his voice trailing off.

"And what?"

"If someone knew someone, palms might be getting greased."

She shrugged. "It's possible."

When they reached the area in question, there were no boats and no sign of chum. A current line did snake through it. An oil-smooth ribbon of water carrying a few coconuts, a plastic fishing float, and a barnacle-covered Coke bottle. Minnow's mind was aflame with the possibility of someone drawing sharks to the area with chum. On the Farallones they had permits to use chum when conducting research, and she'd seen firsthand the result. White sharks in feeding mode were all business. It took less than half an hour for one to polish off an entire elephant seal. She shivered at the thought.

From the journal of Minnow Gray

Hawai'i, February 26, 1998

On one of the walls here at Hale Niuhi, there is an old yellowed page of the Hawaiian Gazette *from 1902, which says the following:*

> *But frequently the fishermen take sharks with spears. Diving to a favorable spot in about five or six fathoms of water, the fisherman places himself in a half-crouching posture against a large coral rock and waits for the shark to appear. When one comes, he darts the spear into a vital spot if possible. Should he fail to kill the fish with the spear, he watches for an opportunity and completes the operation with his knife, fearlessly engaging in close quarters. Should the shark appear while he is descending or ascending, a battle royale is on at once, with the chances largely in favor of the shark.*

CHAPTER 21

The Weather

***ʻŌpua**: puffy clouds, as banked up near the horizon, often interpreted as omens*

As soon as she got in, Minnow called Woody to ask if he knew anyone running shark dives. She figured he probably didn't or he would have said something, but she had to ask. And Nalu was probably right; someone would have seen them. But she also wanted to know if he'd seen anything on the news. Being at Hale Niuhi with no television or easy access to a newspaper was frustrating, while on the other hand it was a dream—being in this place she wished she could hole up in and never leave, living on coconuts, seaweed and rainwater until her dying days.

Woody knew nothing about shark dives, nor did he have any news updates. Next she called Mayor Lum's office to find out if he'd made any decisions. She got his secretary, who told her to watch the five o'clock news—he'd be making an announcement then. Minnow tried not to slam down the phone. So much for personally notifying the task force members.

The thunder of coconuts falling drew her outside. A whole bundle of brown ones had scattered at the base of the nearest tree.

"Watch for falling coconuts."

Nalu was thirty feet up the trunk with a machete dangling from his belt loop. One slip and he'd be dead.

"I can't even look at you up there," she called.

"And watch out for rats too. I disturbed a nest."

"Fabulous," she mumbled.

He shimmied down using a strap, looking completely at ease. Once on the ground, he scanned his loot, then walked over to an older coconut with a tiny shoot coming out of it, held it in his palm and hacked at it with the machete. "The other ones can wait. I bet you've never had coconut sprout before."

"You would be correct."

With his hand miraculously intact, he opened the nut to reveal a white spongy inside that resembled a sea urchin.

"Geez, don't cut off your hand on my account."

He offered it to her with a smile. "*Lolo* it's called. Best thing south of heaven."

Minnow took the piece and tentatively licked it while she watched him devour his. It was both sweet and salty, foamy and slightly crunchy.

"What do you think?" he asked.

She didn't love it.

"It's . . . interesting."

He laughed. "Maybe it's an acquired taste, but the Polynesians used to stock up on coconuts on their voyages. They're like the perfect boat food. Full of all the good kine stuff—electrolytes, natural sugar, vitamins, fat."

"I do like regular coconut meat."

"All g. I'll eat yours."

When he was done inhaling the *lolo,* they collected the other coconuts he'd felled and set them out in a line on the lanai table, and then he left her alone and went off to ask around at Honokohau Harbor if anyone had seen people chumming in the waters north of the Kiawe.

It was almost four in the afternoon, and Minnow had just enough time to shower and clean up before heading to the resort to catch the five o'clock news. Dread knocked around inside her, causing a heaviness to her movements, as though maybe if she didn't watch the news, a shark hunt would not happen.

The air was thick and slippery on her skin. While it had been hot before, now a new level of humidity pressed down on her. The kind of tropical heat where the only possible place to be was in the ocean. Later, back at the house, she would swim, no matter how dark the sky.

Almost every table was taken, so Minnow sat at the bar, which had the best view of the television anyway. She prayed she wouldn't see Luke, and then the next minute she skimmed the whole place, including the beach, looking for him. His boat was there, which to her consternation pleased her. Beyond it, the sun had disappeared behind that same wall of clouds that had been there this morning, and the whole ocean had turned silver.

No doubt Luke had his own kind of animal magic, built up from pheromones and charm and mystery. He was definitely someone she could get lost in, but all she had to do was think about his answer last night and his allure faded away. *It's complicated.* Bullshit. There was nothing complicated about it. Either you were for the sharks or you were against them.

George poured drinks behind the bar, and she watched with bated breath as the beads of perspiration on his forehead threatened to fall into said drinks. Despite a fan, despite the open air, there seemed to be no escaping the heat.

He smiled when he saw her. "Be right with you, my dear."

It was four forty-five. The Dallas Mavericks were playing the Orlando Magic, but the sound was off and she really couldn't care less, so she pulled out her notebook and jotted down notes from today.

"You here for the news?"

Minnow looked up. It was Sawyer, sweating profusely in a linen suit.

"Yes."

"Mind if I join you? I got a call from the mayor's secretary telling me to tune in," he said, lowering onto the stool next to her without waiting for an answer. "Drinks on me. What are you having?"

She needed something stiff for this. "Cadillac margarita?"

"You got it. George, bro, two Patrón margaritas, please."

They sat there for a while in awkward silence, both looking up at the basketball game. Minnow had nothing against the man personally but was in no mood to pretend to be interested in anything he had to say.

Eventually Sawyer broke. "So what's it like staying down at Kaupiko's?"

"I love it."

He reached over the counter and produced a cup of chopped pineapple, popping a chunk into his mouth. "Given the choice, would you rather stay there or here?"

No hesitation. "There, definitely."

"Ouch."

"Nothing against the Kiawe. It's beautiful, but I enjoy my solitude. And Hale Niuhi just feels so . . ." Putting the feeling she got there into words was harder than expected. "I guess it feels like it's been there forever, like it's just a part of the island. It has roots. And I feel strangely at home when I'm there."

"Before I built the Kiawe, I stayed there for a week with Woody. The place gets under your skin, for sure. Did you know he helped me design this?" he asked, waving his hand around.

Her brow pinched together. "*Woody* did?"

"Yeah. I had it in my mind to do something like Rockefeller did at Mauna Kea. A five- or six-story building. He told me no way, that the only way to make something work down here was to do it like the Hawaiians, only better. And so I did."

"Thank God you listened to him," Minnow said, unable to imagine a big boxy structure here.

George slid two margaritas in front of them, and Sawyer held his up. "To no more shark attacks."

At least she could drink to that. She clinked his glass and took a sip, then gagged.

He smiled. "George knows how I like my drinks—just like my women. Strong."

Minnow had no response to that kind of weirdness, so she took another sip. This one went down easier and she savored the icy coolness, then pressed the glass to her forehead. *Let's get on with this.* Sawyer went on about his hotel, and she nodded along, all the while feeling the tequila spreading out into her limbs, loosening the cords of tension that had been twisting all afternoon.

Then he said something that chilled her. "I know it may look like we're raking in the dough, but you'd be surprised. A lot in this business is smoke and mirrors. A few sparse months could put us under."

She was about to ask him to elaborate, but the news came on and George turned up the volume. The first story was about a tornado in Florida that left at least forty-two dead. Tornadoes were much more dangerous than sharks, that was for certain. The local anchorman Stan Jones wore a toupee and had at least an inch of pancake makeup on. He stared solemnly into the camera and said, "And now, we have an announcement from Mayor Lum on the recent deadly shark attacks on the Big Island that have made national headlines, and what the state is doing about them. Linda, over to you."

It was getting harder and harder to take a breath.

Linda Moore was standing out front of a green wooden house with Mayor Lum flanked by two men in aloha shirts. "Stan, the mayor is just about to go live, and as you can see, we have a lot of interest here."

The camera panned to an army of reporters jockeying for position. Mayor Lum tapped the mic. "Aloha. I want to thank you all for being here, and also thank the task force who met to determine the best course of action in the wake of these tragic incidents."

She sat up straighter. "At least he said *incident* rather than *attack*. He gets a point for that," Minnow said with a burst of hope. Maybe he had heard her after all.

Sawyer did not take his eyes from the TV. "What's the difference?"

There was no time to answer, as Lum got right to the point. "We heard from all parties with a stake in this—Ocean Safety, Hawai'i Fire Department, DLWA, the Hawaiian community, business owners, family members of the victims, a white shark expert from the mainland—and we looked at this thing from all sides. In the end, the team decided it is in our best interest to go ahead with a controlled shark hunt, to begin this Saturday morning."

The team decided? His words pierced, stung, sliced through her.

"And so it is," Sawyer said.

"Fuck," was all she could think to say.

Minnow slid off her stool and made a run for the beach. She knew her behavior was not very professional, but that's what happened when your passion became your profession. The lines blurred and you cared more than you should. It made her think of Luke's cryptic comment. *I care too, probably too much.* She walked to the far end of the beach and sank down into the sand, feeling broken. She had failed at the one thing she came here to accomplish.

She never expected the journey here to be smooth, and all along a hunt had been a real possibility, but this news felt like an execution, a slaying. Maybe she was irrational, or more probably, insane. What kind of person chooses sharks over people? That was the question that often reared up at times like this. Even as a young girl, she had been more interested in what was underwater than above it. She was flawed and weird and unfixable. A freak of nature with an indelible connection to these ancient animals. If she thought the hunt would do any good, it would be another story.

She lay back and spread her arms out wide, looking up at orange feathers streaking across the sky. The beauty did nothing for her. Coming here had been a waste of time, she now realized. Sidetracking her own work, putting off therapy and running off here with grand notions of enlightening the world about sharks. All for nothing. She'd call Joe in the morning and let him know she was leaving. It was the only thing to do that made sense. Because the truth of the matter was, staying for the hunt would ruin her.

An eye for an eye.

The sand cradled her head and she grabbed handfuls of it, letting it pour through her fingers. She lay there panting in the heat, haunted by the memory of the dead shark at Catalina. As the sky darkened, she settled to the wingbeats of herons, crabs digging holes all around her and a mongoose slithering in and out of the bush nearby. The world and its creatures were good at carrying on even when it felt like she couldn't. Maybe there was a lesson in there.

On down the beach a ways, footsteps vibrated through the ground. She turned her head to see. Luke. Of course it was. He seemed to be everywhere. In the half dark, she watched him wade out into the water, pull off his shirt, step out of his shorts and stuff them in a dry bag. Only in a Speedo, he somehow looked leaner. And hotter. He didn't look her way, and she was glad for it. In this vulnerable state, who knew what might happen.

Swimming out, he lay on his back and kicked, holding the bag on his stomach like a sea otter. It was a short swim, but the water was black and eerie. Something about this weather raised the hair on her arms. Storm weather. She hoped Luke knew what he was doing. By the time he made it to the boat, she could just make out his silhouette. The anchor chain clanked against the boat and she heard the anchor fall heavy on the fiberglass. Then the motor sputtered to life, running lights went on, and instead of heading out, he came straight for shore. Straight for *her.*

From the journal of Minnow Gray

January 7, 1998

Memory is nonlinear and is strongly tied to our emotions. It is commonly believed that when we experience a highly emotional event, our brains are more likely to encode and store it vividly. Our amygdala and hippocampus working hand in hand. Yet it also turns out that some memories are so painful, they hide out in our brain, unable to be accessed. This dissociation is designed to protect us, but it also causes distress down the road.

My therapist says that we need to root out the memory of my father's death in order for me to fully heal, but my question is: Does anyone ever fully heal? I really just want to know what happened. I know that's probably simplistic, and there's got to be all kinds of trauma and weirdness buried in my subconscious mind that I'm scared to set free. When I think about all this, what stands out the most to me is that our brains are little miracles (I say little *because an adult white shark brain is about two feet long). They are imperfectly perfect and I love mine for fighting so hard to keep me safe.*

I think Emily Dickinson said it best: "The brain is wider than the sky."

CHAPTER 22

The Ride

***Hekili**: thunder; to thunder;*
figuratively, passion or rage

Minnow sat upright, wiping her eyes as sand poured down her back. Even more reason to swim when she got home. Luke was still headed to her end of the beach and she figured he must have forgotten something. Just before hitting the sand, he cut the engine and tilted the prop up.

He was looking right at her. "Come on, I'll take you home."

There was no question in his voice.

She stood and dusted off her rear. "How did you know I was down here?"

"Just a hunch."

"No, really. Tell me."

"I went to the bar to grab some nuts and a bag of chips for my ride and saw Sawyer. He told me."

Minnow went to the water's edge. Fortunately, she was wearing jean shorts, because the tiniest wave splashed up on her legs, soaking them.

"Where are you going at this hour?" she asked.

"I was hoping to see some of the meteor shower before that bank of clouds moves in."

She hadn't heard anything of a meteor shower, and stars had begun to show but only in the northeastern part of the sky. The rest was a blank slate of gunmetal ready to swallow them up.

"Fine. I'll come. As long as you're not going to be fishing."

"Cross my heart. Not tonight."

She didn't have it in her to ask anything else, so she waded in deeper, grabbed his hand and let him pull her into the boat. He lifted her as though she weighed no more than a leaf and was just as precious.

"Do you want a life vest?" he asked.

She was quick to answer. "What do you think?"

"Just had to ask. Safety first."

It was hard to tell if he was serious, but just being on the water made her feel a little lighter, and she leaned against the center console, grabbing on to a leaning post for support. This boat felt so much more substantial than the little Whaler she and Nalu had been tootling around in. There was room to spread out, and she made sure to keep a safe distance between herself and Luke. Already she could feel the heat coming off his skin and hear the soft *whoosh* of his heartbeat.

As a girl, she had thought that everyone could hear the things she could. She remembered asking her father when the eggs would hatch as they passed underneath a heron's nest high in cypress.

"How do you know there are eggs up there?" he'd asked.

"I can hear the babies wiggling around inside them. They're almost ready."

He gave her a strange look, then said, "How about we come check every morning? That way we'll know for sure."

They hatched three days later. The earth and the animals spoke to those who were willing to listen. That's what her father told her. Her mother, on the other hand, would tell her what a great imagination she had when Minnow said she could hear chirps of the bats hanging in the attic or fish nibbling on kelp. Eventually she stopped mentioning it and the heightened sensitivity became a secret she held close to her heart.

In the boat neither spoke as Luke navigated them out of the bay. The engine purred along, and as they headed seaward she watched the lights from the resort grow smaller and smaller. She kept waiting for Luke to turn south, but he didn't.

"Hale Niuhi is that way," she finally said.

"Are you in a hurry?"

She sighed and resigned herself to let him take her wherever he wanted. "No, I guess not."

"How about we just pretend the world back there doesn't exist and enjoy this stunning evening," he said. "Have you eaten yet?"

"No."

"Good."

It felt nice to be on a boat at night without wearing ten layers and a wool beanie. Even with the light wind on her face, she was perfectly comfortable. But she felt on edge—mad at herself and mad at this crazy world that couldn't seem to see beyond the immediate and how the entire planet was all one beautiful and troubled organism.

"Why is that good? Are you going to share your nuts and chips with me? Or do you have *'opihi*?" she asked.

He slowed the boat down to a crawl. "I only eat *'opihi* fresh, and believe it or not, I have a big sandwich and a tub of mac salad in that cooler back there. Only one fork, though."

A tiny crack formed in her armor. "Do you do this often? Go out just to eat and watch the stars?"

"Lately, yeah. There's something about this island that makes me want to be outside all the time. I feel restless when I'm indoors, like I might be missing something spectacular. Have you noticed?"

Why did he have to sound like such a kindred spirit? It made her like him even more, when she wanted not to like him at all. "All hours of the day and night. I think it's the warmth and the color of the water."

"That, but more. If you had asked me five years ago if I ever wanted to live in Hawai'i, I would have shaken my head. But now that I'm here, I'm not sure I'll be able to leave. The pull is physical."

She understood. She'd felt it too. "Like an umbilical cord."

He shot her a glance. "You could say that, yeah."

"Strange how it's all the same ocean but so different than the West Coast, like another planet. But as magical as it is here, I'll never leave my sharks."

He went quiet for a bit, and Minnow turned to look back at the land. There were only tiny patches of lights here and there, and the four tall mountains stood dark against the stars, cutouts of massive pyramids.

"Did you know they have orcas in these waters?" Luke asked.

"I'd heard they occasionally visit."

"Every few years. Last month I got lucky and ran into a small pod about five miles south of here. Four females and three males."

"What a shocker that must have been. Do they come all the way from the mainland, like the white sharks?" she asked.

"Nah, we believe there's a Central Pacific population—you can tell them apart by their markings—and they veer into the island chain now and then."

"*We*?" she asked.

A pause. "Those of us who . . . know about orcas. They're in my blood, what can I say?"

Her heart sang for him because there was a sadness in the way he said it, almost an apology. And she knew that feeling well. Being misunderstood. Apart.

"You don't have to say anything. I get that," she said.

"Most people don't."

"Would you rather be in the water with an orca or a white shark?" she asked, wanting to lighten the mood, both for his sake and her own.

He leaned sideways toward her. "You must not know much about orcas, ma'am."

She had to laugh. "Excuse me, but do you know who you're talking to?"

"A gorgeous and arguably mad marine biologist who has a bunch of fancy letters at the end of her name."

Heat collected on her neck and the hidden places on her body. "*Gorgeous* and *mad* are both debatable, and I do know some about orcas, but not as much as I'd like."

He leaned back, head tilting skyward. "To answer your question, give me an orca any day. As the largest member of the dolphin family, they are quite possibly the most intelligent animal in the water and they rarely attack humans in the wild. I hate to break it to you, but I think you might be one of the only people alive who would rather swim with *Carcharodon carcharias* than *Orcinus orca*."

There was something so appealing about a man who spoke Latin to her, and she felt a deep longing for him to show her his northern undersea world and the giant dolphins that inhabited it. Something she understood would probably never happen, and yet a vision of them both in full wet suits staring down a curious orca flitted across her mind like an old black-and-white film. So clear it unsettled her.

"I've seen a few pods in Northern California, just passing through, but never had the chance to go down with them. Their size is shocking after getting used to bottlenose dolphins. Maybe in another life I'll get to know them better."

"Yeah," was all he said.

They finally veered south, and they rode for another fifteen minutes or so before Luke cut the engine. Her eyes had adjusted to the night sky, and she watched him go to the built-in cooler and pull out a plastic bag and two bottles, then lay a sunscreen-infused towel on top of the cooler.

"Sorry, it's a little damp. I wasn't expecting company," he said, popping open the caps of the bottles in a one-two *pop* and handing her one.

His hand brushed against hers, and something about his rough skin gave her a rush between her thighs. Whatever this was between them had a life of its own, and it felt like the more she resisted, the more she was drawn to him. The dangerous unknown had always appealed to her, and Luke in his own beautiful way was just that.

Minnow sat on one side of the food bag, Luke on the other. The sound of deep ocean rose from below them, a blue and insistent hum.

"Do you hear that?" Luke asked, tilting his head away from her and listening.

"Hear what?"

"The abyss. It has its own language. When I was a kid, my pops would take me out in this old canoe he found on the beach and restored, and we would paddle straight for the horizon. It was a Salish canoe, I think, with no outrigger. One wrong move and you were toast. We'd only go out on calm days, and I remember my dad talking about the silence and how much he loved it. I remember thinking to myself that it was far from silent. Water lapping on wood, distant gulls and the sound of the ocean breathing."

Minnow felt her heart swell. She wanted to tell him that she heard it too, along with the singing of the stars, but she had held it in for so long that no words would come. Instead, she took a gulp of the ice-cold beer.

Luke went on. "I know it sounds crazy, but when you spend your whole life outside like I did, it's just natural. Anyway, sorry for rambling, you're probably starving."

"No, I like to hear you talk."

It was the plain and simple truth, but saying it out loud gave it life—*it* being this thing that was growing between them. In the dark it was hard to read his expression, but she thought he might have smiled.

Carefully, he pulled out a sandwich and unwrapped it, handing her half. "I hope you like jalapeños."

"What kind of sandwich is it?"

"Jalapeño."

"This will be a first."

"You can give them to me if you don't like 'em."

"Who doesn't love jalapeño?"

"Plenty of people, but I'm an addict. And just so you know, there's some veggies and provolone thrown in too," he said.

They ate and talked, and Minnow had to quench the fire in her mouth with the beer, which went down too easily. He told her more about the San Juan Islands and she told him about her travels, and they kept it real but safe. They shared the same fork without question and steered clear of the news and the shark hunt. It was too raw to even think about, let alone discuss with Luke. Nor did Minnow mention she would be leaving the island as soon as she could get a ticket. The moment felt perfect and peaceful and she didn't want to ruin it. There would be time for that later.

"Where are these meteors you speak of?" she asked. She'd kept an eye out for the past half hour and hadn't seen anything.

"It might be too early. Middle of the night is when the show is really supposed to start."

They sat with that for a while, and she imagined lying with him somewhere entangled under the stars, the feeling of his sandpapery hands running down her body.

As if he'd read her mind, he stuffed the trash in the bag and stood up. "We should probably head in."

She was disappointed, not ready for this to end. "Sure, okay."

They motored in the direction of distant lights. A few minutes later, something flashed behind them. Minnow spun around, but the horizon was black.

"Lightning," she said.

"Yeah. Those clouds have been lurking all day, but I think they're finally moving in."

Another flash, and the whole horizon lit up neon blue and electric white. There was no place more terrifying to be in a lightning storm than on a boat, which she guessed Luke knew too.

Instead, he said, "We have time."

She wasn't sure if he was trying to convince her or himself, but either way, he was wrong. Minnow kept an eye on the storm cloud, which looked to be larger than the whole island. With the next explosion, a streak of lightning shot down to the water, spilling out in all directions. Every hair on her body stood on end. "I don't know about that. I'd gun it in," she said.

"I think you're right. Hang on."

He shoved the throttle forward and they hurtled toward land. The first thunder came when they were about a half mile offshore, a low and faraway rumble.

Woody had wedged a solar light into the rocks that stuck out on the north end of the bay and had planted a couple under the coconut trees, and Minnow scanned the dark coastline south of the Kiawe for them. It would have been easier to go in at the resort, but that was another ten minutes away. The wind on her face cooled some, but the water stayed smooth as glass.

"There," she said. "Can you see the Whaler?"

A flash turned everything white. The boat, the house, the trees.

"Affirmative."

Luke flipped on a bright light mounted on the bimini top. "I hate to use this, but sometimes you have to."

Minnow pointed. "There's another mooring over there. If I were you, I'd tie off and swim in with me."

Their eyes met and held. It was madness to invite him into the house. She didn't trust herself alone in a storm with this man, but what choice did she have?

"I should be fine."

Another bright flash, and two air masses slammed together not far away, rendering the air staticky and charged with energy.

"Leave everything. Let's go," she said, grabbing his hand.

He didn't argue, turning the light off and letting her pull him aft. They jumped in the water together, fully clothed. This mooring was farther out than the other and it suddenly seemed a long way to shore. Minnow put her head down and went for it, oblivious to what might be beneath, hunting in the dark waters. Luke stayed next to her the whole way in. When her hand hit the sand and pebbles, she stood up.

"Follow me," she said, out of breath.

The first raindrop hit her shoulders then, and by the time they made it to the house, it was pouring down in sheets. She ducked under the eave and felt around the sliding door for the handle. Luke bumped up against her, one hand settling on her hip. His closeness gave her goose bumps, and she expected him to move his hand away, but he didn't. He just stood there, a few inches away, smelling like rain and thunder.

She found the indentation and slid the door open, moving through the dark to distance herself from him.

"There's a generator, but it's out by the pond in the back," she said, lighting the glass lantern in the center of the table.

"What do we need a generator for?"

"So we can see."

"I can see just fine."

Without Luke standing right there, she would have peeled off her wet clothes, but she ducked into the bathroom and stripped naked, then wrapped herself in one of the many bright pareos that the Kaupikos kept on a shelf. She took one for Luke too.

"Here," she said, handing it to him.

He was no longer wearing a shirt, and her gaze slid down over his sleek, wet body. In the hurricane-lamp light, he was the color of burnt ochre.

"What is this?" he asked.

Rain on the metal roof made it hard to hear him.

"A pareo, Woody calls it. He wears it around his waist in the mornings," she said, raising her voice.

At first she thought he would refuse it, but he went into the bathroom and came out a few minutes later. "I'm not big on wearing skirts, but when in Hawai'i . . ."

Minnow laughed. "I like the look on you."

He stepped toward her. "Do you?"

She swayed a little, and not just from having been on a boat. More like Luke was drawing her into his gravitational field. "Definitely."

Another step. Minnow remained planted and swallowed hard. This was happening and there was nothing she could do to stop it. Nor did she want to. Luke came toward her until he was close enough to kiss if she just leaned in. Her heart pounded wildly.

"I like the look on you too. Maybe a little too much," he said, setting both hands lightly on her shoulders and dropping down to press his forehead against hers.

Minnow inhaled his breath as one of his hands ran up the back of her neck and into her hair, getting stuck in her wet curls. He pulled back and smiled, and the way he looked so searchingly into her eyes made her feel raw and exposed.

His mouth moved to her ear. "Tell me I can kiss you."

Their lips came together, feather soft. She wasn't really sure who kissed whom, all she knew was he tasted salty and a little like mint. Her fingers gripped his back and she held on, trying to pull him closer until every inch of her was touching every inch of him, if that were possible. His tongue worked slowly around her mouth, exploring, teasing, then moving on to kiss her jawline and trace down her throat and collarbone, leaving a trail of heat in his wake.

Luke spoke into her skin and it sounded something like, "You taste like ocean."

Around them, lightning flashed through the house, followed closely by a thunderclap that rattled her teeth. Luke jumped higher than she did.

"There's a metal windmill behind the pond, where the well is. It's taller than the roof, so let's hope if lightning hits, it'll hit that," she said.

"I'm not worried."

Before she knew it, he was kissing her again and pressing her hard against the counter. She felt ragged with want and barely noticed the wood in her back. They were both still damp, and Minnow could have sworn that steam lifted off him, he was that hot. A small voice of reason tried to question if being with Luke was the best course of action, but the sound of driving rain and his heartbeat drowned it out.

His palm slid inside her pareo and he traced circles on her bare belly. She had nothing on besides the piece of material. Neither did he. This knowledge felt both dangerous and thrilling at the same time. She melted into him even further and gasped when his hand brushed the bottom of one breast, and then the next.

There was something about his closeness that caused a dent in her field, an opening and a flooding of feelings. Suddenly her whole body started trembling.

He pulled his hand away. "You're shaking. Are you okay?"

He was backlit by the lamp, and concern filled his eyes.

"I'm fine, just cold," she lied.

Luke wrapped her in his arms and she rested her cheek against his chest, letting the rise and fall of his breath calm her.

He rubbed her back. "I'm sorry if I came on too strong. It's just . . . I haven't been able to stop thinking about you since that first morning at the Saltwater Bar."

Minnow knew the feeling. "Don't apologize."

"But I—"

She held a finger up to his lips and led him toward the bed. She sat down on the edge and he knelt in front of her. Her legs parted and she still felt a tremor in them. She wanted him to squelch the fear. Luke leaned in with both hands high on her thighs. He kissed her again. This time, soft as feather boa kelp. She ran her hands down his chest, then traced the indentations of his abdomen. His whole body tensed up when she got to the top of his pareo, which was slung low on his waist, but she stopped there.

Whatever this was, it seemed like so much more than plain old physical longing. Minnow felt bound to him inextricably, like he was a mooring and she a boat. Tied on and floating around him but never quite touching.

The rain came down even harder now, but the thunder and lightning had moved off a ways. Luke kneaded her thighs with rising force, then stood and swept her legs onto the bed and lay her down. He lay next to her on his side, propped up on his elbow. Shadows flicked around his face, and one side of his mouth curved up in a smile that went straight to her core.

"It feels like a dream, doesn't it?" he said, motioning around them. "This. You."

He seemed so happy, it made her feel bad.

"I'm leaving tomorrow," she said.

The words slipped out on their own accord, and the minute she spoke them, she regretted it. The thought of not seeing him again turned her heart dark, but she couldn't hold it in any longer.

Luke went rigid. "What?"

"Well, tomorrow or the next day. Before the weekend. As soon as I can. I can't be here for the hunt," she said, looking out at the falling rain.

He let out a long breath while Minnow held hers, waiting for him to say something. A new heaviness surrounded them and she knew that bringing him in here had been a mistake.

"So you're running away. I guess I had you pegged wrong," he said, sitting up and running his hands through his hair.

His words hit a nerve, and Minnow slid out of the bed. "I came here on a dime and have poured my soul into trying to figure out what's happening and stop a mass culling. I've done everything I could to prevent mass hysteria. But why are you here, Luke? There's something you haven't told me—I can feel it loud and clear."

Luke stood up and his pareo slid off his hip, exposing his bone-white skin. He tugged it back up. “You wouldn’t understand. Any of it.”

He went to the sliding door and stared out at the dark ocean, running his hands through his hair and tugging at it. Minnow got the feeling he was weighing his options: reveal whatever it was he was holding on to or make a run for it. The rush of rain on the roof had lightened, but it was still coming down with a steady hiss.

“Try me,” she said.

“You’re leaving. It doesn’t matter.”

She pressed him. “It *does* matter. I’m so confused, Luke. You obviously know a lot about marine life and you care about orcas and turtles. But what about sharks? Are they somehow different?”

“No. They aren’t different,” he said, quietly.

“Then what?”

For the first time, she saw his shoulders sag, like someone let all his air out, and she felt bad for a few heartbeats, but then he turned and said, “I’m not the man you think I am. I should probably go. I’m sorry, Minnow. I really am.”

He made a run for it.

Minnow stumbled back onto the bed.

The shivers started up again.

Haiku

by Minnow Gray, age 18

Swimming down
with eyes closed, I hear her.
She wears my father's shadow.

CHAPTER 23

The Guardian

__ʻAumakua__: family or personal gods,
deified ancestors who might assume
the shape of animals or plants

Rain fell all through the night. Minnow knew because she had flopped around like a dying fish, awake and thinking about Luke and wondering what kind of crazy she had gotten herself into. Maybe his leaving had been a blessing, but it sure didn't feel that way. It felt hurtful and sharp and sad. What was he so afraid of that he couldn't tell her? Whatever it was, it felt big.

The clouds were still there, thick as mountains, and it almost didn't feel like morning. She dragged herself out of bed and looked toward Mauna Kea. There was no sign of the sun trying to shine through. Her hair felt as though a slither of serpents had nested in it overnight, and she could still feel the residue of Luke's palm against her scalp.

She knew she should call Joe and tell him she was leaving, and see when she could get out on Hawaiian Airlines, but it was early yet. Instead, she ate a banana, put on her swimsuit, grabbed her mask, fins and dive knife and headed out onto the seawall. The air was so still and the water so smooth, it felt like stepping into a black-and-white photograph, worn around the edges. And that reminded her to look through the photo album Woody had left on the counter when she got back from her swim. He must have pulled it out for a reason.

With lips raw from all the kissing, the snorkel chafed as she put it on. She waded into the water, headed south since she'd already gone north, and the cold water woke her up immediately. Without the bright sun, or any sun really, everything was void of color. Minnow had been studying the framed coral reef fish poster on the wall and now it paid off. A family of rockmover wrasse poked around in the sand. A large cloud of yellow tang drifted near the boat. Several juvenile yellowtail coris darted in and out of a coral head, orange and white and bearing no resemblance to their purple and spotted future selves.

As soon as she rounded the south end of the bay, a cluster of lava fingers gave way to more of a clean shelf that dropped straight into the water. The vertical rock was about fifteen feet high and met with sand or smooth black pebbles at the bottom. Even in the low light, the water was so clear, she could easily see for sixty or more feet. There was something ethereal about it all and she felt no apprehension, only wonder. That was the secret of the ocean. It could make you forget about what existed above.

As Minnow swam along, she could hear the *humuhumunukunukuāpua'a* grinding on coral, little sand makers that they were. And when she dove down, a faint whale song reached her ears. She wondered what whales thought of lightning. From deep underwater, it was probably lovely. She poked her head up and looked around, checking for any flashes. The stillness and dense clouds made conditions ripe for another thunderstorm, but there was no sign of one, just a dab of red over Mauna Kea. *Red skies at morning, sailor take warning.* The saying was etched into her mind, as it probably was with most seafaring folk.

Minnow kept going. Over fields of finger coral full of delicate snowflake eels. Across a deeper trench where four turtles floated near the bottom, surrounded by fish. There was abundant life and beauty here, but it was so much more than that. Most people had no idea that at least half the oxygen on earth comes from marine plants in the form of tiny phytoplankton floating near the surface. Whales loved it and so did manta rays. Upset the balance of the ocean and you upset the balance of all life on earth.

Even as she swam along, she went through bursts of plankton. It was almost like swimming through fairy dust. Every so often she also came upon a shadowy cave in the shelf, but without a dive light, it was impossible to tell how far in they went. Nor was she about to find out on her own, especially with the toothy moray eel hanging out of one of them, mouth opening and closing.

The farther she went, the more the knots in her neck and shoulders loosened, but try as she might, she couldn't entirely shake thoughts of the hunt and of Luke Greenwood. His words kept playing over and over in her mind. *So you're running away. I guess I had you pegged wrong.* She could see how, from his perspective, leaving seemed like a cowardly thing to do. But what did he really know of her? Judging was easy when you didn't know the full story. That was her fault as much as his.

At the next little inlet, she came upon a crack in the shelf full of humpback cowries as large as her hand. Smooth and shiny and a rich coffee brown with speckled tops. She never took live shells, so she hung there admiring them for a while. When she turned to go, her eye caught something on the bottom lying in the sand. She dove down and picked up a whole cowrie, bigger than any of the ones in the crack, but this one was heavy with an animal inside it too.

She was about to kick back up for air when the water around her lit up silver. The fish around her froze for a few seconds, then disappeared into nearby coral heads. Minnow dropped the cowrie and shot up. At the surface, she looked at her watch. Forty minutes had passed since she left the house, which meant she had a long swim back. Thunder rumbled in the distance, but she had a feeling it was coming closer. The clouds had darkened and electricity tickled her skin. Swimming this far down the coast under such dark skies had probably been reckless, but it was too late to worry about it now.

Fish near the surface could get electrocuted, which meant she could too. In her boat captain class, Minnow had learned that when lightning strikes the ocean, its current spreads out over the water, potentially harming or killing anything near the surface. Keenly aware of this, she took off toward the house, staying close to the rocks and keeping an eye out for any possible caves in the water or on land. She found when she was coming from the other direction, things often appeared that she may have missed on her first pass.

She was swimming hard but evenly, trying to remain calm. Sending off fear vibes would not serve her well. A ruffle appeared on the water, and soon there were whitecaps. She had to move to slightly deeper water to avoid being pushed onto the urchin-infested rocks or jagged lava. She wished Woody was here. Or Nalu. Or even Luke. Especially Luke. There was something about him, even after last night, that made her crave him in a way she had never craved a man.

Ever.

Ten minutes into her return, as the lightning moved closer, she noticed the gaping mouth of a lava tube just above the surface of the water. It would have been easy to miss if she hadn't been poking her head up at regular intervals, taking stock of the sky. Maybe it would be worth it to try to scale the rocks and wait out the storm. She swam in for a closer look. Black *wana* with footlong spines blocked the immediate area. It was getting harder to see with the rough conditions.

She kept going, looking for an out, when she sensed something behind her. She turned and did a quick three-sixty. There, on the periphery, her eyes snagged on a dark shadow. She squinted for a better look, but a small whitecap broke on her head, filling the water with bubbles. Minnow sank down, her back toward the rocks. This time the outline was clearer.

Large shark.

Her hand went to her dive knife. She came up for air, keeping her eyes locked on the animal.

The next flash of lightning showed the shark in all its splendor. Broad head, vertical stripes, pale underbelly. At least fourteen feet. Big but nothing like a Sister. No claspers, so it was female, and the fact that she was still out there was a good sign. She was curious. Minnow was close enough to the rocks, where she could make a scramble for it, but this shark displayed no aggressive behavior. Propelled by the slow side to side of its tail, the animal kept moving in her direction but was ten yards or so out.

As she approached, she dropped beneath the surface, watching Minnow. There was no doubt about that. Minnow let out all her air and dropped to the ocean bottom, hair floating around her. When the shark passed by, she noticed a deep scar up near its mouth. Her hand squeezed the knife handle as her heart banged around in her chest. She maintained composure, staring it down the same way it stared her down. They were two intelligent beings sizing each other up. Both predators, both wary.

But this was a special moment and she knew it. The shark kept swimming, and Minnow watched its three-foot-high tail slowly disappear into the dark beyond. She felt a rush of relief combined with wishing she could have frozen time for a few moments and just taken it all in. When she came up for air, the rain was spilling down hard, dappling the surface of the ocean. The wind stopped as quickly as it had whipped up, and Minnow headed in the same direction the shark had. Toward the house.

A few minutes on, the water turned blurry and noticeably colder, as happened around freshwater springs. There was a cave, too, one she had missed on the way down. Sandy bottom, blue light at the far end. Had she not just encountered the tiger shark, she might have gone in, but she remembered Woody talking about a sacred cave around here. A home to his family's revered *'aumakua*. Maybe this was where her tiger had gone. The opening was wide but low, and she could hear the sound of water scraping on rock.

Then out of the side of her eye, she caught a flash of movement and turned to see that the shark had swung around and was swimming back her way. Not ten yards out but in a line that would bring it right to Minnow. Its energy had changed and she could tell by the way its pectoral fins were down that the shark was coming back for another look. Or perhaps a taste. Instinctively she backed toward the rocks. *I come as a friend,* Minnow repeated over and over in her mind.

The shark shot toward her, and though she held up the knife, it was laughable. There was nothing a small blade of steel could do against four thousand pounds of muscle and cartilage. Still, she would die fighting. Hit it right in the nose, and the animal might retreat. Miss the nose, and it would swallow her arm. But instead of colliding with Minnow, the shark passed within a foot of her, smacking her shoulder with its tail. Minnow spun around just in time to see its jaws open wide and its gills ventilate as it clamped down on a small turtle. Lightning flashed down and for a moment everything turned red. Minnow felt for the turtle, but her relief was bone-deep and pungent. Immense.

She swam for home.

From the journal of Minnow Gray

Guadalupe Island, July 9, 1993

Most of the time when we see these white sharks swimming around the boat and the dive cage, they're in cruise mode and it's easy to forget how fast they can move–like underwater bullets. Today one of the sharks blew by us in a flash of black. This high speed is partly made possible because of their unusual skin. They have what are called "dermal denticles," almost like teeth, with a pulp on the inside and dentine on the outside. These denticles reduce drag and add stealth by limiting the turbulence their large masses can create. I like to think of them as having their own underwater suit of armor.

CHAPTER 24

The Story

***Mahina**: moon, month, moonlight*

When Minnow walked out of the water, her legs were weak and she could still feel the sway of the ocean. She stumbled, then caught herself. Woody and another man were standing on the wall, watching her. She was surprised to see him back so soon.

"Hey," she said, attempting a smile.

Neither of them smiled back.

"I thought you were smarter than that," Woody said.

"What do you mean?"

Though she knew exactly what he meant.

"Going out in a thunderstorm. By yourself. No note, no nothing."

The man next to him was a younger, long-haired version of Woody, with streaks of silver. Both men were barefoot and held steaming coffee mugs in their hands.

"I had my knife," she said, as if that meant anything in these waters.

"What's that gonna do against lightning?"

"I know. It was dumb. But I *had* to swim. And I didn't think you'd be here."

When she reached the wall, Woody offered her a hand and pulled her up. The skies were still dark and a powdery rain fell, almost like snow.

Woody nodded to the house. "Come, we go inside."

In the house she wrapped her now-shivering body in the thickest towel she could find and went to the counter, where Woody filled a mug with coffee and handed it to her.

"Here, drink. And tell us what happened. You're white as a sheet," he said.

No one had introduced her yet to who she figured was Cliff, so she smiled and said, "I'm Minnow."

He nodded. "Cliff."

She turned to Woody. "What happened to the job you were working on?"

"Canceled. It's flooding all up and down Hamakua side and the road is closed. Better I'm down here anyway, and my brother wanted to come."

"I'm glad you're here."

"Now talk, though I got a feeling I already know what you goin' to say."

Her teeth started chattering and she took a sip of the coffee to try to warm herself up. It burned her tongue. She took another sip, and another, letting the hot liquid spread to her limbs. Still, the cold permeated through her skin, muscle and bone, and she realized her chill wasn't something that could be warmed by coffee.

"I woke up feeling like shit, bummed about the mayor's announcement last night and wanting to clear my head. When I left the house, there was no thunder or lightning, just a dark sky. So I went for it."

"And?"

"And it was beautiful and I could have kept going forever, but the lightning moved in, so I turned around. I was about halfway back when I noticed the freshwater and the cave opening on the bottom. And then the tiger shark was there. I felt it behind me, but it was just checking me out—"

"How big?"

"About fourteen feet."

"Male or female?"

"Female."

Minnow told them about the encounter and how she never felt threatened, until the turtle. But that had been misplaced.

Cliff spoke for the first time. "Mahina."

"You're lucky, she doesn't show herself to many people," Woody said.

"Is Mahina your *'aumakua*?"

"Hina is what we call her. She's an old shark. We grew up together. She never bothered us, we never bothered her. She keeps these waters clean and watches out for us."

Cliff kept watching her with an animal intensity that made her uncomfortable. Like he was trying to see inside her. "Hina is the shark your mother had a run-in with," he said.

Minnow felt a sheet of ice forming on her skin. "Excuse me?"

The two men swapped looks. "I left the photo album on the counter. Did you not see it?" Woody asked.

"I was going to look when I got back. What are you talking about? My mother?"

"Your mother came here with your uncle Jimmy just before you were born."

It was such an odd thing to say, she almost laughed. "I think I would have heard about that." But what did she really know about her parents' life before her? Only fragments of stories, and ones they had chosen to tell. Minnow had been so young.

"She came here to figure things out. She was six months pregnant and thinking about leaving your dad."

A lead weight fell through her. "That's not possible."

"Obviously she went back and made it work, but she was soul-searching and trying to do right by you."

"But why? Why has no one ever mentioned this?" she asked.

Absurd as this notion was, though, there was something familiar about it. Something real.

"I have no idea, but probably because things straightened out once she went back. Cliff spent more time with her than I did, so he can tell you more."

Minnow looked at Cliff. "Why was my mom here?"

He didn't say anything, just stood unmoving. A stunned fish.

"Please, tell me what you know," she begged.

"The first thing I thought when she and Jimmy showed up was that she was too skinny. She had this basketball stomach, but the rest was bones. And she had these bruises under her eyes, looked like she nevah slept. We was supah worried. All Jimmy told us was that she was pregnant and depressed. But when they came and we got to talking, Layla told me your dad was drinking too much and he had slapped her one night. The next day she was outta there. She told him she was leaving and that she may or may not be coming back. I admired her spirit. You could tell she meant it."

It was hard for Minnow to imagine her father hitting her mother, much less while she'd been pregnant. Just the thought made her want to turn around and walk away. Catch that plane back to California. Minnow shook her head. "You're wrong. My parents didn't drink."

"Not after her trip here, no. When your mom went back to Catalina, Bruce promised he would stop and he did. Layla and I kept in touch for a while. There was no funny business or anything between us, but we clicked right away. She was a fine *wahine,* but she had her demons, same as me."

Minnow knew of her mother's demons, partly from living with them and partly from Uncle Jimmy. The mood swings, the dark periods, the inconsolable sadness. They had always been there. And when Bruce had died, she went down a hole she couldn't climb out of. Even having a young daughter could not save her.

"I don't understand why no one told me. This is a big fucking thing to swallow," she said, setting down her mug and backing away.

Bruce had hit Layla. Layla had been here, pregnant. Which meant Minnow had been here too. Breaths became hard to take in, and she floundered, unable to speak.

Woody jumped in. "When Jimmy asked if you could stay here, he warned me they never told you. It was such a short time in their lives, and your dad changed. He went cold turkey and never touched another drop, for you and your mother. Not many people can say that."

She looked at Cliff, hungry for more information. "What else do you know?"

"I know you look just like her," Cliff said, picking up the photo album and taking it to the table, where he then sat.

Minnow joined him. He flipped to a few pages in, and there she was. Her beautiful waif of a mother. Sitting on the wall sideways, knees bent and arms wrapped around her legs. She had turned to smile at the photographer but without emotion. As though to lift the edges of her mouth took every last bit of strength and there was nothing left inside her.

"Your mom was desperate when she came. Desperate to stay with Bruce but also desperate to make sure you wouldn't be in danger. You could tell Jimmy was scared for her. We all were," Woody said, sitting across the table.

"Why here, though?"

He shrugged. "Jimmy suggested it. He knew if anywhere could pull her out of her funk, it would be here."

Cliff turned the page and Minnow's eyes went to another series of photos. Layla and Jimmy and Woody, all wearing the woven hats, standing on the wall, holding up big cowrie shells. In these shots, her mom's smile was real.

"Being here was good for her. You could see the changes day to day. Color on her face, and by the weekend she was shoveling food down like one vacuum cleanah. 'Cause of my mom. She came down and cooked all day long. Eggs, bacon, banana pancakes, beef stew, mac salad, *'ōhelo* berry pie, fish tacos. Layla couldn't get enough," Cliff said.

Cliff spoke so softly, Minnow had to lean in to hear him. But each word came out as though it was quite possibly the most important thing he had ever said.

He went on. "At first she refused to go in the water. She said she almost drowned as a kid and it made her nervous. She wanted to get over it—you could see it in her eyes. The way she'd sit on the wall and watch us. Mom told her that the ocean was a pregnant woman's best friend and she liked that. After that, she came in with Jimmy and me and swam around right in front, nice and easy. After that, you couldn't get her out. She would float there all morning and then again for an hour or two before sunset."

Minnow tried to imagine her unborn self hovering in these waters, being lulled into peace. Weightless. Water lapping against her mother, holding her. Rocking her.

"What about the shark?"

His eyes flicked over to Woody, who dropped his chin almost imperceptibly.

"It was a dark morning, like today. *Malie* water, the kind you see your reflection in. We was up here getting ready for fishing, and your mom was on the wall. I saw her sitting there, kinda peaceful-looking. Jimmy and Woody was out in the shed collecting gear, and I was wrapped up in making sure we had the right lures and all. When Jimmy came back, ten, fifteen minutes later, he asked where Layla was. She was gone."

Far off, thunder grumbled. Cliff looked out over the water, where the gray had turned a bruised purple. A strange flicker moved across Minnow's eyes. As though if she looked hard enough, she could see the shimmering outline of her mother on the wall.

"We all scrambled around, looking for her because, well, there was this unspoken feeling that she might do something . . . unsafe. There were these times when she shut down and no one could reach her and like maybe she didn't know what she was doing or even know where she was. All the sudden, we heard this scream." His hand moved to his hair and he began to twist a lock around his finger. "Layla was way out in the ocean and you could see this giant fin slicing through the water—moving away from her but damn close. Then it did this slow turn and went under the surface. Jimmy was yelling at her to swim to the boat, which was the closest thing to her, but she wouldn't have been able to get in, not in her shape."

Woody cut in. "Right off the bat I knew it was Hina and that Layla would be okay, but your uncle was beside himself. Finally convinced him, and your mom made it in no problem. But we had to help her out of the water and her eyes were a different kind of wild."

Understanding dawned. No wonder her mother was so afraid of her going in the water. And she remembered those periods when her mom had been almost catatonic. It had scared her to no end.

"What did she have to say about it?" she asked.

"She said suddenly the shark was just there, swimming by, looking at her. Layla said she stared back and was almost hypnotized for a few seconds and then realized it wasn't a whale or a dolphin. That's when she screamed." Woody looked Minnow in the eye. "But still, you ask me, the ocean saved your mother's life."

And mine.

As she let this new information filter into her, everything she knew to be true shifted a few degrees to the west. The hitting. Her mother being here. The shark. The possibility of her mother drowning with Minnow inside her. But her mother had come back to shore. Back to California. Back to her father. She chose life, at least in that moment.

Minnow stood. "Excuse me. I really need to be alone right now."

She went to the wall and sat on the cold hard concrete, oblivious to the light rain now falling. How strange that this was where she ended up all these years later, in the company of the same two men and eye to eye with the same tiger shark. Whoever thought that there was no synchronicity in this world was dead wrong.

Seven Ways of Looking at a White Shark
by Minnow Gray, age 20
(Many thanks to Wallace Stevens)

Beneath a following sea
my favorite moving thing
was the eye of a white shark.

I was of infinite minds,
like an ocean
in which there are white sharks roaming.

The white shark bulleted in the winter seas.
She was a small speck in a big picture.

A girl and a fish
are one.
A girl and a fish and a white shark
are one.

When the white shark swam out of sight,
it marked the start
of a long migration.

The current is moving.
The white shark must be swimming.

It was morning all day.
It was raining
and there would be thunder.
The white shark swam
in between the stipes of kelp.

CHAPTER 25

The Guest Book

***Ohana**: family, relative, kin group*

Nalu called an hour later asking what Minnow wanted to do since the weather was so crappy. She didn't think it was crappy at all. Actually she loved it, but most people wanted blue skies and sunshine. The weather fit her mood too. Surly and haunting. Dark.

"Oh, and by the way, I found out something interesting yesterday at the harbor," he said, a glimmer in his voice. "I tried to call you, but there was no answer."

She was only half listening. "What'd you hear?"

"There are these guys who raise seahorses over near the airport, and I talked to them when they were rinsing down their boat. The captain said they go along the coast from time to time and let some out in the wild, trying to repopulate. So a few weeks ago, on the way back from Kawaihae, they were farther out than usual and came upon what looked like a bunch of fishing floats, but when they got closer, he said there was a metal framed cage hanging at the surface of the water. And get this—it was in the same general area as the chum."

Minnow's mind whirled. "How big was the cage?"

"Eighteen to twenty feet. Not any kind of fish trap I can think of."

There was only one thing it could be, really. But none of this mattered because she was leaving. A long moment passed before she could get the words out. "Tell Joe, because I'm going back to Santa Barbara this afternoon or tomorrow. There's nothing I can do about it."

The line went silent. She waited. He said nothing. "Nalu? Are you there?"

"Whoa. Dude. How can you just bail on us like that?"

Us?

"We did our best, but the hunt is on and I'm not staying for it. I can't. And who is this *us*? It's been just you and me all along here, fighting a losing battle," she said.

"Me and the sharks."

"Joe and the rest of the team should be able to take over. Aren't they back from Australia today?"

"I think so. But I talked to Joe last night. He's taking a leave of absence to take care of his wife and baby. I guess there's been more complications. Sounds like their daughter has a heart defect and is going to need open heart surgery."

"Oh my gosh, I'm so sorry to hear that."

"Her chances are good, but he said he needs boots on the ground at home for the foreseeable future."

"I'll give him a call," she said.

"Doc, you can't go, not when we might finally have our answer. At least stay through the weekend," he said.

Minnow could feel his desperation through the phone line, tense and wiry, and it caught her off guard. Had she been too self-absorbed to notice how important this whole thing was to him? She wanted to say *okay*. Didn't want to let him down, or let the ocean down. But she already had, hadn't she?

"Why don't you take the day off? Woody and Cliff are here, and I can get them to go out there with me. I'll let you know what we find out."

"I want to go out there with you."

"I don't have time to wait if I want to catch a red-eye. I'll call you at three p.m. Stand by," she said, then quietly hung up the phone.

Nalu had been such a faithful companion, it felt cruel to shut him out like this. But maybe that was the point. It was easier to push people away than let them in.

As soon as she hung up with Nalu, she called Hawaiian Airlines. Woody and Cliff were somewhere out back, rustling around in the bushes across the pond, so she wouldn't have to explain to them. Not now. There was a red-eye out of Honolulu at ten p.m., so she booked a connecting flight at seven thirty. Which meant she'd have to leave here at around five thirty, to be safe. She could get a cab or shuttle from the Kiawe if it came down to that.

She put down the handset and eyed the photo album on the table, fighting the pull to open it again and spend a hundred years staring at the pictures of her mother. There were only a few, but Minnow had thought she'd seen every picture of her mother in existence. So each one was like a tiny window into the past. Next to the album, she noticed a book sitting open. It hadn't been there earlier. Its pages were lined in handwriting. Minnow took a closer look. A guest book.

September, 1967.

Her legs gave way and she found herself sitting in the chair, eyes searching for what she knew must be there. The first entry was written by someone named Marilyn Carlsmith, who filled up almost a whole page about fish. A woman after her own heart. Then Minnow's eyes swung to the handwriting at the bottom of the opposite page and she knew right away whose it was.

> *This is a very short tale of a girl who was almost gone. I came here not knowing how I could go on in this world, but being here in your shark house has been the greatest gift. The hush of the*

night. Your sweet ukulele playing. The magic food that Mrs. K cooked in her tiny kitchen full of love. The shells. The fish. The whales! I truly believe they were wrapping me in their song and weaving some kind of spell. The shark, well, that was another story. Quite honestly, it was the biggest fright I've had in my life.

The main thing is, I came here with questions, and I'm leaving with answers and a renewed sense of hope. It's my wish that I can bring my daughter here one day. I have a feeling she will be a much braver soul than me. (Don't ask me how, but I just know I'm having a girl.)

Layla O'Donnell. September 7, 1967

When Minnow finished reading, she sat there in a stupor. Tears slid down her cheeks and one of them landed on the page, blurring the word *shark*. She had just found the thread that had sewn together her distant past with her present, plus the revelation that her life in the ocean started far earlier than she ever knew. She was born of whale song and tiger shark and undersea things. Of her mother's fear and love and hope. Of this very place.

The back door slammed and she jumped, placing a soothing hand over her heart. Woody came over and saw the guest book in front of her, still open to her mother's entry.

"Straight from the seahorse's mouth," he said, squeezing her shoulder. "How you holding up, kid?"

"Hanging in there. This has all come out of left field, and it might take a while to sink in. How you explained it, it makes sense, and then reading this helps. I just can't believe no one told me. And why didn't she bring me here?" She leaned back in the chair and looked up at the cracks in the ceiling, fighting back more tears.

"Cliff can tell you some."

His brother was just walking in the sliding screen door, holding a machete. There were twigs and leaves in his hair, and for the first time she realized just how handsome he was, in a very jungly, wild man kind of way.

"Tell her what?" he asked.

"Why Layla never came back with Minnow, and your theory on . . . everything."

"Not sure if she wants my theory on everything. That might take a while. But like I said, your mother and I kept in touch. She wrote me letters and I sent her postcards. I wanted it to be out in the open, not like we had some secret thing going on. One day your dad found the postcards and went off the rails. So she asked me not to write anymore," he said, shrugging as if it was no big deal. But the hurt was still there. She could see it in the lines of his face and the way his body contracted as that last sentence bled out.

He had loved her.

"And that was that?" Minnow asked.

He bit his lip and gave her a sad smile. "That was that. I never heard from her again, and I honored her wish."

She felt a warmth for this man. Such a kind soul, it was hard to imagine him firing a gun at boats in the bay, or snapping, like Woody said he could. He was like Minnow—he cared deeply. Maybe too deeply. It made her think of Luke for a few heartbeats, but she recovered and stayed in this lane.

"Do you still have her letters?" She had to ask.

It took him a few moments to answer. "I think so, somewhere."

Yes.

"Can I see them someday? If they aren't too private?"

"I'll see if I can dig them up."

Minnow had a feeling he knew exactly where they were, but didn't push. He had lost something too, long ago as it was. But love and time were independent of each other. Anyone who had ever loved knew that.

When she told them about the chum, both were genuinely surprised. Woody agreed it was an area not often traveled. Far from any boat ramps, and most fishermen were either farther out or farther in. But they were eager to go have a look.

"We didn't see any metal cage or buoys when we drove through, but we could have easily missed it," she said.

"What if they take the cage in?" Woody asked.

"Where would they take it?"

Neither of them had an answer for that.

They loaded up the boat with boiled peanuts, poke, a peanut butter and honey sandwich for Minnow, and enough Coca-Cola to last a week. But when Woody went to start the motor, it sputtered and she smelled gas. He lifted the can to make sure it was full, then said, "Whoa, what happened here?"

Minnow and Cliff both came over. Woody was holding the fuel line, which had been severed.

"We had no trouble with it yesterday. Though Nalu was driving so I didn't actually pay much attention."

The edges were neatly cut through. Was it possible something on the boat had sliced it? She glanced around, but there was nothing sharp in sight. They all stared at the line for a moment.

"Sabotage. Guaranteed," Cliff said.

"Gotta be. Unless you or Nalu accidentally cut it?"

She thought back. Neither of them had used their dive knives while last in the boat. Had they?

"Something could have been resting against it and we didn't notice," she said, not sounding very convincing.

"Possible," Woody said.

Cliff frowned. "My ass. Someone doesn't want you, us, poking around."

"So what do we do?" she asked.

"Keep our eyes wide open."

Uneasy, she fumbled around in the toolbox for the roll of heavy-duty duct tape. "For now, we can use this to patch it, and I'll ask Nalu to bring another line when he comes back."

Woody drove, with Minnow standing next to him at the center console, and Cliff sat on the cooler. Skies were a blue gray and clouds seemed to be thinning toward Maui. Here and there, light poured down to the surface of the ocean in pillars of amber.

Once underway, Minnow asked, "Can you tell me more about Hina? When did you guys first encounter her?"

"When we was young, really small, like *hanabata* days, there was this old shark called Umi. Whenever my pops and his friends went out diving and they came back in, there was always talk of this shark. A few years later, I remember suddenly it was gone. Pops was always asking if anyone saw Umi, but he must have died. My father mourned that thing like it was a pet dog or something. But Umi had been around forever by then, so it was just the natural order of things, you know? I never saw him, but not long after, Hina showed up."

Cliff called from the back. "I saw Umi. Once. He was like one pit bull under watah. Fat."

Woody smirked and said to Minnow, "Yeah. Cliff's claim to fame. First time we saw Hina, he walked on water to get to the nearest coral head." He threw his head back and laughed. "She was interested in us for real, and my dad said we had to keep our eye on her. He and I went back to back and she circled a few times at a distance, then swam into the cave, and from then on she was just around. Sometimes we gave her fish, sometimes she stole it from our lines. But she nevah bothered anyone."

"I didn't realize tiger sharks lived in one particular area, especially a cave. From what we know, they roam," she said.

He shrugged. "I don't know what happens in the rest of the world, but here at Kalaemanō they do. Umi and Hina, at least. I'm sure they travel, but this is where they return to."

"What do their names mean?"

"Umi-a-Liloa was a Hawaiian chief who united the all the islands and Hina is the silver light of the moon."

Cliff added, "Don't forget she is also the goddess of the ocean."

Minnow got full body chills. Anyone who named individual sharks and revered them as these two brothers did were her people.

"When I was young, on Catalina, I fell under the spell of a white shark I named Luna. She was huge and scraped up, but she was mine. Or so it felt."

Woody nodded, as though this was the kind of thing he heard every day. His eyes were on the ocean ahead, reading every ripple and current.

She went on. "I never told anyone about her or that I named her. I think I had enough sense to keep all this to myself. I knew my mom was not into me swimming alone and my dad might have understood, but he was so busy. So it was just me and Luna, best friends forever."

"How old were you when you left the island?"

"Seven."

"It's not every day a white shark becomes your guardian. It's a high honor," he said.

Minnow had never thought of Luna as a guardian, but it made sense. And now she was returning the favor. Trying to, at least.

They rode on in silence, every so often spotting a whale in the distance or a burst of flying fish—*mālolo,* as Cliff called them. Iridescent winged creatures whose tails left a zigzag pattern on the glassy surface before they lifted off. More gliders than fliers, they were one of her favorite fish.

Minnow was still buzzing from the morning encounter with Hina and this new information about her mother. Like someone had plugged her into an outlet in the wall at Hale Niuhi and she couldn't unplug herself.

Twenty minutes later, Cliff said, "Look, over there."

She and Woody turned. It looked like debris scattered along a current line. Plastic bottles, branches, coconuts. When they reached it, they turned and followed it out, staying just beyond it. Minnow had the binoculars and was looking for any sign of floats or a cage.

"Glass ball weather—keep an eye out. The Kona storms bring them in and we gotta get them before they hit the rocks," Woody said.

"That's not what we're here for," she said, sounding bitchier than she intended.

"When the ocean offers up treasure, you take it, girl."

"Sorry, you're right. I'm just feeling pressure to find something that might give us answers and maybe stop the hunt."

"Nothing we find is going to stop these guys. They pretend to listen to everyone, but they made up their minds already," he said.

"'They'? Isn't it all on Mayor Lum?"

"I think there's more going on behind the scenes."

"Like what?"

Cliff was suddenly on the other side of Woody. "Money. Guaranteed, one of these parties is paying someone off."

"That's a big allegation and would be hard to prove," she said.

"I know people who know people who say Lum is a crook. A ranch down South Point and fancy trips and cars, and who's paying?"

Woody thrust out his chin. "He don't care nothing about the *'āina,* I tell you that."

He turned to her and their eyes met. There was anger there but also a fire that made her feel like she had someone on her team. An ally in the truest sense of the word.

"So if the mayor and his nephew were taking money—say, from these shark tours—it would definitely be in their best interest to clean things up, and fast," she said, not liking where this was going.

"Damn straight."

Minnow brought them roughly to the location where she and Nalu had seen the chum, which she had triangulated in order to find it again. The current line was like a huge conveyor belt of flotsam and jetsam, running through the area.

"You'd think we would notice a cage that big with floats," she said.

They drove in and out, back and forth, covering a large grid, but there was no evidence of a shark cage or chum.

"Maybe the guy was mistaken. Coulda been something that got loose and was traveling in this current," Cliff said. "There's all kinds of weird shit in the ocean these days."

Sad but true. The sea was home to unimaginable amounts of trash, from microplastics to airplane parts to automobiles. Minnow had seen it all. On the surface, you would never know it, but go below and strange things turned up.

"Or maybe whoever's cage it was pulled it up because of the storm," she mused.

"Two o'clock," Woody said, nodding starboard and veering that way.

There was something small and round, glowing a pale aqua green, and beyond that, two similar objects. He throttled down and put the boat in neutral. They all leaned over the edge, tilting so far that Minnow had to grab onto the rail.

"Glass balls!" they all cried.

Cliff grabbed the net and gently scooped them each into the boat. Baseball-sized and covered in barnacles.

"One for each of us," Woody said, smiling like a kid who had just reeled in his first fish.

"What's that down there?" Cliff said, pointing up ahead.

Minnow squinted to see into the dark water. There, a foot or two below the surface, was something round and whitish. Woody pulled forward, and again they all peered over the side. Cliff tried to scoop the thing in, but it soon became apparent that it was attached to a line.

"It's a buoy," he said, eyes glinting in a ray of sun.

Something passed among the three of them, sparking inside Minnow. A sureness. "They tie off on this buoy and they can take the cage in when they need to. Maybe they brought it in because of the storm," she said.

"Could be."

"If someone is really running a shark dive operation here, this would absolutely draw large sharks to the area and keep them hanging around. This is the break we needed."

Woody scratched the silver stubble on his chin. "How are they getting customers, though? It's not like they can advertise."

"Fakkahs," Cliff muttered.

"That's not our problem."

"We need to catch them in the act," Cliff said.

"What about the cage? How would no one see it on the boat?" Woody asked, then emphasized, "I'm not doubting someone is doing this, just trying to figure how no one has seen 'um."

"Maybe they stopped when they realized people were getting bit," Minnow said.

"You saw chum the other day, though, didn't you?"

"Yeah."

Cliff cleared his throat, gazing in at the coastline with a stormy look on his face. "*Auwe.* They not gonna get away with this. Not in our waters. "

Minnow smiled for the first time today and felt her salt-soaked lips cracking.

From the journal of Minnow Gray

Hawai'i, February 27, 1998

Pay attention and notice everything around you, for the universe is always showing you the way. A new word I learned. Hōʻailona. *Sign, symbol, omen, portent.*

CHAPTER 26

The Call

***Naʻauao**: learning, knowledge, wisdom, science; literally, "daylight mind"*

Minnow waited until they were back at the house to tell them. Brooding skies made it appear to be almost nighttime, when in reality it was only a little before three o'clock. She would pass on all the evidence in her possession to Nalu, who could then share with whoever took over for Joe. Likely one of the scientists who had just returned from the conference in Australia. It was a lonely and sad thought, and she tried to brush it away.

But before she could gather the courage to break the news, the phone rang. "Hello, Kaupikos," she answered.

Cliff was out front sharpening a machete and Woody was picking up downed coconut fronds.

"Dr. Gray? Minnow?" a woman asked.

She recognized the voice right away. "Angela?"

"Call me Angie, please."

"I've been meaning to come by. How are you doing?" Minnow asked.

"A little better each day, I think. Less pain meds, so the walls have stopped breathing, so that's good."

Minnow had to laugh. "A good sign, for sure."

"Listen, I heard they called on a shark hunt, and I saw you on the news pleading against that. Is there anything I can do to help? Talk to the press, go see Lum, anything?"

"I'm sure the press would be all over that, and the world would love to hear from you and hear that you're doing well. But to be honest, I don't know that you'd be able to stop the hunt."

Angela sighed. "I'm sure that leg doesn't help."

"The leg?"

"Did you not hear?"

A sick feeling bubbled up. "No, I was out on the water most of the day. What happened?"

"Some divers found a human leg wedged in a crack in the rocks and called the fire department. They went and recovered it somewhere not too far north of the Kiawe, and they're speculating that it belongs to Hank, the missing swimmer. I watch TV all day, so I just saw it on the news."

Minnow sat there, unable to form any words. It was entirely possible the leg had been severed after he drowned, but that would require a medical examiner to determine. Until then, the hype would just keep building.

"Thank you for telling me. If it is his leg and he was bit before he died, that does not bode well for the hunt. It'll just give them more fuel."

"Which is why I want to do something. Please. It would make me feel useful and I love a good fight."

A strange contradiction often occurred with shark bite survivors. Many of them could not wait to get back in the water, did not hold anything against the shark and even went on to become advocates for the animals. The exact opposite of the hysteria everyone else was experiencing.

"I think the best thing you can do is to call the press and tell them what you told me the other day, and just be honest with them. Remind them—"

"Will you come up here and join me on it? That would be more powerful. 'Two girls who give a shit,' we'll call ourselves."

Minnow fumbled for an answer, then came out with the truth. "I would love to, but I'm leaving tonight."

"Why?" Angela sounded baffled and even a little hurt.

"My work here is done. The rest of the Hawai'i shark team arrives today, back from a conference, and they can take over."

"When is your flight?"

"Tonight."

Some rustling of crisp bedsheets, then, "Stay at least until tomorrow. I'll pay for your change fees and any extra expenses."

She wished she could say yes. A braver person would. "I can't."

"What is this really about? You know your work here isn't done. Far from it. This goes deeper, doesn't it?"

Minnow looked out to sea as two frigate birds hovered high above the boat, their distinctive shapes dark against the already dark clouds.

Cliff burst in. "*Hō'ailona,*" he said, nodding toward the birds.

She held her hand over the phone. "What does that mean?"

"A sign."

Then he blew out as fast as he came in, binoculars in hand and leaving a trail of smoke in his wake.

"Minnow?" Angie said.

"I'm here."

"I know you hardly know me, but I feel like we can help each other. We both know the kind of devastation that can ruin a person, but you've been running from it your whole life. You can't keep running, love. Stay at least until tomorrow. Please?"

Her words were tender but fierce, and they brought up a memory of the morning Minnow's father died.

She is standing on the shore screaming and flailing as her mother tries to pull her away. The squeeze of Layla's fingers burn as they dig into her bony arms. A waterfall of tears blocks her from seeing anything, but Minnow keeps breaking free and running toward the icy water. Layla keeps dragging her back until Minnow collapses into a tiny heap on the beach. There isn't enough air to breathe and her mother shakes her hard, rocking her back and forth.

"What did you do?" she screams.

But it's the look in Layla's eyes that scares Minnow more than anything. A cold hard fear that is animal in its nature. Primal and raw and wild.

Unforgiving.

"Will you?" Angela asked, breaking the spell.

And in that moment she knew. "Yes, I'll stay."

There was no other choice. Running away with her tail between her legs would never allow her to face the unthinkable and maybe move beyond it. That little piece of memory she had been mining for her whole life.

"Attagirl. You are stronger than you think. Remember that. And I'll be here for you, whatever you need. Can you come up to the hospital in the morning?"

"Just tell me when."

"Let's do it early, say eight? That'll give them enough time to run the interview on the mainland. I'll have my agent reach out to Josh Brown and anyone else who's here on the island."

"I'll be there."

Minnow hung up and let out a long breath.

Nalu hadn't been in his room when she called, so she went outside to see what Cliff was doing with the binoculars. She spotted him on the south end of the bay, sitting on a rock out on the point. She put on her rubber slippers and walked out there, careful not to twist an ankle on the rough and crumbly lava. In the still air, the briny smell of the brackish ponds filled her head. Every so often he would pick up the binoculars and scan the waters, then scan the sky.

When she got close, she said, "Can I help you?"

He didn't turn. "No."

She stood there for a few moments, debating whether to turn around and leave, but she was curious about what he was doing. And what he'd meant by *hōʻailona.*

"Get ovah here," he finally said.

Minnow noticed a line of smooth rocks and hopped from one to the next, then had to stretch her legs as far as she could to reach the high rock he was on, surrounded by water. To fall in would mean landing in a bed of black spiny *wana*.

"What are you looking for?" she asked.

He patted a spot next to him. "Come, sit."

She sat on a flat and worn place.

"Those *ʻiwa* birds that flew by are now way up the coast in the same spot we found the buoy. Can you see?"

She held a hand up over her eyes to lessen the glare but still couldn't see anything. "No."

Cliff grunted, then handed her the binocs. She swept across the sky a few times, then saw two black shapes circling, wings wide.

"Do you think they could be out there now, chumming?" she asked.

"The *ʻiwa* birds always come in close with the storms, but you can bet they're checking out that buoy and maybe something left ovah floating in the area. Something we missed. Their eyesight is outta this world."

A ridge of lava on the north side of the bay blocked the ocean from view.

"What did you mean by *hōʻailona*?" she asked.

"That we gotta pay attention."

From the side, his features looked stronger, like a fierce warrior. Thick eyebrows, jaw jutting out. He kept his gaze on the water.

"To the birds?"

He nodded. "They warn of something to come. Something *hauna*—stinking. Something we must not back down from."

Minnow felt her throat constrict. She had come so close to leaving, and now she worried about living through a shark hunt. Seeing one shark killed had wrecked her. Boatloads of them might push her over the edge. Hooks and hollow eyes, creatures never meant to leave the sea.

Cliff slowly turned to her. "You feel it too, huh?"

His words threw her, but she knew exactly what he meant. "I do."

"The bond passed on to me from my grandfather. Woody and our pops didn't get it, even though they are caretakers. You got it, too, somehow."

Being here on this rock with someone who understood her was comforting, hard as it was. Silver-blue water lapped around them. "It's both a burden and a blessing, I think. It tears at my heart but also makes me feel like the luckiest girl in the world," she said.

"My mother always said those who swam in the abyss were the only ones who could also soar with *'io*, the hawk," he said.

"I love your way of thinking."

He shrugged. "Old wisdom."

They sat shoulder to shoulder, looking out at a wall of rain on the horizon edging closer, and after a while she told him about the leg.

"I already knew he was bit. Woody told me about the fin you found and I could just *feel* it. The shark that's out there has been here before. I seen her six years back or so and a couple years before that. She usually minds her own business."

"Maybe it's a different one?" Minnow suggested.

"Not this big. I only saw her at a distance both times. A long shadow on the periphery, checking me out, cruising like one nuclear submarine. Brah, my heart was going off the Richter. You see something like that, you *nevah* forget it."

Something about the cadence of his words, and his pidgin, gave everything he said an exclamation point after it.

"Oh, I know."

"So what we goin' do about it? That is the question."

"Tomorrow I'm going up to the hospital to support Angela as she makes a statement," Minnow said.

"That's her deal. But you and me and Woody, we gotta make a stand," he said, unfolding his legs and standing. He held a hand and pulled her up. "We'll *hui* tonight at the Kiawe. Make a plan, roll some heads."

Whatever that meant, she was in.

From the journal of Minnow Gray

September 29, 1992

Things found in a shark's stomach: a whole reindeer, an unopened bottle of wine, a human arm covered in tattoos, license plates, car tires, porcupine spines, a dog with a collar still on, a drum, a camera, a boat propeller. This is obviously just the tip of the iceberg, but it goes to show you that sharks use their mouths to sample and explore things. We might do the same if we had no hands.

CHAPTER 27

The Meeting

***Ua**: rain, to rain; rainy*

They piled into Woody's truck before sunset, even though there was no sign of the sun, and drove to the Kiawe. Nalu had shown up an hour earlier, thinking he would be taking her to the airport, so he joined them. On the way, Minnow learned that the Kaupiko family had once owned the land where the resort sat, so Woody and Cliff could eat for free there until the day they died. A deal brokered by their father and one they took full advantage of whenever they were at the house. Things now made more sense.

She had tried to talk them out of going, blaming the approaching squall, but Cliff had his mind set on curry and coconut cake. Of course it was Luke she didn't want to run into, but she wasn't about to tell them that. Thoughts of last night kept dropping into her mind. It scared her how strongly she had reacted to him.

When the four of them rolled into the Saltwater Bar, every head in the room swung in their direction, as though a band of outlaws had just ridden into town. Minnow wasn't sure why at first, but it dawned on her that her three companions gave off a kind of subtle energy, powerful as the sun. Especially Cliff with his shock of unruly silver-streaked hair and fire in his eyes. One look his way and you could tell he was not someone to be messed with.

They grabbed a table closest to the ocean and Minnow sat facing out, noticing Luke's boat was not there. Dixie was working and zeroed in on them right away. When she pulled up, Nalu stood and kissed her in front of everyone. It was sweet to see him so tender with her and not worried about what anyone thought.

After handing out menus, Dixie lowered her voice. "Y'all might want to know that Josh Brown is all giddy because he got to interview the Search & Rescue guys about a leg that was found. Did you hear about that?" she asked, scrunching up her face.

"We did," Minnow said.

"Everyone really wants this shark hunt, but I'm with you guys. Anything that swims in the ocean does so at their own risk. My motto is *be ready for anything to happen out there,* and I do mean *anything.*"

Woody nudged Nalu's shoulder. "This one is a keeper."

Nalu grinned. "Yeah, I know."

Cliff ordered a round of mai tais for the table and Minnow saw a look of concern pass across Woody's face. "Just water for me, thanks," he said.

Minnow held up her hand. "Same."

Nalu seemed to catch on. "None for me, either. I'm not a big drinker."

As much as she liked the guy, she could see that Cliff on alcohol might not be a good thing. There was a volatility coiled beneath his skin that she wasn't sure she wanted to see unleashed. At least not now.

He looked dejected. "Shoots. Water for me then too."

They ordered dinner, and Woody and Cliff shared stories about their childhood and how they once hiked with their father from Kona to Kawaihae along the old trail used by the Hawaiians, surviving on fish, seaweed and coconuts. Minnow found herself half paying attention and half thinking about her mother being here all those years ago, a baby in her belly, coming face-to-face with a large tiger shark. How that experience had shaped her and how in turn that had shaped Minnow.

When the food arrived, they got down to business.

"So, I been thinking about how to approach this," Woody said in between bites. "We can make a last plea to Mayor Lum and talk to this Josh Brown guy and get ourselves on national TV, explaining in more detail how a shark hunt goes against all of our cultural values. In the old days, families had their day of the week they fished on and they couldn't fish any other day. Kept things in balance."

Minnow hadn't heard that before, but she liked their way of thinking. "We could also try to get a judge to halt it on the grounds of animal cruelty or some other law, but we'd have to move fast," she added. The idea had been brewing in the back of her mind, far-fetched as it was. "Do you know any judges on the island we could call on?"

"Judge Carlsmith. She would know if it was even feasible," Woody said.

"Where have I heard that name?"

"The guest book. She's a family friend. Tough *wahine*."

Right. The woman who knew all the fish. "Can you call her first thing in the morning?"

"Rajah."

"I also want to talk to the medical examiner once I'm done with Angela and find out what I can about the leg. I'd like to get a look at it myself," she said, sick at the thought.

Cliff, who had been quietly stirring his curry all this time, finally lifted his head. "You folks do that. I'm going to put some feelers out and see if I can rally the troops."

"Rally them for what?" Minnow asked.

"You let me worry about that. I don't want to get anyone's hopes up. But we gotta have something in place to stop these guys if all else fails."

Woody frowned. "No violence, Cliff."

"They the one bringing violence."

"Yeah, but we take the high road, no matter what. No 'eye for an eye' or any of that kind of bull crap."

"Easy for you to say," Cliff said, squeezing his fork with a balled fist.

"No, it's not easy for me to say. But we do what we can, say our prayers and trust God to do the rest."

Cliff's leg bounced up and down, and he shot his brother a dangerous look. "Only people I trust around here are you and maybe this *wahine* here next to me. How many times we let the so-called people in power make stupid decisions that serve only them or their special interests? Not us, nevah us."

It surprised Minnow to be included in his small circle of trust. "If we can prove that there's chumming, I think we have a shot at stopping the hunt, so let's focus on that," she said, trying to sound more upbeat than she felt.

"All these guys, they need smacks upside the head."

Woody shook his head. "You do that, you're no better than them."

For a moment Cliff looked like he might break down in tears, and she felt for him. There was nothing worse than being backed into a cave and the only way out was to fight and claw and scream. Her nightmares contained a similar vein of powerlessness.

Nalu nodded toward the bar television. "Sorry to interrupt, but . . . news time."

She and Nalu hurried over to the two empty bar seats in order to hear better, leaving the brothers some time alone.

A young local guy named Keone Kern was just introducing fire department spokesman Cyril Macadangdang.

"What can you tell us about this possible new development in the disappearance of Hank Johnson?"

"Keone, it's too early to tell, but divers found a leg wedged in a crack in about fifteen feet of water. This was in the general area where Hank was last seen. And because we're looking at over two weeks since he went missing, there has unfortunately been significant decomposition. It's still uncertain if the leg was severed before or after the owner died. But I can tell you this: There are tooth imprints on the bone. Large ones."

"Oh shit," Minnow said.

"No one left me a message. That sucks," Nalu said.

They'd given the intern's number to Lum's secretary since Hale Niuhi had no answering machine and they were hardly ever in the house.

"At this point we're just noise," she said, standing up to return to the table, but she couldn't bring herself to leave.

Keone wore a solemn look. "Any estimation how long it will take to find out?"

"Couple days max. This is being expedited, especially with the shark hunt to begin Saturday."

"As someone with a long history of experience in this kind of thing, what else can you tell us, Cyril?"

"There are no other missing people in the area, and we know with a hundred percent certainty of a large predatory shark cruising this coastline, so that tells me this person was most likely hit while still alive."

What kind of faulty logic is that? Minnow felt like shouting.

"Were there any signs of clothing or goggles or fins, anything like that?" Keone asked.

"Nope, but based on the size of the bones and the foot, the deceased appears to be male. We should have our answer soon. And in the meantime, if you do swim, stay close to shore."

Keone nodded and stared back into the camera. "Thank you so much, Cyril. Now back to you, Joe."

Nalu shot her a look. "What the hell was that?"

Minnow had no answer. When she was halfway back to the table, she caught a glimpse of a man sitting on the beach staring out at the squall now just offshore. Wide shoulders and wet, scruffy hair.

Luke.

But where was his boat? Her first instinct was to go out there and sit down next to him, lean in and wait for the rain to come, tell him she wasn't leaving after all. Then she remembered his words.

I'm not the man you think I am.

"Who are you, Luke Greenwood?" she whispered.

Minnow picked at her salad, borrowed a few french fries from Nalu, and drank four glasses of water. Her mind was whirling with so many thoughts in so many directions, it was hard to concentrate on anything anyone was saying. Also, she could hear the approaching raindrops falling hard on the ocean surface, a loud rush of freshwater into salt. So loud she covered her ears with her hands.

"You okay, Doc?" Nalu asked.

She attempted a smile. "Fine, it's just so loud."

"The music?"

Two musicians had started up in the corner, but they were pure background.

"The rain."

Suddenly Luke stood up and made a dash toward them. She tracked his every effortless step, and he made it to shelter a few seconds before the sky opened up and unleashed raindrops the size of jellyfish. There were plenty of places he could have looked, but he half turned toward their table and locked eyes with Minnow. His face went from surprise to the stirrings of a smile to something darker. She had to rip her gaze away.

"Isn't that your friend?" Nalu said.

No way was she going to get into it now.

"Yeah, that's Luke."

Her heart hurt and was beating too fast, like tiny bird wings fighting for flight.

"You not going to invite him over?"

Minnow gave him a cold glare. "There's no room at the table."

Cliff pushed out his seat and stood. "We *pau* anyway. Let's head back. I got some things to take care of."

Woody swallowed his last piece of coconut cake and Minnow put hers in a to-go box. When they walked out, Luke was still standing there—she could see him out of the side of her eye. This time she forced herself not to look. His pull was too strong and she couldn't be swayed right now. Not that he wanted anything to do with her anyway. But as she passed, she swore he said her name out loud. Or maybe it was just the song of the rain on the roof.

From the journal of Minnow Gray

Hawai'i, February 28, 1998

Woody told me that to dream of sharks often signifies the spirit of a loved one coming to visit, usually to give guidance or offer protection—especially in times of heightened significance. I might not have believed him a month ago, but I do now.

CHAPTER 28

The Gift

***Makana**: gift, present; reward, award, donation, prize*

The dreams came all night long. Storms and sharks and Layla. In one of them Minnow was standing on a coral head, pregnant and ready to give birth. It was peculiar, though, because she had no idea who the father was. Contractions started and she sat down on the rock, spread her legs and a rush of baby sharks poured out, splashing into the water and swimming all around her. They kept coming and coming, their small fins all tipped in red. Soon she was surrounded by hundreds or maybe thousands of tiny sharks and her heart swelled with a fullness she had never known before.

In the morning Woody was working on a leak in the roof, while Cliff had driven off last night sometime after Minnow had fallen into bed exhausted. Now she and Nalu were on the way to the hospital and she felt even less rested. With all the tossing and turning and dry mouth, her sleep had been shitty, to say the least.

She rubbed her eyes. "When we get there, pull around back. I don't want to run into anyone on the way in."

Nalu was quiet for a moment, then said, "Did something happen between you and Greenwood? That look you two gave each other last night. It felt . . ." He paused, fishing for the right word.

Minnow finished his sentence. "Complicated."

"Maybe. But I was going to say loaded. He's into you, for real kine."

She wished she didn't care, but she did. "We had a hot moment a couple of nights ago but I told him I was leaving and it's like he went numb. His entire vibe changed, and then he told me he's not the man I think he is."

He hit the steering wheel. "See, I told you. I like the guy, but something is off about him being here. Staying at the hotel and that fancy boat. What fisherman can afford that?"

"I know. And he said he grew up with orcas in the San Juans. He seems so connected to them and the islands. Which makes me wonder why he would leave that for Hawai'i."

"Who knows. Maybe he's running from something."

"I think he is."

One shoulder lifted. "You should ask him point-blank."

"I already have."

"He does seem like a badass, though, in and out of the water. I can see why you would dig him."

She shrugged, again feeling weird about talking to Nalu about this, but she had no one else.

"But you know what?" he said.

"What?"

He gave her a sideways glance. "You're even more of a badass, and he would be lucky to have you. Any guy would."

"Thank you, Nalu. I'm glad you're here."

"Wouldn't miss it for the world."

"And about Luke, one thing I can say is, whatever he's not telling me is haunting him. He carries it with him in his eyes."

"Yeah. I could see that. Like he's always got something heavy on his mind."

Doesn't everyone.

They passed over a bridge, a stream of reddish water raging below. Then the hospital sign. An image of Luke's incredibly potent stare came into her mind, sending a line of warmth up her neck. As much as she'd wanted to get out of his sphere as fast as possible last night, part of her had hoped he'd come after her. For all he knew, she was leaving and that could've been the last time he'd see her. *It's better this way,* she told herself. Luke was a distraction to leave behind. A small blip on her radar.

At the hospital the parking lot was packed with vans and people milling about the entrance. Rows of agapanthus bloomed in small purple explosions, full of bees. A light drizzle was falling. Minnow had gone as far as brushing her hair, putting on lipstick and mascara, and wearing a beaded necklace, one of her mother's.

Angela was standing by the window when they walked in, dressed in a white fleece jacket and wearing red lipstick. She turned and smiled. "You ready?"

Minnow and Nalu both stood there, gaping. Gone was the severely wounded and drugged hospital patient. This was the Angela the world knew and loved. Makeup seamlessly covered the scar on her face, and her eyes were much clearer than the last time Minnow had seen her.

"I told them no more pain meds. I don't know what was worse, those or the shark bite," Angela said with a sly smile. "I'm still feeling weak, but it's nice to have a reason to pull myself together."

"Thank you for agreeing to do this."

"It's the least I can do. Zach was wholeheartedly against it—he's still mad at the sharks. I told him he could go back to California if he didn't support me."

Sadly, there were lots of people like Zach. "Did he go?"

"No. He thinks I'm still off my rocker from the meds, but I was serious. I'm all in to help you and I don't want his disapproving looks and bullying," Angie said, lifting her arm and looking down, as if checking her watch. But the sleeve was empty and flopped down. She blinked hard; then her eyes met Minnow's.

Minnow walked over and gave her a hug, careful not to press too hard.

Angie melted in her arms. "It's been so fucking hard."

"I know."

"One moment you're having the time of your life, the next you're fighting for it with everything you've got. We all live with this illusion that *it*—that horrible, most feared thing—could never happen to us, but I'm here to tell you that it can. And miracle of miracles, I survived. So what now?"

"Now you live, the same as before. Only better. With eyes wide open."

"Eyes and heart and soul. I feel so raw, like I've been skinned alive. It's hard to explain."

Minnow stepped away, letting go. "*From the ashes,* isn't that what they say?"

Angie smiled again, this time wide and radiant. "Hell yes. Let's do this."

Nalu pushed her in the wheelchair through the maze of hallways and out to the front, her personal security guy trailing behind. She could walk, but all that blood loss had weakened her, and it would take a while to regain her strength. They paused at the double sliding doors and she looked at Minnow.

"I hope you're ready for this," Angie said.

Minnow was never ready to be on TV, but she forced a smile. "Absolutely."

The three of them went out into the cold, hard wind. Angie was the only one dressed for the occasion and goose bumps spread over Minnow's whole body. Cameras snapped and reporters crowded around them.

"There she is!"

"Angela!"

"Ms. Crawford!"

Angie smiled graciously. A corner of the building was blocked from the wind and they moved their way over. Josh Brown followed them closely, and soon the rest crowded around, remarkably respectful. They must have sensed they were about to get something good.

"Thank you all for coming. I have a few things I want to share with the world, and I need your help in doing it. First, though, I want to thank you all for your well-wishes and outpouring of love. It's given me strength. And so you know, I can walk. My legs are fine, I'm still just a bit weak. A little over a week ago, I lost part of my left arm to a shark. I had been swimming off a boat near a pod of dolphins, which I now know is not only illegal but dangerous. I'm lucky I survived, but I'm also deeply troubled by what is about to take place tomorrow down along the coast."

She paused, slowly sweeping her gaze across all the cameras. Everyone was hanging on her next word.

"The mayor and some members of a shark task force, though strongly advised against it by shark researchers, are launching a shark hunt that will likely decimate the local shark population and upset the balance of the ocean. They say it's to make the ocean safer for the international swim and because spring break is coming up, but according to experts like Dr. Minnow Gray here with me, there is no evidence to support what they're doing. In fact, she believes the shark who bit me is long gone. There have always been sharks here. We know that each time we enter the water. All they are doing is trying to survive. I hold no ill will toward the shark and I will go back in the ocean as soon as I can."

She lifted what was left of her arm and let the sleeve dangle down for effect. Camera shutters snapped all around. Angie's delivery was smooth and impassioned, and Minnow wished she had just a fraction of her composure. The featherlight rain falling around her only added to the woman's otherworldly aura.

"Basing decisions on fear never leads to good things. Did you know the military used to fly helicopters over Kailua Bay on O'ahu with a sniper and a high-powered rifle? Any sharks they saw, they'd shoot. No questions asked. I'd like to believe we have evolved since then, and it's our duty to take a stand. I urge you to call the Big Island mayor's office and tell him so. Are the events of the past few weeks tragic? Yes. But allowing the culling of countless sharks would also be tragic. Did you know that more people die each year from elephants, bees, dogs, and falling coconuts?"

Another long pause was filled with murmurs from the group, and then a surprise caught Minnow wholly off guard.

"In support of Dr. Gray and all that she's doing to learn about these important apex predators, I'm donating a hundred thousand dollars to her nonprofit Sea Trust so we can deepen our understanding of these beautiful creatures. I believe that knowledge is our secret weapon and the more we know about sharks, the more we can lessen our chances of getting hurt in the water."

It took a moment to register. *A hundred thousand dollars. To Sea Trust.*

Suddenly all eyes were on Minnow, and the questions came all at once.

"What will you do with the money?"

"What about the roughwater swim?"

"What if they call off the hunt and someone else dies?"

Minnow rested a hand on Angie's shoulder. "You have no idea what this means to me. Defending sharks can feel lonely, so I appreciate the support more than you know," she said quietly.

"I did my research," Angie whispered back.

Josh Brown held the mic up in front of her. "One question, Dr. Gray. Will you be entering the roughwater swim next week?"

The crowd fell silent. Minnow had no plans to enter the race. Why would she? But there was no other answer than, "Yes, and I'm looking forward to it."

That pretty much sealed it. She wouldn't be leaving anytime soon.

From the journal of Minnow Gray

Farallon Islands, September 29, 1996

My shark Luna came and went with the tides or the cycles of the moon or on some mysterious shark schedule. She would be there one day and sometimes hang around for a week, and other times and I wouldn't see her for months. But she always returned. I told myself it was because she and I had this special relationship. Some kids have imaginary friends, and in some ways I guess Luna was an imaginary friend because although she was very real, our friendship was one sided—I loved her and she was curious about me (at best).

The social lives of white sharks are murky. For the most part, they are solitary animals, but the ones we've observed and gotten to know can have some pretty distinct personalities. Some are pushy and direct, others more shy and cautious. Some seem angry, others almost playful. We also know that they often appear at the Farallones or Guadalupe with the same sharks several years in a row, as though they might travel together. And when they lift their head out of the water to look at you, you get the feeling that some kind of connection is being made. Like they are observing you in the same way you are observing them. It gives me goose bumps every time.

CHAPTER 29

The Friend

***Hoaloha**: friend; literally, "beloved companion"*

After the hospital, Nalu drove Minnow to the medical examiner's office in Kona, but the secretary refused to let them in to talk to him. There was a box of malasadas on her desk and she offered them up, as though that might somehow make up for her lack of cooperation.

Minnow set her hands on her hips. "But I'm part of the shark task force. I'm *the* white shark researcher on the case. I need to look at any imprints on the bone."

"I'm sorry. You'll have to wait for Dr. Tenby's report. Strict orders."

"Orders from who?"

"Direct from Mayor Lum."

Nalu shook his head. "Now he's playing dirty. What a kook."

Minnow stepped toward the desk. "Thank you, Renee. And actually, I will take one of those malasadas."

Nalu followed suit, and by the time they reached the truck both of them had sugar lips and beards and Minnow was wishing she'd grabbed two more. They were hot and doughy and oh so delicious.

"Lum is so typically passive-aggressive, it's almost a joke. Don't play his way and you get slowly iced out. Whatever," she said, feeling worn out.

Nalu opened her door for her. "It's not like the results will change anything, though, will they?"

"No, but I want to know if our shark is still around. Bite marks could tell us that, if they're clear enough."

"And if she is?"

"Even more reason to shut them down tomorrow."

A beautiful shark—maybe even a Sister—taken by some dumb fisherman who couldn't think for himself would slay her.

They regrouped at the house, and then Nalu left to pick up the other scientist. Minnow felt a sense of impending doom. The gray skies didn't help her shadowy mood. Woody was on the beach scrubbing off the barnacles from the glass balls they'd found yesterday. When she came to the wall, he was so engrossed in his work, he didn't look up.

"Hey," Minnow said.

"How'd it go?"

She told him.

Finished with the glass balls, he walked over and handed her one. "A souvenir. Oh, and I called a few of my die-hard fishing buddies and heard something interesting."

"Yeah, what?"

He hopped up onto the wall and started walking back toward the house, cradling the two other now shiny green orbs against this body. "Joe Apuakehau said there have been a couple boats anchored up the way in Pāpapa Bay. Couple old fishing shacks down there, only accessed by a rough jeep road or by sea. If someone has the gate codes, they could be running a dive operation out of there."

"Do you know the families?"

"Yeah, but one of them sold to a guy from Oʻahu a few years back.

No idea about him. Keep in mind, taking people out to swim with sharks isn't illegal."

"I know. But chumming is."

"So, how you gonna prove that?"

She wasn't sure exactly. "Like you said, catch them in the act and take photos. Ask for witnesses to step forward."

"You mess with someone's livelihood, it could get ugly."

"Maybe we go out with a bunch of other boats as backup. You must know people," she said, unable to keep the desperation from her voice.

"If I trusted DLWA, I would report it, but I don't."

It was feeling more and more like the Wild West out here. Vast and lawless and full of shady characters. The only thing missing was cactus, but the thorny kiawe trees were good stand-ins.

"Is Cliff going to come back? Did he tell you what he's doing?" she asked.

"All he said was to trust him, which makes me nervous. Because with him, things could either go really good or really bad. It's usually nothing in between."

Wonderful.

Minnow went back inside and set her glass ball on the table and surrounded it by a few cowrie shells so it wouldn't roll off. She wondered how long the hand-blown float had been riding the ocean currents and how far it had traveled. Decades and probably thousands of miles. Japanese fisherman were said to have stopped using them in the eighties. Replaced with plastic. Like everything else.

She sat down, pulled out her address book and found Doc Finnegan's number. "Hey, can I make a long distance call? I'm good for it," she asked Woody, who was rustling around in the kitchen.

"Shoots."

She dialed, enjoying the feel of the old rotary phone. It made her feel like she'd walked back in time to when her mother was here. Like maybe Layla would come through the door at any moment, dripping wet and sun-kissed.

He picked up right away. "Pete Finnegan."

It was how he always answered, and my God, she wished he were here, big ego and all. He had a way about him that made people listen.

"Doc, it's me, Minnow."

"My favorite student calling from Hawai'i. What the hell is going on over there?" he boomed.

"I don't know how much you've been following the news, but I gave it my all and they're still sending out a fleet of boats tomorrow and all through the weekend to kill as many sharks as they can," she said with a quivering voice.

"I got back three days ago and I've seen the news, but I want to hear it from you."

She told him everything. Her secret hope was that he would hop on a plane and come to her rescue. That he would somehow know what to do.

Instead, he said, "All you can do is all you can do, kid. Sounds like you put up a good fight, but you also have to know when to throw in the towel."

His words sparked a rage inside her. "Not yet."

"What are you going to do?"

"I don't know."

Nalu called and said the flight from Honolulu was delayed, and it would be a couple more hours before the other scientist arrived. Thunderstorms had settled over O'ahu. Minnow was at a loss for what to do, so she lay on the bed leafing through the photo album. Layla looked so young and innocent. Cheeks full and round. Hair just as wild as Minnow's, only hers was blonde and down to her waist. She'd been six years younger than Minnow was now. A babe with a babe in her womb. Minnow ran a finger over the photo in which her belly looked so round and ripe.

A flurry of inner warmth spread through her and for a few moments the fear and guilt of the past few days melted away. She was swaddled in feathers and radiant sunshine and a mother's undying love. The sensation was intense and comforting, but the minute she grasped at it, it slipped away. If only she could bottle the feeling and drink from it whenever life became too much.

She kept turning the pages, studying her mother for some sign of instability, when all she could see was this undiluted happiness. It was hard to imagine her coming here in despair and considering leaving Minnow's father. How quickly things changed. But that was the way of her mind. Cycling through hills and valleys and mountaintops. And then falling into the abyss.

Woody walked in a few minutes later. "Think I'm going to head out too. I want to check in on Cliff and make sure he's not going to cause more trouble than good. But I'll be back early in the morning. Wait for me."

Minnow shut the album. "What kind of trouble are we talking about?"

He shrugged. "Oh, I don't know. Burn all the boats, slash the tires of the trailers. He has no trouble waving that rifle of his around, either."

Yeah, not good at all.

"He would do that?"

"Maybe."

Maybe it was time someone did something radical if it was the only way to be heard. Animals and plant species were becoming extinct by the hour, or something like that, and she suddenly knew how those Greenpeace guys felt, or the woman who'd camped out for two years perched in the top of a redwood tree.

What happens if it never stops?

Alone with time on her hands, Minnow decided to take the boat to Pāpapa Bay and nose around for any signs of a shark-diving operation.

If nothing else, she could see the little black sand cove Woody said was a slice out of old Hawai'i. The seas were quiet today and she opened up the throttle, appreciating the warm wind against her skin. About twenty minutes later, once she hit the spot on the coast that was in from the sunken buoy, she slowed. Up ahead she could see the green of treetops, and soon the cliffs gave way to a wide, flat shelf of tidal pools.

She drove in so she was hugging the rocks and putted along in amazement. According to Woody, *pāpapa* was a flat and expansive reef, and she could already see a proliferation of purples, golds and blues lining the shallows beneath her. Fish swam in multitudes.

Once in the bay itself, she swung in along the sandy beach and spotted three semi-dilapidated houses tucked away in the trees. Two boats were anchored—a small metal skiff with a ten-horsepower motor and sunbaked oars that no one would be using for shark dives, and a twenty-eight- or thirty-foot Radon, anchored deeper in the middle of the bay. Was it big enough to carry a shark cage on its long flat aft section? Maybe.

No one was in sight and the beach was clear of footprints, though with the tide high that wasn't saying much. She passed close to the Radon and saw nothing out of the ordinary. It was old but looked to be well maintained. There were traces of diesel fuel in the air, as though the boat had been driven recently. She wished she could talk to someone, but she scanned the shacks again and there was no sign of life. Weekday, early afternoon, gloomy weather. It made sense. The setting did resemble something out of a painting, rusted tin roofs under coconut and kamani trees, and the black sand made it even more exotic.

Discouraged and not ready to go home, she beelined it back out to the buoy area. Today the current line was less obvious, so she had to rely on her landmarks to find the submerged float. It took a bit of back-and-forth, but she finally found it. She turned off the engine and floated for a while as a few random shafts of light beamed down from the heavens. Dark and light, sea and sky doing their dance. In theory if someone had been chumming, the sound of a boat engine should draw sharks since they'd be habituated.

She waited, looking down into the depths, hoping for a visitor or two. The water was remarkably clear and dusted with plankton and the occasional jellyfish. In the distance a whale slapped its tail on the water, making loud smacking sounds that Minnow was surprised she could hear. It was too much to be out here and not in the water, so before she knew it, she was grabbing the bowline and her mask and fins and slipping beneath the surface. Cool but not cold. Silky. She did a one-eighty to check her surroundings and then tied off to the buoy.

There was something about floating in the open sea that calmed her. A tiny speck of life in a vast underworld. She dove down a few times, seeing how far she could follow the line. Woody estimated it was probably a few hundred feet to the bottom, maybe more, so she was barely making a dent. On her third dive down, she thought she heard something. She hung in place for a few moments, listening. The sound of water swirling and an overwhelming feeling that she was not alone. She slowly spiraled up for air, took several deep breaths, then dove down again.

The boat offered only a small measure of safety, but her gut told her she was in no danger. Whatever was coming was coming leisurely. When the shape appeared far below her, she relaxed. It was a baby whale. The animal was so far below, it was merely a shadow before disappearing into the blue. Minnow hung on to the edge of the boat, watching and waiting and hoping for more. A few minutes later, it came back into her vision, probably thirty feet below her.

Not a baby whale.

A Sister.

It had to be.

The world went quiet, save for the insistent thrum of her heart. There was something familiar in the movements of this shark. This graceful and ragged-toothed beauty. This behemoth. As white sharks often did, the animal swam loops beneath her, coolly observing. Minnow observed back as the shark slowly rose higher and higher. As if orchestrated by a higher power, sunlight pierced the water around them, illuminating a network of gashes and scars across its flank.

Closer and closer it swam, languidly, as though it had all day to suss her out. No tag was visible. This one had eluded all the curious scientists out there. Then Minnow's eyes darted to the fin, where she saw four deep slices. Impossible, and yet there they were, exactly as she'd remembered them.

Luna.

Her shark.

Now at least eight feet wide and taller than she was, the Sister of all Sisters.

Minnow forgot about breathing until her lungs let her know it was time. She surfaced again, never once taking her eye off this smoothly circling shark. The one who started it all.

"My friend," she said, going back under and speaking into her snorkel what would have been gibberish to anyone around.

On the next go-around, Luna came right for her. Minnow didn't flinch. She knew enough about white shark body language to tell that this interaction was not an attack. Had Luna wanted to attack her, she would be dead already. They passed within feet of each other and that dark and intelligent eye locked on with hers. She was close enough to touch, and Minnow held out her hand, wanting so badly to feel her, but she pulled back. Touching animals in the wild was frowned upon in her circles, and she didn't want to do anything to ruin the moment.

A moment she would relive again and again for the rest of her life. It felt like meeting a long-lost relative or finding a brother you never knew you had. Not only was Luna a Sister, but she felt like Minnow's sister. Flesh and blood. Fin and tail.

This time when the shark swam away, she angled down and dropped into the depths. Minnow waited for what felt like hours, hoping for another round, but Luna was gone.

"Go away from here and don't come back. It's not safe," she said, wishing her words would carry through the water and translate into shark.

Two smaller sharks showed up a few minutes later. They moved in fast and furious, just as Minnow was climbing into the boat. She sat on the cooler in a daze, watching their fins zigzag around her. Galapagos sharks. Pups compared to Luna.

As much as she hated to think about it, the chances of another twenty-foot white shark in the area were almost nil. Which meant that Luna was responsible for the bites.

It's Luna they want in the hunt.

All other sharks would be collateral damage.

There was a reason chumming was illegal within three miles of shore. It attracted large predators. Groomed them, even. Whoever these fuckers were, they had blood on their hands.

Minnow closed her eyes and balled her fists, lying back on the cooler and trying to calm the surge of adrenaline flooding into her body. Here she was, witness to sharks appearing at the sound of an engine, and yet there was no cage, no boat, no one red-handed. The hunt would still go on in the morning.

"Get out of here, all of you!" she called out. "Swim away and stay away from all boats, do you hear me?"

Only water sounds and a Hawaiian Airlines jet approaching from Kawaihae. Planes were usually farther out to sea, but this one was hugging the coastline. Must have been the shift in wind direction.

"Do you hear me?" she screamed. "You have to listen. You have to go. Now!"

Her voice cracked. Still wet from her swim, a chill ran through her. Something about the cold brought her back to Catalina.

Instead of stopping where it had last time, the memory continued to unfold.

She is standing in the icy water. She turns and sees her father sprinting toward her, pointing. The kayak must have been washed out with the tide. He stops next to her for a second and she can smell his wet suit rubber as he zips up.

He points and she follows his line of sight to see the yellow kayak float-

ing toward open water in a strong current. Her father dives in and swims as fast as he can toward it.

Minnow watches with no apprehension. As far as she's concerned, her father is of the sea.

When he is almost there, she notices a disturbance in the water. Bruce seems to lift up and slam down again, then disappears entirely. A moment later, he pops up and lets out a terrible and unhuman sound. She covers her ears. This time a tall fin splashes around him and the water clouds red.

"Papa!" she yells.

No answer.

"Papaaaaaaa!"

Now she's howling on the shore, pacing back and forth, wanting to go out there to help him but terrified. She begins to swim out anyway, but her arms and legs aren't working properly. They've turned to lead, and she has to turn back. It's then she sees her mother running toward her at an all-out sprint. Minnow turns to look for her father, weeping and unable to breathe.

"What happened?" Layla yells, wild-eyed.

Words will not come, so Minnow just stands there shivering. Her mom begins screaming and at some point Minnow tries to swim out again, but her mother drags her back. Takes her to the house and calls 911.

Her mother bends down so they're eye to eye, both hands digging into her shoulders. "You have to tell me. What were you doing out there?"

All hollowed out, Minnow still has no voice.

"Why would you take the kayak?"

Minnow musters, "I didn't."

"Don't lie to me."

"I'm not."

Layla shakes her hard and Minnow squeezes her eyes shut and retreats into that underwater cavern in her mind. The place she goes when her parents fight or when others tease her or she just wants to be alone with her imagination. The place she buries her hurts and wishes and secrets.

A bird screech somewhere above drew her out of the daydream.

Above, a handful of *'iwa* birds circled, swooping and diving and hunting for fish. Dark feathered crosses in the sky. Same as the sharks, maybe they came for the chopped-up fish parts or whatever else the chummers were throwing into the ocean. Great frigate birds couldn't swim or submerge themselves, so they were known as the scavengers of the sea.

Hō'ailona.

Even with the thick cloud cover, she could feel herself burning, so she put on Woody's straw hat and wrapped a towel around herself. Then she sunk down and wept. All this time, every single moment of her life, she'd been shouldering the burden of her father's death and her mother's fury. Her pain and sorrow and eventual crumbling into oblivion.

All your fault.

You should have listened to me.

Why, Minnow, why?

But no. It was all a bitter misunderstanding. Minnow had been rolling around in the shore break, not out paddling around in the kayak as her mother had believed. Bruce must have been yelling for Minnow to get it, but she couldn't hear what he was saying against the roar of the waves, so when he came down to the beach, the kayak had already been swept out. It was not Minnow he was going out to rescue; it was his trusty kayak. He would have been swimming frantically to reach it before it was lost for good. The shark hit him on the way out. One bite.

But one bite was often all it took.

A light ruffle of a breeze began to blow in from the south, rocking the boat from side to side, but she barely noticed. It felt like her skin had just been ripped off, exposing every nerve to the elements of nature and time.

"I'm sorry, Papa. I wish I had heard you," she said aloud.

One weight had lifted, ever so slightly, but another had flattened her. The sharks had always been there, circling, and she needed a way to keep them alive. Whatever the cost.

From the journal of Minnow Gray

February 8, 1990

The Vivid Dancer. *My father told me they were fairies, and I believed him. I remember having this mini-obsession with them. And at night on Catalina I would sit by my window once the lights were out and watch for their tiny bodies to circle the moon. To a young girl their iridescent blue color and finely veined wings matched perfectly with what I thought a fairy should be. Later, in school, I learned that they were damselflies. Similar to dragonflies, only daintier, and their wings fold back when at rest. Whenever I see one, I feel like my father is near.*

CHAPTER 30

The Note

***Koa**: brave, bold, fearless, valiant; bravery, courage*

When she returned, the property felt oddly quiet and empty without the Kaupiko brothers, like the soul of the house was missing. After a quick rinse, Minnow was about to enter the house when she noticed a piece of paper under a lava rock in front of the door. She bent down to pick it up, thinking maybe Woody had left it for her and she'd missed it earlier since she went out the other door. But it was not from Woody.

SHARK LADY

GO BACK TO CALIFORNIA

BEFORE SOMETING BAD HAPPENS

YOUR NOT WELCOME HERE

Luna and the recent memory of her father were immediately forgotten as a sharp wind hit her from behind. She read the paper again, noting the misspelled word. Had that been on purpose? What kind of nut job would leave a threatening note here on the doorstep at Hale Niuhi? Someone bold, obviously. She spun around, eyeing the bushes and rocky outcrops, keenly aware of her dive knife on the table with her mask and snorkel. Slowly, she walked over and grabbed it, taking the blade in the house with her. On the table was a small, shimmering dead fish. She leaned in closer to inspect it, thinking at first it was a reef fish.

"Oh . . . my gosh," she said, picking the little thing up by the tail to make sure it was what she thought it was.

A minnow, of all creepy things.

That someone would go to the trouble to find an actual *minnow* freaked her out. Did they even have them here in Hawai'i?

Chilled, she tossed the poor fish into the pond, then filled the kettle and set it on the stove. She wrapped herself in a blanket and lay on the bed with the phone, dialing Nalu's hotel room even though she knew he wouldn't be there. She was right. He and the scientist were probably en route to Hilo to see Lum. Minnow had declined the offer to join them. For a brief moment she contemplated calling the police but decided to consult with Woody first. No one answered at his main house either. She looked up Cliff in the phone book, but he wasn't listed. It figured.

Her mind began to run through possibilities of who might be behind this. Lum and Warren had pushed hard for the hunt, but they didn't have much skin in the game, did they? And the note felt personal. Sawyer and the open-water swim officials maybe. Both stood to lose a lot of money if nothing was done to appease the public. But she'd never gotten an unhinged vibe from Sawyer. She also thought of Stuart Callahan and his immense grief, and Angela and Zach, but their tragedies had already happened. Minnow being here would have no bearing on them. Maybe she'd inadvertently pissed off some local who just wanted her off their turf? Whatever the case, Minnow was not leaving.

When the tea was ready, she took her mug outside and sat on the lanai, watching the whitecaps form on the water. So much had happened in the past few days that it felt like she'd been here for months, years even.

The memory from earlier was still fresh in her mind, and she re-examined it from all angles. The kayak had been left on the beach by her father the previous evening, and when he ran into the water to get it, she hadn't been able to hear him. All she was guilty of was not noticing that the kayak had been swept out and not hearing him.

Two things beyond her control. Six-year-old Minnow moving through life believing that she had killed her father. It was going to take a while to undo the wound in her soul, but the awareness felt liberating. Because how could you heal from something you couldn't remember? The sweaty, heart-thumping nightmares, the isolation, the pushing away of men she thought she loved. All of it.

A loud bang came from somewhere behind the house, and she startled. It sounded like a door slamming or something big falling. She peered around the house to the shed out back, but that door was locked. A gunshot? Jumpy and skittish from the note, she grabbed the machete that Cliff had been using and circled the house. The wind now whipped in a frenzy and she had to pull the hair out of her eyes to see anything. She wished Woody had stayed.

On the other side of the house, she discovered one of the wooden boards that covered the windows when no one was there had fallen against the siding. Relieved, she went back inside and pulled it up with the rope, securing it more tightly this time. Suddenly a thought came to her: There was no one around to hear her if she screamed. She tried to tell herself she was just being paranoid, but it was hard to ignore the warning, especially with the dead minnow.

Nalu called ten minutes later from a pay phone to tell her that their drive to Hilo to see Lum had been a waste of time, and he and Chip, the other scientist, were going to grab some food and head back to the hotel.

"I don't know what Chip was thinking, but he was adamant that Lum might listen to him over you, since he grew up on Maui. A braddah-braddah kind of thing."

"What you really mean is because he's a man?"

He paused awhile. "Maybe. Yeah, probably."

She was about to tell him about the note but decided not to. If he knew, he'd insist on coming over and bringing Chip, and she wanted to be alone. *Needed* to be alone. They agreed to meet at five in the morning at the house and hung up.

Not really hungry, Minnow took a Sierra Nevada from the fridge, snagged a half-full bag of Fritos and scrambled out to the rocks where Cliff had been sitting. Wind blasted in off the ocean, but she'd tied her hair in a tight knot at the base of her neck and she gripped the bag of chips as though it were a lifeline. Within minutes a thin layer of salt covered her whole body. She felt like she should be doing something, anything, to put off the shark hunt, but no one would be out there in this weather. Tomorrow was her last hope.

Here at the far end of the wild Pacific Ocean, she watched the clouds fade from gunmetal to black. She finished the beer and the chips and thought about her parents and how much she still loved them all these years later. That love had a life of its own—this astonishing, full-bodied love that ran in her veins. But maybe that was the way of real love: It never left you, not even in death. Especially in death.

When her clothes became soaked from the salt spray and she realized she was shivering, she fumbled back to the house in the near-dark. She had just reached the lanai when she swore she could hear the sound of shoes crunching on lava rock. She stood still and listened.

Crunch. Crunch. Crunch.

Instinctively, she crouched low and ran toward the house, going straight for the machete. It felt heavy and dangerous in her hand, and she wasn't sure she could actually use it on a person. But if she had to, she would. Back against the wall, she waited.

Crunch.

Whoever it was stopped. Minnow held her breath.

"Hello?"

The voice was nearly stolen by the wind. She remained where she was, breathing in time with her heart.

"Minnow?"

Louder this time. That voice, she knew it well.

What the hell was Luke Greenwood doing here?

She had no desire to see him, but his presence was better than some hired thug to send her off with her tail between her legs, or worse. Maybe if she stayed where she was, he would just turn around and leave. She closed her eyes and willed him away.

"Ah, come on. I know you're here, I saw you on the rock," he said, then added, "I got here a while ago. I was just trying to work up the nerve to talk to you."

She grabbed the lantern from the table and stepped around to the front, where he stood. Orange light spilled across his face and he offered up a half smile.

"What do you want?" she asked.

"Sorry to intrude on you, but we need to talk," he said.

"About what?"

The question seemed to throw him. "About the sharks. And us. Me. There are things I have to tell you that I should have just come out with on day one."

"The sharks I want to hear about, but there is no *us*."

He bit his lip. "Yeah, I thought you might say something like that. But hear me out at least, please. I need to get this off my chest."

Standing there in surf shorts and a long-sleeved aloha shirt with boots on, he looked ridiculous. But there was a new vulnerability to him. The wind tossed his hair around like dried grass.

"Fine, tell me," she said.

"Can we go inside?"

Having Luke in the house again was probably not a good idea, but she was cold, so she turned and walked in. He followed. She sat at the table and offered him nothing, motioning to the chair across from her. She flicked on the lantern.

His eyes bore into her as he sank down. "Minnow," was all he said.

"Yes?"

"You have no idea how badly I've screwed things up."

"Do I really need to know?"

"I think you do."

"Then I want to hear it all. No more of this vague bullshit. Promise?"

He reached out and pulled the large, smooth cowrie toward him and his hand covered it. "It's a long story, so bear with me."

Being in such close proximity to him threw her equilibrium off and she didn't say anything.

"I studied marine biology in grad school. Orcas, to be specific. And later I worked with a team in the San Juan Islands for eight years studying and documenting their migration patterns. I loved them as much as you love your sharks. But then there was an accident."

He paused and wiped his eye and Minnow wasn't sure if there was a bug in there or he was crying.

"We were out on a rough day," he continued, "like this, only way wilder and bitter cold. I was driving and there were three of us. Me, my research partner Sandra and an intern who wasn't any good in the boat. He was always distracted and hanging over the edge and generally unaware of his surroundings, no matter how often you tried to teach him. I didn't want him with us, but Sandra was his adviser and thought he could learn. We were looking for a pod of orca and Jimmy must have seen something, because he ran to the rail, yelled something, and as the boat slammed into a wave he went overboard. It all happened so fast, and I cut the engine, but it was too late. Sandra jumped in and we pulled him into the boat, but his neck had been cut open. He was already dead."

A fever dream. "Devastating. I'm so sorry."

He shook his head. "Devastating doesn't even describe it. And it was my fault. I knew the kid was a liability and I let him on the boat. Nice guy. Smart. But super impulsive. He would get so excited whenever we saw anything that you never knew what he might do. I should have listened to my gut, but I didn't. You want to know why?"

She wasn't sure she did, but he continued.

"Because I had a thing for Sandra and I let it cloud my judgment. Hell, she was married. I don't know what I was thinking. But I knew she wasn't happy and I had this fantasy that maybe she would leave him for me."

He let out a breath and eyed her almost apologetically.

"It still doesn't sound like your fault," she said.

"Tell that to Jimmy's parents. They sued the university and me personally, and I lost my job and had to sell my house to pay for legal fees. Of course I deserved it, but no one in the Pacific Northwest would hire me, and everywhere I went I got stares and whispers. His dad was the high school football coach and everyone loved him. Even though the judge ruled in my favor." His hand on the cowrie was shaking. "Do you know what it's like to have someone die because of you?"

"I do," she whispered.

His eyes searched hers for more. Minnow met his stare but did not give him anything. She was still wondering where all of this was heading.

"It will live in me forever. I accept that, but it's been rough as hell. Bad enough that I sold everything and came over here hoping for a fresh start. Leaving my orca pods was probably the hardest thing I've ever done, but I knew I had to get out of there or I might not survive. Sawyer and I were friends from high school and he offered me a room here while I tried to figure shit out—it's their quiet season, so there were extra bungalows."

As he spoke the wind died down and the night turned quiet. He hugged himself as though cold, rubbing his arms and shivering.

"How long ago did this happen?" she asked.

"Last year."

Although their situations had been drastically different, she ached for him. That kind of guilt would gnaw on your bones until they were bare and white.

"I'm sorry that you had to go through this, but how does this relate to the sharks?"

"A couple months after I got here, Stuart Callahan died—talk about heartbreak. Then Hank disappeared. Two mornings later, I was approached by a guy at the Saltwater Bar who asked if I wanted to take a ride on the boat anchored in the bay, maybe see some whales or dolphins. It seemed a little odd, but the boat was nice and I figured, what the hell. I'd bought a fourteen-foot Whaler from the dark ages that barely ran, so I was drooling over the Robalo. He let me drive it, then asked if I would be open to making a deal."

Oh, hell no!

"Said if I would be willing to land any big sharks in the area, the boat would be mine."

Minnow stood up and backed away. "What the fuck, Luke? How could you?"

His face turned crimson. "He also offered an extra ten grand for any shark over fifteen feet. And fifteen grand for a white shark. I had just lost everything, Minnow, and this would have given me the boost I needed. I was desperate."

Shame and guilt were smeared all over his face.

"So you said yes?"

He nodded.

Minnow wanted him out and away from her. "Just leave now. I've heard enough. This is disgusting, horrendous. You study sea creatures, for fuck sake. You're supposed to protect them!"

He stood but didn't move. "Obviously I was conflicted, but I convinced myself that it would be worth it."

"Go!" she yelled, pointing.

"Please, I need to finish."

She glared at him but didn't say anything.

He continued. "As soon as I got out there in the water with all the fishing gear, ready to lay lines and troll, I realized I may not be able to go through with it. I made up excuses to buy myself time, but I wanted that boat and I was carrying on this monumental battle in my mind about pulling in one big shark so I could keep it.

"When the guy checked in with me, I lied. I told him I had caught two big ones but they both cut the line and got away. By then I'd found out he was ex–Special Forces, and he was pretty intimidating. I started hating myself again and I knew if I actually did catch a shark, I'd have sold my soul." He looked like someone had let all the air out of him. His eyes watered. "Then you showed up."

All this talk of killing sharks caused a cramp in her side and she had to sit back down, this time on the edge of a bed. "So you never got one?"

"Not one."

Minnow flashed back on those first encounters with him. The gold reels and the smell of baitfish. The odd hours. That sense that something weird was going on with him. Suddenly she needed to know who was behind this.

"Who hired you, Luke?"

He stiffened slightly. "That's the thing. The guy who took me out on the boat was just the middle man. His name was Bob, but I think he was working for Callahan. Who else around here has that kind of money?"

It didn't add up. "Sam Callahan?"

"Yeah."

"Why wouldn't he just ask you himself?"

"I'm guessing he was worried about upsetting the Hawaiians. From what I hear, down at Koholā there's a cultural practitioner who educates all the billionaires about protocol and what to do and what not to do. Killing the family guardians is not good PR. I'm sure you know from Woody that a lot of the locals are not happy about a hunt along this coastline. Also, Bob told me in no uncertain terms to keep this whole thing quiet."

She tried to make sense of this bizarre new turn. "So why are you telling me?"

"Because I walked away."

"What about the boat?"

"It's gone. I told Bob I was out."

Hope nudged at her. "How did he react?"

"Didn't seem too bothered since a whole fleet is going out tomorrow."

She glanced over at the note sitting by the telephone just as a gecko on the outside of the screen caught a moth. The moth was bigger than its mouth, but the lizard hung on dearly and soon swallowed the whole thing. Eat or be eaten—one of nature's most brutal truths.

She went over, lifted the note and handed it to him. "When I got back today, this was on the doorstep."

Luke held it up to the light and read. "What the—"

"Your man Bob?"

"He's not my man, but I don't know. Bob knows how to spell. Did you tell anyone about this?"

"Not yet. It's been a crazy afternoon."

His eyes flickered. "Where are your two brother friends?"

"They went home for the night. But honestly, I'm having a hard time imagining Sam Callahan as the guy behind this. When I spoke to him, he seemed like such a reasonable guy. Even in his devastation, he was quite matter-of-fact."

"I looked into the guy. People say he can be ruthless. It's why he's made so much money. In this case that shark took what was most important from him."

"That still doesn't mean he hired you. And if he did, how would you find out?"

"I think Sawyer might know. I went to find him this morning, but I guess he was on Maui for the day."

"Would he tell you if he did?"

"Maybe. I got a call from the front desk this morning saying I had to move out today." He snapped his fingers. "Just like that. No warning. I had kind of wondered about being able to stay here this long. When I first came, Sawyer had told me I could stay for a week or two max. And then they moved me to a nicer hut and said I could be there as long as I needed. Same time Bob approached me."

"Interesting."

"What Callahan did was shady and self-serving, even if not quite illegal."

Minnow thought back to her meeting with Sam and the way he so needed to be the expert. The one in charge. She still wasn't convinced, but who knew? And then another idea came to her. "If he was paying you, I wonder if he was paying anyone else? *That* would be illegal."

"I've thought about that."

"Woody and Cliff brought it up too."

Luke leaned back and stretched his arms out, wide as albatross wings, and Minnow felt for him. Coming here to the house had taken guts after how things had left off between them. There was so much new information to digest, her mind just wanted to shut down. Stare at the stars. Get in the water and swim away.

"It's never simple, is it? Life, I mean," she said in almost a whisper.

A small shake of his head. "Never. Never, ever."

"I thought I was coming out here to look into a few shark incidents and now everything I knew to be true has been turned upside down." She looked into his eyes and was hit with the feeling that he could see right through her. "There are things you don't know about me too."

Maybe now wasn't the best time to tell him, it was such long story, but she had this pressing need to share what had happened today, and Luke happened to be sitting here in front of her having just bared his soul.

"Go on, I want to hear everything," he said.

So she told him about Luna and about Wally, and how everything with Wally still haunted her. Luke was silent as she spoke and even wiped his eyes a few times. When she finished, he stood up and came around the table, reaching a hand out.

"Come," he said, softly.

Minnow stood and he folded himself around her in a way that made her want to weep. Her cheek fell on his shoulder. Their closeness was electric, and static seemed to form wherever they touched. In all the years since her father died, she had never allowed herself to be so fully held, like this was exactly where she belonged—in time and space and heart. Like Luke was the door she needed to walk through to get to the other side. Or maybe he was the other side.

Out behind the house, a strange humming started up. Minnow cocked an ear, trying to understand what she was hearing.

Tiny wingbeats?

"Do you hear that?" she asked.

"Hear what?"

She grabbed him by the hand and pulled him out back. The clouds had all been swept away, and the sky was salted with stars. They moved toward the pond, carefully walking across the uneven ground. The sound grew louder. In the faint light from the lantern in her hand, they saw a cloud of shimmering red dragonflies—no, damselflies—hovering over the water, wings delicate as lace spun from spiderwebs. Hundreds of them, maybe more.

"What are they doing?" Luke asked.

"I don't know. I've never seen them swarm like this. I know that Hawai'i has several of its own species of damselflies, so maybe this is something they do?"

He looked at her and ran the side of his hand down her cheek. "Dear God, you're sexy."

"These guys are the sexy ones. Look how they shimmer."

His hand paused on her jawline and she leaned in, wanting more but afraid to admit it.

"Most people I know will never know the difference between a dragonfly and a damselfly. But you, you can hear them, can't you?" he said.

They were on the small wooden deck built over the corner of the pond and she sat down, dangling her legs in the water. The damselflies kept on buzzing, doing their damselfly thing, and Luke sat next to her, shoulder touching hers, thigh too. Coconut lotion lifted off him in waves.

"I do. I hear their wings the same way I hear the stars singing or the beating heart of a fish. Is that weird?" she asked.

His hand went to her thigh and rested there, big and warm. "Not weird. It's your special gift. I think we're all born with these kinds of abilities or intuitions, but most people shed them along the way when they're still too young to remember."

"It took me a while to realize that no one heard what I was hearing, and that not everyone loved sharks and sea creatures the same way I did."

"A real live mermaid."

"I like to think of myself more as a fish."

He laughed. "Of course you do. A fish that has led quite a life. To go through what you did and still have love in your heart, that says something about your resilience. Another gift."

"I did what any kid would do."

"No, you didn't."

She kicked her feet in the water, enjoying its coolness. "I had the sharks."

The damselflies were giving off their own light, if that were possible, and the surface of the pond glowed as red as a lava lake. It was beautiful, and eerie. They sat for a while in silence, Minnow wondering what was coming next. Because when insects swarmed or animals behaved oddly, it often portended some kind of impending disaster. She tried to tell herself it was only her imagination conjuring up some doomsday scenario.

But of course a disaster was coming. Tomorrow morning, bright and early.

Eventually they ended up back in the house, and she realized she didn't want Luke to leave. The note had shaken her up and the idea of being alone here all night was causing shortness of breath.

She worked up the nerve to ask him. "Would you stay here tonight? It just feels kind of scary knowing there's possibly someone who is ex–Special Forces out there somewhere. And if not him, then someone else."

"Trust me, I would have slept on that wall out front if I had to. I'm glad you asked."

"Thank you—"

"And don't worry, I'll sleep in my own bed."

He had nothing with him, though.

"Where's all your stuff?" she asked.

"In my truck back at the hotel. George said I could stay in an old coffee shed on his property in Hōlualoa for a while, so I'll probably take him up on that."

"Where's Hōlualoa?"

"Up the mountain, above Kona. It's gorgeous, like another world up there."

She motioned across the room. "Well, take your pick of beds. That one over there will leave you swaybacked, though, and the one by the door is completely lopsided. And that one is made out of bricks, but it may be your best bet."

He grinned and his smile sent shock waves through her. Minnow shook it off. They washed up and luckily for Luke there was a box full of extra toothbrushes. When he came out of the bathroom, he wasn't wearing a shirt. She was already lying in bed in nothing but a skimpy tank top and underwear. Any more clothes than that and she'd wake up in a pool of sweat. The lantern was next to her on a stool that doubled as a bedside table. She watched him flip back the quilt and ease in between the sheets, lying on his back with his hands folded behind his head.

He stared up at the ceiling. "So what's our plan for tomorrow morning?"

"*Our* plan?"

"I'm a hundred percent Team Shark, Minnow. Whatever you tell me to do, I'll do."

"You don't have—"

He cut her off. "I need to do this for my own peace of mind. I still kind of hate myself for what I thought I was capable of doing, all in the name of getting my feet back on the ground." He rolled onto his side and faced her, one bed between them. "Plus, I want to make it up to you."

Whatever was happening here, she couldn't fight it.

Right then, the phone rang. Minnow had no choice but to climb out of bed in her undies and sheer top and get it. "Kaupiko's," she said.

"It's me, Woody. Sorry to call so late, but I wanted to tell you not to wait for me in the morning. Just drive the boat to Honokohau and get there before sunup. Bring Nalu with you, and also get ahold of Josh Brown and tell him to get down there, crack of dawn."

"What's happening?"

"Trust me on this. You'll see."

She wanted to ask more, but he'd already hung up.

When she looked over at Luke, he was sitting up. "Everything okay?"

She told him.

"These guys are obviously going to protest. I just hope it doesn't get out of hand," he said.

"I would hate for it to backfire. Cliff has a reputation as being kind of a wild card, but I like him. He's connected."

She then called the resort and left a message at the front desk for Josh, saying it was urgent.

When she walked back to her bed, Luke's eyes followed her every move. They both lay down again and this time she flicked off the lantern. Woody's call had sobered her and she lay there in the dark hoping she'd be able to sleep. The humming of the damselflies had stopped, but she could hear the soft sounds of Luke breathing and the crinkling of starched sheets. Her mind revisited the day's events, especially the encounter with Luna, while at the same time being hyperaware of Luke's presence in the room.

"Good night," she finally said.

"Sweet dreams."

Twenty minutes later, she could tell he was still awake by the way he kept flipping from side to side. Would it be so bad to crawl into bed with him and nestle her head in the crook of his neck?

"Minnow?" he whispered.

"Yes?"

"I can't sleep."

"Me neither."

Without another thought—because sometimes thinking really got in the way of living—she went to his bed and lay down facing him, an inch or two away. He kissed her lightly on the nose and pressed his forehead to hers.

"Turn around," he said, rolling her so her back was to him.

He wrapped an arm around her and pulled her into him. Every surface of their bodies touched and she felt her whole being relax.

"There, better. Now maybe we can sleep," he said, holding on to her as though he needed this as much as she did.

Something deep and unshakable passed between them. Minnow drifted off within minutes, sure of only one thing: Tomorrow would test her beyond measure.

From the journal of Minnow Gray

San Francisco, August 24, 1995

This guy on the airplane today told me, "I know your type. You're one of those outspoken hippies who puts animals and plants ahead of humans and then you think you're so much more enlightened than everyone else."

I was rendered mute by his rudeness and then finally said, "You don't know the first thing about me."

CHAPTER 31

The Reckoning

***Pono**: goodness, uprightness, morality, true condition or nature, virtuous, fair*

They left in darkness. Minnow had told Nalu to meet her at the harbor—it would be easier that way. Luke drove the boat and they were hauling ass with Minnow holding on tight. After a while the sky lightened in the east, pale blue slowly spreading until she could just make out the coastline not too far inside of them. All lava. Then two white sand beaches. Five minutes later, they passed the airport as a jet airplane took off above them, steeply ascending and then banking off to the right.

Luke looked at his watch. "We should be there in fifteen minutes or so." There was no chop on the water and they'd been flying along without a hitch.

Minnow was ready for anything yet had no idea what to expect. She noticed breaths were becoming harder to draw in. She tried to reassure herself that she was okay, that everything would be fine. A ways on, she had to sit down on the cooler to try to catch a breath.

"Are you sure you're okay?" Luke asked, into the wind.

"Just nervous."

So nervous that a pain in her stomach started up and she had to lean forward to try to ease the burning.

"I have a feeling these guys know what they're doing," he said.

"I sure hope so."

Maybe she ought to ask him to turn around. This was too much for her to take. But that would mean giving in, and she couldn't do it.

A few minutes later. "Almost there now."

Minnow forced herself to sit up.

"I'm ready," she said, although she felt anything but.

Get it together.

The sun was still behind Hualālai, but they could see the lay of the land now, passing another long beach with a thatched A-frame hut at the end of it. The harbor buoys came into sight, but there were no other boats in the water. Odd for such a busy harbor. When Luke turned around the red buoy and headed into the boulder-lined harbor mouth, Minnow saw that a crowd had gathered on the wall. Several flags hung flat in the still of the morning. Below the people, boats were lined up side to side across the entire entrance.

"What the—" Luke said.

A surge of adrenaline ran through her. "Oh my God! They're blocking the harbor."

Luke put the boat in neutral, and they floated there, unsure what to do. Then someone from the wall whistled and waved his arms and pointed at Minnow and Luke. He was trying to gain the attention of one of the boat drivers. That ratty coconut frond hat was hard to miss.

"It's Woody," she said.

The boat in the middle backed up, and a guy standing in the bow of the boat next to it yelled, "Hooey. You. In here." He motioned for them to slip through the space between.

The shortness of breath and pain in her midsection faded. "Go. They're letting us through," she said.

Luke was already maneuvering them in. They squeaked into the harbor and up to an open spot where boats rinsed. Woody was standing on the edge and he offered Minnow a hand.

"Is this your doing?" she asked.

"Cliff."

"Where is he?"

Woody nodded toward a row of trucks over by the boat ramp. This time she could see that the flags were Hawaiian but upside down.

"He's over there talking to the news. And the cops."

The harbor was not a big one as far as harbors went, but with all the fishing tours in Kona, there were still a lot of charter boats whose captains were probably pissed off right now.

"Are they letting anyone out into the ocean?"

"Just a couple of the regulars who go down south. Bruddahs we trust. Come."

As they made their way to the trucks, Minnow couldn't help but smile inside. This was exactly the thing they needed. Grassroots all the way. A middle finger to Lum and his shitty decision-making.

Newspeople had crowded around the trucks and a chaos of boats on trailers had collected in a wide asphalt parking area. Every now and then someone honked or yelled. But these trucks were big and so were the men who owned them. Some stood in their beds, others were on the ground being interviewed or looking intimidating. Heat swelled in the morning air and Minnow felt lightheaded amid it all. She counted five cop cars, but the cops didn't seem to be doing much other than standing around talking. As though this kind of thing was routine.

Up ahead Cliff was talking with Josh Brown and the cameraman. His silver-streaked hair flowed halfway down his back and he wore a piece of fabric wrapped around him and tied on his shoulder. He held a big conch shell in his hand. When he saw Minnow, he raised his chin slightly in acknowledgment. Josh had his back to her and he didn't turn, so she and Woody stopped behind him, eavesdropping.

Cliff spoke softly but with conviction. ". . . On this whole coastline, we only have a handful of beaches and hotels. If you do the math, there are so few people utilizing these waters that it makes no sense to go out there and start raping the ocean. This place belongs to the sharks, not the people."

Woody leaned over and whispered, "He can talk *haole* when he wants to."

"What about the other boat ramps up the coast? Are you folks blocking them too?" Josh asked.

"Yep."

"How long do you plan on being here?"

"As long as we need to be."

Minnow wanted to run up and hug him. The metallic taste of blood in her mouth was fading and she felt stronger and more alert. Boundless, almost.

"I assume you realize you are breaking the law. Are you willing to go to jail for this?" Josh asked.

"Our *'aumakua* protect us, we protect them. So yes, if that's what it comes to. You know, I don't think the mayor thought this through. Even with all the research stacked against a hunt, he goes ahead and calls one anyway. All just to cover his *okole.*" Cliff paused and looked up at the mountain, his profile backlit by the sun. "That is not *pono*—not right."

Josh seemed to sense someone behind him and he turned around. When he saw Minnow, his eyebrows went up. "Speaking of research, what do you think of all this, Dr. Gray?"

"I support the people who have lived here longest. They are the ones we need to listen to. More than research and more than me or any other scientist. They have hundreds of years of experience in these waters. To be honest, these guys are my heroes."

She smiled at Cliff and he winked; then she turned and walked away. This was no longer her story and she wanted no part of the spotlight. It was bigger and older and deeper. The story of a people keeping watch over their own.

Woody came with her and she headed toward Luke, who was waiting by the Whaler. Along the way, they passed several people holding signs that said *Shark Mana* and *Their Water, Not Ours*.

"You must be proud of Cliff for orchestrating such a huge deal," she said.

"One thing about my brother, he's all or nothing. Neither of us slept a wink last night. I don't know how long we can keep this up, but I'm hoping those bruddahs in power are paying attention."

"I'm sure they are."

On the boat ride over, Minnow had been thinking about how to catch the chummers in the act. An idea had dropped into her head in the middle of the night, waking her with a start. Now she told Woody.

"I'm there. I'll tell Cliff and we'll bring some friends," he said with a nod.

Someone grabbed her shoulder from behind and she spun. "Nalu! You made it."

The brightest smile spread across his face. "This is rad. I had no idea."

"Neither did I."

It was the best kind of surprise.

A wavy-haired man with wire-rim glasses stood next to him and held out a hand. "Dr. Gray, I'm Chip Young. I'm an admirer of your work."

Minnow had heard of him too. "I wish you could have come sooner, but I'm glad you made it."

He nodded. "Nalu's filled me in and it sounds like you've made a valiant effort. I applaud you on that. My whole department does," he said.

"There's still plenty of work to be done, so I hope you're ready for a long day—and an even longer night," she said.

His mouth lifted on one side. "Absolutely."

At four the following morning, three boats left from Hale Niuhi under the cover of darkness. Minnow reasoned that whoever was doing the chumming must have been doing it at night. And all those lights she'd seen in the early morning hours, maybe it had been them. Luke, Nalu and Minnow rode in the Whaler, while Woody and two brothers from Hawi named Dean and Liloa took the *Midnight Blue,* a yellow fishing boat. Cliff, Chip Young and an ex-cop named Kamaki were in a twenty-six-foot Zodiac with more horsepower than a jet airliner.

They'd all duct-taped their running lights so they'd be invisible, and they headed north toward Pāpapa. Each of the boat drivers wore different color glow sticks around their wrists—green, purple, pink—so they could keep track of one another. They also knew the coordinates of their destination. Minnow and Chip both had cameras and Kamaki packed a pistol and his old badge. No one needed to know he was retired. The plan was to float around in the dark just beyond the buoy and wait.

For most of the way out, Minnow imagined Luna swimming in the deep beneath them, listening for engine sounds and homing in. Sharks had good hearing and sensed vibration from a long way off, and Luna and others had obviously been lured in and were now programmed. She didn't like that word in use with animals, but it was accurate for what was going on here.

Once they hit the coordinates, they drove slowly out to sea for a couple of minutes, then cut their motors. The outline of land and mountains stood dark against the starry sky. There were sprinkles of lights here and there, but it was only four thirty, so much of the world still slept. Minnow loved the silence and listened for anything large passing under them but heard only the lap of water on fiberglass.

This could all be for nothing—she knew that, and she tried not to get her hopes up. One of her defense mechanisms. *If you prepare for the bad, you'll never be disappointed.* Only it didn't work that way. Instead, it made unwanted outcomes live in her head for much longer than they needed to.

"I'm scared," she whispered to Luke.

He reached out and fumbled for her hand. "Imagine what you want, not what you don't want. It's my new mantra."

They were sitting on the bow and Nalu pointed out constellations the Hawaiians used for celestial navigation. Some were the same as the ones Minnow knew—the Pleiades were called *Makali'i* and the Big Dipper was known as *Na Hiku*, for the seven stars that made it up.

"When the Makali'i rises in the east, it's the start of the Hawaiian new year," he told them.

A few minutes later, she heard a faint buzzing and her whole body lit up.

"A boat," she said, loud enough for the others to hear.

No lights were visible yet and the guys were all mumbling excitedly.

"Where?" someone called out.

"Near the shore."

They all went silent again, and soon running lights appeared in the direction of Pāpapa.

Luke squeezed her hand. "It's them."

"Gotta be," Nalu added.

They all sat quietly as Minnow counted her breaths, trying to slow them down. She could smell the boat as it drew near. Fish and blood and rankness. It made her head swim. When the Radon got up to the buoy, a bright light flashed on. The shark cage sat precariously on the back. Minnow shrunk back, sure that if the people on the boat looked their way, they'd see them. But they were all business. Two men and a woman.

The driver began shouting orders and they lowered the cage into the water. The woman then lay on the deck with a big pole and looped a rope around what must have been the buoy. The guy next to her slid into the water briefly, holding a spear. All of them oblivious to what surrounded them. When the guy got back in the boat, he and the woman started dumping out buckets into the ocean.

"Game on," Nalu said quietly.

Behind them Minnow heard the birdcall, and off to the side another. The signal. This moment was everything she had come here for, and a feeling of love for the guys with her welled up. In an instant all three boats started their motors and turned on the blue lights Kamaki had given them. Minnow's job was to tear the duct tape off the running lights, which she did with lightning speed. Cliff pointed a strobe light into the driver's eyes.

"Stay where you are," Kamaki said through a bullhorn.

The guy and girl whipped the buckets down, and the driver held an arm over his eyes and ducked away from the helm.

"Chumming within three miles from shore is illegal. You are breaking the law," Kamaki shouted.

The boats were closing in now, and Minnow caught sight of Cliff standing up on the bow holding a three-prong spear. He looked like a fierce warrior with an aura of ancient grace. She then glanced at the boat driver of the Radon and saw that he was starting up the boat again.

"They're going to make a run for it," she said to Luke.

"I'd love to see 'em try."

They were within earshot now and Cliff yelled, "Turn off your engine. We have you surrounded and I promise, brah, you don't want to mess with us."

The driver paused and Minnow could see the gears of his mind churning, but he stepped away from the helm and the engine sputtered. All three of them were lined up, squinting, unsure where to look and wondering who their adversaries were. No one had said *police,* but the blue lights were suggestive.

Nalu bounced up and down, excited. "Red-fucking-handed."

Cliff's and Woody's boats pulled up alongside the Radon and Nalu pulled in front of the bow a little ways off.

"What, you gonna arrest us? I want to see your badges," the driver said.

Kamaki held up a badge, but never did he touch the gun in his holster.

"So, what, you chumming and doing shark dives? Bringing tourists out?" Cliff said.

"So what? We're not bothering anyone. This is boonies, man."

Beer-bellied and a lot older than the other two, he seemed to be the ringleader. His pale, blotchy skin had seen better days.

"Tell that to the three people who were attacked by a shark recently just down the coast. You've got blood on your hands. All of you," Woody said in a cutting voice.

While the brothers and Kamaki were busy with that, Minnow began snapping photos, zeroing in on the culprits' faces, the boat name, and the fish parts and blood in the water. Luke held the light for her since sunrise was still a long ways off.

"And now, because of your stupidity, every shark along this coast is in danger. All those sharks that you feed and your customers swim with will be brutally pulled out of the water and killed. You ever stop to think about that?" Cliff said.

Of course not every shark would be caught, but even one was too many.

The three of them just stood there, blank-faced, mute.

Luke nudged Minnow gently. "Ten o'clock. Fin."

Minnow looked out into the darkness behind the boat and saw a tall fin making a smooth arc through the water. It was too dark to tell what kind it was, but whatever it was, it was very large. *Leave,* Minnow called out in her mind.

Cliff pounded the dull side of his spear onto the boat next to him. "This is how it's going to go from here on. We take your cage and you will never, ever chum in these waters again. Our eyes are everywhere, on land and in the water. If you disrespect the *'āina* again, we will not be so forgiving. Consider this fair warning."

Kamaki pointed at the driver. "You, what's your name?"

"Alex."

"Last name."

He muttered something under his breath, then said, "Dickerson."

Minnow burned their names into memory.

Kamaki, who had been holding on to the side of their boat, let go. "We have photos, and DLWA will be paying you a visit. Now get out of here."

Alex gave him a smug look. "Go ahead."

"Not just DLWA, but the Feds too."

This time Alex glanced at the girl, and Minnow saw real fear in their eyes. So they weren't scared of the DLWA, but they were of the Feds. It gave Minnow pause. Of course Kamaki was bluffing, but they didn't know that.

"Brah, that cage was expensive. You can't take it," Alex said.

"We can and we will."

Cliff pointed to shore. "The harm you have caused is irreversible. Now go."

Alex looked like he was dying to say something more, but Woody and Dean and Liloa had closed in on them and stood in solidarity with Cliff. Alex started the motor and sped off toward Pāpapa Bay.

The three boats floated for a while, no one saying anything. Luke found Minnow's hand and squeezed.

"Sometimes you can't undo the wrongs of others, but I'd say this is a darn good start," he said.

Minnow squeezed back, thankful to no longer feel alone in this. She'd found her tribe in the last place she would have expected. But that was life wasn't it? One minute you were swimming alone, the next you had a big, beautiful shiver of sharks alongside you.

From the journal of Minnow Gray

February 1, 1998

Grief can take many forms, one of them being rage.

CHAPTER 32

The Bad Guys

***Pono'ole**: unjust, unrighteous, dishonest, unprincipled*

The harbor blockade lasted three days, giving Minnow and Woody and Chip enough time to give the police and Judge Carlsmith their photos and written testimony. They also went to the media so that the whole world knew what had been going on—that sharks were being lured into the area by illegal chumming of nearshore waters. Woody also wanted to make sure the story couldn't be swept under the rug by a questionable administration.

Luke met with Josh Brown to tell his story about being hired by an anonymous ex-military guy to bring in as many big sharks as he could. And then there was Minnow's threatening note. Brown, true to his investigative journalist nature, smelled a story and looked into all involved. It turned out Sam Callahan *had* hired Bob to hire Luke, but they hadn't been behind the note. That was someone working with Alex and the shark tours. Jess, the woman on board, had spilled in order to save herself from jail time, telling how their operation was conducting several shark dives throughout the day, some in the cage and some not, and they were chumming each time they went out. Money had been pouring in, and the only way they'd been able to keep doing it was paying off Warren, who in turn was giving a cut to Lum. No wonder they needed this whole thing over with. Within days the story made headlines and the shark hunt was overshadowed by the scandal.

Suddenly the sharks were no longer the bad guys.

From the journal of Minnow Gray

July 29, 1993

The two-chambered heart of a white shark is S-shaped and proportionately slightly smaller than a human's. The interesting thing about them, though, is that unlike most fish and even other sharks, their exceptionally muscular ventricle wall allows them to operate like a fine-tuned athlete, almost mammalian in nature. Their heart rate is believed to be somewhere in the neighborhood of eight to twelve beats per minute. I know because when I quiet my mind, I can hear that slow and insistent thump.

CHAPTER 33

The Race

***Laulima**: cooperation, joint action;*
group of people working together;
literally, "many hands"

Five days later

Minnow stood on the far end of the beach in front of the Kiawe, staring out at the satin blue water. Men in Speedos and women in one-piece suits with goggles on their heads had begun to trickle down steadily, as the pre-race meeting neared. She had walked down early from Hale Niuhi with the rising sun. Woody would be escorting the race with his friend, and had offered to drop her off, but these early mornings were magic and her favorite time of day here. A few last stars were out and she listened for their song.

Behind her, the kiawe trees gave off an earthy, nutty smell that would forever remind her of this trip. She inhaled deeply as she stretched her shoulders, back and hamstrings. Open-water swim races had never been her thing, but she was looking forward to just being out there in the water and swimming with no other purpose than to enjoy the ocean and finish the race. Not that she was under any illusions of doing well, but the world was watching her, and she had to show them that she was not afraid. Especially now.

"Excuse me, miss," said a girl, maybe around eighteen. "Are you that shark expert?"

The question caught her off guard and part of her wanted to say no, but others would be bound to recognize her and she was not in this for herself.

"Yes, I'm Dr. Gray."

The girl had dark hair pulled tight in a bun and her skin was a beautiful golden brown. She looked strong in the way of a swimmer or surfer. "I just wanted to thank you for taking a stand for the ocean," she said, looking down at the sand as if too shy to meet Minnow's eyes. "I want to be a marine biologist and study sharks someday too."

Minnow melted. "What's your name?"

"Mahina. Hina, for short."

Hearing her name was like a sucker punch.

"Well, Hina, we definitely could use more women like you in the field, so please look me up if you need anything. I would be more than happy to help."

"Really?"

"A hundred percent."

"Good luck in the race," Hina said, standing a little taller now.

"You too. I'm just in it to sightsee and prove to everyone that shark bites are flukes, not the norm."

"The crowd seems thinner than last year, though. That's a bummer."

"Not surprising. How did you do in the swim last year?" Minnow asked.

Hina shrugged and smiled. "I came in first."

Minnow gasped. "First in the whole thing?"

She nodded.

"You are a legend, Hina. Now I'm the one who's impressed. I'll wave when you pass me on your way back," Minnow said.

"Insider tip—pay close attention to the current and move in or out, depending."

"Thank you."

Hina went off toward the crowd, and Minnow spotted Luke milling about, wearing a Speedo himself. He had not seen her yet and he was clearly searching for someone. She watched him, feeling like the luckiest girl in the world that it was probably her he was looking for. The moment their eyes met, he smiled. Minnow waved and he came over, leaning down and giving her a long, slow kiss. She held on to his shoulders and let her mouth linger on his lightly sugared lips.

"You've been eating malasadas again, haven't you?" she asked once they pulled apart.

He wiped his chin. "That obvious, huh?"

"Not the best pre-race meal."

"I'm addicted, what can I say?"

"How many?"

"Just one."

"Liar."

He laughed. "Okay, three."

Luke glanced beyond her and she turned to see a boat approaching. It was Woody and his captain friend Jay, but there were two other men aboard who looked a lot like Nalu and Cliff. Twenty feet off the beach, the two jumped into the water and swam ashore.

"What are you guys doing here?" Minnow asked when they walked up, dripping wet, Nalu also in a Speedo.

"Solidarity," Cliff said.

"We figured we may as well join you in the race," Nalu said with a shake of his hair.

"Been a while since I done a swim this long, but Woody said he'd rescue me if I need rescuing. Just don't expect me to wear those bikini bottoms. Ever," Cliff said, nodding toward Luke and Nalu.

She couldn't help but laugh. "Wear whatever you want. I'm just glad you're both here."

"And I fed Hina on the way here, so we're good to go," he said in all seriousness.

"Perfect."

There was nothing to worry about.

Even with fewer entrants than in past years, the beach ended up rock to rock full of people. Everyone had a large number written in black grease on the side of their thigh, and Minnow was number seventy-seven. Photographers had lined up on the rocky bluff, setting up their large telephoto cameras. Minnow heard the word *shark* floating around a few times and shook her head. These guys were probably hoping someone would get bit, sending ratings through the roof.

As she struggled to tuck her hair into her swim cap—something she hardly wore—she felt a tug on her arm. A tall, pale woman with short blonde hair, a Panama hat and aviators stood next to her, smiling.

"Minnow," the woman said.

There was something familiar about her. "Yes?"

The woman glanced around, then lifted her glasses for a second. "It's me."

Angela Crawford.

"Oh my gosh, I didn't recognize you."

Of course that was the point, and she felt stupid for saying it.

"I wanted to pretend I'm a normal person for a few hours and cheer you on. This is courageous of you. Everything you've done these past few weeks has been so brave and inspiring. Can I be you when I grow up?"

Angela was wearing a long-sleeved white bohemian shirt, and it was impossible to tell she was missing part of her arm. And with the large camera around her neck, she easily passed for a journalist there for a story.

Minnow grinned. "I'm glad you came. It must be nice to be out and about and in the fresh air. You're looking stronger."

"I still hurt everywhere, but less so. I also wanted to tell you some top-secret news. Can I trust you not to tell a soul?"

Minnow nodded.

"We're meeting a Realtor tomorrow to look at a few houses in Koholā. I feel a strong connection to this place now, like I lost my arm but gained perspective. Hard to explain, but I'd love to have you come visit when it all pans out and when I'm healed up. What do you say?"

It was just a feeling, since she hardly knew this woman, but she liked her a lot.

"I would love to."

Angela's face broke into a thousand-watt smile. "Go. I know you have a swim to do. Who knows, maybe next year I'll do it with you," she said with a wink.

They all lined up together, men and women starting at the same time. When the horn went off, they all rushed into the water like newly hatched turtles.

The beginning was chaos. All bubbles and arms and legs, kicking and scratching to get ahead. A few people almost ran Minnow over and she had to kick them away. She was in no big hurry, though, so she kept a steady pace and took an outside line like Hina had suggested. Soon the pack thinned and there were a few swimmers up ahead, barely visible, and two behind her. Nalu and Cliff. She knew because it was habit to check behind her regularly. The depth varied between thirty and fifty feet, and she swam over coral fields and big ravines full of boulders and schools of fish.

In water this warm, she could swim forever if she had to. Luke had given her a few tips yesterday, suggesting more of a body rotation and a lighter flutter kick. She was moving along, absorbed by the colors below and soaking up the winter sun on her back. This would be her last long swim in the Hawaiian ocean and she wanted to savor every sun-dappled moment. Every now and then she would dive down and listen to the whale song or get a closer look at an eel or octopus—or as Woody would say, *puhi* or *heʻe*.

With every stroke she could feel the presence of her father with her. A guide and guardian angel. And the water became as nurturing as her mother's womb. Minnow had this strange new awareness that humans really did live forever. She might be her own soul, but both of her parents were *in* her. Not just their cells but their hearts and their voices and their stories. Their loves and their fears. The way they saw things and felt things. She was them and they were her and there was no end to their love.

A while on, she poked her head up and finally spotted the turnaround buoy way in the distance. A giant red triangle floaty. At that same moment two swimmers shot past her on the inside. It took a moment to register that it was Luke followed by Hina in her strappy red one-piece suit. Minnow turned and watched their bubbles fade, letting Nalu and Cliff close in. Cliff came up for air and got his bearings.

"Next time, I'm escorting," he said, then put his head down and kicked away.

It wasn't until they rounded the buoy that Minnow realized their little pack of three had grown to four. There was another swimmer outside of them. She didn't pay too much attention as they began the long swim back. As the sun climbed higher, the ocean grew clearer and everything beneath the surface shone in Technicolor. Stroke after stroke, she swam. A moving meditation. Scattered light. Shadows on the ocean floor.

You did it.

The voice was not her own. She glanced around.

Did what?

You smashed your darkest fear and found the truth.

A turtle rested on the ocean bottom.

And now what?

Stay.

My life is waiting for me back home. Everything I've worked for, everything I know.

It's all one ocean.

The water had been scraping her bare of all that no longer served her. Every barnacle and crab and seaweed falling away, returning to the source. Lungs almost empty, she came up and gulped in oxygen for a few moments. Nalu and Cliff kept going. Then she felt a presence moving up behind her. She turned and saw someone right on her tail. He stopped when he got to her.

It was Luke.

"Are you okay?" he asked.

"Didn't I see you swim past me like twenty minutes ago, in the lead?" she asked, confused.

"I'd rather swim with you."

Her mask began to fog. "That was you outside of me this whole way?"

He nodded.

Minnow could have stayed in that moment for a long time, but instead she grabbed his hand, ducked under and pulled him along. A few minutes later, they caught up to Nalu and Cliff, and the four of them swam along in a wide formation. Somewhere up ahead a long submarine shadow swam before them. For all any of them could tell, it could have been a shadow or it could have been a shark.

Except Minnow. She could hear the beating of a very large heart.

When they came to the beach, they walked out together. Her legs were jelly, the way they always were after a long and vigorous swim. Cliff stumbled a few times and Luke and Nalu caught his arms and helped him keep upright. The warm sand felt good on her feet, but she was almost sad to finish, wishing they had kept going all the way to Hale Niuhi.

The Shark House.

From the journal of Minnow Gray

February 11, 1998

My mother took her own life using the same pills they gave her to treat the depression she couldn't climb out of. Something about that seems very wrong to me. I was at school and Billy Jo, her friend from the art gallery, found her in the bathtub with all the life drained out of her. They were supposed to have lunch together and I know Billy Jo was worried about Mom—everyone was. She said that when Mom didn't come to the door, she had this horrible feeling that she should come in and check.

Billy Jo came to the school and they pulled me out of art class. At first I was excited to think I could leave early, but then I saw the haunted look on Billy Jo's face. There was no note, no good-bye, and I was left with only my memories of my mother and this preternatural sense that I was suddenly very, very alone. Not in the physical sense, because even back then I loved being alone, but my heart felt completely untethered to any other living hearts. The only source of love I'd known was gone forever. All along I thought it broke me, but now I'm beginning to realize it made me stronger.

CHAPTER 34

Gone to California

***Hokū**: star*

On the plane ride back to California a few days after the rough-water swim, Minnow leaned her forehead against the cool window and stared down at feathery white cloud fields opening to patches of ocean far below. Her mother's card burned a hole in her thigh. Cliff had given it to her this morning, suggesting she read it alone.

The goodbye had been rough. How could she even thank the Kaupiko brothers? In all honesty, it felt as though they had given Minnow her life back. In such a short time, the Kaupikos had become family to her. And for a girl with hardly any family, that was a big deal. Some said it was a Hawai'i thing, and that Hawaiians, if they like you, will welcome you into their homes with more *aloha* than you'd know what to do with. Maybe that was true, but Minnow knew it had more to do with the ocean. The same salt water ran through all three of their veins. Nalu's too. She loved that kid—man—whatever. And then there was Luke. Leaving him had felt unnatural in a way that caused an actual physical ache beneath her ribs.

"Water or passion-orange juice?" the flight attendant asked.

"Passion-orange, thank you."

Minnow downed the juice, wiped her hands and pulled the card out from the envelope. On the front was a quote from Søren Kierkegaard.

Life can only be understood backwards;
but it must be lived forwards.

When she opened the card, a photo fell out into her lap. Square, black-and-white, faded. Right away Minnow recognized it was a baby picture of herself, wide eyes looking into the camera with uncanny awareness. Layla had always said Minnow was an old soul, and that picture made her think that, yes, maybe she was.

Dear Cliff,

It feels like another lifetime ago that I was in Hawai'i, even though only a few months have passed. I know I said I wouldn't be writing anymore, but I couldn't help myself. My daughter is here and she's perfect! She came out kicking, literally, and moving her arms like she was trying to swim, which she probably was. They tell me babies do that. As far as newborns go, she has been remarkably easy. She is quiet and watchful and she loves to lie in her crib and listen to the birds sing, especially the crows. All mothers think their babies are special, but I swear, mine really is. How did I get so lucky?

When I take her for walks on the beach, her eyes track the waves and she reaches out, grabbing for the water. There is such wonder there, it seems unusual. And maybe I'm crazy (actually, I know I am), but I think she remembers our swims out front of your house. She wants to get back in the water—I can see it in her eyes. I have to be honest, it both thrills me and terrifies me. I have never understood the ocean, never trusted it or loved it the way you do and the way Bruce does. I envy that.

So I'll get to the point. Would you give her a Hawaiian middle name? Please! I might have to fight Bruce on this, because he wants her middle name to be Sofia, after his grandmother, but it would mean so much to me. A child can have more than one middle name, can't they?

All my love.

XO,
Layla and Minnow

Minnow read the letter again and again, as though she might be able to absorb her mother by osmosis. The love Layla had felt for her oozed off the page. Humbling. All-encompassing. Immense and bright as an exploding star.

But what of a Hawaiian middle name? All her life, Minnow only had one middle name: Sofia. So what had happened? Did he ever send one? Surely he would have said something about it. Or maybe not. Cliff operated by a different set of rules. Unpredictable and unknowable.

A while later, when she slid the card back in the envelope, it caught on something. A small piece of folded paper. She pulled it out. On it were the words:

Ka'ahupahau. Shark goddess. Guardian to the entrance of Pearl Harbor. I believe she will live up to this name.

Beneath that he had written:

What I never sent your mother but should have. You live up to it.
Aloha, CK

At that moment the plane shuddered, rocking and bucking and creaking through a patch of turbulence, as though the universe was trying to get her attention. As soon as they made it through, Minnow made a promise to return to Hawai'i as soon as she could, to that rough and ragged stretch of coastline that would never let her go. And now, looking backward, she understood why.

CHAPTER 35

The Swimmer

***Mana**: supernatural or divine power; spiritual energy, universal life force*

Carpinteria, California

A bright April sun reflected on the water and scattered down into the kelp. Minnow had been back now for over a month and in that time had christened her new boat, *Luna,* a used Boston Whaler Outrage 26. It was not much longer than a large white shark but was exactly what she needed. Solid, spacious, maneuverable. She'd also budgeted out half of Angela's donation and would be using it for shark tags, cutting-edge underwater camera and video equipment, and a new computer with the latest software that would enable her to better manage all of her data. The rest of the funds she would save for the future, maybe even for research trips. To Guadalupe. Or Hawai'i.

The island was never far from her mind, even when she was sleeping. Her dreams were all over the place. From friendly run-ins with Hina, to thunderstorms that rained down baby sharks, to moonlight swims with Luke. Stupidly, she had thought that with the distance between them, her feelings might fade. In actuality the opposite had happened. She craved him in a way that slanted her whole world. They had fallen into the habit of having long and leisurely conversations every Sunday evening, catching up on their weeks. They talked about everything and nothing, and Minnow was content just to hear the sound of his voice. The one thing neither spoke of was the future.

It was too soon for that. Or was it? Minnow felt the pull to hop a plane back to Kona, but Luke sounded busy trying to find work that was meaningful to him. For now, to make ends meet, he had a gig at a new seahorse farm, raising seahorses. He was also still at George's place on Hualālai, but he worried about overstaying his welcome. Part of her wanted to suggest he come to California for a while, but she knew he had to find his own way.

Today three undergrads from UC Santa Barbara were on the boat with her. Nothing formal, just an outing to count juvenile white sharks in waters off of Carpinteria. Pupping season was in full swing, and Minnow had always had this unyielding dream to see a newborn white shark—even though no one had ever seen one. There was always a first for everything. These girls were all marine biology majors but still early in their studies. None of them had ever been in the water with a white shark. Minnow almost envied them their first encounter.

They floated just outside the surf line, waiting and watching. The girls were all so eager and excited to be out there, and it brought Minnow back to her days in school, when everything was so fresh.

"What is the one thing you love most about white sharks?" asked Beverly, the quietly observant one.

"Just one thing?"

"Yes."

Minnow thought for a while. "If I had to pick, it might be the power of their presence and how you can feel them even when you can't see them. They really do activate some primal part of our brains, as though we were somehow wired together. Someday maybe we'll discover that they have an energetic field. A big one."

"Like an aura, you mean?" Bev asked.

"I guess you could call it that."

Beck added, "My mom says horses have big auras, so why not white sharks?"

Why not indeed?

Over the next two hours they spotted two eight or nine footers cruising through a shallow, sandy spot just inside of them, fins cutting through the surface with their telltale triangular shape. The girls were mesmerized.

"Can we jump in and swim with them?" Shelly asked, as she hung half her body over the edge of the boat.

Beck nudged her. "Don't be stupid. That's how you get munched."

Shelly pulled herself up and looked to Minnow. "Would the juveniles really hurt us? They're so cute."

Minnow couldn't help but smile. "Generally, the juveniles are non-aggressive, but we still wouldn't jump in. Mainly because we don't want to bother them."

"But you've swum with them, haven't you?"

"I have but under different circumstances."

"Tell us what it's like."

And so she did. By the end of their conversation, she guessed that out of the three of them, Beverly might be the only one who actually would go on to become a shark scientist. Shelly and Beck were intrigued by the idea of big sharks, but neither actually knew anything about them. Beverly, on the other hand, had done her research and reminded Minnow a little bit of herself.

Their last stop was near a popular point break. A small swell brought in knee-high and peeling waves, and a few surfers were out, so they pulled farther into the cove and dropped anchor. Minnow knew they had a better chance at seeing leopard sharks than white sharks, but she figured the girls would be thrilled to see any kind of shark.

"You guys want to swim toward shore and snorkel for a bit?" Minnow asked.

Their faces all lit up. "Yes!"

They suited up and jumped in, all staying close to Minnow, and soon were in the shallows floating over a scattering of leopard sharks. Small, spotted and stunning, the sharks had a completely different vibe than white sharks. Kittens versus lions. It was still hard to get used to the bite of the cold water after spending so much time in the warm waters of Hawai'i, but Minnow acclimated. The sharks darted this way and that on the bottom, shy creatures that they were.

Minnow hung suspended, watching the girls study the sharks, when she felt a presence behind her. She spun around and saw a large shape in the turbulence of a small breaking wave. After that first jolt of adrenaline that she usually got when encountering a large creature in the ocean, she relaxed. It was just some crazy guy out for a swim wearing only surf trunks in fifty-three-degree water. He kept coming, and Minnow kicked to get out of his way, but he followed. Did he not see her? She popped her head up. The man did the same. They were face-to-face, and when she realized who it was she tore off her mask.

"Oh my gosh, you scared me! What are you doing here?" she said, unable to keep a smile from spreading throughout her whole body.

Luke seemed almost nervous. "You told me you'd be here, and I wanted to see you. I hope you don't mind."

She let herself float into him and he wrapped his arms around her, giving her a long saltwater kiss.

"I missed you," he whispered. "Badly."

"I missed you too. We're going to need to figure something out," she said, staring deep into his kelp-flecked eyes.

One side of his mouth lifted. "I have a proposition for you."

CHAPTER 36

The Gathering

***Hui**: to join, unite, combine, mix*

Big Island, Hawai'i

Seven months later

Coconut fronds rustled and crab feet scurried. Minnow sat at the head of the big table on the lanai at Hale Niuhi as orange faded to blue above the horizon. She wore several lei around her neck that smelled like forest and honey and vanilla, and she wished she could bottle the scent. It was her favorite time of day, and she glanced around at all the faces in the candlelight. Good faces. Courageous faces. Faces of substance. Luke Greenwood, Woody and his wife, Anna—a strong woman with a radiant smile—Cliff and his lanky new dog, Boo, Nalu and Dixie. The two had become as inseparable as Luke and Minnow. As soon as Nalu finished his thesis, he'd be moving here.

They were gathered to celebrate Minnow's birthday. Having a party had been all Luke's idea. Minnow had never been big on birthdays, never really had had a tribe of her own to celebrate with.

Woody held up a beer can. "Cheers, to one of the most fearless *wahine* I know."

Everyone else raised their glasses and bottles, clinking with each and every person at the table.

"To someone who walks the walk. Or should I say, swims the swim?" Nalu said with a sly grin.

Luke didn't say anything, but his eyes bored into her, turning up the heat. She still found it incredible how he loved her so unflinchingly and how she felt the same way about him.

"Aw, thanks, guys. You have no idea how much it means to be back here with you all. It feels like home, really and truly."

When Luke had come to California in April, he'd come with news of two things—ideas that had been brewing but he'd wanted to be certain of before he shared anything with Minnow. The first was that Sawyer had hired him to manage the resort's beach and ocean activities, as well as to run educational whale-watching tours on the boat. While the job didn't involve orcas, he was where he wanted to be, and humpback whales were quickly becoming an obsession for him.

As for a place to live, Woody asked if Luke wanted to caretake Hale Niuhi in exchange for living in the small guest cabin in the back. Woody and Cliff needed the help and it would be good to have someone there to keep an eye on things. The only stipulation was that Luke would get to travel to Santa Barbara several months out of the year to help Minnow with her research. That was nonnegotiable. And Minnow would spend her off months with Luke on the Big Island, tracking white sharks in the months they migrated to the Hawaiian Islands.

So what if there might be an ocean between them? They were both committed to making it work, and that was all that mattered. Both hearts were in it two hundred percent. And it made Minnow strangely happy to know that if they were to swim far enough, they would meet in the middle of the deep blue abyss.

The sharks had given all this to her, and she would be forever grateful.

AUTHOR'S NOTE

When I was fourteen, I saw my first shark in a small bay in South Kona—a five- or six-foot white tip reef shark resting on the sandy bottom of a cave. The experience was peaceful and nonthreatening, and nothing like I had imagined a shark encounter would be. I've spent much of my life in the ocean and have only once seen a large shark: a hammerhead, while I was out bodyboarding. It turned slowly away the moment it saw me. On another occasion, I was swimming in Waimea Bay with friends, far from shore, when people began yelling, "Shark!" The water was a bit cloudy, and I immediately imagined a massive shark bulleting toward me. That swim back to shore was the longest of my life—but I made it, and no one was harmed. The shark in question turned out to be a six-foot hammerhead that postured briefly at my friend Daniel and another man, then left them alone. On Hawai'i Island, I see smaller reef sharks now and then, but they always mind their own business.

The idea for this novel has been swimming around in my mind for ages, and I'm thrilled to finally bring it to life. One of the early sparks of inspiration came from a book my father gave me years ago: *The Devil's Teeth* by journalist Susan Casey. Her true story about white sharks and the scientists of the Farallon Islands brought these incredible animals to life so vividly I couldn't put it down. I became a fan of both Susan and the sharks. Much of what I learned about the Farallones and shark studies there came from her book, and I highly recommend it.

While *The Shark House* is pure fiction, there are real places and events that I borrowed from. About six years ago there was an incident along the coast here where a twenty-five-year-old man lost part of his leg to a shark in a place near where we often surf. I think it was that moment, when we heard what had happened as we were driving to surf, that I realized this could have easily been any of us. It felt very close to home, and we knew many of the people involved in the rescue. Whenever someone dies in the ocean here in the islands, there is a collective feeling of loss, because the ocean connects us in such a deep way. That this man survived is incredible.

In writing this novel, I really wanted to understand sharks more, and also to understand their place in Hawai'i. While it's the tiger shark we usually worry about, great white sharks do travel here regularly. Hawaiian culture, the ocean and sharks are also tightly interwoven, and I wanted to explore that as well. Many of our friends are divers and fishermen, and they all have their stories. As do most surfers. We humans enter into the ocean knowing that there are sharks and other possible dangers out there. It is a choice we make. The sharks do not have a choice. They live there. And we must honor that. I hope this book opens your eyes to the magnificent creatures that they are.

ACKNOWLEDGMENTS

My deepest, heartfelt thanks to all the people who helped shape this book in one way or another.

To my steadfast agent, Elaine Spencer, who was all in from the moment I first broached the idea—and who did an amazing job helping me whip it into shape for submission, and then again later when my first draft was done.

A huge thanks to my new publisher, Harper Muse! I am so grateful to Amanda Bostic and Lizzie Poteet for believing in this story—and in me as an author. Lizzie challenged me to dive deep to make this book shine. Her suggestions were always insightful and grounded, and the story is so much stronger because of her. I'm also deeply thankful to Kimberly Carlton, who enthusiastically took on this project and offered expert guidance in steering it toward publication. I feel so fortunate to have such a gifted team behind me. And to the cover designer, James W. Hall—when I first saw this cover, it was love at first sight.

I'm also grateful to early reader Maya LeGrande for her expert scientific eye and deep knowledge of Hawai'i and its language. Thanks to Marilyn Carlsmith for an early read as well—Marilyn is the woman who helped me fall in love with the undersea world, and I only wish I could be as fearless as she is. And to Jen Homcy, marine biologist and ocean advocate, who inspires me and graciously gave me a quote for the book—thank you.

The Kaupiko brothers in this novel are fictional, but their last name comes from a real family with deep ties to the ocean and traditional

Hawaiian fishing practices on the island. I was honored to receive permission to use the name.

And where would I be without all my mermaid sisters—who swim, surf and play in the sea with me regularly? Thank you, Leesa Robertson, Jennifer Freitas, Mahea Holzman, Malia White Eversole, Nicole Pedersen, Mary Smolenski, Vivian Varney, Shelly Batha, Crystal Thornburg-Homcy, Barbara Haight and so many more over the years. And of course Todd, too, though he's more of a merman and I love that about him. The ocean truly sustains us.

Of course, too, I am thankful for the sharks.

DISCUSSION QUESTIONS

1. What did you learn or feel differently about sharks and the ocean after reading this book? Did it challenge any assumptions?

2. In what ways does Hawai'i function not just as a setting, but almost as a character in the book? How does the island shape Minnow's experience?

3. Given the opportunity, would you rather stay at Hale Niuhi (the Shark House) or the Kiawe, and why?

4. Minnow Gray is both a scientist and a "shark whisperer." How does her relationship with sharks reflect her inner life and emotional journey?

5. How does the 1998 setting influence the story? Could this novel have taken place in today's world, or does the time period add something unique?

6. How do family secrets and unresolved grief shape Minnow's identity? What does she learn about her past that shifts her perspective?

7. Could you relate to the Kaupiko brothers and their deep connection to the ocean and the sharks?

8. How did you feel about Minnow's heightened ability to hear? Do you enjoy stories with a hint of magic to them?

9. Would you be for or against a shark hunt?

10. Have you seen the movie *Jaws*, and how did it affect you?

11. Sharks in this story are both real and symbolic. What do you think the great white shark represents for Minnow? For the larger community?

ABOUT THE AUTHOR

Photo by Sarah Anderson

Sara Ackerman is the Hawai'i-born, bestselling author of historical novels set in the islands. Her books have been labeled "unforgettable" by Apple Books and "empowering & deliciously visceral" by *Book Riot. New York Times* bestselling authors Kate Quinn and Madeline Martin have praised Sara's novels as "fresh and delightful" and "brilliantly written." Amazon chose *Radar Girls* as a best book of the month, and ALA Booklist gave *The Codebreaker's Secret* a starred review.